CW01638035

PRAIS *ATE*

"Kakande unc the burden of expectations, political corruption across nations, racism, and the dangers and temptations of power."

— Publishers Weekly

"A work of fiction told with the force of truth."

— The Niche

"Kakande's *A Murder of Hate* is a truly remarkable work of crime fiction; it thrills, it tantalizes, it refreshes, it hums with harmonious rhymes."

— The Nation

"Fast-paced, thought-provoking, lanced with sexual passion and utterly original."

— Bookwormwhitlock86

"*A Murder of Hate* is a compelling read that transcends the boundaries of a traditional crime thriller."

— The Financial World

ALSO BY YASIN KAKANDE

The Ambitious Struggle
(2013)

Slave States
(2015)

Why We Are Coming
(2020)

Green Card Brides
(2024)

A Murder of Hate
(2024)

The Missing Corpse

The General's Project Series 2 of 3

Yasin Kakande

BLACK WRITERS INK LLC
Boxborough, MA, 2025

BLACK WRITERS INK LLC
318 Codman Hill Road
Boxborough, Massachusetts

www.blackwritersink.com

First Edition 2025
Copyright ©2025 by Yasin Kakande
All rights reserved

This book is a work of fiction. Names, characters, places, and incidents are either products of the author's imagination or used fictitiously. Any resemblance to actual events or persons, living or dead, is purely coincidental.

Book design: Pablo Capra

ISBN
Paperback 979-8-9909844-4-8
Ebook 979-8-9909844-5-5

Printed in the United States of America

Contents

Dedication

To all Africans and their enduring struggle to break free from imperialism and its puppet leaders.

Warning

The Missing Corpse contains depictions of murder, sexual violence, kidnappings, torture, and graphic language. Reader discretion is advised.

Prologue

JESSICA Nanjovu, First Lady of Uganda, stood in the immigration line at Washington Dulles International Airport, her heartbeat a slow, hammering drum against her ribs. The air inside the terminal was thick with the scent of overworked bodies and stale coffee, and somewhere in the distance, a child was wailing, the sound needling its way into her skull.

Seventy years of life had taught her many things—how to keep secrets, how to wield power like a well-sharpened blade, how to smile while gutting a man's ambitions—but nothing had prepared her for this.

She adjusted the brim of her hat with a trembling hand.

Beside her, two aides hovered, their suits impeccable, their faces locked in the neutral expressions of men who had long since learned that survival depended on how well they could fade into the background. At their feet, five suitcases bulged at the seams, each one crammed with crisp, fragrant U.S. dollars. Ten million, to be exact.

Jessica stepped forward.

The immigration officer barely glanced at her as he took her passport and those of her aides, flipping through them with practiced boredom. A stamp came down. Another. He was halfway through the third when something made him pause. His eyes flicked up, studying her face with the sharp, hawk-like gaze of a man who had seen more than his fair share of liars.

"Are you carrying anything you want to declare to U.S. Customs?"

"Yes," she said. "I have ten million U.S. dollars in those suitcases."

For a moment, the world seemed to stop. The officer blinked. His fingers twitched, hesitating over the passport before flipping back to the first page.

He cleared his throat. "What do you do for work?"

"I'm the first lady of Uganda."

Another pause. Longer this time. The officer's eyes darted to the passport again. His lips pursed, forming the question before he even spoke it.

"It says here you're the minister of education."

Jessica inhaled slowly, keeping her voice steady. "My passport says I'm the minister of education, but I'm also the first lady. It's allowed in my family to hold two government offices."

The officer's expression didn't change, but the way he shifted in his seat, the subtle tightening of his jaw—she had seen that before. The moment when a man realizes he's holding something bigger than he knows how to handle.

He reached beneath the counter and tapped a button.

Red. Panic.

Jessica's stomach turned to ice.

The lead officer arrived, a man with graying temples and the jaded look of someone who had seen everything from drug mules to human traffickers trying to weasel their way past him. The first officer turned to him, voice measured but thick with something resembling disbelief.

"She's the first lady of Uganda," he said, "and she's carrying ten million dollars in those suitcases."

The lead officer let out a low breath. "Jesus."

He stepped closer, lowering his voice. "Ma'am, do you want to donate all this money to the poor U.S. government?"

Jessica's smile was tight, humorless. "It's my money. I want to deposit it into U.S. banks."

"Ma'am," the lead officer said, his tone shifting into something colder, more authoritative. "We're going to have to detain you. It's not permitted to transport such large sums of money without proper authorization."

She felt the room tilt slightly. Not with panic—Jessica Nanjovu did not panic—but with the sheer weight of the stakes pressing down on her.

"I have a diplomatic passport. Can I speak to Taylor, my lobbyist?"

"No, ma'am. Only a lawyer."

"Then can I speak to the head of the CIA? They know I'm coming. I have important news for the U.S. government."

"Are you on a CIA assignment? Do you have a code I can use to verify your identity?"

"No. Just bring the CIA boss here."

The officer exchanged glances with his colleagues.

A silent decision was made.

"Okay, ma'am," he said, stepping back. "We're going to have to hold you here until the CIA arrives."

She didn't resist when they escorted her away, past the wide-eyed passengers, past the curious glances of tourists and businessmen and people who would never understand the game she was playing.

The holding room was cold. Sterile. A place meant to make people feel small.

Jessica did not feel small.

Hours bled away. Outside, the afternoon light dimmed into the gold-tinged hues of early evening. The clock ticked. The door remained shut.

And then, finally, it swung open.

Taylor, her lobbyist, stepped inside first, his face pale but composed. And behind him, a man she had met only once before but whose presence she had never forgotten—the head of the CIA African desk.

Jessica exhaled.

The weight of everything she carried—her mission, the secrets that could burn down entire governments—settled onto her shoulders.

It was time.

CHAPTER 1:

Shawn

SHAWN Wayles stepped off the crowded bus and into the seething, sweating chaos of the Malaba border, where Uganda and Kenya bled into each other like a bad wound. The heat hit him first, thick and merciless, turning his shirt into a second skin. The air smelled of diesel, fried food, and the sour tang of unwashed bodies.

The road ahead was a clogged artery, lined with trucks that stretched back into Kenya, their engines growling low like hungry animals. They carried everything—fuel, electronics, sacks of grain—whatever kept Uganda breathing. Drivers leaned against their rusted rigs, smoking cheap cigarettes, their eyes dull with boredom or something darker.

Shawn fit right in. Or, at least, that was the plan.

He had traded his usual sharp suits for faded jeans and a sweat-streaked t-shirt, his backpack light but packed with what he needed. No one would mistake him for a tourist. He looked like a man with somewhere to be and nothing to prove. Which was exactly the point.

The border pulsed with life. Vendors shoved plastic bags of roasted peanuts at passing travelers. Men waved tattered currency in the air, promising the "best exchange rate" in rapid-fire Swahili. Somewhere in the distance, a truck horn blared, long and angry.

Shawn moved through the crowd like a shadow, his eyes scanning for trouble without making it obvious. He avoided the main customs checkpoint—it was for the clueless and the unlucky. Instead, he slipped toward the footpath where locals crossed in a steady, unbothered flow.

That was when he spotted the boda bodas, a swarm of motorcycle taxis waiting like vultures at the edge of the road. Their riders—young, wiry men with hard eyes and quick hands—scanned the crowd, looking for fares.

One of them stood out. Not because of his face, but because of his shirt. It was old, sun-faded, the red almost pink now, but Shawn recognized the logo immediately.

Boston Red Sox.

Jesus Christ.

Thousands of miles from Fenway Park, and here it was, stitched across a stranger's chest in the middle of a border town.

Shawn walked up, swung his leg over the back of the motorcycle, and settled in.

"You a Red Sox fan?" he asked.

The driver glanced back, confused. "I don't know what that is."

Shawn smirked, tapping the logo. "The team on your shirt."

The guy looked down like he was seeing it for the first time.

"Oh, this. I don't read everything on my clothes, but yes, I like Red Sox."

"Who's your favorite player?"

"I don't know the players. I bought this shirt in the used market. Maybe someone else wore it before."

That stopped Shawn cold. *Maybe someone else wore it before.*

The words sat heavy in his mind. The driver had no idea what Red Sox meant, no connection to the game, to the city, to the culture—but he was wearing it anyway.

It wasn't his. It never had been.

Shawn felt something shift in his gut, an old instinct waking up. The world was full of things that didn't belong where they were. Sometimes they were harmless. Sometimes they weren't.

"Fair enough," he said, slapping the driver's shoulder. "Let's go."

The engine growled as they shot forward, dodging potholes and weaving through foot traffic. Shawn stayed loose, but his mind was already ticking through possibilities, mapping exits, counting the faces around him.

The driver made a sharp turn. Too sharp. And then they stopped.

Shawn's stomach went cold.

A group of men stepped forward from the side of the road, moving fast, surrounding them before he could react. The driver said something in Luganda.

The men grinned. Then, all at once, they started shouting.

"Sir! Best rates! Best rates!"

Money changers.

Jesus. Shawn let out the breath he'd been holding.

They were just hustlers, not thugs.

The men held out bundles of Ugandan shillings, waving them like bait. But Shawn wasn't interested in the loud ones. His eyes locked onto a man who stood a little apart from the chaos.

He wasn't shouting. He wasn't desperate. And in his hand, gleaming in the dusty afternoon light, was an iPhone 15 Pro Max.

Shawn blinked. Something about it made his skin itch. Not the phone itself—hell, he had the same model sitting back in a hotel safe—but the way it looked here, in this place. It was too new. Too clean. Like it had never seen a day of struggle in its life.

"Nice phone," Shawn said, stepping forward.

The man looked up, smiling slow.

"We're making money here, boy," he said, his English smooth, his accent thick. "That's why we have these iPhones."

Shawn reached into his pocket, pulled out a few Kenyan notes. The man took them, his fingers moving fast over the iPhone screen, calculating.

For a moment, it felt like something had shifted. Like two worlds had scraped against each other in a way they shouldn't have.

The latest tech in the oldest kind of hustle.

Shawn took the Ugandan shillings, sliding them into

his pocket.

"Fair exchange," the man said, grinning.

Shawn nodded.

The boda boda driver, his mission complete, barely acknowledged Shawn as he wove through the crowd and disappeared into the sea of bodies. Shawn didn't watch him go. He had other things to worry about.

He moved through the throng, scanning the taxi park. The place looked like a graveyard for vehicles that had survived one too many bad roads. The shouts of conductors filled the air—sharp, urgent calls of destinations, names spat like warnings.

"Kampala! Kampala! Full van, we move now!"

That was a lie. The van was never full. Not yet. But it was the game they played.

A young conductor, sweat glistening on his forehead, shoved his way toward Shawn. "Forty thousand to Kampala," he announced.

Shawn dug into his pocket and handed over the shillings. Eight dollars, give or take. A small price to pay for blending in.

The van waiting for him was a relic from another era, its paint peeling in great, jagged patches, as if the vehicle had given up trying to hold itself together. The sliding door shrieked in protest as Shawn pulled it open. Inside, fourteen seats—at least, in theory. He settled into the front, close to the driver.

"Full soon?" Shawn asked.

The driver, a wiry man with a sunken face and a grin too wide for his weary eyes, nodded. "Soon, soon," he promised, but they both knew what that meant.

"Five minutes" could be an hour.

He settled in, his back pressed against the cracked vinyl seat, and watched as passengers trickled in. A mother cradling a sleeping child. A man with a bundle of sugarcane strapped to his back. A teenager carrying a live chicken that flapped once in protest before settling into miserable silence.

The van creaked under the weight of its occupants, but still, they waited. Another twenty minutes passed before the conductor slammed the door shut and smacked the side of the van with his palm. "Tugende!" *Let's go.*

The driver gave a satisfied grunt, twisted the key in the ignition, and the van shuddered to life.

They lurched forward, coughing up dust as they escaped the border town's tangled streets. Shawn let his gaze drift to the window.

As they rumbled forward, Uganda unfolded around him. The landscape changed from dry, choking red earth to something lush and alive. Banana trees stretched toward the sky, their broad leaves swaying in the afternoon breeze. Tea and coffee plantations rolled by in endless rows, green against the dark soil. Small villages dotted the roadside, their thatched roofs barely visible through the dense foliage. Shawn let himself admire it, but only for a moment.

It was beautiful. Almost peaceful. But Shawn had learned the hard way—beauty was a liar.

You could admire the rolling hills, the endless green, the postcard-perfect scenery, but it didn't change what lurked beneath. Power, greed, the silent violence that kept men in charge and others buried beneath them.

The driver hummed tunelessly under his breath.

Shawn shifted in his seat.

He could feel it, even here, in the quiet hum of the van's engine. That weight pressing against his ribs, that old, familiar whisper in the back of his mind. Something was waiting for him in Kampala.

Shawn let his head rest against the rattling window, eyes half-lidded, watching the Ugandan countryside unspool like an old film reel. Even the banana trees seemed to drop under the weight of the humid air, the occasional mud-brick house blurring past, laundry flapping on sagging lines. The road hummed beneath the tires of the ancient taxi van, and his mind drifted back—not to the present, but to that cold goddamn room on the sixth floor in Langley, Virginia.

It had smelled like fresh carpet cleaner and stale coffee. The kind of place that tried too hard to look nondescript, as if the weight of its secrets didn't saturate every inch.

*

Boylston Aldrich had been waiting, stiff-backed in his chair, his expression grave. That in itself was unsettling. The man had the face of someone who had spent years in the game, someone who had seen regimes rise and fall over scotch and cigars, never losing sleep over the bodies left behind. But that day? That day, he looked rattled.

"Shawn, we have an urgent assignment for you."

The words came heavy, like stones dropped into deep water.

Beside him sat Taylor, part-time swamp creature, full-time lobbyist, and—when the stars aligned just right—a seasoned CIA case manager for Africa. He had silver hair that looked combed by ambition and fingers that had once tucked government-grade bribes under mahogany desks like love notes. For three decades, he'd played footsie with African warlords, cutting deals over whiskey and blood. But today, even Taylor looked like a man who'd just realized the coffin he was building might be his own.

"What's the situation?" Shawn had asked, already knowing it was bad.

Boylston exhaled through his nose. "We have unconfirmed reports that Uganda's president, Joel Katila Muaji, is dead."

The air in the room changed. Like something unseen had slithered under the table.

Shawn stayed quiet, waiting for more.

"He was 82. His health's been failing. But here's the problem—the Ugandan government hasn't announced anything. No leaks. No mourning. No goddamn sign that anything's wrong."

Shawn nodded slowly. "So, either they're covering it up… or they don't know what to do next."

"That's our concern," Boylston said. "We think they're stalling, figuring out succession before making it public. But we're the biggest funders and intelligence providers for that government. We should've been informed first."

It made sense. Uganda was a keystone in the region. If Muaji was dead, the power vacuum could spiral into something ugly—civil unrest, military takeovers, or worse, another Russian- or Chinese-backed dictator stepping in to claim the throne.

Shawn leaned forward. "Who's the source?"

Boylston glanced at Taylor, who finally looked up from his phone.

"Pilooto Kaguume," Taylor said, his voice dry. "The president of their tiny neighbor in the south. His intelligence service is the best in the region, second only to Uganda's. If they say Muaji's dead, we take it seriously."

Shawn processed that. Kaguume had been a useful ally in the past—sharp, paranoid, and always looking to climb another rung up the global political chain. He wouldn't risk feeding the CIA bad intel.

"And then," Boylston added, his fingers drumming on the desk, "there's the matter of the first lady."

Shawn raised an eyebrow.

"She showed up at Washington Dulles yesterday. Ten million in cash. Says she wants asylum. Claims her husband was overthrown in a coup. Says she doesn't even know if he's alive or dead."

That got Shawn's attention. Ten million wasn't just an escape fund—it was a goddamn war chest.

"Her stepson," Boylston continued, "General Mlevi Kainewaragi, is trying to force parliament and the cabinet to swear him in as the next president."

Shawn knew the name. Hell, anyone who had worked in African intelligence knew the name. *The General.* A man raised in blood and steel, rumored to have a taste for power—and for eliminating anything that stood in his way.

"We don't want another intelligence failure," Boylston said, his voice going sharp. "No repeats of the Afghanistan debacle in '79. No Iranian Shah collapse. We can't afford another black eye."

Shawn exhaled. He understood. Intelligence agencies lived in the shadow of their own failures. And every agent who came after was expected to clean up the mess of the past.

"So," Shawn said, "what's my role?"

Boylston leaned in. "We need you inside Uganda. Inside the State House in Nakasero. Find Muaji. Get it from his mouth—if he's alive, if he's ceding power, if he's being forced out. And if he's dead…" Boylston's mouth curled into something cold. "We need proof."

Shawn's stomach tightened. "Proof?"

"Photos. Documents. If you have to steal the goddamn corpse, do it."

Taylor, still gripping his phone, suddenly straightened. His face was a mask of concentration. Then he spoke, low and controlled.

"Oh, someone's answered."

Shawn watched as he brought the phone to his ear.

Boylston leaned closer. "Who is it?"

Taylor hesitated, then put the call on speaker.

A voice slithered through the receiver, thick with amusement and something else.

"Uncle Taylor," it crooned.

Shawn felt something tighten in his chest.

Mlevi Kainewaragi.

"The General."

There was something off about his voice. It was slurred, like he'd been drinking. Or worse.

Taylor cleared his throat. "Can I speak to your father?"

A pause. Then, a quiet chuckle.

"Oh," the General purred, "you don't know yet, do you?"

Shawn could almost hear the smirk on his face.

"My dad's been unwell," the General continued. "Some… health issues. He asked me to take his calls."

Taylor's jaw clenched. "Tell him to call me when he gets better."

The General just laughed. And then the line went dead.

Boylston cursed under his breath.

"That son of a bitch," he growled. Then, to Shawn: "You're on the next flight to Kenya, then slipping into Uganda by road."

Shawn nodded, the weight of the mission settling into his bones.

By the time he left that office, his new identity was already waiting on the fifth floor.

A Zimbabwean passport. A Zimbabwean national ID.

And now Shawn was heading into the heart of Uganda. The road ahead was long and uncertain, but the mission was clear. As they drove through the countryside, the beauty of Uganda was impossible to ignore. Small villages dotted the landscape, their thatched roofs a picturesque reminder of simpler times.

The van's conductor was still shouting out destinations at every intersection, trying to coax more passengers into the already full vehicle.

Uganda was beautiful, no doubt about it. But beneath the surface of this serene landscape lay a complex and potentially volatile political situation. The next hours would bring him closer to Kampala, closer to the truth, and closer to the heart of a nation teetering on the edge of uncertainty.

Four hours later, the outskirts of Kampala came into view. The city was a sprawling metropolis, a mix of modern buildings and chaotic markets, where the old and the new collided in a vibrant symphony. Shawn's fixer would be waiting for him at the old taxi park, ready to provide the information he needed.

CHAPTER 2:

The General

THE Nile Hotel loomed over Kampala like a golden beast, its glass windows reflecting the flickering city lights, its corridors humming with the whispers of politicians, foreign spies, and the occasional lost tourist. But beneath all that luxury—beneath the silk curtains, the crystal chandeliers, the expensive perfume—lay something rotten.

And tonight, General Mlevi Kainewaragi, aka *the General,* was at the center of it.

He sat at the head of a long, polished mahogany table in the hotel's basement conference room, a seat meant for his father. The chair was old, carved with lions along its arms, its high back towering over the men gathered before him. His father had ruled from this chair many times. But not tonight.

No, his father was elsewhere. Cold. Still. Unburdened.

The General adjusted his cuffs, glancing around the room as ministers and top military officials took their seats. They had been searched, their weapons stripped from them. That was the first step—making them vulnerable. Men without guns were just men. And men, when faced with uncertainty, always revealed their fears.

To his right, Douglas Mwesigye stood, speaking in his quick, clipped way. He had once been a radio journalist, his words falling from his mouth like machine-gun fire. Now, he was the General's mouthpiece. His voice filled the room, giving shape to the message the General had already decided upon.

"As many of you know, our nation is at a crossroads," Douglas said. "The president believes that now is the time for strong leadership and unity."

The General barely listened. He pulled out his phone instead, letting the screen's glow light his face. He knew the effect it would have—how it would make him seem detached, above the noise. Let them think he wasn't paying attention. Let them think he was just a son sitting in for his father.

They had no idea.

Douglas started talking like a man with a ticking bomb strapped to his chest and a stopwatch in his throat.

"The reason you're all here," he said, his voice cracking like a cheap speaker at a doomed wedding, "is simple. We're beginning—no, we're *completing*—a peaceful transition of power. Or at least that's what we're going to *call* it."

He wiped sweat from his upper lip with a trembling finger, then steamrolled on.

"The president wants you to draw up the papers naming his beloved son, *His Holiness the General*, as the next vice president. Then, in a glorious act of democratic cosplay, the president will step down and—poof!—the General becomes our new commander-in-chief. Just like that. An old man exits, a military brat enters. Bloodline politics, gentlemen. The purest African tradition."

Douglas added that they were also supposed to whip up a bill to rewrite the constitution—nothing big, just a little tweak so presidents would be elected by parliament instead of the filthy, mud-caked peasants. The party with the fattest flock of MPs would simply hatch a president like an egg. The General, doesn't have the patience to go door to door kissing babies sticky with porridge or pretending to care about dirt farmers' pigsties.

"No one leaves this hotel until the ink dries and the oath is sworn. Not even for a single day."

At that, the General raised his eyes from his phone he was pretending to read. Just one look. Cold. Calculated. Like a crocodile eyeing a goat near the riverbank.

The look said, *Easy, Douglas. You're giving away too much too fast.*

Douglas caught it mid-rant, stuttered, swallowed, and slowed his tongue like a man realizing he was about to say the wrong thing in front of God… or a firing squad.

The ministers exchanged glances. Some nervous, others calculating. They had come expecting a direct order from the president himself.

Kenneth Mugabi, the minister of defense, and lifelong friend of President Muaji was sitting stiff-backed, hands clasped on the table like a man holding onto the edge of a cliff. His lips were pressed tight, his eyes flicking between the General and Douglas like a man watching vultures circle.

Mugabi had been calling the president for days. No answer. And now here he was, in this dimly lit hotel basement, listening to the General's aide speak where his friend should have been. His nostrils flared. His jaw clenched. It was coming.

"Tell us exactly why we are here," Mugabi finally said, his voice sharp enough to cut through the General's thoughts. He stood up slowly, hands flat on the table. "Where is the president?"

Douglas kept talking, flipping a page in his notebook, ignoring the question.

Mugabi slammed his fist down. "Enough! Why is his phone off? Why has no one seen him? Tell us what's going on in this country!"

The silence stretched, too thick now, like the air before a thunderstorm.

The General exhaled and rose from his chair. The weight of the pistol in his hand was familiar, comforting. He turned it over lazily, running a thumb along the barrel. It caught the light in a sharp, silver flash.

"Sit down, Mugabi," the General said.

"Don't try to scare me, kid," Mugabi snapped. "You know I raised you. If your father were here, he'd have you flat on your stomach while I flogged you myself."

The General smiled. A slow, deliberate smile that didn't reach his eyes.

Mugabi squared his shoulders. "Go on then. Shoot me, boy."

The General pulled the trigger.

The shot cracked like a bolt of lightning, splitting the stale air. Mugabi's skull jerked backward, a red mist blooming in the dim light. For a second, he was still standing, his body deciding whether or not to obey physics. Then his knees buckled, and he collapsed onto the table, sliding off in a graceless heap. The smell of gunpowder and blood seeped into the room.

Someone gasped. Another whimpered. But no one moved.

The General turned, his face as unreadable as stone. He motioned to the security aide near the door. "Clean this up."

The man hesitated only for a breath before moving, dragging Mugabi's corpse away like a sack of grain. Another aide scurried in with a rag and a bucket, scrubbing away the blood. The sound of it—the wet slosh, the squeak of fabric against polished wood—was the only noise in the room.

Douglas adjusted his tie and cleared his throat. "Okay," he said, his voice only slightly shaky. "Let's focus back on the important things."

The ministers sat frozen, their expressions carved from fear. Their breathing was shallow, their hands tight on their laps. A few nodded mechanically.

The General sat back down, flipping open his phone, scrolling through messages like he had just finished a mildly inconvenient chore.

Douglas continued, his voice lower now, darker. "You have all seen that the General will not tolerate any bullshit here."

No one dared look at Mugabi's empty chair.

The General felt the weight of their stares, the sheer terror pressing against him like a wave. He inhaled it, fed on it. The room had changed now.

This was no longer a meeting. This was his kingdom.

The whiskey in his hand caught the dim light, its amber glow flickering in the crystal glass like a dying fire. The General watched it swirl, slow and hypnotic, before taking a measured sip. The burn coiled its way down his throat, warming the cold pit in his stomach. A man in his position should always drink slowly, should always savor the moment—because any moment could be the last.

Across the room, Douglas was in his element, words spilling from his mouth again in a relentless volley, sharp and unstoppable. He stood tall, his voice bouncing off the paneled walls, commanding every eye in the room.

"Let me emphasize this, we're here on the wishes of the president of our beautiful country," Douglas declared. "To see that his favorite son, who has worked so hard all his life, gets rewarded with the biggest reward in this country."

The General smirked into his whiskey, the amber stuff swirling like a storm in a glass. *Favorite son.* Now, that was a punchline if he'd ever heard one. If his old man had gotten his way, he wouldn't even be breathing right now. The true golden child—the apple of Daddy Dictator's dead eye—was Enock Rugasira, the secret bastard stashed like a loaded gun in the opposition party, just waiting for the family business to change logos.

The ministers sat stiff-backed around the table, their faces carefully composed. But he saw it. The fear. The barely contained tremor in their fingers, the glances exchanged when they thought he wasn't looking. They knew. They didn't know the details, not yet, but they felt the shift in the air. It was like the pressure drop before a storm.

Douglas kept talking, piece by piece, feeding the room a carefully crafted illusion of order.

"Our target is to be here for three days," he said. "Each of you will have a bedroom, which will also serve as your office. You will work on the necessary paperwork. We will stay here, working tirelessly, ensuring this transition is complete."

The General let his gaze wander. He could feel the room shrink as the weight of those words settled on the ministers like a wet, suffocating blanket. Three days. It wasn't a request. It was a sentence.

The ministers shifted in their seats, the bravest among them nodding like good little soldiers. They knew better than to argue.

Douglas pressed on.

"We're having tough times," he said, his tone darkening. "It seems the foreigners will try to conspire against our government. The General has ordered that all opposition leaders working with them be arrested until this process is complete. As we speak, our men are making those arrests."

Silence. Cold and thick. The room had turned into a tomb.

The General took another slow sip of whiskey, watching their reactions over the rim of his glass. Some of them clenched their jaws. Others kept their faces blank, though their hands betrayed them—fingers curled too tightly, nails pressing white against skin.

"We also need to be vigilant," Douglas continued. "Watch the neighbors. Rwanda. Kenya. The CIA has been visiting them too often, re-assigning our previous assignments to them."

There was no more pretending now. The tension in the room was thick enough to choke on. Some of them had friends in those countries. Some of them had business dealings. Some of them, he knew, had already thought about running.

That was amusing. There was nowhere to run.

Douglas delivered the final blow.

"So, any ideas that foreigners will try to stop this transfer of power with things like negotiations?" He let out a dry chuckle. "We are not going to accept that. That's why we will do everything here, in this hotel. And only go public after everything is complete."

Finality. No way out.

The General drained his glass. The whiskey left a pleasant sting, but it was nothing compared to the fear now radiating from the men in the room. It was in their eyes. That quiet, gnawing dread.

They knew now.

The doors had closed. The walls had drawn in. This was not a transition. It was a purge.

CHAPTER 3:

Joanne

JOANNE Nambatya caught her own gaze in the cracked mirror, a jagged line splitting her reflection in two. The glass had seen better days—just like this room, just like this life—but it would do. She adjusted the dress, the golden fabric clinging to her like a whispered promise, like something alive, something waiting. It shimmered in the dim light, accentuating the deep curve of her waist, the swell of her hips, the soft, treacherous flesh of her thighs. A dress like this wasn't just worn—it demanded attention. It beckoned, it lured, it threatened.

Behind her, Helen Namusoke muttered curses at the heap of clothes spilling from the makeshift wardrobe, the wooden planks nailed together in haste, in desperation. Joanne barely heard her. She turned, watching her reflection shift and distort with the fractured glass, watching herself become something else—someone else. She traced the edge of her neckline with a slow finger, feeling the fabric stretch just enough to remind her that she was still in control. For now.

"How is this?" she asked, her voice a little too casual, a little too knowing.

Helen looked up, and for a moment, there was silence. Then, a slow grin stretched across her face, the kind of grin that knew things, that understood the game.

"Damn, girl," Helen said. "You look like a problem."

Joanne smirked, feeling the heat of approval settle in her chest.

Helen yanked a skirt from the chaos, pairing it with a tight white blouse that barely survived the stretch of her curves. She stepped beside Joanne, tilting her head, studying their reflections side by side.

"Move," she said, nudging Joanne. "Let me see myself."

Joanne crossed her arms. "You don't need the mirror. I've seen for you."

"Still. Need to make sure."

Helen twisted, adjusted, scrutinized, the mirror catching her in that same fractured way, as if she were two women at once—the real one and the one she showed the world. Joanne understood that. More than she liked to admit.

She turned away, stepping toward the battered wooden dresser, its surface scarred from years of restless hands and impatient nights. She sifted through the tangled mass of undergarments, fingers brushing over lace, satin, cheap cotton. Some were old, frayed at the edges, ghosts of past nights that clung in ways even memory couldn't shake.

Others were bold, untouched, waiting. She reached for a simple, safe choice, something that wouldn't whisper too much about her intentions.

Helen caught her wrist.

"Not that one," she murmured.

Joanne barely had time to react before Helen plucked something from the pile—a flash of red, delicate, sinful. A thong, the kind that belonged to someone braver, someone who didn't hesitate. Helen held it up to the light, the lace almost glowing, threads catching in the dim bulb's flickering breath.

"This," Helen said, voice rich with meaning.

Joanne hesitated, a flush creeping up her throat. Something inside her recoiled; something else leaned forward, curious.

She took it from Helen's hand.

Tonight, she decided, was not a night for hesitation.

She slid the thong up her legs, the fabric vanishing beneath the golden dress, a whisper against her skin. It disappeared, leaving behind only the ghost of itself, faint red lines tracing its path along her hips, marking her, claiming her. The dress settled over her like a second skin, but she could still feel it, a secret only she knew, a quiet, electric thrill humming beneath the shimmer of gold.

Once they were satisfied with their outfits, it was time to sort out their hair. In the corner of the room, their small collection of wigs lay piled like discarded dreams, strands tangled together like lovers whispering secrets. Joanne plucked a synthetic blonde wig from the heap—Swedish hair, too perfect, too foreign—and pulled it on, adjusting it until it sat just right. It transformed her, made her someone else, someone untouchable.

Helen reached for a monofilament crown wig, one that clung closer to her real hair. She fumbled with it, hands shaking slightly, before turning to Joanne with a plea in her eyes.

"Joanne, can you help me with this?"

Joanne nodded, stepping forward, fingers working expertly, securing the wig in place. Then she turned to the lashes—Helen liked them long, dark, dramatic, as if they could blink away the world. Joanne applied them carefully, each movement precise, sculpting beauty with an artist's touch.

"Close your eyes," she instructed, sweeping crème powder over Helen's face, blending, enhancing. Helen obeyed without question, trust settling between them like an unspoken bond.

"There, all done," Joanne murmured, stepping back to admire her work.

Helen opened her eyes, blinking at her reflection. "We look amazing."

They checked their shoes next—high heels, towering, dangerous. But the slums of Nateete weren't built for stilettos. The ground outside was cracked and uneven, littered with puddles that swallowed light and spat back shadows. No, the shoes would stay in their handbags until they reached their destination. Only then would they step into the night, transformed.

Joanne gave the room one last glance, eyes landing on the small form curled in the corner. Her son, Anselm Mutebi. Seven years old, already accustomed to a life of whispered goodbyes and late returns. He stirred in his sleep, murmuring something lost to dreams. She moved to him, tucked the thin blanket tighter around his small body, pressed a silent promise to his forehead.

Helen clutched her tiny purse, and Joanne grabbed her handbag. One last look. One deep breath. Then they stepped out into the night, the cool air wrapping around them, heavy with the scent of rain and secrets. The city pulsed ahead, hungry and waiting.

CHAPTER 4:

Shawn

SHAWN checked into a modest hotel in downtown Kampala, the kind of place that didn't ask too many questions. The sign above the reception desk was faded, the letters peeling away like dead skin, and the air inside carried the musty scent of a thousand transient lives passing through. The lobby was nearly barren—just a couple of sagging chairs and a desk that looked like it had been scavenged from a government auction. A ceiling fan creaked overhead, struggling against the thick night air.

He wasn't one for television, but curiosity got the better of him. He grabbed the remote, flipped it on. The screen flickered to life—Netflix, Disney+, all the American staples. It amused him. No matter where he went, America was always there first. Even in the heart of Africa, Hollywood had set up camp. The thought made him grin, a cynical twist to his lips. Maybe the world really was getting smaller. Or maybe it was just America getting bigger.

After a quick, lukewarm shower that smelled faintly of rust and chlorine, he dressed in dark jeans and a fitted shirt, something that wouldn't make him stand out too much. He stepped out into the night, the Kampala air thick with heat and life. At the reception, a middle-aged woman with tired eyes and a warm smile barely looked up as he approached.

"Excuse me," he said. "Know any good places for a drink?"

She glanced up, sizing him up the way people did when they were deciding whether to tell the truth or the version you wanted to hear. Finally, she nodded. "There's Seniors Pub just around the corner. You can walk."

"How late is too late to come back?"

"There is no late time. Our night staff will let you in."

He thanked her and stepped outside. The city was alive in a way that was almost primal—bodies moving, voic es rising, neon signs buzzing like electric insects. Vendors called out, selling everything from grilled meat to cell-phone minutes, and motorcycles weaved through the traffic with reckless confidence. He followed her directions, his senses on high alert, tracking the ebb and flow of the night.

Seniors Pub wasn't hard to find. The place had a pulse to it, a low throb of bass that vibrated through the air. A handful of women lingered outside, their dresses tight, their eyes sharp, scanning the street like hunters waiting for prey. As he approached, their gazes locked onto him, sizing him up like he was merchandise on display. The place had the feel of something between a nightclub and a brothel—maybe both.

He remembered something one of his instructors back at Langley had told him, an African operative with a grin full of secrets. "In Africa, when you sleep with someone, you've got yourself a new family. That's why all the mothers' exes are 'taata' (dad), and all the fathers' exes are 'maama' (mom)."

The memory made him chuckle. He wasn't just here for a drink. He was here to blend in, to sink into the city's undercurrent, to disappear into the kind of connections that couldn't be traced on paper. If that meant being laid and creating a cover family for the night, so be it.

Shawn stepped forward, and the mountain of a man blocking his path barely moved. Built like a linebacker, he had a face carved from granite, but something in his eyes softened—a flicker of amusement, maybe, or just the resigned patience of a man who'd seen it all before.

"Welcome," the bouncer rumbled, his voice like distant thunder. He ran a handheld metal detector over Shawn's body, slow and thorough, before giving him the kind of pat-down that suggested he wasn't afraid to crack ribs if necessary. Satisfied, he gave a curt nod toward the door.

Inside, the club hit him like a punch to the senses. The music wasn't just loud; it lived in the walls, in the floors, in his chest. It was a pounding, relentless rhythm that synced disturbingly well with his own heartbeat. The air was thick, a heady cocktail of cigarette smoke, sweat, and the cloying perfume of too many people in too small a space. The dance floor churned with bodies lost in the music, faces caught somewhere between ecstasy and oblivion.

Shawn moved toward the bar, sliding into a space that had barely opened up before the bartender was already on him—a wiry man with quick hands and a sharper smile.

"What can I get you?" he yelled over the noise.

"Nile Special," Shawn said, knowing better than to hesitate. Foreigners hesitated. Foreigners got noticed.

The bartender nodded, grabbed a bottle, and slid it across the counter. Shawn took a swig, letting the beer settle on his tongue. It was rich, malty, strong enough to remind him he was on duty in Uganda.

He turned, scanning the room, his eyes drawn to a pool table where a game was in full swing. The players were serious, their movements calculated, but the laughter that followed every shot was easy, unforced. He leaned against the wall, watching, blending.

And then, she appeared.

A woman in a yellowish dress rose from her seat, stretching like a cat waking from a nap. She reached for her friend's hand, helping her up, and the whole goddamn room seemed to hold its breath. Shawn wasn't the only one watching. Every pair of eyes around the pool table trailed her as she moved toward the dance floor.

Her dress clung to her body like it had been painted on, outlining curves that made conversation irrelevant. The fabric molded to her hips, highlighting the roundness of her ass—a sway so hypnotic that even the music seemed to fall in step with it. The outline of her thong was unmistakable, the thin straps riding high on her waist before vanishing between toned cheeks. She wasn't dancing yet, but she was already commanding the room.

When she did start to move, it was something close to

witchcraft. Her hips rolled with a slow, deliberate rhythm, her body flowing with the music like she was born from it. The men muttered in Luganda, their words lost in the noise, but their tone wasn't.

Admiration. Hunger. Maybe a little fear. Shawn wasn't sure which one he felt more.

He realized, with absolute certainty, that he needed to talk to her.

Blending in wasn't just about drinking the local beer. It was about reading the room, knowing who mattered. And this woman, with her golden dress and a presence that could halt time, mattered.

He waited. Watched. Let the song play out, let her and her friend drift back to their table. Her laughter rang over the music, a bright, clear note in the club's dark symphony. She was magnetic, pulling people in without even trying.

Shawn drained the last of his beer and stepped forward.

"Hi," he said, flashing his most effortless smile. "Mind if I join you?"

She looked up, her gaze locking onto his. Up close, she was even more striking. Confidence radiated from her like body heat, the shimmer of her dress catching the dim light and casting gold along her smooth skin. Her friend barely glanced up, too caught up in her phone to care.

"So, do you come here often?" Shawn asked.

"Every now and then," she said. "Good place to unwind after a long week. What about you? You don't sound like you're from around here."

"You got me. I'm new in town, just exploring the nightlife. And I have to say, I'm impressed."

She laughed—a sound that was damn near musical. Heads turned at the sound of it, like it was a melody people wanted to follow.

"Well, welcome to Kampala, sir. Stick with me, and you'll see all the best spots."

The club was a living thing. The bass thumped like a giant's heartbeat, rattling bones, making promises it had no intention of keeping. Shawn leaned in closer to her, the only way to speak without shouting. It brought him near enough to catch the faint scent of coconut in her hair wig, near enough that he could feel the heat rolling off her skin.

"What's your name?" he asked.

"Sasha," she said, her lips curling at the edges. That kind of smile that knew too much and gave too little.

"Sasha, like President Obama's daughter?"

"That's the one. Do you like her?"

Shawn let out a short chuckle, shaking his head. "Oh no, I like you more."

That made her laugh—light, teasing, but it carried weight. She tilted her head slightly, studying him like she was trying to peel back the layers with her eyes.

"Are you American?" she asked. "You sound like that actor—the big one, the one who slapped a presenter on stage. What's his name again?"

"Will Smith," Shawn supplied. "But I'm Zimbabwean, not American."

Her gaze flickered—interest, curiosity, maybe even a little suspicion.

Shawn felt a shift in the air. Small, almost imperceptible, but it was there. If she could pick up on his accent, others could too. And that wasn't good. Disguising his background was crucial. He was supposed to be invisible. Ghosts didn't have nationalities.

"So, Sasha," he said, his tone easy, reeling the conversation back before it strayed too far. "What brings you to a place like this?"

She lifted one shoulder in a slow shrug, her movements effortless, hypnotic.

"Just looking for some fun, like everyone else. And you, Mr. Zimbabwean? What's your story?"

He let the question hang for a moment, taking a deliberate sip of his beer. She was testing him. That much was clear.

"Call me Shawn," he said finally. "I'm just a traveler, passing through. I like to explore new places, meet new people."

Her eyes narrowed just a fraction, but her smile never wavered.

"Is that so?" she mused. "You don't seem like the typical traveler. There's something different about you."

Shawn felt something tighten in his gut. Not fear—no, that was too strong a word. Awareness. Like stepping into a room and realizing the walls have ears. He forced an easy grin.

"Is that a good thing or a bad thing?"

"Definitely good," she purred, leaning in, closing the space between them. "I like a man with a bit of mystery."

Shawn raised his bottle, tapped it lightly against her glass.

"Here's to mystery then."

The clink of glass was drowned in the music, lost in the

hum of conversations pressing in from all sides. But for a second, just a second, there was only the two of them in that crowded, pulsating room. Shawn had the feeling he'd just stepped onto a path he couldn't turn back from.

And Sasha—if that was even her real name—she was either the start of something dangerous or something worse. Maybe both.

Shawn slumped in his chair, his eyes discreetly tracking Sasha's friend as she whispered with another man. It was a quiet negotiation, subtle nods and murmurs exchanged like spies in an underworld deal. Then, as if reaching an unspoken agreement, they stood and drifted toward the narrow staircase at the back of the club, vanishing into the shadows above.

He turned to Sasha. "Where's your friend gone?"

"You're a grown man. You figure it out," she said. "Do you want to go and play too?"

"Wouldn't say no."

"Then why didn't you ask earlier? Shy?"

"Didn't want to offend you."

"You care about offending strangers?"

"Strangers are still human."

Her lips curled into something between amusement and mild curiosity. She leaned in, close enough that he could smell the liquor on her breath.

"So, how much do you wanna give me?"

Shawn met her gaze. "Depends on what's on offer."

She smiled again, but this time it felt calculated, like the precise movement of a chess piece.

"Everything. Any fantasy, any desire. You'll remember me forever."

Shawn thought, *Jesus, this girl could sell sand in the desert.* If she'd been born in another world, she'd be pulling six figures in a high-rise office, running a sales team for some Fortune 500. But here she was, a marketing genius stuck selling her own skin. He kept those thoughts buried.

Instead, he said, "I'll pay whatever the market rate is."

"I hate that word," she said. "I don't sell in 'the market.' What I give you is tailored, made for you. If you want 'market rates,' pick another girl."

"Fair enough. Name your price."

"Fifty thousand shillings."

Shawn did the math—around fifteen bucks. Not bad, though he knew damn well she'd tacked on a foreigner tax. He glanced around; the locals seemed to be paying less. Still, he nodded.

"Okay. Do I pay you here?"

"No," she said, standing. "Upstairs."

As they ascended the stairs, a man sat at the top like a troll guarding a bridge. Before him, a small wooden table displayed a scatter of condoms and tissues—standard issue supplies, courtesy of the establishment. Shawn's eyes flicked to a pack of Durex, the only recognizable brand among the cheaper local ones. The gatekeeper glanced at him and, as if reading his mind, muttered, "Durex costs extra. Ugandan brands are free."

For the briefest moment, a ridiculous thought crossed Shawn's mind. He was American. Durex was American. Shouldn't he get a discount? If locals got their brands for free, why not him? But the thought passed as quickly as it came. This wasn't a game. His cover depended on blending in, not flashing entitlement.

Sasha nudged him to pay, and he forked over the extra ten thousand shillings for the room.

The man jerked a thumb down the hallway. "Two doors left."

Shawn followed Sasha down the corridor, a narrow passage lined with peeling paint and doors that had seen too much. From behind them came the sounds—low moans, sharp whispers, the rhythmic creak of bed springs, like some unholy symphony of lust and loneliness.

Sasha stopped at the designated door and turned to him, eyes dark and unreadable.

"Here we are."

She pushed the door open, and the room swallowed them whole.

It was small, barely more than a closet with a bed. An old iron frame, one leg propped up on a stack of bricks. The sheets—once white, now a tired, yellowed gray—lay in disarray, their fabric stiff with the ghosts of past encounters. The mattress sagged in the center, a concave pit of surrender. A single pillow, lumpy and sweat-stained, bore the imprint of too many heads pressed against it for too many nights.

Sasha moved to the bed, sat down, patted the spot beside her.

"Come on," she murmured.

Shawn hesitated, a moment's pause before stepping forward, closing the door behind him.

The lock clicked.

Inside the room, Sasha wasted no time. She slid her thong down with a quick, practiced flick of her wrist, letting it slither to the floor before scooping it up, wrapping it tight around her fingers like a silk noose.

Shawn watched, his mind buzzing in that strange space between lust and unease. She lay back on the bed, dress bunched up to her stomach, eyes locked onto him with a smile that didn't quite reach them.

"You're not waiting for me to undress you, are you?" she said. "That's not part of the package."

He fumbled with his pants, urgency mixed with an odd sense of guilt. The buckle clattered against the floor as he kicked them off, leaving his shirt on. His hands were unsteady as he reached for the condoms she had already laid out like bullets in a chamber. He tore one open with his teeth, rolling it on with expert efficiency.

But as he moved onto the bed, inching closer, something shifted. Her eyes were closed. Her face was blank, empty, like a mannequin discarded in a darkened store window.

"Please be quick," she murmured, her voice devoid of everything—desire, anticipation, even boredom. Just a flat, empty space.

A cold tendril of something—not quite fear, not quite disgust—coiled in Shawn's stomach.

He moved, obeying the command, but the rhythm felt wrong, the air in the room suddenly heavy, oppressive, like the walls themselves were closing in. Sasha lay still beneath him, stiff as rigor mortis.

He hesitated. "Am I hurting you?"

"Just be quick and get it over with."

Her voice was a dead thing, hollow and brittle.

Even through the fog of heat and adrenaline, Shawn felt something crack inside him. He stopped. Pulled back.

The silence in the room pressed down like an unseen hand. He reached for the tissues on the small table beside her bag, stripping off the condom and tossing it into the trash bag—already half-full with the ghosts of other men.

Sasha's eyes flickered open, confusion flashing across her face.

"Are you done?"

"No," Shawn said, shaking his head. "I just didn't want to hurt you."

She blinked, then laughed—a short, sharp sound, like a blade scraping against bone.

"You Zimbabwean? Why do you care about hurting a stranger you've paid?"

Her laughter was light, almost dismissive, as she pulled her dress back down, slipped into her knickers, and grabbed her bag. She scanned the room in that meticulous way women do, making sure she hadn't left a piece of herself behind.

As she moved to leave, Shawn reached out, tapped her shoulder.

"I want to ask you something."

She turned, one eyebrow raised. "Sure, go ahead."

"Can I pay you to stay with me for a night?"

"How much do you pay for a full night?"

"It's your territory, name the price again."

"You will pay me 100,000 shillings"

Shawn calculated the figure to be double, around $30. He agreed.

"Where's the hotel?" she asked.

"Agripina Inn. It's just a few blocks away, a walking area."

She nodded, seemingly considering it.

"Right, let's go down. I need to tell my friend where I'm going, and then we can head out."

With that, they left the room, descending the narrow staircase that seemed to creak under their weight. The atmosphere was thick with unspoken words, but for now, Shawn was focused on getting her to a place where they could talk—really talk—away from the transactional nature of this dim, claustrophobic room.

CHAPTER 5:

Joanne

JOANNE lay awake in the dim glow of the hotel room, listening to the steady rhythm of Shawn's breathing. After everything that had happened the night before, she had expected him to reach for her, to demand something in return for the money exchanged. But instead, he had collapsed onto the bed and drifted into sleep, as if she were nothing more than a shadow in the room. That unsettled her more than if he had tried something.

For a long time, she just watched him. There was something about the way he slept—completely unguarded, mouth slightly open, fingers curled loosely against his chest—that made him seem almost… harmless. That was dangerous. It was always the quiet ones, the gentle ones, who hid the deepest scars.

By the time the faintest hint of dawn seeped through the curtains, she had made up her mind. She reached out and shook his shoulder, just enough to pull him from whatever dreams had been keeping him under.

"Hey," she whispered. "I've got to go. I have a son I need to prepare for school."

Shawn blinked sluggishly, rubbing his eyes like a man who had just crawled out of a grave. "Oh, you're a mother?" he asked, sounding genuinely surprised. "I'm a father too—of one boy."

"How old is your son?" she asked.

"He's four," he replied. "He's staying with his mother."

A small shift, barely noticeable, passed between them. Joanne wasn't sure what it was—maybe recognition, maybe something closer to regret.

"What about you? How old is your boy?" he asked.

"He's seven," she said. "So, you're married in Zimbabwe?"

"No, no," he answered quickly, shaking his head. "We just had a baby together back in college. Now we're just co-parenting."

Silence settled in, thick and uncertain. It was the kind of silence that wrapped around you when you stood too close to a choice you weren't sure you should make.

Then he spoke again, his voice quieter, almost hesitant. "Can I ask for your mobile number?"

She stiffened. This was the part where things usually turned sour. She didn't mix business with pleasure. That was a rule she had built walls around. But something about the way he asked—tentative, almost like he needed it for more than just convenience—made her pause.

"I don't usually go out with clients," she said. "It's just not what I do."

"Please," he begged. "I'll be gentle. I just need a local connection, someone who knows their way around."

She sighed, already regretting what she was about to do. But the words left her lips before she could stop them.

"Okay," she relented. "But you can call me Joanne. That's my real name. 'Sasha' was just for work."

She saw the flicker in his eyes—surprise, curiosity, maybe even a little bit of hope. That last part was what worried her.

Shawn nodded, accepting the unspoken terms.

"What are you going to do during the day?" she asked.

"I've got a few meetings with my company's colleagues until around three," he said. "But I'll be free most of the evening."

"Okay," she said, standing up and gathering her things. "Call me later once you're done with work."

With that, she picked up her bag and quietly slipped out of the room.

CHAPTER 6:

Shawn

THE journey to becoming a CIA spook didn't start with a gun or a mission—it started with a cell. Concrete, cold, and full of urine-stained regrets. Shawn had been locked up for a murder he didn't commit, and if that didn't sound cliché, well, the murdered girl was his Ugandan girlfriend and classmate, Sheila. Boston PD had slapped the cuffs on him so fast, you'd think he'd confessed in his sleep.

Turns out, Sheila had made enemies beyond the bedroom. The real killer was some racist white boy with a God complex and a dull blade. When the detectives finally pulled their heads out of their paperwork and caught the bastard, Shawn got released with a formal apology and a free bus pass. Justice, American-style.

He went back to Essex University in downtown Boston like a ghost haunting his old life. Studied creative writing, because fiction was the only place people told the truth. By graduation, he had a degree and a baby. Katie, his girlfriend—now very much *not* Sheila—had delivered a healthy, screaming boy the same week Shawn walked across the stage. They named him Gabriel. Shawn called him "Gabe the Tax Deduction" when no one was listening.

And yet, even while holding his newborn son, Shawn had this itchy idea that writing stories wasn't enough. "Saving the world" had a better ring to it than submitting to literary journals run by sad white men with cardigans and inferiority complexes.

So, on a random Tuesday that felt like a Monday, he walked into the U.S. Army recruitment office in Dorchester. A sergeant with a buzzcut and a smile sharp enough to cut drywall looked him up and down.

"You look like you can handle a ruck march, boy," the sergeant said, eyeing Shawn's gym-built shoulders. "Ever think about serving your country?"

"Sure. Why not?"

He figured it'd be sit-ups, patriotism, and maybe a free tank ride.

The Army wanted citizens between 17 and 35 who weren't full-on felons and could pass a physical. Shawn fit the bill. Sort of. After being acquitted of murdering his girlfriend—turns out being creepy wasn't a felony—his only real crimes were swiping a Red Bull in high school and abandoning CrossFit the day his intestines tried to exit through his mouth mid-burpee.

First came the ASVAB, a test with all the charm of a DMV line. He crushed the verbal sections, flopped on the mechanical stuff—he figured Google could explain pulleys better than he ever could. Still, his score of 62 got him into the infantry. He chose 11B because it sounded like a cheat code and he'd watched *Black Hawk Down* like it was scripture.

MEPS was a carnival of needles, urine tests, and personal questions. One doctor with the bedside manner of a parking ticket asked if he'd ever smoked weed. Shawn said no. A lie, obviously, but the truth involved coughing like a Dickens orphan after one hit.

Basic Training at Fort Benning—now called Fort Moore, thanks to the Army's PR makeover—was a 10-week exercise in misery. The drill sergeant screamed like a banshee on meth. "You move slower than my grandma with a broken hip, O'Connor!" he roared as Shawn face-planted in Georgia mud.

The Army Combat Fitness Test was biblical punishment. Deadlifts, sprints, carries, and a two-mile run that made Shawn negotiate with God around mile one. Somehow, he survived. Barely. Then came AIT, where he learned not to shoot his own team and developed a disturbing enthusiasm for marksmanship. Every paper target wore his old economics professor's smug little face.

Two years at Fort Bragg followed. Rifles, boredom, and the slow rot of disillusionment. Katie called him with an ultimatum: come home and be a family man, or stay gone and join the honorable brotherhood of child-support deadbeats. Shawn chose career over crib. He told himself Gabe would understand someday. That was a lie too.

Then came Afghanistan. And the CIA.

One afternoon, during a boring patrol through beige hell, a man in civilian clothes strolled up to him like he was buying tomatoes at a farmer's market. He looked like an LL Bean model with secrets.

"Ever think about doing something bigger?" the man said, handing him a card with nothing on it but a phone number.

Shawn, tired of sand in his boots and poop-in-a-bag meals, made the call.

A week later, he was sitting in a hotel room in D.C., across from a guy in a charcoal suit with the smile of a funeral director.

"Do you believe in loyalty?" the man asked. "Are you okay with lying for a living?"

Shawn said yes. Because truth hadn't done him many favors.

The CIA application process was like enlisting in the Army, but with more coffee and more paranoia. MyLINK asked for a resume, transcripts, and three essays on "Why I Want to Be a Spy." Shawn typed out something noble about "defending liberty," while secretly hoping for a cool codename like "Shadow Hawk."

The background check was surgical. They talked to everyone—his high school janitor, his ex-girlfriend's mom, even the Dunkin' guy who always forgot his cream. The polygraph was a medieval ordeal. Three hours of questions like, "Have you ever betrayed your country?" and, "Do you enjoy taking risks?" He almost failed just thinking about nachos.

Medical check? Passed. Psych eval? Also passed, although the shrink side-eyed him when he said he sometimes dreamed in first-person shooter mode.

Then came training. Eighteen months at "The Farm,"

also known as Camp Peary. Less James Bond, more *Hunger Games* with paperwork. Tradecraft, surveillance, recruiting assets, making dead drops in porta-potties. Physical training involved hand-to-hand combat and being hunted through the woods like a deer wearing Nikes.

Classroom work taught him to lie professionally and write reports that didn't read like Facebook rants. His instructors were ex-SEALs, former NSA nerds, and at least one guy who looked suspiciously like the janitor from *Stranger Things.*

The final test? A simulated hostile-city operation. Steal intel. Escape. Live. Shawn pulled it off by hiding in a dumpster behind a fake pizzeria while his "pursuers" argued about lunch.

And then—just like that—he was a CIA officer. Badge, gun, and a one-way ticket to hell in a tailored suit.

His latest assignment: Operation Black Tiger.

Target country: Uganda.

Objective: Rescue the president.

Threat level? Somewhere between "mild inconvenience" and "biblical bloodbath."

And Shawn? He was ready. Or so he told himself.

*

Now this morning in Uganda, Shawn slept like the dead—except the dead probably got better rest. Two hours ticked by after Joanne left, and still he lay there, sprawled like a man who'd lost a boxing match with jet lag. The transatlantic shuffle from the U.S. to Kenya had wrung him out like a bar rag. When he finally hit the pillow, it hit back and pinned him there.

He dreamed of weird things: a president with no face giving a speech underwater, Katie holding Gabe while floating past on a mattress shaped like a coffin, and a goat that spoke fluent Swahili asking him if he remembered the safe word. His subconscious, always a little theatrical, was in rare form.

Then came the knock.

Three taps. Not urgent, not lazy. Just… deliberate. Like someone trying not to wake the devil, but needing to borrow his lighter.

Shawn stirred, one eye crusted shut, the other barely tracking the dim light seeping through the curtains. His body screamed in six languages. For a second, he thought it might be Katie. Maybe Gabe. Maybe the past had caught up with him, wearing Joanne's perfume and tapping like it belonged.

The knock came again. This time, a little louder.

He reached for the Glock tucked under his shirt on the nightstand—standard spy habit, born of too many nights in places where the welcome mat came with land mines. He didn't call out. He never did. You don't shout, "Who is it?" when you're in a country where the wrong name could earn you a plastic bag over the head and a one-way trip to Lake Victoria.

He padded to the door in bare feet, each step like walking on rusty nails. The knock had stopped. Now there was only the breathless pause of someone on the other side, waiting to see if they'd made a terrible mistake.

Shawn unlatched the lock, cracked the door, and peeked through the gap.

The man outside smiled sheepishly and mumbled an apology—wrong door, his bad. Shawn shut the door in his face without a word, turned, and practically dove back into bed like it owed him money. Sleep grabbed him the second his head hit the pillow, dragging him under like a jealous lover. Within moments, he was out cold again—dead to the world and determined to stay that way.

He was dreaming again—this time of a forest full of corpses singing gospel songs in reverse. One of them looked like Sheila. Another had his father's eyes. One tried to hand him a phone that wouldn't stop ringing. When he finally took it, the voice on the other end whispered: "They know you're here."

Shawn jolted awake.

It was his alarm ringing at 7:30, a wheezing little banshee that clearly didn't care about his suffering. He ignored it and sank back into sleep. It screamed again fifteen minutes later—more insistent this time, like a rat scratching behind the walls of his skull. He considered silencing it with a violent swipe or maybe a bullet, but in the end, he did nothing. It eventually gave up. Most things do, if you ignore them long enough.

Then came the call at 8:00. His contact was downstairs, waiting. No hellos. No good mornings. Just the quiet implication: *Get moving or you're already dead.*

Shawn groaned, muttered a half-hearted apology, and peeled himself out of bed like an old sticker off a rusty bumper.

The bathroom light buzzed, flickering weakly, as he rinsed his face in the chipped porcelain sink of his hotel room. Water pooled in the basin, slow to drain, a murky swirl of last night's grime circling the gaping mouth of the rusted pipe. His eyes landed on a tube of Colgate toothpaste lying on the counter. The cap was missing, a hardened crust forming at the opening.

He picked it up, rolling the soft metal between his fingers, squeezing out a perfect coil of red and white onto his toothbrush. The colors twisted together like a candy cane, or, more fittingly, like the American flag. He smirked. So, this was African independence? A country clawing its way out from beneath the boot of colonial rule, yet still brushing its teeth with a Western brand. It was laughable, really—the grand speeches, the nationalist pride, the rage against foreign influence—all while their very breath carried the scent of America.

The irony was bitter on his tongue as he scrubbed his teeth, the bristles sawing against his gums. A taste of blood, faint and metallic, pooled in his mouth. He spat it out, watching it spiral into the drain, red vanishing into the darkness below.

He slid into a pair of blue jeans that still smelled faintly of airplane and desperation, then tugged on a white long-sleeved t-shirt that had seen better days—probably sometime around the Bush administration. Casual was the uniform of ghosts and men trying not to be noticed. If you wanted to blend in on the dusty streets of Uganda, you didn't dress like a tourist. You dressed like someone nobody remembered seeing.

He slung a small laptop bag over his shoulder—not that there was a laptop in it. Just some forged documents, a dog-eared novel for cover, and a few secrets he prayed no one would ever ask about.

Then he stepped out, slow and measured, moving with the casual rhythm of a man who looked like he had nothing to hide—though, of course, he was hiding everything. The trick was in the pace. Men with secrets didn't run. Dead men did. And Shawn wasn't planning on dying today. Not before lunch anyway. Maybe after, if things went sideways.

His contact was already in the lobby. Walusimbi—or whatever he was calling himself this week. The name was about as real as a stage prop, just something to hang on for the sake of conversation. Shawn had been in the game long enough to know names were like breath on glass: there for a second, gone in a blink. Hell, even *he* wasn't Shawn today. He was Michael—quiet, forgettable Michael, who asked no questions and didn't exist in any system that mattered.

Walusimbi wore a suit so stiff it could've walked itself across the room, and his eyes flicked around like they had somewhere else to be. He knew. Of course he knew. But they played the game anyway. That's how this world worked. Lies wrapped in suits, walking side by side, pretending they weren't both armed to the teeth with truths they couldn't afford to say out loud.

The drive through Kampala was a slow, suffocating crawl through dust-choked streets. The city felt restless, unsettled. The elections had been brutal, the violence as thick in the air as the smoke rising from burning tires. Soldiers loomed on street corners, their rifles slung casually over their shoulders, eyes scanning the crowds with the kind of detachment that only came from knowing they had the power to kill without consequence.

Vendors barked out prices from wooden stalls, their voices rising above the cacophony of honking boda bodas weaving through traffic like insects on a carcass. A newspaper headline caught Shawn's eye as they idled at a stoplight: *PRESIDENTIAL VICTORY OR MILITARY COUP?* A grainy photo of the old but newly "re-elected for the tenth time" president scowled up at him, his face carved from stone. The man had won again, alright—if you counted stolen ballots and bodies dumped in ditches as votes.

As they left the city center, the roads grew worse, the asphalt crumbling into jagged potholes that sent shocks through Shawn's spine with every bump. Buildings leaned against one another, their facades scarred with bullet holes from conflicts no one spoke about.

Shawn turned his thoughts to Joanne—or Sasha, as she had introduced herself. He had slipped up, given her his real name. A stupid mistake. He told himself it didn't mean anything, that it was just exhaustion, just habit. But deep down, he knew better. He had let something about her get under his skin, and in this line of work, that was a dangerous thing.

The car jolted as they turned onto a narrow dirt road, the city shrinking behind them. Mulago Hospital loomed ahead, its blue and white walls streaked with grime, a place that smelled of death even from a distance. They pulled up beside a squat five-story building, its windows dark and watchful. Walusimbi didn't say a word as he climbed out, motioning for Shawn to follow.

Inside, the air was stale, thick with the scent of old paper and sweat. A single bulb swung from the ceiling, casting sickly yellow light across the bare room. A desk. A few chairs. A door leading to some unseen place beyond. Walusimbi gestured for him to sit. "Wait here," he said, before disappearing into the shadows.

Shawn exhaled, rolling his shoulders. The real work was about to begin. Outside, in the dying light of morning, Kampala pulsed with uneasy energy, the city holding its breath, waiting for whatever came next.

Before the meeting, Shawn stood on the fifth floor of the high-rise, staring out through the grimy window at the shifting mass of humanity below.

From five stories up, Kampala sprawled out before him, a tangled mess of roads and shanties, high-rise towers and crumbling colonial relics, all drowning under the weight of the sun. But his eyes weren't on the city. The crowd below had swelled—an undulating mass of bodies, fists raised, voices lifted in defiance. The protests had been relentless since the election, since the announcement that Joel Katila Muaji—the decrepit, 82-year-old dictator—had won yet another term. The people weren't buying it.

The sound of revolution drifted upward in waves—chanting, singing, the rhythmic pounding of fists against anything that would carry the echo. Music blasted from unseen speakers, tinny but defiant, the lyrics sharpened by rage and years of suffocated hope. Down in the streets, the colors of the Ugandan flag bled together in the humid air, bright swaths of red, yellow, and black caught in the midday glare. At first glance, it looked almost jubilant, like a national celebration rather than a demand for justice.

It almost looked beautiful. Almost. Then came the sirens.

Shrill. Mechanical. Shrieked like a death rattle through the streets. The celebratory fervor curdled into something else—fear, thick and cloying.

Gunfire erupted.

Shawn ducked on instinct, pressing his back against the wall as the first cracks of automatic weapons tore through the chanting. The glass didn't shatter—the building was too expensive for that—but it rattled in the frame, vibrating with each shot. He swallowed hard, forcing himself to move, to look.

Outside, chaos bloomed like a disease. The crowd scattered, some running, others dropping where they stood, clutching at wounds that hadn't even begun to bleed out yet. The police—no, not just police, these were something else, men in riot gear, JATT faces masked behind dark visors—descended like wolves. They moved in formation, shields raised, batons swinging, boots crushing fallen banners underfoot. The peaceful march had dissolved into screaming, into bodies trampled in the crush of fear.

Tear gas plumed in thick white clouds, curling through the streets, stinging even from this distance. Shawn's throat tightened, his lungs rejecting the air. He had smelled this before—in Caracas, in Cairo, in places where democracy was just another word for the promises men made before loading their guns.

Shawn watched the chaos unfold like a low-budget apocalypse. Protesters had turned the road into a minefield of rubble, hurling stones like toddlers on a sugar high, jamming traffic and common sense alike. The cars behind them jerked and stumbled, their pursuers more frustrated than a mosquito trapped behind glass.

But then came the crown jewel of the freak show.

A lone protester staggered into view, cradling a bucket like it was the Holy Grail. Shawn squinted. The kid looked possessed—or high, which was pretty much the same thing in that part of town. The police were on him in a heartbeat, shouting, pointing, reaching for something unpleasant.

And then—like a magician pulling a rabbit from a particularly disgusting hat—he dumped the contents of the bucket over his own head.

It wasn't water. *Oh no*. Shawn gagged as realization hit.

Feces. Human waste. Homemade horror soup.

The cops skidded to a halt, visibly recoiling, their uniforms not nearly thick enough for this brand of biological warfare. One of them made the sign of the cross. Another whimpered.

The poor bastard ran while they were still deciding whether to chase him or just call a priest.

He almost made it. Almost.

A gun cracked—sharp, final—and the protester dropped like a puppet with its strings cut, a steaming mess in more ways than one.

"Damn," Shawn muttered. "That's one hell of a shitty way to go."

Another man went down hard, tripping over another who had already collapsed, his face pressed to the asphalt, unmoving. A woman carrying a child staggered, her head jerking back from the force of a baton strike. She crumpled. The child rolled from her grasp, wailing as a boot slammed down next to its tiny body.

Shawn counted. One, two, three, five—too many

to keep up. Bodies hit the ground like felled trees, their blood mingling with the dust.

A young man in a torn football jersey was trying to pull an elderly woman out of the chaos. He didn't make it. An officer's baton cracked against his skull, the sound hollow, too soft for such a devastating blow. He crumpled, arms spasming, fingers twitching in the dirt. The woman screamed, her hands shaking as she reached for him, but another officer shoved her back. She disappeared into the blur of bodies, her cry lost beneath the roar of boots and engines.

And then, as if from the mouth of hell itself, the truck rolled in.

Big, black, armored, it rumbled down the street with the inevitability of a hearse. JATT men jumped down from the back. They carried no weapons, only one task. The dead and dying were lifted—limbs limp, heads lolling—and tossed like sacks of grain into the truck bed.

Some were still alive, moaning weakly, hands twitching. It didn't matter. They were all going to the same place.

One. Two. Five. Ten. The numbers rose with sickening efficiency. No hesitation. No reverence. Just another day, another cleanup job.

Shawn swallowed bile. He knew exactly where those bodies were going.

River Nile.

He'd read it in the files, seen the satellite images, the grainy footage of bloated corpses snagged in reeds.

The president's son—General Mlevi Kainewaragi, the real power behind the throne—had perfected this system. No bodies. No graves. No evidence. If the world couldn't see the dead, then, officially, they didn't exist. Their families would search for them in police stations and morgues, never knowing they had been swallowed whole by the river, their remains picked clean by crocodiles.

A woman in a red dress broke through the crowd, wailing, clutching the arm of a man already slick with blood. Husband? Brother? Lover? Didn't matter. She begged, pleaded, her voice hoarse, hands shaking as she tried to pull him from the fate already decided for him.

A soldier shoved her away. She stumbled, but still she clawed at the corpse. She was screaming now, something raw, something primal, something that made Shawn's ribs feel like they were closing in on his lungs.

The soldier raised his baton.

Shawn turned from the window before it fell.

His breath came sharp and fast, adrenaline buzzing under his skin. He was here for a mission. A job. Intelligence. He had seen worse, but the horror of it never dulled, never became easier to swallow. The air in the room was stale, thick with the residue of sweat and cigarette smoke, and yet it was still cleaner than the air outside, where hope was being choked under a dictator's boot.

Walusimbi was waiting to usher him into a secret meeting.

Shawn wiped his face, exhaled slow, and turned toward the door to a meeting room. The mission was on a start.

CHAPTER 7:

The General

THE General let the silence stretch. The air in the room was thick, humid, laced with the weight of unspoken fears. The ceiling fan overhead churned in slow, lazy circles, pushing the heat around but doing nothing to relieve it. The men around the table—his men—sat rigid, waiting. Some wore the calm of seasoned killers, men who had spent years obeying without question. Others, younger, less bloodied, shifted in their seats, their nervous fingers betraying them. The General saw everything. He always did.

He exhaled slowly, rolling his shoulders. The leather of his chair creaked beneath him. Then, finally, he spoke.

"There's a rumor."

His voice was calm, measured, the voice of a man accustomed to control.

"They're saying the old man is dead."

No one flinched. But he could feel their bodies tighten, their eyes darting to one another. He let that hang in the air for a second, then leaned forward, pressing his thick fingers against the polished mahogany table.

"We all know how dangerous that kind of talk is," he continued, his tone sharpening, slicing through the oppressive heat like a razor.

"A rumor like this is a match to dry grass. It spreads. It burns. And it does not stop until the whole fucking country is on fire."

He let the words settle, savoring the way the room seemed to shrink under their weight. Then he laid it out for them.

"This is what happens now," he said. "You hear someone whispering about the president's death? You put them down. Right there. No trials, no arrests. No fucking mercy."

He flicked his gaze over his officers, one by one, letting them feel it.

"I don't care if it's a journalist. A blogger. A priest in a pulpit. If they speak of the president in the past tense, they are ghosts already."

He paused, picking up his glass of wine, swirling the deep red liquid in slow, hypnotic circles. Then he took a sip, let the bitterness settle on his tongue, and smiled.

"Except for one." He sneered. "Bob Omubanda. The musician. That fool has too many eyes watching him. The American media have a soft spot for his kind, and I have no interest in watching CNN turn him into a martyr. But he needs to understand that even untouchables can bleed. Make sure he's reminded of that."

A slow nod passed around the table. They understood. There were ways to break a man without spilling his blood.

"To be specific," he said, "let that guitar-humping clown turned politician know he loses *everything* if he opens that mouth of his. And I mean *everything*—the mansions, the SUVs, the stupid American scholarships for his ungrateful little bastards. Poof. Gone. We don't just ruin careers, gentlemen—we *unmake* lives."

There was a pause, thick and heavy, like a hangman tying a final knot.

"Not just him," the General went on. "The whole family. Every cousin, every baby mama, every uncle laundering our kindness in real estate and Range Rovers—we take it all back. And we do it *loudly.* We let the public know exactly who made them rich. Us. The regime. Midnight deals signed in whispers and handshakes while the rest of the country slept on empty stomachs. Let the people know just how dumb they've been all these years, worshipping these opposition conmen who talk revolution by day and cash government checks by night."

He chuckled—low and bitter. A sound like a coffin lid creaking shut.

"Let's be real. You really think someone gets rich by shouting 'dictator' into a microphone? No, my father—God rest that iron soul—he wasn't just a president, he was Uganda's original mob boss. And he *shared.* That's the secret to staying in power, boys. You don't kill your loudest enemies. You *feed* them."

The soldiers shifted, some stifling grins, others dead silent, absorbing the dark gospel.

"Every time a new rebel rose up with a mouth too big

and a crowd too loud, Daddy would send a messenger. Not a threat. Not a bullet. A *sack of money.* Just enough to buy silence… or at least turn the fire into smoke. They'd take it. Every single one. Set up businesses, buy land, build towers with their siblings' names carved in stone. And in return? They played opposition like it was theater. Great actors. No plot."

He leaned forward now, voice dropping to a near-whisper.

"Except for *one fool.* Barigye Kato. A man with the ego of a demigod and the brains of a wet brick. Took my father's money—then still tried to take the throne."

The room stiffened. The General smiled like a man about to rip the wings off a fly.

"Since we're all here, and I'm feeling generous, let me tell you Barigye's real problem with my father. It wasn't politics. It was *personal.* It started in the bedroom."

A few of the men laughed uneasily.

"Barigye was once my father's personal doctor. That means he saw *everything*, if you catch my drift. Claimed to one of my dad's high-school flings—Evelyn Basiima, fine legs, poor judgment—that he was, shall we say, *better equipped.* Bigger stick. Better hammer. Evelyn, ever the scientist, decided to investigate. Opened the lab. Ran her tests."

He paused, letting the vulgarity linger like a ghost in the room.

"But after a while, the novelty wore off. A big tool's nice, she said, but it doesn't get you into the State House. She started missing the presidential treatment—motorcades, bodyguards, silk sheets. She wanted a president, not a penis. And that's when Barigye made the dumbest promise of his life. He told her, 'I'll become president of Uganda.' He *resigned* from government. Started calling himself a revolutionary."

"He sold the same old pitch to the voters—that he had the biggest hammer in the country. The campaign crowds, started calling him *Sseyondo*, like he was some mythical blacksmith sent to fix the nation by smashing its skull."

The General's voice hardened.

"He ran against my father—again and again. Got votes, sure. But votes don't count if you don't *count* the votes. My old man didn't waste time charming the masses. He charmed the *counters.* That was the game.

"But Barigye... He got desperate. When ballots failed, he went for the nuclear button. He reached out to the very machine that put my father in power: MI6. Yes, London's invisible hand. The men who planted the seed and watered it with blood and oil."

He spat on the floor.

"You can take my dad's woman. Maybe. But you don't take his *power.* That's sacred. MI6 didn't like that. Daddy was their Frankenstein. They don't take kindly to rebels trying to smash their toys. So, they baited Barigye, set a neat little trap, then wrapped him up in ribbon and handed him back. *Return to sender.*"

Now the General's face was stone.

"And that, my friends, is the true story. Not the garbage in newspapers. Not the whispered lies on X Spaces. This is the story you remember. This is why Barigye will *pay.* One way or the other, he *will* kneel—apologize to my father's ghost for breaking his heart and disrespecting his throne. Or he'll learn the hard way that some mistakes get you more than killed."

Silence followed. Not out of fear—but reverence. The kind of silence that hangs in the air right before the thunder cracks.

The General straightened, his fingers tapping against the table.

"Now, these protests."

He allowed himself a small chuckle. A joyless thing, like the scrape of metal against stone.

"They're demanding proof of life. They want to see the old man, but we all know that's not possible."

He lifted his eyes to the far end of the table, where Douglas sat stiff-backed, a thin sheen of sweat on his forehead.

"Start tweeting like him—same tone, same words." the General said. "The president is alive. He is recovering. He sends his love. You know the tone—call them his grandchildren, just like always. Keep them calm, keep them waiting."

He stood now, his movements slow, deliberate, like a beast rising from the depths of a murky river. The chair scraped against the floor.

"But for those who won't be pacified," he said, rolling his shoulders, "for the ones who take to the streets, who scream for change, who think they can defy us…"

He let out a quiet breath, shaking his head.

"You crush them. No rubber bullets, no tear gas, no warnings. You shoot to kill."

The room absorbed his words like a dying thing taking its last breath. No one dared look away.

"And when they fall," the General continued, "you don't leave them there for the world to see. We will not be another headline. A truck follows behind. The bodies go in the truck. No photos. No videos. No evidence."

A slow inhale, a moment of silence, then the final command.

"When the truck is full," he said, his voice almost a whisper, "you take it to Jinja. To River Nile."

No one moved.

"The river will take them," he murmured. "The crocodiles will do the rest."

He straightened his cuffs, then reached for his wine again. The meeting was over. The orders had been given. His men would do what needed to be done. Because that was the way of things. The old man had built this empire with blood and fire, and the General would ensure it endured.

He took one last sip of his wine. Then, without another word, he turned and walked out of the room.

The General had just dismissed his officers, the room still smelling of fear, cheap cologne, and burnt coffee when one of them—a bony little man with too many medals and not enough common sense—scurried after him down the Nile Hotel's dim corridor.

"Sir! A word, sir—a quick word!"

The General stopped walking, mostly because he wanted to see which shade of terror the man would turn when he answered.

He pivoted slowly, like a villain in a badly lit soap opera.

"What… do you want to say?"

The officer swallowed hard, his Adam's apple bobbing like a trapped animal.

"Sir, the protesters' bodies are piling up… in the morgues."

For a moment, the General said nothing. Just stared at the man like he'd farted during a funeral.

"Morgues?" the General finally said, his voice low, syrupy with sarcasm. "Who told you to give those pests *dignity*? Why are you wasting refrigeration on traitors?"

"Sir…" the officer stammered, "the ones we dumped in the river… some of them are floating back. The crocodiles—uh—they can't eat fast enough. Too much meat. Too little appetite."

The General sighed like a disappointed father watching his son fail at hiding a body.

"So now we're making the crocodiles look lazy. Great. Anything else?"

"Yes, sir. We've got ten trucks full of corpses parked in Jinja. Drivers say they can't offload everything at once—the riverbank's getting crowded, and the crocs are starting to get… overwhelmed."

"Well, *is* the Nile the only goddamn river in this banana republic?" the General barked. "There's a whole country full of water. Lakes! Streams! Drainage ditches! Get creative, soldier. Use Google Maps. Just don't bring me logistics about dead people again. I pay you to make them disappear, not give them scenic tours."

"Yes, sir! Of course, sir! I'll find another river. Maybe even Lake Kyoga."

The officer saluted and fled like a man escaping a burning outhouse.

The General kept walking, but the gears in his skull had started to creak and grind—old, rusted things that only turned when the dead refused to stay buried. The corpses were piling up, and unlike unpaid bills or crusty socks, you couldn't just shove them under the bed and forget. They were floating now—bloated, smug, showing off on riverbanks like they were auditioning for a horror film. Worse, some nosy do-gooders had started dragging them out of the Nile like lost treasure. That was dangerous. These bodies weren't supposed to be found. They were supposed to vanish—like secrets, or shame, or whistleblowers.

He'd have to get ahead of this mess before someone made a Netflix documentary.

Still, he wasn't too worried. Western media had the attention span of a kitten on cocaine. And his lobbyist friends in Washington? They'd smother any headlines with a donation and a wink. As long as the story stayed on social media—lost in a sea of selfies, conspiracy theories, and political relatives wailing into their phone cameras—he could manage it.

Dead men don't talk. That was the whole damn point. And the ones gunned down on the cracked streets of Kampala and dumped in River Nile? They barely had time to float before the crocodiles clocked in for lunch. Bones, blood, silence. That was the cycle. Efficient. Final.

And the opposition! *Ha!* The General nearly smiled—an expression so rare it might've triggered a coup if anyone saw it. Thinking about them always tickled something dark in his ribs. Like rain in the Sahara, or remorse at a firing squad. *God's own joke*, he called them.

No country on Earth had a more neutered, housebroken opposition than Uganda. If cowardice were a currency, theirs would've bought the moon.

Their leader—oh, the leader—led from a throne of upholstery, hunched over a smartphone, barking revolution from his living room on X Spaces like a prophet with a Wi-Fi signal.

He'd warn his followers not to take to the streets. "It's dangerous," he'd say, as if that was news. *No kidding, sunshine—people get killed in revolutions. That's the point.*

The General relished the absurdity. They demanded that the government stop killing their supporters—stop throwing them into the Nile like unwanted furniture, stop torturing them in safe houses that were neither safe nor houses. But the moment things got hot, they curled up like scared cats and decided maybe antagonizing the government wasn't such a good idea after all.

Didn't matter. The government still came for them. Dragged them from their beds at 3 a.m. like bad dreams you couldn't quite shake. Picked them like ripe fruit, bruised or not. No one stopped them. No one dared.

And when the opposition's fearless leader staged his online "protests," the General would nod to the IT guys—just a slight tilt of the head—and they'd scramble the signal a little. Nothing major. Just enough static to make the livestream stutter. Then the dear leader would turn to his fans and whisper in dramatic tones, "They're scared. Look, the government is trying to stop us. They're *terrified*."

Terrified, the General thought, nearly laughing now. *Of buffering?*

According to them, online protest was the most powerful tool to make a tyrant listen. The best way to resist was to tweet hard and refresh often.

Good fools. The best kind.

Any government lucky enough to have an opposition like Uganda's could rule forever. Hell, even death wouldn't interrupt it. They'd probably tweet the funeral.

The General could hardly believe his luck. The pop singer had turned revolution into a traveling circus, and the clowns weren't even aware they were clowns. No more street protests, no more tear gas. Just boat rides, disco lights, and champagne sprayed on rented decks. From his rat-hole in Kamwokya to South Africa, Boston, Toronto, the man presided over parties like some glitter-soaked prophet. The bastard probably will throw a rave on the moon if Elon Musk sold him a ticket.

Whenever some sour-faced exile had the audacity to say, "*Maybe less dancing—our brothers are rotting in basements back home*," they were smacked down as jealous nobodies, accused of envying the singer's fame as the great *Opposer-in-Chief.* That part always made the General chuckle. Fame—built not on fire and fury, but on white girls clinging to the singer's son at each party and fashion choices dissected like holy scripture.

The General's favorite act in the opposition circus was watching how his old man handpicked the ringmasters. The man didn't just run the country like a dictator; he ran the opposition too, like a ventriloquist with a fist shoved so far up their spines they burped talking points.

Old Muaji wasn't playing politics. He was playing goddamn 4D chess in a country where most folks were still chewing on the checker pieces. Always one move ahead, sometimes two, and if a few pawns had to bleed out on the board—well, you don't win by being squeamish.

His greatest checkmate? Smuggling his bastard son Enock Rugasira into the opposition like a diseased organ into a body already on life support. Enock sat there smiling in press conferences, pretending to fight the regime—while the regime tucked him in at night and read him bedtime reports. It was beautiful. Ugly, treacherous, gut-wrenching—but beautiful.

Officially, Enock was just the "Secretary General"—the opposition's Mr. Fix-It-All. But everyone who mattered knew the plan: if the regime ever started crumbling—say, under international pressure or one too many bodies dumped in the Nile—Enock would be in the right chair to catch the falling crown.

The headlines would scream *"Opposition Takes Power in Uganda!"* The world would clap like trained seals. CNN would run soft-focus segments on reconciliation. Maybe even a Nobel Peace Prize. But under all that glitter and bullshit, one fact would remain: the president's son will still be the president.

*

But then there was *him*. That one mosquito still buzzing after the spray. A refugee-turned-journalist somewhere in cold, forgettable America, flapping his mouth about names, lists, books—*history*.

The General knew his name. John Katende.

The General had seen his fair share of stupid. He'd watched a man try to bribe a traffic cop with a pineapple.

He'd seen ministers who believed loyalty could be bought with hugs and shared whiskey. One colonel once tried to smuggle gold inside a goat—*inside* the goat. But this Katende… He was in a league of his own.

A Shakespearean idiot, the General thought. The kind who walks into a lion's den, waving a torch, quoting Hamlet, then wonders why his legs are missing.

Katende, the man with ink in his veins and no survival instinct in his brain, had the audacity to approach the opposition leaders about writing a book. Not just any book. No, not something polite like *A Brief History of Mango Farming*. This fool wanted to write a bloody memorial—*Profiles in Martyrdom: The Nile's Dead*—documenting every poor bastard the Ugandan government had "helped relocate" to the afterlife via crocodile courier service.

Katende pitched the book like it was a holy mission, some sacred calling scribbled on the back of a napkin in exile. First to the opposition in the diaspora—America, specifically, where they wore African grief like designer coats in D.C. air-conditioned think tanks. He expected urgency. Fire. Maybe even a hallelujah. What he got was silence. Cold, polished, bureaucratic silence.

So, he dialed Uganda—where the opposition ran its little revolution from a rented bungalow and paraded its "foot soldiers" like toy generals in hand-me-down boots, more bark than bullet. He asked for names. Just names, he said. Of the missing. Of the dead. Of the ones dragged out of beds and into those black "drone" vans, dumped later into the Nile like unwanted secrets. Two hundred, maybe three hundred souls. Names, phone numbers of surviving family members, anything. He'd do the rest. He'd call them, interview them, stitch together their last known moments. Then he'd bind it all in a book—a permanent testament, he said, to the tyranny and the terror. A ghost ledger.

He made it sound noble. Easy, even. Just a roll call of the damned, and a tribute to their suffering. A journalist's duty. A record for the day truth finally mattered again.

But the opposition didn't bite. Not these ones.

If they were real freedom fighters, they'd have jumped at the idea like it was the last chopper out of hell. But these weren't freedom fighters. These were night-crawlers—political opportunists with polished statements by day and secret meetings with government men in untucked shirts and bribe breath by night. They didn't want a book. They wanted candidacies—shiny seats in Parliament with opposition logos slapped on like bumper stickers, the kind of power you could taste but never use.

The General didn't just roll his eyes at this report; he almost popped a blood vessel. The only good thing? The opposition, bless their greedy little hearts, reported Katende right back to the government.

"He's dangerous," they told the General. "We'll keep our mouths shut."

Good dogs. Well-fed dogs. Funded dogs.

Still, the General couldn't shake the unease. Katende was like a cockroach dipped in holy water—he kept surviving. The journalist even whispered about writing prisoner testimonies. Stories from the Naguru and Kololo safe houses. Tales from the padded rooms with no windows and all the screaming. Who the hell did this little ink-stained twit think he was? Just because he'd been deported from Dubai for writing things that made sheikhs squirm didn't mean he was out of reach.

The General didn't deport people. That was for bureaucrats and cowards. The General preferred a more… permanent edit.

So, he sent a messenger. A honey trap with cheekbones you could slice steak on. She asked Katende to meet her at a café in Boston. She said she admired his writing, wanted him to help pen her asylum story. The fool showed up like it was a Tinder date and not a setup for a chemical kiss of death.

The General almost regretted not being ready. If she'd only carried Nexumbra—that neat little synthetic neurotoxin the boys in the lab cooked up in the shadow of the Alps—Katende would've been dead before dessert. Nexumbra: no smell, no color, dissolves in the blood like sugar in tea. Just one handshake, one gel-coated glove, and you've got blurred vision, heart flutters, and death in a week. Long enough to confuse the coroner and silence the press. The poisoner walks away clean, takes a shot of Vitarin-7 from a fake fountain pen, and that's that. A masterpiece in murder.

But the young woman only carried words.

She sat across from Katende like a bad omen in a tight dress—legs crossed, lipstick lethal, eyes that said *I've memorized your obituary*. The coffee shop was warm, cozy even, but the chill in her voice could've flash-frozen a pond.

She leaned in, smiling like a woman selling salvation in a house on fire.

"The General will kill you," she said, every syllable as crisp as a gunshot. "Forget your little book. No one's going to connect you to the victims' families, sweetheart. Because no one wants the victims remembered. Dead men don't vote, and the living don't want to know how close they came."

Katende swallowed hard, suddenly aware of the sweat under his arms and the fact that no one in this café knew he was marked for death except the woman across from him—and she seemed oddly at peace with it.

"You think the opposition cared about your book?" she asked, sipping her tea as if it didn't taste like betrayal. "They told you to send your proposal in writing. And you—God bless your hopeful little refugee soul—you did. Didn't even spell-check it. They passed it to the General faster than a church plate on Easter. They didn't read a damn word."

She picked a crumb off the table and inspected it like it might squeal secrets.

"Their plan," she continued, "isn't justice. It's airtime. Sympathy equals votes, and votes equal seats in Parliament where they can play dress-up as freedom fighters while cashing government checks. They don't want the regime gone—they want to inherit its wardrobe."

Katende's throat had gone dry. His mind was sprinting toward the exit, but his body sat paralyzed.

"And protests?" she laughed softly, like someone telling a bedtime story with a twist ending. "Those were rerouted to X. Digital outrage—very clean, very safe. Anyone who still marched in the streets did so on their own. And when the bullets came, it was convenient—for everyone. The government buried the bodies. The opposition buried their names."

She stood, smooth as silk and twice as sharp.

"Good luck with your book, Mr. Katende," she said, adjusting her coat like a funeral mourner. "Just remember: memoirs are only worth something if the author survives to sign copies."

Simple. Honest. Like a knife with no handle.

And Katende, like the idiot he was, smiled back.

"Tell the General," he said, "everyone dies."

The lady left.

The General watched the footage three times, sipping something strong and red.

He could admire the journalist's balls, even as he planned to feed them to a crocodile one day.

"He's a cheap kill," the General muttered, half to himself, half to the empty room. "And one day, I'll get my chance."

CHAPTER 8:

Joanne

JOANNE shut the door like it was a secret she didn't want escaping. The latch clicked soft and final, barely a whisper, because Helen was asleep in the room, sprawled out like roadkill beneath a thin kitenge. Helen hated being woken up, especially during the day—night shifts had twisted her clock until sunlight felt like an insult.

Outside, the Kampala air hit Joanne's face like an open oven. She tied her headscarf tighter and started toward Nateete Primary, where Anselm would be tumbling out of class in his too-big uniform and busted shoes, grinning like he ruled the world. Ten minutes, if she didn't stop to chat or dodge any boda bodas riding like they had death on speed dial.

But Joanne wasn't just walking toward her son today. Her thoughts kept wandering off toward that strange man from the other night—the one with a soft American accent and eyes like he was always halfway through crying.

Shawn, he'd said. Zimbabwean, he claimed. Which was laughable—his American accent was too clear to even a toddler.

He'd left her a number. Of course he had. Like all men do when they're either too sure of themselves or too damn lonely. She hadn't meant to think about him again. But there he was, camped out in her thoughts like a mosquito you hear but can't see.

She'd debated calling him, then decided against it, then decided for it, and then again against it.

But now she was thinking: maybe just lunch. Just conversation.

Maybe she'd tell him what she told every man eventually: *"I'm not here to be saved or screwed. I'm just here."* But they never listened. Most men couldn't hear through their own breathing.

And worse, he hadn't even tried to touch her that night. Paid for a hotel, passed out cold, and didn't so much as graze her thigh. That unsettled her more than if he had. What kind of man does that? And why did it make her curious?

She reached into her small purse, dug out her battered phone, and scrolled until she saw his name: *Shawn Maybe*. That's what she'd saved him as. Maybe he was okay. Maybe not.

Then, with a sigh, she dialed. One ring. Two.

"Hi, sweet pie," came his voice, sticky-sweet and entirely too hopeful.

Joanne almost hung up. Her thumb hovered. But her mouth beat her to it.

"Nope," she said. "I'm not your sweet pie. Let's set that straight now. If you want a sweet pie, go to Café Javas. I'm just a friend."

"Oh—shit. My bad. Hi, friend," he stammered, like a kid caught stealing a cookie. "I'm just really glad you called."

"You don't sound like someone with a lot of female friends."

"You're not wrong."

"I told you I don't make promises I can't keep, so I had to call you."

"So... lunch?" he asked, like a man asking for more than just food. "You think you could meet me in the city?"

"I can be there around four. But listen—lunch is food. Not code. Not metaphor. Actual food. No funny business."

"Oh, very clear," Shawn said. "I want to eat. I mean—lunch. Not you. I mean—Jesus, I'll shut up now."

She couldn't help but laugh, which annoyed her a little. Liking this man would be like adopting a stray cat you couldn't afford to feed.

"Uhuru Restaurant. Mutaasa Kafeero Plaza. You can walk there from your hotel. Unless you're scared of potholes."

"I'll find it. I'll be there."

She was about to hang up when something in her chest nudged her.

"Shawn... I'm bringing my son. Anselm. He's seven. If that bothers you, let's call the whole thing off now."

"Are you kidding?" Shawn said. "I'd be honored to meet him. Maybe he'll like me more than you do."

"Don't count on it," she said. "He's got good instincts."

The line went quiet. Then died.

Joanne stared at the blank screen a second longer than she needed to. Then she tucked the phone back in her purse and kept walking, dust rising at her heels like whispers.

Maybe, she thought, *just maybe, this stranger with sleepy eyes and a broken accent would turn out to be the first man who heard her say "just friends" and actually meant it.*

She doubted it. But, hell, a girl could dream.

*

Joanne arrived at Mutaasa Kafeero Plaza with Anselm's hand folded neatly into hers like a secret. The boy's fingers were warm, always too warm, like he ran on a small fire of his own. She could hear his shoes slapping rhythmically against the tile steps as they climbed the narrow, chipped staircase—an artery of old concrete curling up toward Uhuru Restaurant like a forgotten vein of the building.

This was one of those places in Kampala where the scent of spices beat louder than the noise of traffic. Pilao rice and fried meat sang from the kitchens in waves. She'd eaten here once or twice before. It was cheap, busy, and carried no shame about its cracked walls or plastic chairs. Places like this didn't need to pretend.

Shawn was easy to find.

He sat alone on the balcony, leaning over the railing like he wanted to touch the pulse of the city itself. His eyes were scanning the crowd—searching. Still hoping. That made Joanne pause at the threshold for half a second longer than she needed to. He was probably looking for the woman from the club: a swirl of synthetic hair and lip gloss, with perfume that entered a room five seconds before she did.

But that woman didn't show up today.

Today, Joanne was plain. A t-shirt faded from too many washes. Loose trousers. Her hair pulled back into a knot, no wig, no games. A scarf tied it all up in a no-nonsense bow. She wore just enough lip balm to keep her lips from cracking. That was it. She didn't come to impress him. She came to make a point.

"Shawn," she called gently, walking toward him like someone who knew who she was—and what she wasn't going to be.

He jumped. That startled little flicker in his shoulders betrayed something soft inside him. Then he smiled—wide and hungry. His eyes darted over her quickly, then slower, like his brain was adjusting to a different temperature.

"There you are," he said, standing and motioning to the chair beside him. There was only one.

No seat for Anselm.

Before Joanne could say anything, Shawn dropped to a crouch, opened his arms, and pulled Anselm into a hug—an awkward, over-eager thing. The boy stiffened, unsure, but let it happen. Then Shawn lifted him briefly into the air like a prize and set him down with exaggerated care.

"I'll get you a chair, young man," he said. "Don't worry."

"Don't stress," Joanne told him. "We'll call the waiter."

But Shawn's eyes were already back on her. They glinted in a way she didn't like—like he was peeling back her clothes with his mind, layering them back on, then peeling again.

She shifted in her seat, then broke the silence before it got worse.

"So," she said, "how were your meetings? You told me today was going to be busy. Honestly, I didn't think you'd make it."

"For you?" he said, with a grin like melted butter. "I'd cancel everything. Hell, I'd burn the calendar."

She chuckled without warmth.

"Please don't cancel anything. Like we agreed… we're just—" her voice dipped as she glanced at Anselm, "—friends."

"Oh, right. Friends." He leaned in and dropped his voice to a gravelly whisper. "You're even hotter today. I mean it. No makeup, no wig… Damn. You're just so naturally fucking beautiful."

"Shawn." Her voice turned to ice.

"Yes?" He blinked, still smiling.

"This is my son. You don't curse in front of my son."

"Oh God—I'm sorry. I'm really, really sorry."

"And don't talk to him about last night."

"I wasn't going to."

"You know, Shawn," she said, narrowing her eyes, "you can lie about Zimbabwe all you want. But no African swears like you do. That's an American thing. I watch too many movies. You *are* American. Why don't you just own it?"

He didn't answer. Just waved over a waitress, like he could wash her words off the table with a new topic.

The waitress approached with a shy smile, her eyes dancing between Joanne and Shawn like she was watching a soap opera unfold.

Anselm ordered confidently: pilao and chicken. Fanta. The boy had taste.

Joanne asked for matooke with beef stew and a small plate of pilao on the side. Then she grinned slyly.

"And you, Shawn? Let me guess—French fries and chicken like you people do back home?"

Shawn raised both hands in protest. "No, no—give me whatever you're having. Local me."

"Same as mine," she told the waitress. "And some passion fruit juice for him."

The waitress nodded, and that smile of hers grew a little. New lovers, it said. She didn't believe in *just friends* either.

As they waited, Joanne took a sip of her warm bottled water, let her fingers tap idly against the plastic. She glanced at Anselm, who had already taken out a toy car from his pocket and was rolling it gently across the table's edge.

"I'll take him home after this," she said casually. "Then maybe I'll take you somewhere. A place we sometimes work. Good spot for tourists. Real Ugandan."

"Like a bar?"

"Yes, of course. A real one. You said you wanted to see Uganda."

His smile softened then. Less like a man trying to get lucky. More like a man starting to realize luck might look different than he expected.

"All right," he said. "Lead the way."

CHAPTER 9:

Shawn

JOANNE practically dragged Shawn through the crowded streets of Kampala, her excitement bubbling over like a shaken beer can. He could feel it vibrating off her, infecting the air between them. She talked a mile a minute, waving her hands as if she were leading him to some grand revelation.

"This place," Joanne said, her voice low and soaked in something that wasn't quite sadness and wasn't quite rage, "is the biggest brothel in Africa. Maybe even the world."

She wasn't joking. Not even close. The way her lips barely moved, the way her eyes stayed locked on the city outside like it had just confessed something filthy—it all said she meant every word.

"Feels like the whole country works here," she added, a brittle laugh cracking at the edges. "No employer in Uganda hires more people than this brothel. This—this is the real 'Made in Uganda.' The last thing we still produce. Everything else comes from outside. Phones from China. Aid from Europe. Policies from Washington. Morality from imported pastors. But sex?" She turned to him with a sad little shrug. "Sex is our local industry."

Shawn didn't argue. What would be the point? Joanne wasn't citing statistics—she was testifying. Uganda was her reality, not some place on a map but a long, painful story she'd lived one chapter at a time. And if she said the whole nation was one sprawling, sweat-slick brothel, he believed her.

She didn't say it with pride. It wasn't rebellion or revelation. It was resignation. The kind you find in the eyes of people who know the system isn't broken—it was built that way.

"Every Tuesday, we work here," she said, hopping over a pothole like it was second nature.

"You and who?" Shawn asked, playing dumb, watching her reaction.

She didn't even flinch. Just kept moving and talking too—explaining the damn place with the same calm you'd use to describe a bus schedule or the ingredients on a cereal box.

"This whole area is called Nateete. That's where I stay too. The brothel is called Nateete Best Motel—got everything: steam, sauna, a restaurant, a VIP lounge where all the girls walk around naked. And the rooms—about a thousand of them. Every one of 'em sees action, nonstop."

A thousand rooms of paid fucking. Jesus. Shawn wasn't sure whether to be impressed or sick.

"Are they like the one we had last night?" he asked, still

tasting the stench of stale sex from the closet-sized hellhole they'd fucked in.

She glanced at him.

"What do you mean?"

"Never mind," he muttered. "Just keep talking."

And she did.

"Me and Helen—she's the other girl you met last night."

Shawn let out a dry laugh. "Met? That's generous. She barely looked up from her phone before some guy hauled her upstairs."

Joanne smiled.

"Don't be like that. Helen's the best. You'll see. I'll introduce you properly tonight."

He wasn't sure he wanted a proper introduction to Helen, but he let it slide.

"How are we getting there?" he asked.

She was already scanning the road.

"I'll get us a boda."

Of course she would.

Before he could respond, she'd flagged one down. The driver rolled up, his bike rattling like it was held together by prayers. Joanne hopped on like she was mounting a goddamn throne.

"Come on," she called, slapping the seat behind her.

Shawn sighed, then swung his leg over. Joanne fit against him like she belonged there, her body warm, familiar.

The driver glanced back, took her instructions, then kicked the bike to life. They shot forward, weaving through traffic.

The city blurred past in streaks of neon, diesel, and dust. Shawn tightened his grip—whether on Joanne or just for balance, he wasn't sure.

Joanne tilted her head back, her voice carrying over the roar of the engine.

"You're gonna love it, Shawn. Just wait and see."

He doubted that. But then again, he'd come this far.

The boda boda sputtered to a stop, coughing out a final breath of exhaust before the driver jerked his thumb toward the towering, sun-bleached sign: *Nateete Best Motel.* The letters were big, bold, and unapologetic, like a drunk shouting his own name.

Joanne didn't hesitate—just grabbed Shawn's wrist and pulled him toward the back gate, where the real business happened, where secrets slipped in unseen and sins walked out with their pockets full.

The main entrance was a spectacle for the reckless—men who didn't care who saw them, women who had long stopped pretending to give a damn. But here, in the shadows, was where secrets festered, where the world's filthiest desires slipped through the cracks unnoticed.

*

Joanne led the way like she belonged, like she had walked these halls so many times that the walls knew her scent. But as he followed her, something gnawed at the base of his skull, that primal warning system that whispered: *This is different.*

"This is where the girls enter," Joanne said over her shoulder. "Less conspicuous than the front."

A joke. Like there was anything subtle about this place.

The courtyard was alive with its own kind of chaos. Wooden benches packed with men and women, drinks sloshing, hands grabbing, mouths laughing at jokes that weren't funny. The air was thick with the greasy aroma of grilled meat and the tang of cheap liquor. A low, bass-heavy beat thumped through the speakers, rattling through Shawn's chest like a second heartbeat. Girls drifted through the crowd—some carrying trays of beer, some giggling in men's laps, others wordlessly disappearing through the doors lining the compound, leading their patrons into whatever hell awaited them inside.

Joanne moved through it all with ease, her hand brushing against Shawn's arm as she guided him forward. She was in her element here, and damn if that didn't make his skin crawl.

Men's eyes trailed her, some full of hunger, others recognition. He didn't like it. He didn't like that she didn't care.

They reached a dimly lit entrance near the back.

The sauna.

"You go on ahead and pay at the reception," she said. "Men's changing room is down the hall. Shower first, then you can relax in the steam rooms. It's good for unwinding."

Unwinding. Yeah, sure. That's what this place was for.

"I'm working the bar tonight," Joanne added. "But Helen's coming. She works in the sauna. You can hang with her."

Shawn turned to her, searching for something—maybe a flicker of jealousy, some sign that this wasn't just another night for her. But all he got was a tired smile.

"Remember," she said, "you're free to have any girl you want. Sauna, rooms—it's up to you."

And just like that, she was gone, swallowed by the crowd.

For the first time in a long while, Shawn felt something unfamiliar slithering through his gut.

Alone.

He stepped up to the receptionist, a woman who looked like she had been carved out of stone—expressionless, mechanical in the way she processed him.

"Do you have any valuables? Phone? Wallet?" she asked, already sliding a plastic bag across the counter.

Shawn hesitated before stuffing his things inside. There was something final about it, like sealing away the last piece of himself that didn't belong to this place.

"What name should I put on it?"

"Michael," he lied, because why the hell not?

The receptionist scrawled it onto a tag, taped it shut, and moved on to the next poor bastard in line.

"Enjoy your time."

He doubted that.

The men's changing room was a different kind of beast. No music, no laughter—just damp air, the slap of bare feet against tile, the low murmur of conversations that died the second he stepped inside.

A gatekeeper stood at the entrance, his arms crossed, eyes dead.

"Receipt," he barked.

Shawn handed it over, watching as the man barely glanced at it before tossing him a pair of plastic sandals and two thin wrappers of cloth. No instructions, no pleasantries—just take this, get naked, get in line.

Shawn stole a glance around. The other men wrapped one cloth around their waists, the second draped lazily over their shoulders or heads, like kings in a kingdom of sin. He did the same, peeling off his clothes and stepping into the uniform of the damned.

The showers were just ahead, steam curling from behind the half-open door. He could hear the water running, the occasional low grunt of someone scrubbing away whatever filth they carried in here. Shawn stepped forward, the tile cold beneath his feet, his skin prickling as he moved into the mist.

His first destination after his shower was the sauna room.

The heat hit him like a goddamn freight train, wrapping around him like a wet blanket left out in the sun. His skin prickled instantly, the sweat rising before he even had time to sit his ass down.

He found a spot in the corner, leaned back, and let himself melt into the haze, listening to the low murmur of voices around him. Men, women—didn't matter. Their words mixed together in a language that felt like static to his ears. Luganda, probably, but to him, it might as well have been ancient hieroglyphs.

The conversation was lively, punctuated by occasional bursts of laughter, but it felt distant, like a song playing on a busted radio—there, but just out of reach. He sat quietly, letting it all wash over him like the humid air, until his skin was slick and his mind was teetering between relaxation and raw fucking paranoia. He didn't belong here. Not in this world of whispered deals and sweaty sins. Five minutes in, and his body was loose, but his nerves were still tight as hell.

Fuck it.

He slipped out of the sauna, the cooler air of the courtyard hitting him like a splash of reality. He dragged in a deep breath, exhaling the tension. This place was alive in a way that made his skin crawl. He flagged down a waitress and ordered a glass of cold water. She nodded, not giving a damn, just another cog in this well-oiled machine of flesh and pleasure.

The compound around him buzzed with activity. Almost everyone was paired off—men draped over women, women curled into men. The two TVs in the corner flickered with distractions—one playing a Premier League match, the other showing the local news, as if anything happening outside these walls actually mattered.

It was just past 7 p.m., and the sky had deepened into a bruised shade of blue. Shawn sipped his water, scanning faces. Some were grinning, some stone-faced, but they all belonged. Unlike him. The energy in the air had shifted—thicker, charged, like something unseen was slithering just beneath the surface, waiting to strike.

Once he cooled down enough, he decided to check out the steam room.

Big mistake.

The moment he stepped inside, the heat punched him in the gut. It wasn't just hot—it was suffocating, a dense, almost medicinal fog swallowing him whole. The darkness was complete. No shadows, no outlines, just thick, choking nothingness. His instincts screamed, *Get the fuck out!* And for once, he listened.

He stepped back out, gulping in the night air, shaking off the suffocating weight.

"Very hot inside?" a female voice asked.

He turned.

A girl stood there, holding a small plastic bucket filled with a bottle of scrub and a stiff brush. She spoke in Luganda first, fast and unfamiliar. When he shook his head, she switched to English, her accent heavy but her meaning crystal clear.

"This steam room is very hot," she repeated, gesturing at the doorway he had just escaped from. "But the other one, opposite side, not so hot." She tilted her head toward a different door.

"Do you want massage extra? I scrub all your body… and extras."

There it was. The offer. Plain as day.

Shawn forced a polite smile, shook his head, and walked away.

She didn't care—just turned and started scanning for the next potential customer.

Curiosity pulled him toward the other steam room.

He stepped inside, and this one was different. The haze was thick, but through it, he could make out shapes. Naked bodies. Sweat-slick skin. Soft moans threading through the humid air like some primal melody.

Men sprawled across the stairs and floor, girls kneeling beside them, scrubbing, rubbing, and in some cases, doing a whole lot more.

It wasn't just a steam room—it was a goddamn buffet of human desire. Inhibitions didn't just take a backseat here; they'd been tossed out the fucking window.

The first thing Shawn saw was a girl—no, a woman—straddling a man, her hands pressed against his chest like she was giving him a goddamn massage. For a second, that's what it looked like, until his eyes adjusted, and he saw the way her hips were moving. Slow, deliberate. Forward. Back. Forward. Back.

She wasn't massaging him. She was fucking him.

And she wasn't the only one.

All around the room, bodies tangled together, sweat-slicked skin against sweat-slicked skin, moving in rhythm, lost in whatever cheap pleasure this place promised. The air was thick with the scent of steam and sex, heavy enough to choke on.

Shawn had seen porn before; hell, who hadn't? But this—this was something else. It wasn't staged. It wasn't glossy. It was raw, primal. Flesh against flesh, no shame, no hesitation.

The only thing that passed for privacy in here was the rhythm of the doors opening and closing.

When the door swung wide, the outside light slashed through the room, revealing another couple, just as naked, just as tangled. When it shut, the place fell into shadow again, a flickering, half-seen world where bodies moved like ghosts in the dark.

His breath hitched. His body reacted. A hard, involuntary response pressing against the flimsy blue wrapper he wore. He swallowed, glancing around. Every other guy looked calm, like they'd mastered the art of detachment. *How the hell are they so composed?* He felt like a teenage boy caught in the middle of a goddamn porno shoot.

Enough.

He turned for the door, but before he could escape, a girl appeared—slim, brown-skinned, completely naked, her eyes dark with silent invitation.

"You want scrub? Massage extra?"

Jesus.

He cleared his throat, shook his head again, more forcefully this time. The heat wasn't just from the steam anymore. He needed out. Now.

As he pushed through the door, another girl approached, making the same offer. "Scrub" and "massage" were just two different ways of saying the same damn thing. He waved her off and stepped back into the courtyard, the night air wrapping around him like an old friend.

And then he noticed it—something small, something that should have been obvious but somehow wasn't.

No condom disposal bins.

His stomach tightened. In a place where bodies tangled like vines, where sweat and sex clung to the air like cigarette smoke, there wasn't a single designated spot for used rubbers.

His gaze flicked to a couple of men walking out of the steam room. They looked… normal. No awkward shuffling, no discreet adjustments. And that's when it hit him, like a gut punch he should have seen coming.

Were they still wearing their used condoms… or had they just not bothered with them at all?

Shawn didn't wait to find out. He was already moving, pushing past the revelers, out of the compound, out of this whole fucking world before it could pull him any deeper.

Back in the courtyard, he sank into a chair, exhaling like he'd just walked out of a war zone.

His body still carried the sticky heat of the steam room, but it wasn't just sweat clinging to his skin—it was something else, something harder to shake. The feeling of watching people fuck like it was just another Tuesday, of knowing this place didn't care who you were or what you thought was normal.

He signaled a waiter and ordered a beer and tea.

Christ, he needed something to clear his head.

Around him, men and women squeezed lemon into their drinks with a casual, practiced ease. He followed suit, mirroring the small, mundane ritual like it might help him feel less like a goddamn outsider.

The tea was hot, bitter, the lemon slicing through it like a blade. It grounded him, but only just.

Music thumped in the background, half-drowned by the murmur of voices, laughter slipping through the cracks like whispers in the dark.

*

Shawn hadn't seen Joanne for a while, and a quiet, nagging part of him wondered where the hell she'd gone. Not that he had any claim over her—hell, that wasn't even the deal—but still.

Then, like she'd materialized out of the humid night, Joanne appeared. That short dress of hers made her stand out, different from the other girls wrapped in their cheap blue and green fabrics. She moved with that easy, knowing confidence, the kind that made men weak and women wary.

She spotted Shawn and smiled, pulling a chair up

close, so close he could smell the faint trace of perfume beneath the sweat and steam.

"You having fun yet?" she asked, leaning in.

Shawn forced a smile. "Oh yeah. This place is… uh, just like you said."

He took a sip of tea, as if that would wash away the discomfort.

"Thanks for bringing me."

"I was looking for you," Joanne said. "A girl told me you were in the steam room. Did someone… massage your snake?"

Shawn nearly choked. The words hit him like a slap, and his face burned like he'd just walked into a furnace.

"No, no," he stammered, shaking his head so fast he probably looked guilty as hell. "It's, uh… tense in there."

Before he could explain, a girl in a blue wrapper strolled up to their table. Shawn barely noticed her until Joanne's voice cut through his thoughts.

"Shawn, this is my friend-sister, Helen. Remember? I told you about her."

Shawn looked up, and there she was—the girl from the nightclub. The one with the sharp eyes and sharper mouth. The one who'd made it real clear she had Joanne wrapped around her little finger.

Joanne rose from her seat and pulled Helen into a hug, holding on longer than necessary.

Then, just when Shawn thought it was over, Helen kissed her.

Not a peck. Not a friendly little thing. A kiss.

And then, as if that wasn't enough to send Shawn's head spinning, Helen grabbed a handful of Joanne's ass, squeezing like she owned it.

Shawn felt something tighten in his gut, something ugly and sharp. Helen caught his eye over Joanne's shoulder, smirking, her expression dripping with smug satisfaction.

See that? her look said. *I have her in ways you never will.*

Joanne finally pulled away, adjusting her dress like nothing had happened.

"Take care of my man," she said, playful, but there was something teasing in her voice, like she was testing both of them.

Helen's smirk widened.

"Sure," she said.

Joanne left, and Helen slid into her chair, turning her attention fully onto Shawn. The amusement in her eyes didn't reach the rest of her face.

"I didn't think you'd actually be following her around like a lost puppy," she said, her voice dripping with sarcasm. "What the fuck are you even doing here?"

Shawn's jaw tensed.

"She asked me to come. I wanted to. What's your problem with that?"

Helen leaned back, stretching out like she owned the whole goddamn courtyard.

"No problem," she said, shrugging. "Just watching out for my sister. You look like her next mistake."

Shawn clenched his teeth.

"I'm not a mistake."

Helen let out a dry little laugh.

"Yeah? Look, you paid her for sex. That's all this is. Don't fool yourself. She doesn't want you. You don't get to turn a one-night stand into a goddamn love story."

Shawn's blood ran cold. He wasn't sure if it was anger or something worse—something he didn't want to name. He stood abruptly, shoving his chair back.

"I don't know why Joanne even brought you to meet me if this is how you feel."

Helen just watched him, expression unreadable, like she was sizing him up, deciding whether he was worth another jab or if she'd already won.

Shawn turned and walked off to find another chair, needing distance, needing air. But his mind was a fucking storm, and no amount of distance was going to clear the wreckage Helen had just left in its wake.

*

The speakers crackled to life with a burst of static, then came the voice—slick, sleazy, dripping with the kind of enthusiasm that made Shawn's skin crawl.

"Attention, gentlemen! Don't miss out on our sauna happy hour! It's a show like no other. Everything is free!"

A ripple went through the crowd, a shift in energy so palpable Shawn could feel it in his gut.

Men peeled off from their seats, moving toward the sauna room like moths to a streetlamp, their anticipation thick in the air.

Girls followed, bare feet padding against the wooden floor, their thin blue wrappers barely clinging to their bodies.

Shawn turned to the girl beside him, a petite thing with dark hair stuck to her damp shoulders.

"What's this happy hour all about?" he asked, keeping his voice casual.

She smirked, eyes gleaming with mischief.

"Go in and watch. Biggest fuck fest in the whole city."

Then she leaned in, voice dropping to a sultry whisper.

"And it's free."

Shawn arched an eyebrow.

"Bullshit. Why would any girl let herself get fucked for free?"

"The manager pays us," she said, like it was the most normal thing in the world.

Shawn said nothing, but something cold coiled in his gut. He wasn't a saint—not even close—but there was something about the transactional nature of it all, the efficiency, that made his skin itch.

Still, curiosity was a bitch, and it had its claws in him.

He moved toward the sauna pavilion, where a man with a graying mustache stood like a goddamn maître d' of debauchery. The manager. The puppet master of this little flesh circus. He greeted the men with a wide, oily smile, gesturing toward the eager, barely wrapped girls like he was seating them at a five-star restaurant.

"Come in, my friend!" he called to Shawn. "You're just in time!"

Shawn shook his head, giving him a polite nod but stepping aside. He needed a vantage point, somewhere he could watch without getting dragged into the madness.

The pavilion was a fever dream of flesh and heat. Men sat along the wooden benches, towels slipping off their laps. Naked girls hovered, hands trailing across thighs, lips whispering negotiations. Some weren't even talking—just climbing on, grinding slow, bodies fusing together like they had all the time in the world.

Then the manager's voice rang out, loud and commanding.

"Off with the wrappers! Time to start the show!"

A ripple of movement passed through the room as men shed their towels, revealing erections lined up like soldiers in formation.

Shawn watched, part of him detached, another part—something buried deeper—disgusted.

The girls got to work, slipping condoms onto stiff cocks with the kind of efficiency that came from practice. Then they mounted, rolling their hips like trained performers.

The manager barked encouragement, his voice slicing through the humid air.

"Water! Water!" he shouted, urging the girls to produce more fluids, like this was some kind of sick competition.

Shawn watched the slick trickle run like a busted motel pipe and chuckled darkly—no wonder Durex skipped this place. Selling lube here would be like selling snow tires in hell. These women came factory-lubed by God—or maybe Satan—with plumbing so efficient it made capitalism cry. Shawn's mind took a wrong turn down memory lane and slammed headfirst into Sheila—the Ugandan firestorm he'd lost back in Boston. Sheila had been the first to baptize him in this miracle of biology, this supernatural slip-and-slide she called *kachabali*. No lube, no warm-up, just nature tearing off its gloves and saying, *Welcome to the jungle, sweetheart.*

The girls mounted the men in unison, like some sick

choreographed dance. The first thrusts were slow, measured—then the room turned into a living, breathing beast of writhing bodies and ragged moans.

Shawn clenched his jaw. This wasn't just fucking. This was a goddamn spectacle.

The sauna heat turned their bodies into human stew—naked and half-naked lumps simmering in their own juices, skin so slick with sweat you'd think someone had basted them for roasting.

He barely noticed the movement at first—a delicate hand slipping beneath the fold of his towel wrapper, smooth and sure like it had done this a hundred times. By the time his brain caught up to what was happening, her fingers were already there—wrapped around him, slick with oil, coaxing a response from his stunned body.

Shawn turned, breath caught somewhere between panic and need. She was there—fully there—pressed against him, her naked body warm, her skin impossibly soft. She whispered something in Luganda, the words breathy, wrapping around his ear like a secret spell.

"I don't speak Luganda," he muttered, his voice hoarse with confusion, maybe guilt.

She smiled like he'd given her permission. Maybe he had. Maybe just not out loud.

Her hands were still moving, slow and deliberate, as if she could rewrite his resistance with every stroke. Shawn knew this wasn't where he was supposed to be—this wasn't the mission, and she definitely wasn't part of the plan. But plans were hard to remember when your senses were hijacked and someone was breathing against your neck like temptation wrapped in honey. Her body moved closer, heat pressing against heat. His resolve was slipping, not all at once, but like a door that couldn't quite latch.

She was gyrating her hips in front of him like a snake that had learned to salsa—smooth, hypnotic, and just a little bit evil. Maybe it was some African dance—maybe twerking, maybe witchcraft—hell, at that point Shawn couldn't tell the difference. Her face, meanwhile, stayed laser-focused on his, eyes sweet as poisoned honey, voice oozing sugar as she cooed him into opening his wallet.

But it was her fingers that scared him the most.

They were down there between them, tucked like contraband in a border crossing, massaging his manhood. She wasn't just touching him; she was *sharpening* him, dragging something soft and deadly across his groin like she was whittling wood with a blade.

Every time her hips ticked left or right, she brushed up against him just enough to send a warning down his spine—like a live wire saying, *you've got about ten seconds before you become a statistic.*

Shawn knew an accident was imminent. He could practically hear sirens. And in that moment, his brain, bless it, decided to flash a warning from back home: those little yellow signs posted in snowy Dorchester, the ones that read:

"CAUTION: SLIPPERY WHEN WET."

Yeah. That.

Except there was no Department of Transportation out here. No cones. No brakes. Just him, her, and the distinct possibility that if he didn't back away soon, he'd skid straight into a big sin.

He told himself to stop. *You're better than this, man.*

You know what this is. But the part of him that cared about consequences had gone quiet—overruled by the animal part of his brain that was convinced nothing bad could come from one more second.

Just one more.

And then he felt it—her entrance brushing against the tip of his erection, close enough to make his whole body stiffen. Skin to skin. No barrier. No logic. Just a slow, dangerous slide into her.

He wasn't inside. Not yet. Just there. At the edge.

Her lips moved near his jawline. "Let us go there. You fuck me. It's free. I just want the money from the manager."

"Please, stop," he hissed, panic clawing up his throat.

This was reckless, stupid. God only knew what he could walk out of here carrying.

"I'm just teasing, sweetheart," she said.

Her fingers tightened on his wrist, trying to pull him toward one of the benches. Shawn exhaled sharply, brain working overtime for an exit.

"I'll give you money. More than the manager pays. But I'm not fucking you here."

That got her attention. She hesitated, studying him like she was weighing the truth in his words.

Finally, she released him, her grip shifting from desperate to businesslike.

"Okay. Come."

Just as Shawn reached for the girl's hand to slip out the door like sinners fleeing a sermon, the sauna manager slammed himself in their path like a bad plot twist. His eyes, slick and judgmental, dropped like a guillotine to

Shawn's midsection.

"Hold up," the manager said, jabbing a stubby finger at the obscene tent pole rising beneath Shawn's soaked wrapper. "You came in here flatter than a deflated tire, and now you're walking out with a damn sword in your pants? That, my friend, is cheating."

The room froze.

Even the writhing couple on the sweat-slick pavilion paused mid-thrust, their bodies forming some obscene statue of judgment. A voice called out from the fog, "Let 'em stay! Give us a show, Pastor Erection!"

Shawn felt the heat rise to his ears, the kind of shame that boiled out of your skin and left you half-hoping for spontaneous combustion. The girl beside him didn't flinch. She leaned in, whispered something into the manager's ear.

The manager blinked. His mouth twitched. Then he turned to his audience, arms raised like Moses parting the Red Sea of perverts.

"The man is religious!" he bellowed. "No sex before marriage. He's taking our girl to church."

A beat of silence. Then someone said, "Amen."

"Amen," said another, mid-thrust again.

"Praise the Lord," the manager declared. "And may they return after the wedding to bless us with holy fornication."

Shawn didn't wait for the chorus of hallelujahs. He grabbed the girl and slipped through the door, his dignity dragging behind him like toilet paper stuck to a shoe.

They walked toward the reception area, the cooler air shocking his senses back into clarity.

Shawn glanced at her as they stepped into the dimly lit hall.

"How much does the manager pay you per fuck?"

"Ten thousand," she said flatly, like the number didn't even mean anything anymore.

Shawn nodded. "Okay. Let's go to the reception. My wallet's there—I'll pay you."

As they walked, he could feel eyes on him. Watching. Judging. But he didn't care. All that mattered was getting out of there with his dignity—and his goddamn health—intact.

After the incident, Shawn returned to his seat in the sauna's reception, his mind churning like a goddamn washing machine on spin cycle. What a fucking night. The so-called "Happy Hour" had wrapped up, and men shuffled back in, sweat-slicked and glassy-eyed, some looking satisfied, some looking like they needed a goddamn priest.

But it wasn't over. Not by a long shot.

The speakers overhead crackled like an old man clearing his throat, then the voice came—oily, eager, promising more depravity like a carnival barker on crack.

"It is Candle Night, boys! Ordinary is 10K, about three dollars, and the VIP is 30K, about ten dollars!"

Shawn raised an eyebrow. Candle Night. Sounded like some cult shit.

Before he could decide whether to stay or walk the hell away, a door at the back of the room swung open, and they started filing in.

The women.

Fifty. Maybe more. Stark naked, each holding a candle, the little flames licking the air, throwing long shadows across their bare skin. It was like watching a slow-moving hallucination—so much flesh and flickering light, moving in perfect rhythm.

Shawn exhaled, rubbing the bridge of his nose. This fucking city.

But he was here. He was watching. And like a man watching a train derail, he couldn't look away.

So, he paid the damn fee.

The Ordinary Lounge was a meat market. Wall-to-wall bodies, heat thick enough to choke on. Most of the women here were older, heavier, their skin slick with sweat, their eyes dull and detached. It was survival, not seduction. The men were no better—drunk, desperate, a few already passed out in the corners.

Shawn didn't linger.

He moved to the VIP lounge, where the real shit was about to go down. This room was different—less sleazy, more surreal. No chairs. Just curved platforms shaped like beds, each one occupied, men and women tangled together like animals, shifting, thrusting, moaning.

The girls were younger here, prettier. The price tag made sense now. The men were waiting their turn, eyes dark with hunger, some rubbing their hands together like they'd just ordered a goddamn steak.

Shawn exhaled sharply and headed for the bar. The bartender was young, barely pushing thirty, and grinning like he'd seen it all.

"What's your poison?"

Shawn skimmed the menu. Uganda Waragi, Nile Special, Heineken, Guinness.

Uganda Waragi. *Kainewaragi.* The name made his

stomach turn. The General was everywhere, lurking like a shadow in the city's bloodstream. Even the fucking liquor had his name.

He passed on it.

"If you don't drink alcohol, we got Red Bull," the bartender offered. Then he leaned in, his grin widening. "And if you need a little… stamina, we got Saba Saba."

Shawn frowned. "What the hell is Saba Saba?"

"Local Viagra juice." The bartender winked. "With Saba Saba, you can fuck this whole room 'til sunrise."

Shawn let out a dry chuckle and ordered a Nile Special and a Red Bull.

Around him, men were already downing their Saba Saba shots, waiting for the magic to kick in, their eyes darting from bed to bed like predators scanning a watering hole.

Then, the speakers blared again.

"Ladies and gentlemen, it's time to stand for the national anthem!"

Shawn almost laughed out loud.

And yet, like well-trained dogs, the men staggered to their feet, swaying but obedient, placing hands over their hearts. The speakers blasted the anthem, a bizarre layer of respectability coating the filth. Some even sang along, voices thick with alcohol and lust.

As soon as the final note died out, the DJ was back, voice booming with the enthusiasm of a man who'd sold his soul and loved every minute of it.

"All the women in this room are fair play now! No one should charge you extra; you already paid!"

Shawn's stomach twisted.

This wasn't sex. This was a goddamn auction.

The show started.

The stage squatted dead-center like a sacrificial altar, with two chrome poles rising from it—twin lightning rods for shame—just like the kind you'd find in any dive strip club where dignity went to die.

The crowd wasn't cheering. They weren't even paying attention. This wasn't a show. This was protocol.

He sat at a wobbly table near the stage, gripping a warm beer, his eyes darting between fascination and horror.

The announcer's voice crackled over a busted speaker, slurring names like they were items on a menu.

"Agnes… Aisha… Nakato…" One by one, the girls took the stage, their faces blank, bodies moving with the rote precision of assembly-line workers. No teasing, no coy glances—just flesh under harsh light, offered up like livestock.

Shawn's stomach churned, but he couldn't look away.

Two men stood center stage, stiff as poles—and not just metaphorically. Naked from the waist up, their dark skin slick with sweat, they glistened like bronzed statues in hell's own showroom. If the chrome poles were decorative, these two were the main event—flesh-and-blood flagpoles with rubber raincoats clumsily rolled down over their business ends, like someone had tried to dress danger in a hurry. Their pants sagged around their knees, dignity abandoned somewhere backstage. These were the real poles the girls would climb—call it exercise, call it sin, call it Tuesday night in a country that had long since stopped pretending.

One man held a bottle of Saba Saba, swigging it between rounds like it was water. They weren't performers; they were machines, built for one purpose.

The first girl—Aisha, maybe?—climbed up, her heels clicking against the wood. No preamble, no seduction. The man with the bottle grabbed her hips, bent her over, and took her in doggy style, his movements mechanical, devoid of passion. The crowd barely blinked.

Agnes joined the stage, and the second man hoisted her into his arms, her legs wrapping around him as he penetrated her, bouncing her like a doll. The rhythm of the music didn't match their pace, but they didn't care. It was all business. Just raw, repetitive sex. Joyless. The kind that stripped humanity down to muscle and motion. They didn't smile. They didn't speak. They just rotated women in and out like dancers at a cursed carousel.

Shawn's grip tightened on his bottle, the glass slick against his palm.

Every two songs, another pair of girls joined them. Different faces, same story.

The host announced them like livestock at auction. "Next up, we got Grace and Leticia… Show some love!"

Nobody clapped. The girls climbed up, eyes flat, like they weren't even inside their bodies anymore. It was sex as sport. Sex as labor. Sex without end.

Shawn blinked hard. His stomach was heavy. It wasn't nausea, it was shame. Not for being there, but for being part of a world that let this place exist.

Then he noticed it. Same condom. Every girl. Every rotation. Same condom.

He felt his heart thud once, like a warning shot fired

inside his chest.

"Jesus Christ…" he muttered.

Shawn scanned the room. No one flinched. On the couches—really just stained mattresses with armrests—couples and clusters were tangled like snakes. A girl rode one man while another behind her thrust into someone else. No privacy. No boundaries. Just a tangle of flesh, sweat, and sound.

Next to him, a teenager—couldn't have been older than twenty—watched with the dead-eyed fascination of someone already too far gone. This wasn't a brothel. This was a graveyard of consent. A slaughterhouse where sex wasn't sold—it was stolen. On repeat.

Who the hell rules this country?

But even he knew the answer. Katila Muaji. Or his drunkard son, the General, which was worse.

The beat throbbed. The lights flickered. The girls rotated again.

Same rhythm. Same condom. Same hell.

Shawn took a long, slow sip of his Nile Special.

This city was rotting.

He wasn't disgusted by the sex. No, that wasn't it. He'd seen things. Done things. But this? This was something else. This was desperation, control, power twisted into its ugliest form.

He downed the rest of his beer, left the Red Bull untouched.

Time to go.

Joanne was somewhere in this madness, but he wasn't about to dig through a pile of sin to find her. Not tonight.

He made his way to the exit, shoving past men who

smelled like sweat and cheap cologne, past girls with tired eyes and forced smiles.

He was intercepted by a man—maybe the manager, maybe just another well-dressed devil in the house of sin—who leaned in with a grin and said, "We also have the VVIP. Jacuzzi, all the girls are naked and wet. Want a peek?"

But Shawn was done. He'd already waded knee-deep through the filth; no need to dive into the deep end. He shook his head, gave the man a cold smile, and walked out—grateful, in some twisted way, to still be ignorant of just how far the rabbit hole went.

When he stepped outside, the night air hit him like a slap—cool, clean, sharp with possibility. He didn't look back. The night was over.

CHAPTER 10:

The General

THE General sat in the cracked leather chair of his makeshift command post on the top floor of the Nile Hotel,

The place reeked of mildew and old secrets—its corridors echoing with the haunted sighs of a country holding its breath. Uganda's transition, he called it. He had summoned parliamentarians and cowed ministers to draft the official paperwork, to pretend this was all legal, all clean, but he knew better. Power didn't arrive with a handshake—it came with a scream.

Outside his curtained windows, the city watched in cautious fear. Inside his skull, the past few days looped like a horror film, each scene stitched with the screams he had learned to ignore. But now, sitting alone in the seat of stolen power, he wasn't so sure the ghosts were done with him.

It had started with a whisper. A single phone call from a sycophant who fed on the decaying remains of power, someone who would have slit his own brother's throat for a sip of whiskey from the president's cabinet. The message was simple, urgent: *Your stepmother is holding a secret cabinet meeting. She's using your father's name. They're choosing a new vice president—her son-in-law.*

That treacherous bitch, Jessica.

The General hadn't hesitated. His informant had helped him bug the conference room, and he sat in the back seat of his black SUV, watching the meeting unfold on his phone as his convoy sped toward the State House. The screen flickered, the grainy footage capturing the figures seated in a semi-circle beneath the opulent chandeliers of the presidential conference room.

His father was there, but barely. The old man slumped forward in his chair, his head bobbing like a drunk in a cathedral pew. His breathing was heavy, labored. Sweat glistened on his dark skin.

Jessica turned toward him, her voice smooth, coaxing.

"Darling, you should rest. The doctors said you need your midday nap."

There was something serpentine in her smile as she patted his arm. *Go sleep, old man. We'll handle everything.*

The General's stomach knotted. He had seen it before—Jessica's way of slowly erasing his father's authority, painting him as feeble, as a relic, while she positioned herself at the center of power.

The old president mumbled something incoherent, then let his head droop. Two aides rushed to help him up, leading him out like a docile animal. And just like that, the presidency was slipping away.

Jessica turned back to the room, barely masking her satisfaction.

"Now," she said, clasping her hands together, "this meeting is to finalize my husband's new cabinet. He will be announcing it after waking up and doing the swearing-in."

There was a rustling of papers. Ministers leaned forward, reviewing the list. Some muttered, nodded. But the first name on the list made the General's blood run cold.

Vice President: Ronald Kuharibika.

Jessica's son-in-law. The first domino in her grand plan. Make him vice president, and in a few months, whisper in the old man's ear—*You're tired. You need rest. Hand over power to someone younger.*

Someone *she* controlled.

There was a brief hesitation. The minister of health, an older woman with sharp eyes, stood. She cleared her throat.

"Mama, I have great respect for your son-in-law. He is a fine man, and I know he will serve the country well. But I must say—your husband and I had an agreement once. We always ensured that the vice presidency went to someone from another family. It prevents accusations of tribalism."

A heavy silence fell over the room. Jessica's lips trembled as she brought a silk handkerchief to her face.

"Why?" she said, her voice thick with feigned emotion. "Why do you people keep reminding us of tribalism? When my husband went to the bush to fight for this country, he went with my brother-in-law, Sayyid. Was there tribalism then?"

There were murmurs of agreement. The prime minister stood quickly, clearing his throat.

"Mama, please, do not be upset. This entire room supports your son-in-law for vice president. We can move forward."

The minister of health sat down, silenced. The decision was made. The coup—because that's what it was, really—was complete.

The General clenched his fists, his vision tunneling. He shut off the video feed. He could hear the roar of the convoy's engine, feel the vibration beneath his feet.

"Faster," he ordered.

He didn't wait for the cars to stop completely before he threw open the door and stormed into the conference hall, boots echoing like gunfire against the marble floor.

The ministers barely had time to react. A dozen soldiers followed behind him, rifles slung over their shoulders, eyes dark and unreadable.

Jessica was still seated at the head of the table, her manicured fingers poised over a stack of papers. She looked up, startled, but quickly masked it with a smile.

"General, what a—"

"Out," he barked.

She blinked. "Excuse me?"

The General pointed at the chair she occupied. "That seat does not belong to you."

The room was deathly silent. A cold, electric fear settled over the ministers.

He turned his gaze to Kuharibika, the man who dared to sit at his father's right hand.

"You too. Out. Now."

The man swallowed hard but didn't move. Jessica straightened, anger flashing across her face.

"You have no right to—"

The General's soldiers shifted behind him, hands tightening around their weapons. Jessica's lips parted slightly, just a fraction of an inch. She saw it then—the line she was about to cross, the one that led to prison or worse. She stood.

Kuharibika hesitated, looking to his mother-in-law for guidance, but she wouldn't meet his eyes. He followed her out of the room, head lowered.

The General took a slow, deliberate step forward and placed his hands on the table, leaning in. The remaining ministers shrank back.

"This meeting," he said, his voice a low growl, "is going to change its venue and agenda."

He turned and walked out, leaving behind a room full of frozen men and women who had just been reminded, with brutal clarity, who *really* held the power.

The General's thoughts drifted—no, spiraled—back to Jessica, the woman who had raised him and now had the gall to snatch his birthright and lay it at another man's feet like a gift wrapped in treason.

Stepmother, yes, though no one dared use the word around her. Jessica, with her hollow eyes and syrupy voice, had nurtured him like one might nurse a venomous snake—carefully, deliberately, with just enough warmth to keep it alive but never tame. Everyone assumed she was his mother. Everyone was wrong.

The truth came in whispers, behind curtains and between the lines of old family photographs.

The General's real mother had been a woman named Hope—a name too bright, too fragile for the life she'd been given. Hope wasn't a mistress. She was a complication. A problem to be solved. And solved she was.

Not by hired men or shady operatives. No lovers' quarrel, no scandal spun out of control. No. Hope had been butchered—systematically, intimately—by the man who had taught the General how to tie his boots and how to slit a throat without flinching. His father. Joel Katila Muaji.

Now, depending on who you asked in the family, the details varied. Like a ghost story passed around a campfire, everyone added their own little spice to the stew. But the most popular version—the bestseller, if you will—went something like this:

Back in the good old days of exile, when Idi Amin was turning Uganda into his personal slaughterhouse, Katila Muaji had been holed up in Dar es Salaam with his good friend Mwesinge Thomas and their respective women. Of course, "women" in that arrangement meant a sort of rotational domestic arrangement—stay-in girlfriends doubling as stay-in wives, because why not?

One of those women was Hope.

And as fate would have it, Hope had given birth to a baby. The General himself, though back then he was just a six-month-old sack of cries and dirty diapers.

Then came the moment that set the whole bloody thing in motion.

Jessica, Mwesinge's official partner, came home early one day. Too early. She found the house unsettlingly empty, except for a rhythmic, unmistakable sound seeping through the walls. The kind of sound that made the blood boil and the heart drop straight into the stomach.

She stood outside Hope's door, listening. Moans. Familiar moans. And not the kind you could mistake for anything else.

She didn't storm in. Didn't scream. No, Jessica had sense. She turned, walked straight to Katila Muaji's shop, and told him exactly what she'd heard.

Katila Muaji, being a man of action (and a rebel, after all), grabbed his pistol and made his way back home with the righteous fury of a man who refused to be the last one to know.

And just like that, boom. One bullet for Mwesinge. One for Hope. Quick, clean, and tied up with a nice little bow. Of course, there was the small issue of explaining two corpses in the house, but Katila Muaji was nothing if not resourceful. He told the Tanzanian police that Idi Amin's men had done it.

That they had come for him too, but lucky for him, he wasn't home. A tragedy, really. The authorities nodded, made a few notes, and promptly looked the other way.

Jessica, ever the opportunist, kept the secret. And in time, what started as a quiet alliance of mutual guilt turned into a romance. A marriage, even. She raised the General as her own. Never told him a damn thing.

Until the day he found out. Now, you have to understand, by then, the General wasn't a boy. He was a man. A man with power, a man with enemies, and most importantly—a man with a gun.

He had walked into his father's house one evening, the

weight of truth sitting heavy in his chest, and pointed a pistol at the old man's head.

"Tell me," he had said. "Tell me what you did."

Katila Muaji had looked at him then, a slow, knowing smile creeping onto his weathered face. Not fear. Not regret. Just the look of a man who had lived long enough to know that everyone, eventually, becomes their father.

The General hadn't pulled the trigger. Not that night. But from that moment on, he never forgave his father.

And the funniest part? Katila Muaji had escaped prison for that murder, and from that moment on, he had a new favorite color—yellow. The color he should have been wearing all his life if he hadn't outsmarted the law that day. The color that would become the banner of his party, the great and mighty Resistance Movement.

The General exhaled, coming back to the present, but only briefly.

His brain—God help it—was like a rat in a maze with a flask of whiskey and a grudge. It wandered again, took wrong turns, circled back, then finally landed on another thought so rancid he almost laughed: How many women had his father… well, not exactly killed, but helped shuffle off this mortal coil, simply because they dared to say, *"I think he's your son,"* or *"She has your ears, Your Excellency"*?

The president had been picky, almost artistic, about who could say they'd carried his sacred seed. Most were silenced. Some were paid off. One or two just vanished like socks in a government laundry.

Then there was Teresa.

Ah, Teresa. A housemaid with hips like a lullaby and bad luck thicker than blood. She'd birthed not one, but *two* presidential spawn. And while the old man privately admitted they were his ("They got my teeth, look!"), he made sure she understood that public acknowledgment came with a price.

"Say it out loud," he told her, "and you'll go the same way Hope did."

He never explained what happened to Hope, but the way he said it—like he was ordering takeout—it stuck with her.

And Teresa—poor woman—believed him. Because when monsters talk, you listen. So she kept scrubbing floors and telling Jessica, the president's *official* wife, that the kids belonged to some fisherman from Jinja. Long gone.

But one day Teresa snapped. Years of pretending to be both invisible and immaculate caught up with her. She'd had enough of scrubbing her baby's father's dirt off marble floors. She wanted her palace. Her throne. Her shot at being something other than the silent uterus in the maid's uniform.

So, she did what any self-respecting woman in a corrupt dynasty would do—she went to Uncle Sayyid.

The General smiled at the memory. Sayyid, the only man the president feared more than a military coup.

The uncle walked into the palace like it was *his* house, looked his brother dead in the eye, and said, "Look, you can kill the whole damn country if you want. But leave the family alone. If the woman has your kids, she's family. Give her a house. Let her raise the brats. And for God's sake, stop making her clean toilets while carrying your DNA."

The president—God rest his lecherous soul—actually listened.

Teresa got her house. A modest one, with a garden and no armed guards at the gate. And in time, her daughter married one of the cousins, as family tradition required. Her son wore a white coat and a stethoscope, whispering Latin names for diseases his old man probably caused in half the nation.

Now, the General had heard the other version. The one whispered like forbidden scripture through generations of security aides and gardeners.

It started, they said, with a towel.

Teresa was headed to the bathroom, her feet bare, towel wrapped tight, when the president cornered her like a cat spotting a mouse in lingerie. He accused her—loudly—of not wearing knickers around his State House. She panicked, probably thinking she was about to get tossed out with her paycheck unpaid.

So, she offered… *compensation.* Nine months later: baby number one.

The second time? Same story, different nightdress. No panties. No escape. The punishment, she said, was "direct." And once again, biology happened.

Jessica—the first lady, by law if not by love—finally drew a line in the sand. She cornered her husband and gave him two choices: fire the help, or marry her. He chose option C: keep both, crown Teresa as wife number two, and let Jessica keep her ceremonial smile and seat at state dinners.

The General never confirmed these stories. You couldn't exactly ask your dad if he was into chasing towel-clad women down dark State House corridors. But some parts rang true. His father had a weakness, and it was breathable fabric—or the lack thereof.

Secretaries, aides, even the health minister once—if they showed up in skirts without reinforcements, he was ready to give them cabinet positions and children in the same week. It was like his libido had a sixth sense.

Strangely, the General's stepmother Jessica never used that particular tactic to keep him faithful. No tight dresses, no panty-less strolls through the kitchen. She walked around in shapeless clothes, as if hiding her curves from a predator—even though the predator was her husband. Maybe she didn't care. Maybe she knew no amount of lace or nudity could keep a man like the president home. Or maybe, just maybe, she knew that monsters don't chase what's already caged.

CHAPTER 11:

The General

THE governor of Uganda's Central Bank, Simon Tumwine, had spent the last week trying to reach the president—like a man stuck in a horror movie, banging on the door of a house that had already burned down. No answer. No call back. Just silence.

Then word got out that the old man was officially… expired. Not that anyone would say it out loud. In this country, even dead presidents tweet daily.

But now, the president's son—the General—was in charge. Which meant Tumwine had a narrow window to save his own neck.

He found the General during his daily evening "power walk" around the Nile Hotel. These weren't leisurely strolls. They were silent military parades with cardio. No running anymore—alcohol had humbled the man—but he walked like he was marching toward a fresh coup every morning.

When Tumwine's presence was announced, the General didn't even pause.

"Tell him to meet me here," the General barked. "If he can't keep up, he loses his job. Or his life. Depending on how dramatic I feel after this walk."

Tumwine came trotting like a banker in a burning building—shirt clinging to his chest, tie flapping, sweat soaking through his government-issue socks.

"Your Excellency," he gasped, dabbing his face with a once-pristine monogrammed handkerchief, "the reserves are… gone. All of them. Dollars. Euros. Pounds. Even the gold. Gone."

The General slowed for the first time. He turned, squinted at the man like he'd spoken in tongues.

Gone?

Tumwine held up a phone. "You need to see this."

The grainy footage played like a nightmare you couldn't rewind: designer heels stomping through the vault, briefcases clicking open, arms scooping piles of wealth into suitcases like they were shopping for apocalypse supplies.

Not soldiers. Not burglars. Family. The first lady. Her daughters. Their idiot husbands. All of them.

On-screen, a handwritten note flickered into view. Denise Kuharibika's perfect cursive.

"General Mlevi, you take the government. We take the economy. A fair split of Daddy's inheritance."

The General stared, jaw clenched, veins quietly conducting symphonies of rage under his skin.

"Vultures," Tumwine said. "They divided the country like it was a carcass."

The General didn't need the footage. He already knew

who orchestrated this opera of betrayal—Ronald Kuharibika. Brother-in-law. Socialite. Saboteur in Gucci loafers.

"He's been funneling funds for years," Tumwine said. "All of them knew the handover was coming. They bled the state dry and set sail before the storm hit."

The General was silent. Then: "Where did it all go?"

Tumwine's laugh was sharp and full of ruin. "Suitcases. Plastic-lined. Military grade. The first lady took twenty million dollars. Flew out on a private jet—Nairobi to Dubai to Zurich. Her final stop? Washington, D.C. Real estate already purchased. Shell company. Offshore lawyer. She's gone."

"And Denise?"

"Munich. Flew out with euros. German citizenship waiting at the gate like a welcome mat. No one stopped her."

"Sandra?"

"London. Seven Samsonites of sterling pounds. Each with diplomatic tags. Customs didn't touch a thing."

"And the boy?" the General finally asked, voice low and deathly calm.

Tumwine grinned, but it was the grin of a man watching a house collapse with him inside. "Ronald tried to smuggle the gold. Idiot wanted to go through Rwanda. The border's closed. He's stuck. Somewhere near Kisoro, last I heard."

The General chuckled—dark and low like thunder warming up. But then the mood snapped cold.

"This will get worse before it turns epic," Tumwine said. "The shilling will crash. Inflation will go berserk. Gas prices are going to riot. Public workers will strike. There'll be hunger. Riots. Corpses."

The General looked at him, amused. "Why are you telling me this?"

"Because they'll blame *you,*" Tumwine said simply. "You're still here. You're visible. You wear the crown now, even if it's made of land mines."

A long pause.

Then the General's voice turned colder than a butcher's freezer. "No word leaves this place. No press. No panic. We stabilize the government first. Then the economy."

He stepped closer, boots crunching gravel. "This country has always run on a dead economy. I don't expect miracles under my reign. What matters to me is power. Military. Continuity of my father's dynasty."

A beat.

"Are you ready to work with me on that, Governor?"

Tumwine nodded, throat dry. "My pleasure, sir."

The General turned to face him. "Because if you're not… you die. Now."

Tumwine swallowed. "I'll work, sir. I'll work."

"Good."

The General turned back to his walk, dismissing the man like a ghost.

"Get out of my face. Go do your job."

Then he called his aide over.

"Get Intelligence on the line. Kuharibika thinks gold is hard to trace. I want every border, every mountain pass, every damn boda boda driver in Kisoro on alert. If he tries to carry a single bar across the line…" He paused, smiling. "We melt it down with him inside it."

The General didn't like to wait. Waiting meant thinking. And thinking meant remembering. And nothing good ever came from memory. So, without skipping a heartbeat—or a step in his brisk, slow-motion power walk around the Nile Hotel—he snapped his fingers and barked, "Call Taylor. Put it on my ear. Left one. Right's still sore from the wax cleanup."

His aide, barely keeping up in size-9 army boots, fumbled with the phone, dialed, and stuck it against the General's ear like a ritual sacrifice.

"Uncle Taylor," the General said as the line clicked alive. "My stepmother. She vanished. With twenty million U.S. dollars. I hear she landed safely in your country. Is she… sleeping on your sofa now? Watching *Netflix* in your bathrobe?"

On the other end, Taylor coughed. Either startled or trying not to laugh.

"Okay, Mlevi. Listen. Your mum—stepmum—is in the U.S., yes. She got snagged at the airport with a lot of money. Declared ten million, but when they counted it, it was just 9.6. Maybe her handbag has a black hole. Or maybe her baggage boys tipped themselves generously. Anyway, the U.S. will return the money… *if* there's a functioning government in Uganda. You might want to look into that."

The General kept walking. A soldier saluted as he passed, nearly falling into a hedge.

"And the balance?" he asked. "Where's the rest of the twenty million? Or are we rounding down now?"

Taylor's pause was long enough to be suspicious. "Who told you it was twenty?"

"The Central Bank governor."

"Well," Taylor said slowly, "you might want to start interrogating him. Just a thought. Mlevi, you're inheriting a country full of thieves. No saints in your dad's government, and trust me—none in yours. Learn to work with the thieves. Or they'll bury you with receipts."

The call ended with a beep that felt more like a gunshot.

The General handed the phone back without looking. Then he turned to the aide on his left. A quiet one. Fast feet. No opinions. Good man.

"Run," the General said casually. "Don't walk. Run and tell the ISO chief to arrest Tumwine before he leaves this compound."

The aide blinked, then bolted. No salute. No "Yes, sir." Just fear-fueled obedience.

The General continued walking.

Above him, vultures circled the parliament dome like they knew something. And maybe they did.

CHAPTER 12:

Shawn

SHAWN left Nateete Best Motel like a man slipping out of a crime scene—silent, swift, and with the stink of regret clinging to his skin. The boda boda ride back to his hotel was a blur of neon-lit streets and potholes deep enough to swallow small animals. Kampala at midnight had a pulse of its own, a restless, throbbing thing that slithered through the alleyways and backstreets.

By the time he reached his hotel room, the grime of the night clung to him like a second skin. The shower was scalding, but no amount of hot water could rinse away what he'd seen, what he'd done. Some stains weren't skin-deep. He scrubbed hard anyway, dressed in fresh clothes, and checked the time. Past midnight. The night of the mission.

Mulago awaited.

The air outside Mulago Hospital's mortuary was thick

and stagnant, like the whole damn city was holding its breath. The few streetlights still working cast long, flickering shadows, turning every shape into something that looked like it had teeth. Shawn stood at the entrance, flanked by Edward or Eddie and Fred, two men who didn't even bother pretending their names were real.

They weren't here for a corpse, though God knew there were plenty inside. No, they were here for something worse—something buried deeper. Beneath the morgue, beneath the weight of a hundred forgotten bodies, lay a tunnel.

A tunnel that led straight to the president's house in Nakasero.

It was a relic of the old days, when paranoia ran hot and heavy, when men like president Joel Katila Muaji still feared bullets in the dark.

Now it was just another dirty secret, a forgotten passage rotting beneath the city like a cancerous vein. It stretched two miles through Kampala's underbelly, from the morgue to the garage of the State House. No exits. No turning back.

If they were caught inside, no one would ever find their bodies.

Shawn pulled his jacket closer, adjusting the weight of the pistol against his ribs. The scent of formaldehyde and something older—something spoiled—curled through the cracks in the walls.

Eddie let out a slow breath beside him. "I don't like this," he muttered, voice barely above a whisper.

"Wasn't aware you had to like it," Shawn said.

The old gatekeeper sat slumped in his chair, watching

them with dull, bloodshot eyes. Shawn pulled out a handful of shillings and slid them across the counter.

"Family business," he said. "Looking for someone."

The old man barely glanced at the money before tucking it into his coat.

"Ain't we all."

Shawn led the way inside. The morgue swallowed them in silence, the walls sweating with condensation, the air thick with the hum of refrigeration units working overtime to keep the dead from turning. It wasn't working.

They walked past the steel drawers, past bodies lying under thin sheets, past the feeling in Shawn's gut that told him to turn the fuck around. But they kept moving, back to the far wall, where the ground changed—smooth tile giving way to rough concrete.

And there it was.

A heavy metal lid, rusted at the edges, worn by time and trembling hands. It sat flush with the floor, unmarked except for the scratches left by men who had pried it open before them. Men who had gone in and—maybe—never came out.

Shawn crouched, ran his fingers along the edge. The steel was ice-cold. It felt like touching a coffin.

Eddie shifted behind him.

"This is a goddamn mistake," he muttered.

Shawn looked up, met his eyes.

"You want to walk? Go ahead."

Eddie didn't move. Didn't say anything either.

With a grunt, Shawn heaved the lid open. The damn thing was heavier than it looked, groaning on rusted hinges as if it hadn't been touched in decades. Beneath it, a hole yawned into the earth, black as sin, the stench of rot curling up like a thing alive. The air that slithered out was damp, thick with the scent of old decay, like something had been buried down there and never quite died.

His gut clenched.

"Jesus Christ," Eddie muttered behind him, pinching his nose.

Shawn ignored him.

"Let's go."

One by one, they climbed down, the ladder screeching under their weight. The deeper they went, the tighter the dark wrapped around them, swallowing up the light from the mortuary above. The last sliver of it disappeared as Shawn pulled the lid shut behind them.

Darkness. Pure, unfiltered, son-of-a-bitch darkness.

Shawn clicked on his flashlight, the beam slicing through the void. The tunnel stretched out ahead, narrow and suffocating, its walls packed with damp earth. Water dripped from above, carving little rivulets through the mud, pooling in uneven craters on the ground. Every breath tasted of mildew and something worse—something sharp.

The silence down here wasn't just silence. It was *wrong*. It clung to the walls like a secret, pressing in from all sides. A silence so thick it felt like it was listening.

Shawn forced his feet forward. One step at a time. The walls seemed to tighten around them as they walked, forcing their shoulders in.

Then came the hissing. Low at first. A whisper of sound against the damp earth.

Shawn stopped.

The flashlight beam swept forward, and the breath hitched in his throat. Something moved in the dirt. A ripple of muscle and gleaming black scales. Beady, unblinking eyes catching the light and throwing it back, cold and dead.

"Fuck me," Eddie whispered. "Snakes."

No shit.

A thick-bodied serpent slithered across the tunnel floor, slow and deliberate, like it had all the time in the goddamn world. It was bigger than any normal snake should be—too big. Too knowing. It coiled slightly, head lifting, tongue flicking. Watching.

Like it was waiting.

"Keep moving," Shawn breathed, voice tight. His pulse hammered in his ears.

They edged past it, careful, slow. The thing didn't strike. Just… watched. Even when they left it behind, he could still *feel* it. The weight of its gaze pressing against his back.

And that was when he heard the voices. At first, they were just echoes. A trick of the tunnel, maybe. But then they grew. Louder. Closer. Whispers—low, garbled, crawling under his skin.

Shawn swallowed hard. He glanced at Eddie and Fred. They heard it too. He could see it in the way their shoulders tensed, their hands clenching tighter around their weapons.

But there was no one there. Just shadows.

"Don't stop," Shawn said. "Keep moving."

The tunnel stretched on, winding and twisting like some living thing burrowed through it long ago. The ground sloped downward, making every step feel heavier, like the earth itself was dragging them deeper.

Then the passage opened into a larger chamber.

And that's when Shawn saw them. Bones. Scattered across the ground like discarded trash. Skulls grinning up from the dirt, hollow sockets staring into nothing. Some still had scraps of fabric clinging to them—rotting, brittle. Military fatigues. Civilian clothes. Some had no clothes at all.

Fred made a choking sound. Eddie turned away and dry-heaved. Shawn just stood there, flashlight beam sweeping over the dead. There were too many. Too fucking many.

"We're in a graveyard," Fred rasped.

No shit.

Shawn swallowed back bile and stepped over a half-buried femur. The tunnel continued on the other side of the chamber, even tighter now. They had to crawl.

The voices were louder now. Snickering. *Mocking.*

They crawled on their hands and knees, the dirt clinging to their palms, sticking under their fingernails. The air grew thick, harder to breathe.

Then the ground *collapsed.*

Shawn didn't even have time to curse before he was falling. His flashlight tumbled from his grip, spinning wildly in the dark. The fall wasn't far—just enough to slam the breath from his lungs as he crashed onto something *hard.*

Something that *crunched.*

Pain flared in his ribs. He wheezed, rolling onto his side. His hand landed on something solid, something smooth. Something that wasn't rock.

Shawn lifted his flashlight, the beam shaking as it swept over the pit. His stomach lurched.

Bones. Dozens of them. Hundreds. Piled deep.

A mass grave.

A *trap*.

His breath came in quick gasps.

Above, Eddie's voice echoed, frantic. "Shawn! You good?"

Shawn forced himself upright.

"I'm alive," he croaked, though his ribs screamed otherwise.

He moved carefully, bones shifting beneath him. Some still had scraps of skin attached.

Fred dropped a rope down, and Shawn didn't hesitate. He climbed. Fast. The moment he reached the top, he collapsed onto solid ground, sucking in breath.

The voices were deafening now. And this time, they weren't whispers. They were screams.

The tunnel had stretched on forever, a gaping wound beneath the State House, swallowing them whole. It stank of damp rot, of things that had been buried and forgotten. But now, at last, they had reached the end.

A door loomed ahead, a massive slab of steel left slightly ajar, like a mouth waiting to snap shut. Shawn's pulse pounded against his ribs as he stepped forward, half-expecting the door to slam in his face. It didn't. Instead, it groaned open just enough for them to slip through.

The shift in the air was instant. The cold, antiseptic sterility of the State House garage was jarring against the tunnel's oppressive humidity. It felt unnatural. Wrong. The kind of wrong that made the hairs on the back of

Shawn's neck stand at attention.

Rows of vehicles sat in the dim light, their sleek surfaces dulled by a thin film of dust. Some had doors left ajar, as if their owners had been in too much of a hurry to close them. Others bore the eerie silence of things abandoned.

Shawn swept his flashlight across the space, his heart hammering. The president had to be nearby. Either alive… or not. There was no time to think. They had to move. Fast.

Shawn signaled to Edward and Fred, keeping low as they crossed the garage. Every step echoed against the concrete, bouncing off the walls like mocking laughter.

Then—a sound. Faint, just a whisper of movement. But enough.

Shawn froze, his breath lodged in his throat. From behind a black SUV, a security guard emerged, his silhouette sharp against the dull fluorescence. His hand twitched toward his holster.

"Wait!" Shawn hissed.

Too late.

The guard's eyes flared wide in a mixture of confusion and fear, his fingers brushing the grip of his gun. Edward moved without hesitation, raising his silenced pistol. A sharp *phut* cut through the silence. The guard jerked once, then crumpled, the dull thud of his body hitting the concrete the only thing left of him.

Edward exhaled, a long, shuddering breath. "I'm sorry."

Shawn laid a firm hand on his shoulder. "You did what you had to do."

They dragged the body aside, shoving it against the garage wall. The State House's emblem on the man's uniform gleamed under the cold lights. Shawn turned to Fred.

"Cover him up."

Fred hesitated, then draped the dead man's jacket over him, a poor shroud for an unnecessary death.

Footsteps.

A second guard appeared at the far end of the garage, stopping dead when he spotted them. His face twisted in fear, his eyes darting between the living and the dead.

Shawn lifted his pistol. "Hands up. Don't move."

The man obeyed instantly, his arms shooting into the air. "I—I don't want trouble."

Shawn's voice was steady. "We're here for the president. If you work for him, help us. If you don't…"

The guard swallowed hard. "I work for him."

"How many more guards inside?" Shawn asked.

"Just one," the guard stammered. "The others—seven or eight—are stationed outside. We used to be a full unit, but the General… He cut us down last week."

A sliver of ice slid down Shawn's spine.

"Why?"

The guard hesitated. Then, barely above a whisper, he said, "Because the president is dead."

A beat of silence. A void, stretching wide enough to swallow them all.

Shawn's heart clenched. "Where's the corpse?"

The guard's gaze flickered toward a stairwell. "I'll show you."

The climb was slow, each step creaking under their weight. The house above loomed like a crypt, every shadow heavy with something unseen, something waiting. The grand living room stretched before them, opulent and frozen in time. Chandeliers gleamed, their light casting fractured reflections along the marble floor. And at the far end—a door.

The guard stopped, pointing. "In there. It's locked. I don't have the keys."

Shawn didn't hesitate. He aimed at the knob and fired. The gun barely made a sound, but the lock exploded inward. The door swung open. The room was deathly still.

A gurney stood at its center. Draped in yellow. Shawn's breath hitched. The president's favorite color. In life, he had worn it with pride. Now, it was his funeral shroud.

A wave of something bitter swelled in Shawn's throat, but he swallowed it down. There was no time for grief. No time for hesitation.

"We need to get him out," Shawn said.

Edward nodded. "How?"

Shawn's mind raced. "Two of you will push the gurney. Edward and I will handle anyone who tries to stop us. The president's toilet truck is outside—it's armored, it's fast, and it's our best shot. We move now."

The guard hesitated. "If they see us—"

"Then we make sure they don't live long enough to raise the alarm."

A chill spread through the room. But no one argued.

They moved. The gurney's wheels squeaked faintly, a sound that burrowed into Shawn's skull like an omen. Every second stretched unbearably long. Every breath felt stolen. The halls seemed narrower now, the weight of their task pressing in from all sides.

Down the stairs. Back through the garage. Toward the

door that would take them outside, into the cold night where danger waited.

Shawn felt the weight of it all. The mission. The risks. The corpse of a man who had once ruled a nation. The president was dead. But their job wasn't finished. Not yet.

The armored vehicle, once the president's private toilet-on-wheels, roared to life, coughing thick, black smoke into the night. The engine growled like a caged animal, and when Edward slammed the gas, the beast lurched forward, tires screeching against the slick pavement.

Shawn stole a glance at the lifeless bundle in the back—the former leader of the nation, now reduced to a stiff corpse wrapped in a yellow sheet. The color of his favorite ties. The color of cowardice. He looked away. The road ahead was more important than the dead.

The State House grounds blurred past in streaks of darkness and fractured moonlight. They had done the impossible, pulled the unthinkable from the jaws of madness, but the real nightmare was only beginning.

Gunfire erupted from the shadows. The night cracked open with muzzle flashes, bright and violent, as the presidential guards realized their fortress had been breached. Bullets clattered against the armored hull, metallic pings echoing inside the cabin like ghostly whispers.

Shawn gritted his teeth. "Keep driving, Edward! Don't slow down!"

Edward's knuckles turned bone-white on the wheel.

"I'm not stopping for anything."

The gate loomed ahead—a monstrous iron maw designed to keep threats out. Or in. Edward didn't hesitate. He gunned the engine, and the vehicle slammed through the barrier. The impact rattled their bones. Metal screamed, twisted, and gave way. The gate folded like wet paper as they burst onto the open road.

"Jesus," Fred muttered from the back. "That's one way to knock."

Shawn twisted in his seat, eyes locked on the rearview mirror. The wrecked gate was already vanishing into the darkness behind them, but the guards weren't giving up. Twin headlights flared to life—two military trucks roaring out of the compound, their engines howling like rabid dogs on the hunt.

"They're coming," Shawn said, reaching for his rifle.

The chase was on. The city streets blurred past in a monochrome nightmare, streetlights flickering like dying stars. Shawn braced himself, steadying his weapon. The first truck closed in fast, soldiers leaning out the open windows, their rifles gleaming in the darkness.

Shawn exhaled. *Aim. Squeeze. Fire.*

The windshield of the first truck shattered, spraying shards of glass across the road. The driver slumped forward, lifeless, and the truck veered sharply to the left, tires screaming. It flipped, metal crumpling as it slammed into a concrete barrier, bursting into a bloom of fire and smoke.

But the second truck was undeterred. It barreled toward them, closing the distance, gunfire rattling from its side doors. Bullets pinged off the armored hull. One round shattered the side mirror. Another embedded itself in the dashboard, inches from Shawn's thigh.

"They don't give up easy, do they?" Fred muttered, reloading his pistol.

Shawn ignored him. He leaned out the window, the

wind roaring in his ears, and took careful aim. The enemy truck was too close now, almost kissing their bumper. He aimed for the tires.

Three quick shots. The first missed. The second grazed rubber. The third struck true.

The tire exploded, shredding itself in a violent burst of rubber and steel. The truck wobbled, fishtailed, and finally flipped, rolling end over end before smashing into the roadside ditch. A thick column of smoke curled into the sky.

Shawn ducked back inside.

"That's the last of them."

Edward didn't slow down. He took the next turn hard, the armored beast skidding onto Jinja Road. The city lights faded behind them, swallowed by the endless black of the countryside. Silence settled in, heavy as a corpse.

"Are we clear?" Edward asked.

Shawn peered into the darkness, the vast emptiness stretching before them.

"For now."

But he knew better. The night wasn't finished with them yet. The armored vehicle devoured the night, its hulking form a shadow in the black expanse, tires chewing up the asphalt with relentless hunger. The rumble of the engine was a low, throaty growl, a beast barely restrained. Inside, Shawn's pulse was still hammering from the chase, the echoes of gunfire and the bright bloom of the explosion burned into his mind. The flames had swallowed their pursuers whole—one moment, the second army vehicle was on their tail, the next it was a screaming fireball, metal shrieking as it twisted into something unrecognizable.

Small victory. Too small. The weight of what they carried pressed down like a tombstone. Mukono loomed ahead, a dark road stretching before them, winding into the unknown. The adrenaline in Shawn's veins began to thin, leaving behind a cold, creeping unease. The vehicle hummed, the only sound now, steady and constant, but inside the cabin, silence stretched taut like a noose. He let his head fall back against the seat, exhaling. But the quiet wasn't peace. It was the breath before the scream.

Then, a vibration in his pocket. His phone. Seven missed calls. Joanne.

Something stirred inside him at the sight of her name. Not love—no, love didn't belong in places like this. But something else. A tether. A pull. The girl from the brothel who had clung to his mind long after he left. It wasn't supposed to be like that. It was supposed to be nothing. He was supposed to be nothing.

And yet, she had been calling.

Shawn hesitated. He shouldn't. He *knew* he shouldn't. But his thumb was already moving, dialing her number. The ring was deafening in the silence.

Then—"Shawn?" Her voice burst through the receiver, laced with relief, panic. "Jesus, where have you been? Are you okay?"

He closed his eyes, the sound of her wrapping around him like an old song.

"I'm fine," he lied.

"I was looking for you in the VIP lounge. You just *vanished.* What happened?"

He hesitated, fingers curling against the phone.

"I had to leave. It's complicated."

There was a pause, a shift in her breathing. Then, softer, "You're in a moving vehicle. Where are you going? I told you it's not safe to move around in Uganda right now. People are disappearing. Being *taken.* Whatever you're involved in—Shawn, please, *be careful.*"

Something in her tone sent a prickle up his spine. He glanced out the window, the darkness pressing in. The road stretched long and empty, but the night had teeth.

"I can't talk about it," he said. "Just… don't worry about me."

Joanne exhaled sharply. "That's bullshit."

He had to end this. *Now.*

"I need to go. I'll call you soon."

He hung up before she could argue. And then—a voice like a blade slicing through the dark: "Do you know what you've just done?"

Shawn turned, his stomach dropping. Fred. The older man's face was carved from stone, his eyes two black pits. The kind of eyes that belonged to men who had seen too much and done worse.

"The vehicle's bugged," Fred said. "They heard everything."

The blood in Shawn's veins turned to ice.

"They'll find her now," Fred continued. "They'll *find* her, Shawn. And you've just put a target on her back."

Shawn's breath came fast, shallow. A thousand things ran through his mind. What they'd do to her. What she'd say when they came for her. How they'd make her talk, even if she didn't know *anything.*

No. No, no, no.

Not her.

"Stop the car," Shawn said. His own voice sounded far away.

Edward shot him a look in the rearview. "What?"

"I said *stop the damn car.*"

The vehicle groaned to a halt on the side of the road, dust curling around them in the headlights.

"What the hell are you doing?" Fred asked. "We have a mission, Shawn. The president's corpse doesn't move itself. We need to get to Jinja. We need to—"

Shawn met his gaze, and Fred stopped talking. Maybe it was something in Shawn's face. Maybe it was the kind of madness that only came when you *knew* you were about to do something incredibly, incredibly stupid.

"I'm going back," Shawn said.

Silence.

Then Fred let out a dry, humorless chuckle. "You're *what?*"

"You heard me." Shawn stepped out of the vehicle. The air outside was thick, heavy. *Waiting.*

Fred was still staring at him, like he couldn't believe what he was seeing.

"You're insane," Fred said.

Shawn didn't argue. Maybe he was.

The armored vehicle rumbled back to life, carrying its dead cargo deeper into the night. Shawn watched it disappear down the road, the red taillights flickering like dying embers before vanishing completely.

Now, he was alone. Alone with the weight of his choices. Alone with the darkness. And somewhere out there, waiting for him, was Joanne. Waiting for the thing that was coming for her. Shawn exhaled and started walking.

CHAPTER 13:

Joanne

JOANNE knew trouble when she smelled it. And right now, it stank like sweat, diesel fumes, and cheap aftershave. As she stepped out of the Nateete Best Motel, her nerves jangled like loose coins in a beggar's cup. Her phone had been making a noise—an unnatural, needling wail that wasn't any normal ringtone. It was the sound of something broken, or maybe warning her that something was about to be.

She flagged down a boda boda, desperate to get the fuck out of there. But just as she swung a leg over the seat, a voice punched through the night.

"She's the one! I have her phone!"

Joanne froze. Not in the way normal people freeze when they forget their wallet or hear a sudden car horn. No, this was a deep, paralyzing kind of freeze—the kind that comes right before death, when your own body decides to abandon ship.

Two men surged toward her like starving dogs on a fresh carcass. She didn't even get to scream before they grabbed her, yanking her off the motorcycle like she was nothing but a sack of beans. The world spun, her feet left the ground, and then—darkness.

A door slamming shut. The reek of sweat and fear inside a moving van. The fists came fast, brutal, and impatient. Knuckles colliding with bone. Her head snapped back. Pain crackled through her skull like static before a storm. Someone shouted at her, but her ears were ringing too hard to catch the words. She tasted blood, thick and coppery.

"You're gonna tell us who the fuck he is," one of them bellowed. "Who the hell is he?"

Joanne whimpered. Not out of fear—no, that was already a given—but because she knew that whatever she said, it wouldn't be enough.

"I don't know him well! Please, forgive me! He just—he just came last night, paid for me. We—" She swallowed, feeling the hot trickle of blood on her lip. "We stayed in his hotel room. I left in the morning. Met him again this afternoon, had lunch with my son. Then I took him to Nateete Best Motel. That's it! That's all I know!"

The men exchanged glances, unreadable in the dim light. The one closest to her leaned in. Joanne could see the yellow of his teeth, the cold deadness in his eyes.

"Take us to the hotel."

She nodded because what the fuck else could she do? They weren't the type of men you reasoned with. They were the type of men who asked questions with their fists and expected answers written in blood.

The drone careened through the night, headlights flashing like hungry eyes. Joanne's own vision was swallowed in fabric, the blindfold scratchy and damp against her skin. The ride felt endless, like a slow descent into something worse than hell. When they finally stopped, they yanked her out, dragging her into the fluorescent glare of a hotel lobby.

The receptionist barely had time to flinch before the men barked their demands. They wanted a room number. They wanted ghosts, and they wanted them now.

When they finally found the room, Joanne let out a silent prayer. It was empty. Shawn was gone. Nothing remained but the stale air and a few wrinkles in the bedsheets.

"He's not here," she whispered, voice hoarse.

They didn't like that answer.

"Back to the drone."

The ride back was worse. The air felt heavier, thicker, like the drone itself had become a coffin. One of them ordered, "Take us to your home."

Joanne felt her stomach plummet into an abyss she hadn't known existed.

"No," she gasped, shaking her head. "Please. My son—he's just a child. Seven years old. Don't—"

"Shut the fuck up."

The drone lurched forward, slicing through the city streets like a hungry blade. Joanne could hear her own breathing, ragged and desperate. Her mind was a swirling mess of fear and calculations. How to survive. How to shield her boy from this.

They crashed into her small room like a wrecking crew. Cabinets flew open, drawers were upended, chairs overturned. Her son's sleepy, frightened cries sliced through the chaos, but the men didn't give a shit. He was background noise. Nothing more.

Joanne watched as they ripped through her life, looking for connections she didn't have. When they found nothing, one of them turned to her son, his face empty, hollow.

"Go back to sleep, kid."

But the boy sobbed harder. His tiny chest rose and fell in frantic little gasps. Joanne ached to reach for him, to shield him, but the men had other plans. They grabbed her again, hauling her toward the door.

"No," she choked out. "Please, don't do this—"

The door slammed shut. The drone roared to life again.

As the city lights blurred past, Joanne felt something ice-cold settle deep in her bones. This wasn't over. This was only the beginning.

Joanne was no longer a woman. She was meat shoved beneath rusted car seats, forced into a shape the human body was never meant to take—spine twisted, rib cage pressing against metal, legs curled like discarded luggage. Her head jutted out between the front and middle rows of the drone car—those infamous grey vans that swallowed people whole and coughed up silence.

The drone car sped through the backroads like it had someplace righteous to be. Inside, there was nothing righteous happening.

A boot—muddy, cracked, and reeking of foot rot and gun oil—pressed hard on her skull. It belonged to the man in the front seat. "Keep your goddamn head down!" he barked, his voice dry and flaked with cheap tobacco. He ground his heel into her scalp as though he was putting out a cigarette. "You want to look at the sun, girl? Huh? You want a sunrise like the others? I'll show you the Nile sunrise—where you float belly up!"

Behind her, her buttocks had somehow become public property. Her short dress had hiked itself up like it, too, had given up. The man in the middle row had stationed himself beside her rear like he was the guest of honor at a flesh banquet.

Out of the corner of her teary eye—blurred but not blind—she caught the striped T-shirt.

White and navy blue. Horizontal. Cheap cotton stretched over a belly stuffed with corruption. She knew that shirt. She had seen it once on a news broadcast. Minister Bafudde—State Minister for Entertainment.

Now, here he was. Slapping her ass with a weapon, she couldn't identify. Could've been a gun. Could've been a baton. Could've been the femur of the last girl who screamed too loud, grunting like a man enjoying a barbecue, his fingers twitching like they wanted to do more than beat.

Each strike made her skin sing with fire, and when she instinctively reached to pull her dress back down, the man beat her fingers like they were snakes. One-two-three, fast and punishing, as if modesty was now treason.

"Keep them hands where they are," Bafudde laughed, "or I'll chop 'em off and feed 'em to the Nile. Crocodiles love finger food."

Her hands recoiled, pulsing with fresh pain, her knuckles swelling like pregnant ticks. She couldn't see the blood, but she could feel the warm syrup of it collecting around her nails.

Two more in the back had claimed her legs as their own. Boots again. Pressed down hard on her calves like she was a live specimen on a metal table. "Try lifting 'em," one said with a giggle. "We dare you. We double-dog-dare you."

Every bump on the road sent a jolt of pain through her bent body. She no longer existed as a whole person. She was a patchwork of bruises and burns, of open skin and broken will. A torso, a head, some legs. None of it hers anymore.

But it was their mouths that did the real damage.

"We've dumped dozens in the Nile," Bafudde said, almost fondly. "The crocs are our brothers. They do the cleanup."

"Ever see a body bloat in the heat? Pop like a tomato," another added, chuckling.

"You're number thirty-four," someone muttered. "Maybe thirty-five. I stopped counting after we fed that journalist to the mud."

Their laughter was a dark lullaby. She closed her eyes—not out of peace, but out of a need to preserve the last flicker of herself that hadn't been stepped on. And in that moment, twisted like a question mark, she understood something horrifying.

She wasn't just Joanne anymore.

She *was* Uganda.

A body beaten into silence. A country forced to lie face down while men in power stepped on its skull, claimed its flesh, mocked its suffering, and dared it to lift a leg. Every bruise on her thighs, every fractured thought in her skull, was a mirror to the nation's torment—an entire people bent double, dress pulled up, dignity shredded, told to smile for the donors.

There would be no justice.

So long as the President stayed useful to America's interests, the drones would keep driving, the crocs would keep feasting, and men like Minister Bafudde would keep wearing striped shirts to torture sessions like it was casual Friday at the ministry.

CHAPTER 14:

Shawn

SHAWN arrived at Joanne's single-room home right on time, but the sight that greeted him made his stomach churn. As he approached the rented building, he noticed a taxi truck—a dreaded "drone car," as the locals called it—parked ominously outside.

Neighbors stood frozen at their windows, peering through thin curtains, powerless to intervene. The presence of the drone car, known to be operated by security or intelligence forces, was a bad omen. These vehicles were infamous for kidnappings, snatching people off the streets or from their homes without warning. Fear kept the neighbors rooted in place, unwilling to challenge the armed men.

Shawn's pulse jackhammered as he saw them—armed men in civilian clothes, packing AK-47s like they were going to war. Two of them dragged Joanne out of her home like she was nothing more than a bag of trash. Her short dress was twisted, barely covering her, but dignity wasn't high on their priority list. When she kicked and struggled, they kicked back harder. One of them cracked her across the jaw, and that was it—Shawn's hesitation snapped like a cheap wire.

The drone car's engine roared to life, tires screeching as they threw Joanne inside. Then it was gone, just like that. Shawn's body took over before his brain could catch up. He bolted to the car—technically not his, but in CIA lingo, that wasn't stealing, just an *unauthorized long-term borrow*. It had been sitting lonely in the parking lot, keys missing, conscience absent. His hands shook as he fumbled with the wires under the dash, praying to the gods of hot-wiring and poor car security.

He peeled out after them, keeping two cars back. The drone weaved through traffic like a demon on wheels, running a red light at the Nateete intersection. Shawn slammed his brakes, snarling, gripping the steering wheel so hard his knuckles went white. He waited, growling at the goddamn eternity it took for the light to change.

Green. Go.

His foot hit the gas like a hammer, tires screaming in protest. The drone car veered onto Nakawuka Road, a winding, dusty nightmare of a stretch. His GPS beeped, but fuck that—his eyes were locked on the bastards up ahead. They turned left onto an unpaved road, heading into Kabojja, the kind of place where screams didn't get answered.

Shawn punched the accelerator, closing in. He rolled down his window, leaned out, and let the bullets fly. The driver took two right in the chest, his hands twitching uselessly as the drone lurched off the road, smashing into a tree with a crunch of metal and breaking glass.

Shawn didn't hesitate. More bullets into the tires, just in case. He stepped out, gun up.

"Drop your weapons, or I'll turn you into Swiss fucking cheese!"

One of the goons, a bulky guy in a yellow and red striped shirt, threw his rifle like it was burning his hands.

"As you said, sir," he mumbled, eyes wide, legs trembling.

But the guy in the blue shirt? He thought he had balls. He reached for his gun, and Shawn put one between his eyes. The man collapsed like a sack of rotten potatoes, his gun falling with a dull thud.

Shawn yanked open the back door. Joanne lay crammed under the seats, mouth taped shut, eyes huge with terror. When she saw him, the fear melted, replaced by something raw and desperate.

"Joanne, you good?" Shawn asked, peeling the tape from her mouth.

She nodded, but her hands shook. No time to process. They had to move. Then there was the last asshole standing—Bulky Shirt.

"Please, sir, my name is Bafudde! I'm the minister of youth and entertainment. I didn't touch her, I swear!" he babbled. "You can ask her! I didn't hurt her!"

Shawn stared at him, unimpressed.

"Yeah? And if I ask her, what's she gonna say? You baked her cookies?"

Bafudde gulped, glancing around like salvation was going to crawl out of the dirt. It wasn't.

Shawn jerked his head toward a thick tree.

"Hug it."

Bafudde looked like he wanted to argue, but one glance at the gun convinced him otherwise. He shuffled over, arms out. Shawn clicked a pair of handcuffs around his wrists, locking him tight. The guy started blubbering, begging, voice climbing in pitch like a squealing pig.

Joanne, dusting herself off, scowled.

"We need to shut him up."

Shawn patted his pockets.

"Where's that tape?"

Joanne checked the discarded roll.

"Won't stick."

Shawn gritted his teeth.

"Well, we need something before he starts singing fucking karaoke."

Joanne exhaled sharply, then, with no warning, reached up her dress and pulled down her underwear. She balled them up and shoved them straight into Bafudde's mouth. The man gagged, eyes bulging like a fish on land. To secure it, she tore a banana leaf strap and tied it around his mouth. The makeshift gag held.

Bafudde's protests were reduced to muffled whimpers, eyes filled with the realization that this was, in fact, the worst day of his life.

Joanne smirked, dusting her hands.

"That should hold him."

Shawn gave her a look—half-impressed, half-bewildered.

"Remind me not to piss you off."

They climbed back into the car. As they sped off, Bafudde's muffled screams faded into the night.

CHAPTER 15:

The General

THE General's breath came in short, ragged gasps as he focused on the young singer beneath him. Sweat slicked his forehead, trickling down his temples, his pulse pounding in rhythm with each thrust. She was young, beautiful, and eager—a dreamer with desperate eyes who had practically thrown herself at him when he whispered the promise of a golden ticket. A visa to the U.S. or Canada, a chance to bear his seed, an anchor baby in a land of opportunity. She had sung for him, soft and sultry, stripping with a slow, teasing grace, her body a melody he intended to conduct.

Power. That was what he loved. The power to bend people to his will, to make them beg, to make them surrender. He grinned as she moaned beneath him, but the illusion shattered with a sharp, insistent knock on the bedroom door.

He ignored it at first, gripping her hips tighter, willing the intrusion away. But the knock came again, harder, relentless.

His pleasure soured. His grip turned punishing.

"Who is that?" he barked, voice low, a blade of warning.

"It's Douglas," came the reply. Urgent. Tense. "We have an emergency."

A growl rumbled in the General's throat. He despised being interrupted.

"What's so urgent you can't handle it yourself?"

"It's a matter of security," Douglas said. "I can't speak freely with… company present. Please, sir. It's critical."

With a hiss of frustration, the General withdrew, feeling his irritation twist into something uglier. The ache in his groin burned, unfulfilled, as he grabbed his robe and stormed to the door. He yanked it open just enough to see Douglas's face, half-lit in the dim glow of the hallway.

The old man leaned in, voice barely above a whisper.

"They've stolen your father's corpse."

For a moment, the words didn't register. They were foreign, meaningless. The General blinked.

"What?"

"The president's corpse, sir. Taken from the State House. The thieves were professionals. They took out five guards, hijacked one of your armored toilet transport vehicles. They disappeared onto the highway before we could stop them."

The General felt something deep inside him fracture. He saw the world dim around the edges, the weight of those words pulling him into a void. This wasn't just a theft. This was an insult. A violation. His father, the man who had ruled with an iron fist, reduced to a stolen corpse in the back of a hijacked toilet truck.

It was an act of war. His fists clenched. His teeth ground together.

"What about the GPS? The trucks have tracking devices."

Douglas's expression darkened.

"Disabled. They knew exactly what they were doing. This was no random raid. This was an inside job. Someone with access. Someone who knew the security layout."

The General's fingers twitched, aching to wrap around a throat. He wanted blood. He wanted screams.

"Any leads?"

Douglas hesitated, then nodded.

"One of them made a mistake. He used his phone inside the truck. Called his woman. We traced the number. Bafudde's men are picking her up now."

A slow, cruel smile spread across the General's lips. Finally, something tangible. A crack in the enemy's armor.

"Bring her to me. I'll handle the interrogation personally."

"Understood, sir. Shall I gather the crisis team? Or... would you prefer to finish here first?" Douglas's eyes flicked toward the half-open door, where the singer lay waiting.

The General's erection had long since vanished. Lust was a trivial thing compared to vengeance. He turned back to the room, saw the girl watching him with wide, questioning eyes. She didn't matter. Not now.

He pulled on his uniform with cold efficiency, ignoring the singer as she sat up, hesitant. She opened her mouth as if to speak, but something in his gaze made her think better of it. The air between them had shifted, pleasure curdled into something sharp and cold. Whatever intimacy had existed moments ago was gone, swallowed by the storm brewing inside him.

The General fastened his belt, adjusted his cap, and turned away. He didn't spare her a second glance as he strode out into the dimly lit hallway, Douglas falling into step beside him.

Outside, the night stretched black and endless, the scent of distant rain thick in the air. Somewhere, his father's corpse was rotting in enemy hands. Someone had dared to challenge him. And someone was going to die screaming for it.

Inside the crisis room, the General sat at the head of the table, his fingers drumming absently on the wood. The room was silent, save for the occasional shuffle of a nervous minister or the faint rustle of papers being smoothed out in anxious hands.

They were waiting for his wrath. And he would not disappoint them. A dull throb pulsed behind his eyes, a cruel reminder of the little blue pill still swimming through his bloodstream. A waste, really. He'd taken enough to power through the night, expecting to drown in the soft flesh of Uganda's most famous singer. Instead, some bastards had decided to steal his father's corpse, yanking him from the promise of pleasure and hurling him into this fucking disaster.

They would pay. Oh, they would pay in ways that would make the devil himself wince. He turned his head slightly, fixing Douglas with a look that sent a shiver through the man's spine. The General could see it, the way his trusted aide's Adam's apple bobbed just a little too fast, like a rat that knows it's being cornered.

"Have the delivery boy bring me a bottle of Waragi," he murmured, then, almost as an afterthought, he added, "Make it two."

Douglas hesitated. A mistake.

"Sir, perhaps—"

The General's fingers twitched, and Douglas wisely shut the hell up. The room held its breath as the order was acknowledged, the weight of it pressing down like the humidity before a storm.

*

The General's mind was somewhere else now, sinking into the past like a corpse dragged beneath the surface of a black river. The loss of his father's corpse was an insult, sure, but what burned, what carved itself into his chest like a fresh wound, was the memory of why that armored toilet truck had existed in the first place.

It had been Arua District. Christ, how could he forget?

A political rally, one of those grandstanding spectacles where loyalty was expected to drip from every villager's pores like sweat from a condemned man's brow. And the president his father—had insisted on attending in person. Of course he had. Because vanity doesn't die with age. It just gets meaner.

His father had been seventy-something then, although no one dared put a number to it. Even the newspapers got cagey. They just called him "mzeei." But mzeei or not, age had started gnawing at him like termites in a coffin plank. His knees cracked, his mind stuttered, and his bladder… Jesus. His bladder had turned into a ticking bomb.

They were halfway through the rally—the part with the staged ululations and fake applause—when the old man started shifting in his seat. At first it was subtle. A twitch here, a grunt there. Then came the glare.

"Find me a hotel," the old man said. "I need to piss."

Right. A hotel. In Arua. In the middle of a campaign rally—or rather, two dueling circuses—the ruling party was yelling into one mic, while just a few blocks away, the opposition leader, a pop star turned politician with more ego than policy, was staging his own show. His supporters, buzzed on cheap waragi and high on broken dreams, swayed like zombies at a disco.

Still, orders were orders.

The hotel stood awkwardly close to the chaos of the opposition rally. But the General didn't flinch. He assembled the presidential convoy with the precision of a funeral director on Red Bull and marched His Excellency straight into the hotel—for a presidential pee. After all, why be afraid of a crowd when you've got more guns than God and a bladder with zero patience?

It was the wrong place at the wrong time—hell, it was the wrong decade. Arua was a pressure cooker of resentment, the people packed tight like beans in a jerrycan, bubbling with rage. They hated the regime. Hated the president. Hated the bulletproof windows that separated them from the man who'd ruled their lives longer than some of them had been alive.

The Guards Brigade tried. God, they tried. They tried

clearing the road. Young men with tight jaws and looser trigger fingers pushed the crowd back with their rifles and elbows. But Arua wasn't Kampala. You couldn't part the sea here. You couldn't even drain it. These people didn't move. They surged. They *spilled* into the convoy's path like a damn flood, wild-eyed and screaming.

The General had turned, eyes on his father, just in time to see him open the door and step out, slow and regal like he still thought he was Moses and the crowd would part for him. The General wanted to scream. *Stay in the god-damn car. I'll get you a bottle. Piss in the backseat, piss in my shoe, piss on me if you want—but not here. Not now.*

But the old man wouldn't listen. Pride is a wicked demon. It whispers stupid things in your ear and dares you to believe them.

Then it happened. The moment history doesn't record but memory never forgets. His father's bladder let go. Just… gave up.

Piss—hot and furious—poured through the man's white ceremonial uniform, darkening the fabric, streaking down his legs like ink from a shattered pen.

And the president, the old lion himself, stood there frozen, his face caught between agony and rage, like he couldn't decide which enemy to kill first: the crowd or his own aging body.

The crowd went silent. There was a beat. Two. And then—laughter. Not just any laughter. Not the kind you hear in bars or movie theaters. This was *violent* laughter. The kind that flays skin from bone. It started like a whisper, then tore through the crowd like wildfire through dry maize.

The General had wanted to shoot every last one of them. Just open fire. Make Arua a memory. But instead, they scrambled back into the car, the wheels spinning, engines growling, shame and dust choking them all the way back to the capital.

The silence in that car was worse than death. The old man didn't speak for miles. Then, at last, in a voice like steel dragged across cement, he said, "You had to shoot."

Not a plea. Not advice. A judgment. A final, bitter lesson.

"They would have run," the old man said.

He never went back to Arua. Not once. Not even when the district begged, not even when they rioted, not even when the damn road needed fixing. As far as the president was concerned, Arua could sink into the Nile and take its memories with it.

The very next morning, the General had a special order drawn up. An armored toilet truck. A throne on wheels. Bulletproof, blast-resistant, chemically sealed. No more humiliations. No more stubborn roadside pit stops.

From then on, His Excellency pissed like a god—in private, in power, and most importantly, in peace.

But the General? He still remembered. Because you never forget the first time your father pees himself in front of a nation. And now, that armored toilet truck was gone. Stolen. Taken by hands that did not deserve to touch it.

The General mourned. His father had been disrespected once, and he had built an armored truck. This time, the offense was far greater. This time, there would be no truck. This time, there would be bodies.

*

The sound of the door creaking open snapped him back to the present, just as Douglas stepped in, carrying two bottles of Waragi like an obedient executioner.

"Sir," Douglas hesitated, his voice carefully measured, "are you certain this is the right time for—"

"Pour it." The General's voice was a blade, slicing through the question before it could take form. He didn't need to hear it. Didn't want to hear it. There was no "right time" for drowning out ghosts, only the necessity of doing so before they tore their way free from his skull and started screaming.

Douglas exhaled softly—defeat, resignation, or both—before twisting open one of the bottles. The clear liquid sloshed into a glass, the scent of ethanol and something medicinal curling up like a specter between them. The General's fingers locked around the glass with something like desperation, and he threw back the first swallow, the burn of it making him feel momentarily alive.

The men around the room—stiff, silent, and terrified—watched him, their gazes flicking like nervous candle flames. Waiting. Expecting. The General knew that look. They wanted him to take control, to tell them what came next. But right now, he was slipping—floating somewhere between rage and regret, between past and present. The Waragi was doing its work, numbing just enough to let him function, but sharpening something else—his anger, his paranoia, his need to make someone pay.

His father's truck. The armored monstrosity, designed to keep him safe, had been stolen. His father's corpse, the corpse of the president, was gone. A fucking joke. A cruel goddamn joke played on him by ghosts he hadn't even met yet. He gritted his teeth and took another drink, the glass trembling slightly in his grip.

His voice, when it came, was a growl—low, dangerous, the kind of voice that made men shift in their boots.

"Now, all of you," he slurred, pointing a crooked finger at no one in particular, "you owe me a fucking explanation. How in the name of every goddamn hell did this happen? How did they steal my father's truck, with my father's corpse in it?"

Silence. The kind that stretched and twisted, suffocating the air itself.

The men looked at each other, at the floor, at the peeling paint on the walls—anywhere but at him.

The General slammed his fist on the table, the sound like a gunshot, his gold-plated pistol rattling in response.

"Are you all dumb?" he snarled. "I hate asking questions and getting nothing but blank fucking stares. I didn't train you cowards to stand there pissing yourselves."

Finally, Colonel Patrick Kakembo, the chief of military intelligence, stepped forward, throat bobbing as he swallowed whatever fear was threatening to choke him.

"Sir… we're moving as fast as possible. We tracked a call from the truck… to a girl. We've sent a team to bring her in."

The General blinked. A girl. A goddamn girl.

The chief nodded, barely. "Yes, sir. But our team should have her soon."

"Good. Bring her to me. I want to see her eyes when she realizes who the fuck she crossed. And where… where the hell is that bastard… General Patrick Katamba?" he mumbled, glaring into the shadows as if the man might materialize from the wallpaper.

Colonel Kakembo, still standing stiff as a lamppost at attention, cleared his throat. "Sir, he's under house arrest. As usual. We lock him up during every election. That was your father's standing order—no general outside the Bachwezi bloodline should be anywhere near the command center."

The General blinked slowly, the information taking its sweet time to land. When it did, he leaned forward, nearly tipping out of his seat. "You mean… I'm staring down the barrel of a damn coup, and my best military brain is locked up like some street thief?"

"We can release him, sir. Bring him here immediately," Kakembo offered, voice steady despite the madness in the room.

"Then do it," the General snapped, swaying as he tried to rise. "And make it quick, before the vultures finish circling."

Kakembo nodded once and disappeared into the hallway. Behind him, the General poured another drink, muttering something about loyalty and the ghost of his father.

Then another officer stepped forward. Cyrus Rukundo, the internal security man. Pale. Sweating. Hands twitching like they wanted to be somewhere else.

"Sir," he started, "we… have a complication."

The General's head tilted slightly.

"Complication?"

"The team… they were attacked, sir." A swallow. A shift. "Two men dead. But Bafudde survived. We found him tied to a tree… with, uh, a girl's underwear stuffed in his mouth."

For a moment, silence. Then, the General let out a long, slow exhale, his fingers flexing against the grip of his pistol.

"And what," he asked, "was that incompetent sack of shit doing instead of finishing the job?"

The officer flinched.

"Sir, the man who interfered—he's dangerous. We believe he may be an American."

That word. That cursed, filthy word.

"An American," the General muttered, almost laughing. Of course. The whole damn world was a casino, and the Americans were always trying to load the dice. "Who?"

"We don't know yet, sir. But he fought like a professional."

The General's grip tightened on the pistol, the tendons in his hand standing out like cables beneath his skin.

"Find him. Find him and bring me his fucking head."

"Yes, sir."

Another knock. Not bold. Not insistent. It was the kind of knock you gave a sleeping bear when you hoped to God it had already eaten.

"What?" the General barked.

The door opened just enough to reveal a young officer—a boy, really, barely old enough to shave without nicking an artery. He stood stiff, like he wasn't sure whether he was reporting news or walking into his own funeral.

"Sir… they found the truck."

The air changed. Even the flies in the corner seemed to pause mid-buzz. Everything went still.

The General didn't move. Just stared at the boy, eyes like twin rifle barrels.

"Where?"

The officer twitched.

"At the Nile, sir. Parked… in the queue."

The queue.

The words dropped like stones into the quiet.

There was only one queue by the Nile. The *other* kind of convoy. The one made of refrigerated trucks and silence. The one no government dared admit existed.

The body trucks.

The General leaned back, slowly. The chair creaked under his weight like it had just remembered every secret it had ever held.

"They want to throw my father in the river?" His voice had dropped to a low rumble, the kind that makes men glance at exits.

The boy shifted like his boots were suddenly too small.

"Sir, we checked. He's… he's not in the truck."

The General's eyebrows lifted a fraction, just enough to make the boy wish he'd lied.

"Not in the truck?" the General repeated, tasting the words like poison.

"No, sir," the officer said. "There are a dozen trucks in front of it, all loaded. Nobody opened the armored one. The drivers said it was parked at night. The man who parked it ran."

The General stood, slow and deliberate, as if gravity had to ask his permission. He crossed the room one step at a time. The boy didn't move. Couldn't. He looked like he was about to piss himself, which would've been fitting, considering. The General stopped inches away, close enough to smell the ghost of fear rising from the boy's collar.

"What are you saying?" His voice was too calm now. The dangerous kind. "Because if I start guessing, things get bad."

The officer forced the words out.

"I'm saying they still have him, sir. Whoever *they* are. They didn't dump him. They're keeping him."

The General went still. The kind of still that made people leave the room and turn off the lights behind them.

"My father," he said, like he was talking to a god that owed him a favor, "is still out there."

"Yes, sir."

A beat passed.

"Find him," the General whispered. "Or I swear on the corpse they *didn't* throw in the Nile, I'll start tossing *yours* in one by one until the crocodiles learn your names."

The boy didn't salute. He didn't breathe. He just turned and bolted like something out of a nightmare was on his heels. And maybe it was.

The room emptied in a flurry of movement, boots scrambling to obey. But the General stayed still, alone with his drink, his ghosts, and the knowledge that something far worse than a corpse was waiting out there in the dark.

Something that had stolen the corpse of a dictator and dared to run.

CHAPTER 16:

Joanne

SITTING in Shawn's car, Joanne felt like a woman who had just crawled out of a shallow grave—alive, but still hearing the dirt settling behind her. Relief, fear, hope, dread—it all twisted together in her gut like a nest of vipers.

The clock had dragged itself past 4 a.m., the blackest hour of the night, and they were racing to find her son. If she could have willed the car to sprout wings and blast off like a goddamn rocket, she would have.

Shawn was at the wheel, jaw clenched, eyes flicking between the road and… her legs.

For a moment, Joanne thought he was just tense from the bloodbath they'd left behind—the gunfire, the dead men, the underwear-gagged official tied to a tree like some grotesque party decoration. But then she caught it. That glance. That flicker of something in his face that had nothing to do with mortal danger and everything to do with the fact that her short dress had ridden up, revealing more thigh than was probably advisable in a high-speed chase.

She yanked the fabric down with a glare.

"Shawn, what the hell? We just outran executioners, and you're about to kill us over a goddamn wardrobe malfunction?"

He blinked like he'd been caught shoplifting in church.

"I—I wasn't—"

"Save it."

She exhaled sharply, a mix of exhaustion and exasperation. Then her stomach lurched. Oh hell.

She remembered.

The panties. Or rather, the lack thereof.

Her last pair of underwear was currently lodged in the mouth of a whimpering bastard back in the wreckage. Joanne's face burned, but she channeled it into anger because embarrassment was a luxury she couldn't afford.

"Oh, I get it now," she snapped. "You think I'm naked, don't you? That's what's short-circuiting your brain?"

Shawn's grip tightened on the steering wheel.

"Jesus, Joanne—"

"No, let's talk about it. You were literally in a VIP room at a brothel today, surrounded by naked women, and now, suddenly, you can't handle a few inches of my legs? Are you serious?"

Shawn swallowed, gripping the wheel like it was the only thing tethering him to reality.

"It's not like that—"

"Then tell me, Shawn—what the hell *is* it like? Enlighten me. Because from where I'm sitting, you've probably seen a hundred naked women today alone, and now, right in the middle of a life-or-death shitshow, you're acting like a hormone-riddled teenager who just found his dad's dirty magazines under the bed."

Silence stretched between them, thick and awkward, like a corpse in the backseat they were both pretending wasn't there. Finally, he muttered, "I can't help it."

Joanne sighed.

"Fine. You're forgiven. Now keep your damn eyes on the road and don't get me killed."

They drove on, the countryside bleeding into the city, trees that loomed like silent witnesses giving way to streetlights. Joanne's nerves stretched tighter with every mile. The weight of everything that had happened—the attack, the chase, the cold edge of death breathing down her neck—crashed over her all at once. Her heart pounded. The questions clawed their way out before she could stop them.

"What's going to happen to us? Where are we going? Are we even safe?"

Shawn didn't answer right away. He just kept driving, his eyes locked on the road like it might give him an answer. When he finally spoke, his voice was low, steady, but carrying that familiar undercurrent of uncertainty that made her stomach twist.

"I'm going to try and take you somewhere safe, Joanne," he said. "I can't promise it'll be one hundred percent safe, but I'll do my best to protect you and your son."

Joanne stared at the dark road ahead, her grip tightening on her lap. *Safe*. A word so simple, so small, and yet so utterly foreign now. Safe was a fantasy, a bedtime story for people who still slept soundly at night. She just hoped to live long enough to tell her son one more story before the monsters came knocking again.

"Well, it's not just me and my son," Joanne said. "There's also Helen. You know that. If she goes back to our home, they'll find her and kill her."

Shawn raised an eyebrow, glancing at her sideways.

"Why do you worry so much about Helen? Is it because she's your roommate?"

Joanne blinked, realizing for the first time that Helen wasn't just a loose end; she was a potential target. Her stomach lurched.

"I need to call her. She has to come with us."

She reached for her phone instinctively, but her hand came up empty. The realization hit her hard.

"Damn it, they took my phone," she muttered, panic starting to creep into her voice. She looked at Shawn.

"Do you have her number?"

"Nope. I don't."

Joanne's mind raced, trying to figure out how they could find Helen before it was too late.

"We have to find her," she said. "We can't just leave her."

Shawn sighed, glancing at her again.

"I gotta be honest with you, Joanne. I don't like that girl."

Joanne stared at him in disbelief.

"What do you mean you don't like her? Why not?"

Without looking away from the road, Shawn replied, "I saw her grabbing your behind when you two hugged at the Nateete Best Hotel."

Joanne's jaw dropped, and then she couldn't help but burst out laughing.

"You're ridiculous! Why were you even looking at my behind?"

"It's kind of hard not to notice when someone's going in for a full-on squeeze!"

"You're being silly. That's just Helen being… Helen."

"She doesn't act normal around me, Joanne. She's always giving me these weird vibes, like she's jealous or something. Like she's not your sister or your friend… whatever."

"That's just how she is. She's been through a lot, okay? And she's protective of me."

"Protective? Or possessive?"

"Shawn!" Joanne gave him a light punch on the arm. "Focus! We're literally running for our lives and you're here overanalyzing Helen's hugs!"

Shawn pulled the car up in front of Joanne's rental home. Joanne glanced nervously around, then turned to Shawn, her face unreadable in the low light of the dashboard.

"Okay, Shawn," she said. "I'm going to tell you something about me and Helen, and please—don't judge us."

Shawn raised an eyebrow but said nothing. He cut the engine, the hum of the car dying down to silence. His eyes flicked toward Joanne, curious but cautious.

Joanne took a breath and continued.

"First, tell me—who are you, Shawn? I don't believe this whole 'I'm from Zimbabwe' bullshit. I think you're American. And those monsters who tried to kidnap me also said you were American."

For a moment, Shawn hesitated, then he sighed, leaning back against the seat.

"You're right, Joanne. I'm American. There's more to my story, and I'll fill you in on all of it soon. But for now, let's focus on this… relationship story with Helen that you're about to drop on me."

Joanne gave him a half-smile, the kind that didn't quite reach her eyes.

"Okay, you see my son, Anselm?"

"Yeah, I remember the boy you had when we did lunch. What about him?"

"Well… Helen is Anselm's biological mother."

"What?"

"That's not all." Joanne paused, bracing herself. "Me and Helen are lovers. And Anselm is our son."

The silence between them stretched out for a moment, thick with the weight of the revelation. Shawn opened his mouth, then closed it, clearly trying to wrap his head around what he'd just heard.

"I don't understand," he said finally. "How does—"

"You will understand," Joanne interrupted. "You're American. You get these things. If you were really from Zimbabwe, like you lied to us about before, I probably wouldn't have told you the truth."

"So, I've been upgraded to confidant because I'm from the States? Good to know."

"No, you've been upgraded because we're in a life-and-death situation, and I need you to understand that this is my family. Helen, Anselm, me—we're all connected. And right now, we need to get Anselm out of that house before those bastards track us down and murder us all."

She didn't wait for a response. Without another word, she yanked open the car door and stepped out, the night air cool against her skin. Shawn quickly followed, still processing the bombshell she'd dropped on him.

As they neared Joanne's home, Shawn slowed down, squinting into the gloom.

"Uh… Joanne?" he muttered.

She followed his gaze and sighed. Just when she thought this night couldn't get any weirder.

On the veranda, in all her soapy, glistening glory, was a woman scrubbing herself down in a dented metal basin like a goddamn Greek statue—if Greek statues had stretch marks and bathed on crumbling porches instead of inside museums. Her bare ass was on full display, a pale moon in the dim light, bobbing slightly as she reached for more soap. Suds clung to her skin in irregular patches, sliding down the backs of her thighs. The rhythmic splash of water was almost hypnotic.

Shawn let out a low chuckle.

"Well, that's not something you see every day."

The woman must have sensed them staring, because she stiffened. Her head turned slightly, just enough to confirm that yes, she had an audience, before she dropped into a deep squat—one of those survival instincts that probably went back to the cavemen. If she couldn't disappear, she'd damn well make sure nobody got a good look.

Joanne cleared her throat and kept walking, her eyes locked on her front door.

"Don't make it weird," she muttered.

"I'm not making it weird," Shawn said, biting back a grin. "It was already weird. I'm just appreciating the dedication to modesty."

They reached the door, and Joanne's hands trembled slightly as she turned the lock. Too much adrenaline, too much goddamn insanity for one night. She barely registered Shawn's voice behind her.

"So let me get this straight," he said, shaking his head like he was still trying to wrap his brain around it. "You and Helen are together, Anselm is your kid, but Helen's his biological mom?"

Joanne sighed.

"Yeah. She carried him, but we made the decision together. We're both his parents."

Shawn let out a low whistle.

"I mean, hey, no judgment. Just… holy shit, Joanne. That's a hell of a fun fact to drop in the middle of a life-or-death situation."

"Tell me about it. My life's basically one long, low-budget soap opera. With more guns."

Shawn grinned.

"Yeah, and apparently more unexpected nudity."

Joanne shot him a look. "You tell anyone about this, and I swear to God, Shawn—"

"Relax," he said. "Your secret's safe with me. Mostly because nobody would believe me anyway."

She rolled her eyes and shoved the door of her home open.

CHAPTER 17:

Shawn

SHAWN'S brain was doing somersaults trying to process this shit. Joanne and Helen. Together. Like, in the biblical sense. It hit him harder than he expected—harder than a sucker punch in a dark alley. He'd been out here dodging bullets for her, risking his goddamn life, and all the while, she had a whole-ass wife waiting in the wings. The jealousy he'd clocked in Helen's eyes earlier made a lot more sense now.

And that led to the bigger, uglier question rattling around in his skull: Was it even worth it? Putting his neck on the line for them?

Inside the house, urgency pressed in on them like a bad smell. Joanne's kid was curled up on the floor where she'd left him, his little body trembling. Silent tears streaked his cheeks. Joanne dropped to her knees, scooping him up, holding him like she could squeeze the fear out of him.

She kissed his face over and over, her own tears mixing with his.

"I'm back, honey pie. Mama's back. Mama will never leave you again," she whispered, voice thick with guilt and love and desperation.

Shawn wanted to let her have the moment, he really did, but they didn't have the luxury of sentimental bullshit right now.

"Joanne, we need to move—fast," he said, trying to keep the tension out of his voice.

They had minutes, maybe less, before the bastards who took her came looking for her again.

Joanne held Anselm tighter, feeling his tiny hands clutch at her like she might disappear again if he let go.

Finally, she pulled back, wiped her face, and turned to Shawn with an expression that was half-exasperation, half-amusement.

"Shawn, do you remember that woman you saw bathing out on the veranda?"

"Yeah, I remember. Hard to forget."

"Can you believe that's our best friend? The woman we trust with our son?" She scoffed, shaking her head. "We take care of her kids when she's off God-knows-where, and she was supposed to be here for Anselm when Helen wasn't. When those men dragged me away, I begged her to look after him. She swore she would. And yet—" she gestured at the boy, still trembling in her lap "—he's been here alone this whole time. Not even a goddamn check-in."

Shawn scratched the back of his neck.

"Maybe… maybe she thought you weren't coming back."

"And you know the saddest part?" she said, voice tight with controlled rage. "While I could've been lying dead in a ditch somewhere, she was out here—having sex."

Shawn blinked.

"Wait, what? How the hell do you know that?"

"She's Muslim. They wash up after sex before morning prayers. She's told us that before. Every time she's out there bathing in the middle of the night, it's because her boyfriend just left."

"Jesus. That's cold. Hard times really show you who your friends are, huh?"

Joanne let out a heavy sigh, rubbing her temples. Before she could say more, Anselm tugged at her shirt, eyes big and pleading.

"Mama, I need to go to the toilet," the boy whimpered.

"You need to pee? Just go outside by the door, baby."

"No, Mama. I need to go to the big toilet."

"Okay, okay," Joanne relented, yanking off a few pieces of toilet paper from a roll and handing them to him. Then she grabbed a rusted key from a nail on the wall and turned to Shawn.

"Can you take him? It's behind the house, up the hill a bit. He'll show you. I need to change and pack."

Shawn sighed and took the kid's hand, but his eyes landed on the toilet paper roll Joanne had just torn from. The brand name *Kleenex* was printed in bold letters. *Kleenex*. An American company. Of course it was.

He almost laughed. Even when taking a dump, these people were funding American capitalism. Somewhere, some rich bastard in Texas was raking in profits off every shit taken in Uganda. The economic choke hold America had on this country was so thorough, so omnipresent, it extended right down to wiping their asses.

It made him think—what the hell would happen if the U.S. just… let this place go? Let them fend for themselves? Would they collapse entirely, crushed under the weight of their own fragility?

Shawn exhaled, shaking off the thought as they stepped outside. The ground was uneven, patches of mud and cracked dirt making every step a gamble.

Anselm led him toward the outhouse—a shack on wooden stilts, built just high enough to avoid flooding when the rains came. Rusted metal sheets held the thing together with more hope than structural integrity. And sure enough, a padlock hung on the door.

Shawn frowned, then pulled out the tiny key Joanne had given him. He hadn't questioned it at first, but now that he thought about it… What kind of third-world horror-show toilet needed to be *locked*?

He turned the key, the padlock popped open, and he swung the door wide.

A blast of stench hit him in the face like a physical force. He gagged.

"Jesus Christ."

Anselm didn't seem fazed. The kid darted inside while Shawn stayed put, trying not to breathe too deep.

He let his mind drift back to Joanne and Helen, to the clusterfuck of emotions tied up in all of it. The jealousy. The unspoken tension. The way Helen had looked at him, like she *knew*.

And that was the worst part, wasn't it? Maybe she'd seen what Shawn himself hadn't wanted to admit—that deep down, he'd been fooling himself. That he wasn't saving Joanne out of some noble duty. That maybe, just maybe, he'd wanted to be *her hero*.

But she'd never needed him. Not in the way he'd wanted.

The door creaked open, and Anselm shuffled out. Shawn locked the outhouse behind them, pocketing the key. As they walked back, the weight in his chest only grew heavier.

CHAPTER 18:

Joanne

JOANNE'S hands trembled slightly as she dressed, her thoughts racing. She had just peeled open the most intimate part of her life like an overripe fruit, spilling its rotten insides before a man she barely knew. The secret she and Helen had buried for years, hidden under layers of caution, fear, and necessity, was now in the open, festering. And the worst part? She hadn't even asked Helen first.

Christ, what would Helen say if she knew? Would she feel betrayed? Exposed? The guilt pressed down on Joanne's chest like a corpse settling into rigor mortis.

They had lived a life of secrecy for so long, accustomed to the whispers, the raised eyebrows, the knowing smirks from older women who thought they understood but really didn't. No one had ever truly questioned why they shared a bed. The default assumption was poverty—two girls too broke to afford separate mattresses, clinging together for warmth. A charmingly pathetic image. The truth was so much worse. It was dangerous.

And all of it had started so innocently. Just schoolgirl foolishness. Harmless giggling in the dark, trading secrets under the covers. Then, one night, everything changed.

Joanne remembered it too well, like a horror movie she could never turn off. The dormitory had been cloaked in the soft, oppressive silence of exhausted bodies. She and Helen lay curled together under their thin blanket, whispering, their noses inches apart. Then Helen kissed her. Not the usual peck, not the silly dares they'd played out before. No, this kiss was different. Deeper. Hungrier.

And Joanne let her.

Helen's mouth traveled lower, her warm breath trailing over sweat-dampened skin. And then, oh God, then—

A moan slipped past Joanne's lips before she could stop it, quiet but damning. A sound with weight. A sound that cut through the dormitory's stillness like a blade. The rustling of blankets. The sharp intake of breath from the next bunk over.

And then—

A scream.

It was a chain reaction. The rustling turned into shifting, the shifting turned into gasps, then gasps into shrieks. Someone ripped the blanket away, and suddenly Joanne and Helen were sprawled out, tangled together like sinners in a Renaissance painting, bathed in the sickly yellow glow of a flickering dormitory bulb.

Joanne never forgot the faces.

Thirty girls, each expression a different shade of horror. Some stared like they'd caught sight of a demon crawling out of a Bible illustration. Others clamped hands over their mouths, their eyes flicking between Joanne's flushed face and Helen's shaking fingers still clutching her thigh.

And then came the words.

"Disgusting."

"Filthy."

"Devils."

Someone threw a shoe. Someone else lunged forward, fist raised, but another girl blocked her path. Chaos exploded around them, voices clashing, bodies shifting. It was a battlefield of disgust and defense, and Joanne and Helen were in the crosshairs.

Trapped. The doors were bolted at night, girls used buckets as toilets. There was nowhere to run, nowhere to hide. The only things keeping them company were the piss buckets at the far end of the room, the acrid stench mingling with sweat and panic, thick enough to choke on.

Then came the guards. The heavy stomp of boots, the metallic clink of keys, and then the door bursting open, revealing the matron in her nightdress, her face twisted into something between confusion and disgust.

"What's going on?" she barked.

Thirty voices piled on top of each other, a cacophony of outrage.

"We caught them!" one girl screamed. "They were… they were doing things."

The matron's eyes found Joanne and Helen, still half-exposed, shame curling their spines like a branding iron. She didn't shout. Didn't scold. Just gave a small, unreadable nod before motioning to the guards.

They were yanked to their feet, bare feet scraping

against the cold cement floor. Joanne didn't struggle. What was the point? They were shoved into a classroom, the door slammed shut behind them. No explanations. No warnings. Just exile.

Joanne sat on the hard wooden floor, knees pulled to her chest, heart hammering against her ribs like a trapped animal. Beside her, Helen reached for her hand, fingers interlocking with hers in the dark.

"We'll be okay," Helen whispered. "They can't kill us for this."

She sounded so sure. Joanne wished she could believe her.

The next morning, they were led, like criminals awaiting execution, to the headmaster's office. But not inside. No, not there. Instead, they were taken to an old supply storehouse on the school grounds, its walls damp with mold, the air thick with something rotting.

And they waited. Again.

Finally, the headmaster arrived, his face a stone slab of disappointment and judgment. He didn't waste words.

"Give me your parents' phone numbers."

Joanne swallowed hard. They had the numbers. They always had the numbers. This was just another layer of humiliation, a reminder that they had no power here, no rights. Just bodies that could be punished, futures that could be discarded.

She forced the words out, her voice barely a whisper. Helen did the same. The headmaster made no comment, just scribbled down the numbers, then stood.

"They'll be here by noon."

And that was it. No indication of what awaited them.

Just the knowledge that the next stage of their hell was only a few hours away.

Joanne's stomach clenched as she stared at Helen, wondering how much worse things could get. But deep down, she already knew the answer.

Much, much worse.

When their parents arrived, the headmaster didn't waste time with pleasantries. He summoned the entire student body, forming a parade of the damned, with Joanne and Helen as the main attraction.

Hundreds of eyes bored into them, greedy for the spectacle. It wasn't enough to expel them behind closed doors. No, this was a lesson, a morality play for the ages. If the girls had known what was coming, maybe they would have screamed, protested, made a run for it. But they were told it was merely a "disciplinary hearing," and like fools, they believed it.

Joanne's father stepped forward first, his face a thundercloud of betrayal. He looked at her like she had personally dug up his ancestors and pissed on their bones. His voice cracked, choked with something dangerously close to emotion—shame, rage, grief, all mashed together like an ugly cocktail.

"You're no daughter of mine," he spat, the words slicing deeper than any cane could.

Helen's father took a more theatrical approach. He rolled up his sleeves and volunteered to beat his daughter in front of the school, as if breaking her ribs might straighten out whatever "wrong" had taken root inside her.

The headmaster, ever the righteous executioner, decided to administer the same punishment to Joanne. The stick came down ten times—each crack against Joanne's skin burning, branding her with shame. The crowd held its breath, waiting for her to cry out. She refused to give them the satisfaction.

Then came the final verdict: expulsion.

The word hit harder than the stick. It wasn't just school they were losing—it was home, security, whatever fragile illusion of safety they had left. Joanne's father turned on his heel and walked away. No ride home. No parting words. Nothing. Just a void where a father used to be.

Helen, battered and bruised, still refused to abandon Joanne. Maybe that was love, or maybe just shared survival instinct. Either way, they left together, dragging their mattresses and suitcases through the jeering crowd. The gates slammed shut behind them, locking them out of their childhoods for good.

They stood on the roadside, blinking against the harsh afternoon sun. The world suddenly felt too big, too loud. A motorcycle taxi slowed beside them, the driver giving them the kind of look men give stray dogs—half-pity, half-annoyance. They pooled their last scraps of pocket change and muttered a destination neither of them truly believed in.

Kampala. The city that ate the desperate alive.

The capital wasn't a place for people like them, girls with nowhere to go and nothing left to lose. They wandered its streets like ghosts, watching the real world move past them. Night swallowed them whole, and eventually, they ended up in a pub—one of those dimly lit places where hope came to die. They sat in the corner, watching, learning. The other girls—girls their age—laughed with men, whispered sweet nothings for a price. Deals were made over cheap beer and smoke-thick air.

Helen suggested it first, voice flat and practical. They needed money. This was how girls like them survived. She didn't ask Joanne to join her. She just went. And Joanne sat there, waiting, listening to the distant hum of the city, trying not to picture what was happening in the backroom.

A few nights later, Joanne followed. At first, it was supposed to be temporary. Just until they figured something else out. Just until they had enough to get a room, some food, a plan. But plans had a way of slipping through fingers, and the city didn't let go once it had its hooks in you. The nights blurred together, a cycle of survival and self-destruction.

Joanne had thought the worst thing that could happen was being expelled, being disowned, being beaten in front of an entire school. But she had been wrong. The worst thing was realizing that, after everything, she was still here. And the city wasn't done with her yet.

Joanne felt the one-room house she shared with Helen suffocating tonight, not because of its size, but because of the weight of her thoughts. Memories, vivid and raw, flooded her mind like an unstoppable tide.

She glanced around, her eyes sweeping over the familiar corners of the room, each space filled with a memory, a story, a piece of the life she and Helen had built together. They had shared this cramped space for almost nine years now, but the most significant memory that clung to her heart was the story of Anselm—how he came into their lives.

She could still remember the day Helen had told her

she was pregnant. The shock, the fear, and the undeniable pull of responsibility that had gripped them both. But it wasn't just the pregnancy—it was the story of how it happened that haunted them.

It had all started at Nateete Best Motel, where Helen had been working as usual, entertaining customers to keep them afloat. That night had been like any other until it wasn't.

Helen had been with a regular patron, a man Joanne vaguely remembered seeing before in the area. He had paid for a session, and everything seemed routine. That was, until the condom had burst.

Joanne remembered the way Helen had told her the story, her voice trembling with a mix of anger and fear. Helen had felt it tear, but instead of stopping, the man had continued. She only realized the extent of the situation when she felt the unmistakable sensation of heat flooding inside her as he climaxed.

When he pulled out, Helen examined the condom, her heart sinking as she saw it had turned into a useless skirt, hanging loosely from his shaft. Her insides clenched with fear and rage as she realized what had just happened. The condom had failed, and the man had made no effort to stop. He had left her exposed, vulnerable in the worst possible way.

She had grabbed the man by his collar and dragged him straight to the brothel's administrator, accusing him of negligence, of continuing when he knew the condom had failed. Her voice had been filled with fury, but beneath that fury was terror—pure, unadulterated terror.

The man had sworn he didn't have AIDS, repeating it

over and over as if that would somehow make things better. But Helen wasn't willing to take his word for it. She demanded to be taken to a clinic, to be tested, to know for sure.

Joanne's stomach twisted as she remembered the moment she had found out. Another girl had come to her while she was working at the bar, breathless and panicked.

"Your sister—Helen—she's at the reception, crying. Something's happened."

Joanne had dropped everything, rushing to the reception. When she found Helen, she was curled up on the sofa, her face buried in her hands, sobbing. Without thinking, Joanne ran to her, pulling her into her arms. Helen had clung to her, her body trembling with fear and exhaustion.

Through her tears, Helen had told her everything—about the condom, about the man, about her fear of contracting HIV. Joanne had never seen her so terrified. Helen had always been the stronger one, the more fearless of the two of them. But that night, she was broken.

They had gone to the clinic together, waiting anxiously for the tests. The tests couldn't be conducted that night, so they had to wait until morning. Joanne had stayed with Helen on the sofa in the reception area, holding her hand, trying to offer whatever comfort she could. She had whispered reassurances, even though she didn't know if they were true. She had prayed silently, hoping that somehow they would get through this without the worst coming to pass.

The next morning, they went to the clinic together, waited for the results together, spent 48 hours in a purgatory of sleepless nights and whispered prayers.

Negative.

They'd dodged one bullet. But there was another one chambered, and neither of them saw it coming.

Two weeks later, Helen started feeling… wrong. Not sick, exactly. Just *off*, like the world had tilted two degrees to the left and no one else had noticed.

Joanne had laughed it off at first. "Stress," she'd said, with a shrug and a half-smile. "Or maybe those street vendor samosas from the guy who wipes his nose with the same hand he serves with."

But then came the test. And the test didn't laugh.

It just stared back. Cold. Unblinking. A little plastic oracle from the drugstore shelf that didn't sugarcoat a damn thing.

Pregnant.

One word. Just one. But it hit like a sledgehammer swung by fate in a bad mood. Helen had looked at Joanne like a woman staring down the edge of a cliff.

"What do I do?"

Joanne had made her choice then and there. No hesitation. No regret.

"We raise this baby together. You'll be the father. I'll be the mother. We'll figure it out."

And somehow, they did. Anselm came into the world screaming, as if he knew exactly what kind of life he was being born into. But from the moment Joanne held him, she knew—she would kill for this child. She would die for him.

To the world, they were sisters. To Anselm, they were his mothers. And if anyone had a problem with that, well… they could go to hell.

*

Joanne kept packing, hands moving on instinct, unsure what to take and what to leave behind in a room that already felt like a museum—one she might never walk through again. Each folded shirt, each zipped pouch stirred ghosts: memories of Helen's laughter, of Anselm's small, sticky fingers clutching her own.

The past came rushing in, uninvited and heavy, like floodwater seeping through cracks she hadn't noticed until now.

It had been nearly three years since she'd last seen her family. A different life. A different Joanne. The moment she pulled off the scam that Anselm was her biological son had been desperate, impulsive, and calculated all at once. But it worked. It had to.

The call had come on a crackling line, her mother's voice carrying urgency and something else—guilt.

"Joanne, your father is sick. Cancer. The doctors say he has only a few months. He wants to see you."

Silence. Joanne could barely breathe, let alone find the words to respond. She had been an exile long before she left. The old man had made sure of that.

Bad behaviors. That's what he called it when he disowned her at school. As if who she was could be boiled down to something she could just stop. Like drinking. Or stealing.

Yet now, she was being summoned. Called back to play the role of a grieving daughter for a father who had never accepted her. Her mother's voice hung in her head long after she had hung up the phone.

There was no choice. She had to go. But she wasn't going alone.

Anselm was just two years old then, a child still too young to understand the weight of secrets. He clung to her like a second skin, his tiny hands reaching for her in the dark. He was hers. At least, that's what she told everyone. What she had to believe.

When she arrived at the hospital, gripping Anselm's small hand in hers, her mother's eyes flicked from her to the boy and back again. A quiet, restrained shock. The rest of the family stared too, their expressions caught somewhere between disbelief and something darker.

"He looks exactly like you when you were young," her mother murmured. "Your dad is going to be so happy to see his grandson."

Joanne nodded, her throat thick with the weight of the lie.

Her father had wasted away into something unrecognizable, a husk of the man who had once loomed large over her life. His skin was paper-thin, his breath labored. When Anselm hid behind Joanne, too young to understand, she whispered to him, coaxing him forward to meet grandpa.

The old man's lips cracked into something resembling a smile.

"Thank you for not denying me the chance to see my grandson," he rasped. "And thank you for stopping those bad behaviors."

Joanne smiled. Lied. "You're welcome, Dad."

"Where's my son-in-law?"

She had been ready for this. Had the script memorized.

"He's away on business, but he'll come soon."

Her father nodded, satisfied. His eyes slid shut. Joanne stood by his bedside, holding Anselm close, watching the old man drift into something like peace. She had given him that, at least. A final, easy lie to carry him into whatever came next.

Two days later, he was gone.

The funeral was suffocating. The village had not forgotten her, nor had they forgiven her. The whispers followed her through the crowd, slithering at the edges of her hearing. Expelled from school. Disgraced. Came back with a child and no husband. But they said nothing to her face. They never did.

She left that same evening. Packed up Anselm and returned to Kampala, and she hadn't been back since.

Now, sitting in the dim room, the weight of those memories pressed against her. She wondered if she would ever return. Or if the General would make sure she never had the choice. Death had been following her ever since she and Shawn had gotten mixed up in this, and she couldn't help but think about her father. About the lie she had left him with. About whether, in his final moments, he had known.

A soft knock at the door snapped her out of it. Shawn and Anselm were back. Time to move again.

"We have to go," Joanne said, grabbing the small bag she had packed. Her mind was already shifting, focusing on the next step. "I know Helen is at Nateete Best Motel. Let's go find her there."

The past would have to wait. For now, survival came first.

CHAPTER 19:

The General

THE room reeked of Waragi, that nasty local gin that smelled like a Molotov cocktail had made sweet, violent love to a rotten mango. The General sat slumped in his massive leather chair, his uniform jacket hanging open like the loose skin of a dead thing, his medals dangling on his chest like cheap Christmas ornaments in a house where no one celebrated. He had not slept. First time in his life, actually. Turns out, paranoia was one hell of an insomniac.

The nearly empty Waragi bottle on the table taunted him, its remaining contents sloshing in silent judgment. Across from him, General Patrick Katamba sat with the rigidity of a corpse at an open-casket funeral—expression blank, uniform crisp, the embodiment of a man who had spent the last few days under house arrest and learned that silence was the best survival strategy.

The rest of the military brass sat around the table, pretending they weren't witnessing an unhinged man talking to himself between gulps of rotgut. Nobody dared interrupt. Not unless they had an exceptionally creative death wish.

The General leaned forward, his bloodshot eyes locking onto Katamba like a predator assessing whether the prey was worth the effort.

"So, Katamba," he slurred, savoring his words like a hyena licking marrow from a cracked bone. "Have they briefed you about the situation?"

"Yes, sir," Katamba said, voice steady, respectful, but carrying the kind of caution one uses when addressing a rabid dog with a grenade in its mouth.

The General scoffed.

"So tell me, Mr. House Arrest. What do you recommend? Enlighten us."

Katamba, ever the dutiful soldier, cleared his throat.

"First, sir, we need to close all roads leading to the embassies. We can't risk anyone slipping through. Border points must scrutinize everyone. We'll distribute images of the suspects immediately."

The General grunted.

"Obviously. Go on."

"We need roadblocks on the Kenyan border. That's their likeliest escape route. If we act fast, we can box them in."

Silence fell over the room. The overhead fan groaned like it, too, was tired of this nonsense. The General leaned back, lips curling into something resembling a smile but carrying all the warmth of a crocodile sunbathing before lunch.

"I want you to know something, Katamba," he said, voice quiet now, conspiratorial. "Your freedom—your entire miserable existence—depends on arresting these bastards. Succeed, and you walk free. Fail..."

He let the word hang, relishing the tension. Katamba nodded once, betraying nothing.

The General's grin vanished. His voice rose like a preacher hitting the climax of a particularly hellfire sermon.

"If you fail, you'll have no reason to keep breathing. You'll be useless to me, to this country, to anyone. And we will get rid of you. Quickly."

He slammed his glass down, making half the room flinch like schoolboys caught stealing from the headmaster's whiskey stash. Katamba remained still, though the sharp scent of Waragi and sweat thickened the air between them.

The General leaned in, close enough for Katamba to smell the death on his breath.

"This won't be like last time, you hear me? My father tried to have you killed with those idiot boda boda snipers—morons couldn't hit a sitting duck. But this time, it'll be different." His grin returned, slow, cruel. "This time, it'll be a firing squad. And guess who gets to pull the trigger?"

The room fell so quiet that even the ghosts of past coups held their breath.

The General chuckled, pouring another glass, Waragi sloshing onto the table like spilled guts.

"That's the beauty of being me," he said, raising his glass in a mock toast. "I say what I want, do what I want, and there's not a damn thing anyone can do about it. Isn't that right, Katamba?"

Katamba nodded.

"Yes, sir."

But inside, his mind was already working. The General was drunk, and drunk men had a habit of thinking they were untouchable. He wouldn't see the fall coming—not until he hit the ground and realized he'd been standing in quicksand all along.

For now, though, Katamba played along. "I understand the gravity of the situation, sir. I'll do everything in my power."

"Good." The General waved his hand dismissively. "Then what the hell are you still sitting here for? Get to work."

Katamba stood, saluted, and left. But as he stepped out into the cool night air, one thought sat heavy in his mind.

Drunk or not, every dictator meets his end. And when that time came, he'd make damn sure Mlevi never saw it coming.

CHAPTER 20:

Shawn

THE Jeep Wrangler idled at the petrol station across from Nateete's Best Motel, its engine purring like a jungle cat ready to strike. The streets of Nateete, even in the wee hours, were as alive as a roach-infested corpse—always twitching, never at peace.

Joanne moved fast, boots crunching gravel as she stepped out. She wove through honking boda bodas and sputtering matatus, eyes locked on the woman waiting on the sidewalk—Helen.

Shawn stayed in the Jeep, fingers drumming the steering wheel, eyes flicking between Joanne and the boy in the back seat. Anselm slept fitfully, head lolling, mouth slack. The kid had no idea how close they all were to dying. But maybe that was a gift.

Joanne returned, tension thick in the air. Helen's voice, sharp as a machete, sliced the moment to ribbons.

"Again, you're with this man?" she spat.

Joanne didn't have patience for a fight. "No time for this, Helen. Get in. Some bad people are on our heels."

Helen hesitated, arms crossed, her mouth a tight line of skepticism. "This guy is going to get us killed," she said climbing into the Jeep.

Shawn turned the key, and the engine growled as they pulled onto the road. Joanne tossed Helen a pair of truck trousers.

"Change," she ordered.

Helen's face twisted in disgust.

"I'm not putting on these—"

"Put them on. Unless you want to be the first thing those drone bastards tear into if they catch us."

The words hung like a noose. Helen grabbed the trousers, grumbling as she wrestled them on in the cramped space. "Where's he taking us?"

"To the American embassy," Shawn said. "Inside, you'll be safe."

It should've been that simple. But then his phone buzzed. He answered with a curt, "Two women and a child. Make sure the gatekeepers know."

The voice on the other end was as cheerful as a funeral. "Don't come. All roads to the embassy are locked down. Same for the British and French. It's a full sweep. Security's on edge. Avoid them."

Shawn exhaled through his nose, like a man realizing he'd stepped into a pit of vipers. He hung up and recalculated.

"There's a change of plans," he announced. "We're driving to Malaba. Out of the country."

Joanne nodded, jaw tight.

Helen, of course, wasn't satisfied.

"Malaba? And what if they're waiting there too? You think you're smarter than them?"

"Not smarter," Shawn said. "Just more desperate."

They rolled into another petrol station. While the tank filled, Shawn stepped out, stretching his legs and scanning the lot for trouble. The kind that didn't announce itself.

Back in the Jeep, he murmured, "Buckle up. And keep your heads down."

The Jeep surged forward, city lights shrinking behind them. The countryside swallowed them whole, an abyss of trees and shadow. The real trouble was waiting ahead.

Near Kakiri town, they hit the first roadblock. The headlights carved long shadows on the pavement as Mabira Forest loomed ahead, ancient and knowing. A bald cop with a belly straining his uniform stepped forward, hand resting on his holster.

"You're the one we're looking for," the cop said. "An American."

Shawn kept his face blank.

"Look, I've got $10,000 in cash. Split it with me, and no one saw anything."

The cop's eyes gleamed like a starving dog spotting an unguarded steak.

"Show me the money. Somewhere private."

"Down there," Shawn gestured toward the tree line.

The cop led the way, his boots crunching leaves. When they were deep enough in the shadows, Shawn acted. One smooth motion. The silencer whispered. The cop's eyes went wide, hands scrabbling at the hole in his chest. He crumpled.

Shawn didn't waste time. He stripped the uniform off the corpse, pulled it over his own clothes. Adjusted the hat. Then strolled back up the slope, slipping into the dead man's gait.

Two more officers lingered by the Jeep, hands twitchy near their weapons. One of them—lean, sharp-eyed, the kind of man who trusted no one, not even his reflection—narrowed his eyes at Shawn.

"Where's Kamya?"

Shawn kept his tone flat, the way you'd speak to a snake and hope it didn't strike.

"Taking a piss."

The officer's gaze dropped to the uniform.

"And why the hell are you wearing his clothes?"

"He gave them to me," Shawn said, deadpan.

The wiry man let out a dry chuckle, more threat than humor.

"Kamya doesn't piss in bushes."

"I'll go get him," Shawn said, gesturing.

They walked together, Shawn's hand drifting to his pistol. When the second cop appeared, Shawn moved. Two quick shots. The second officer folded like bad origami.

The wiry cop trembled.

"I have four kids. Please—"

Shawn wasn't feeling generous.

"Drop your phone. And your AK."

The man obeyed. Shawn shoved him against a tree and stripped him of anything useful. Then he was back in the Jeep, sliding into the driver's seat.

Joanne stared at him, pale. Helen was shaking. Anselm stirred in the back.

"Are you a ninja warrior, Shawn?" Anselm asked.

"Something like that, kid."

He gunned the engine. Then the gunfire erupted. Bullets chewed through the Jeep's tires. The vehicle bucked and skidded, grinding to a halt on its rims.

Joanne screamed, shielding Anselm. Helen shrieked,

"You're getting us killed!"

Shawn scanned the darkness. Two officers emerged, rifles up. One barked, "Throw the weapon! Hands on your heads! All of you, out of the car!"

Shawn's brain whirred. No good options. Joanne's wide eyes begged him. *Don't get us killed, Shawn.*

He exhaled sharply, tossed the gun out, and raised his hands. "We're coming out."

CHAPTER 21:

Joanne

JOANNE sat on the cold slab of floor that pretended to be a jail cell, her spine kissing the moldy cement wall like an old lover she'd hoped never to see again. The place reeked of every bad decision humanity had ever made—urine, sweat, and the stale ghost of forgotten souls. Sleep had left her hours ago—maybe days. The bulb above her head flickered like a dying star, casting epileptic shadows that made the graffiti on the wall twitch like it was laughing at her.

Rats—fat, smug bastards—held meetings in the corners, their slick tails slapping the cracked concrete like tiny leather whips. A puddle in the middle of the cell, dark and suspicious, rippled when cockroaches surfed across it like tiny, godless pirates.

Next to her, Helen clung to her like a shipwrecked sailor clings to driftwood, and between them, little Anselm, her son, curled into himself, shaking like a leaf with a heartbeat. Joanne could feel that frantic rhythm through his skin. It drummed into her arm, a message written in Morse code: *I'm scared, Mama. I'm scared.*

She whispered lies into his ear—comforts she didn't believe—because what else was a mother supposed to do in hell?

Her mind slipped backward, back to that cursed stretch of road near Mabira Forest. Shawn had blasted through an armed roadblock like he was starring in a low-budget action movie and had something to prove—bless his delusional heart. They'd thought they were free. Stupid, hopeful thinking. Then the ambush came—not an ambush, a reckoning.

Armed men burst from the undergrowth like nightmares with a vendetta. Their faces were eaten up by black ski masks, featureless voids except for eyes that glittered like wet stones—dead, but watching. The AK-47s in their hands weren't just weapons; they were extensions of something older and meaner than war, held with the ease of men who'd been born cradling death instead of mothers.

They didn't shout. Didn't bark orders. Just raised their guns and shredded the Jeep's tires like they were popping balloons at a birthday party for psychopaths—one, two, three, four. Flat.

Final.

Then came the walk. Slow. Measured. Boots grinding gravel like bones under a pestle. They moved with the relaxed arrogance of people who knew they were untouchable, immune to the laws that governed the rest of the meat sacks called citizens. Men who knew they wouldn't be punished for anything. Not even murder.

"Stay in the vehicle!" one of them barked, his voice sharp enough to slice skin. Then Shawn's door swung open, and just like that, he was gone—hauled out like a sack of meat by hands that didn't flinch. They cuffed him quick, precise, like they'd done it a hundred times—and they had. The click of metal was loud, final, almost obscene. Joanne wanted to scream, but her throat was stuffed full of panic.

The drone that took him groaned to life and vanished into the green maw of the forest.

They didn't get long to breathe. Another one stepped up—built like a brick wall and wearing a scowl that said he'd seen joy and personally strangled it.

"Out of the car!" he snarled.

Joanne grabbed Anselm, wrapped her arms around him like armor. Helen whimpered, white-faced, but obeyed. Joanne followed, slow, deliberate—but the moment her feet hit the dirt, hands were on her. Rough, calloused, unkind.

The cuffs bit her wrists hard—none of that gentle *"you have the right to remain silent"* crap. These men didn't read rights. They wrote nightmares.

"Don't fight," growled one.

And before she could say a damn thing, a sack was yanked over her head. It smelled like mildew and old onions, and it squeezed her breath down to a damp trickle. Darkness ate her whole.

Somewhere beside her, Helen sobbed. Anselm screamed. Joanne couldn't tell where the noise was coming from anymore.

They were shoved—manhandled, really—into the

back of a van that looked like it had been retired from delivering bread and repurposed for collecting souls. It was one of those dreaded "drones," a boxy, nondescript death rattle on wheels, infamous in whispers and nightmares for swallowing people whole. Nobody ever waved goodbye to a drone van. It wasn't that kind of ride.

The doors slammed shut with the finality of a coffin lid, sealing in a thick, greasy air that smelled like old blood, sweat, and government lies. Then the engine roared to life, coughing like a smoker on his last pack, and they were off—speeding through Kakiri like someone had told the driver hell was paying per mile.

Joanne tried not to gag on the heat or the panic. With the sack over her head still clinging like a sweaty shroud, she strained her ears instead, grabbing at sound like a drowning woman grabs driftwood. Outside, life went on. Motorcycles buzzed by like angry bees. Somewhere, a taxi operator bellowed, "Bweyogerere! Kireka! Mukono!"—the names like breadcrumbs falling into her memory, each one a little more familiar, a little more terrifying.

She built a mental map with those crumbs, trying to figure out where they were being taken. But maps are useless when you're being driven by the devil and your destination's written in code.

The van climbed a hill, its engine groaning like it resented the effort. Joanne imagined it muttering, *Why am I the one hauling dead dreams uphill again?* Then a horn blared, long and impatient, and somewhere ahead, a gate groaned open with the creak of rust and dread. The air changed—quieter, heavier, like the silence was watching them.

The van stopped. Doors flung open. Hands yanked them out like garbage on collection day.

Joanne's legs didn't want to cooperate—jelly would've put up more of a fight—but she gritted her teeth and stayed upright. For Anselm. For whatever god was still pretending to care.

And then: daylight. Or something like it.

The sacks were torn from their heads in one sharp motion, like a magician's trick, except instead of applause, there was only the dead hush of horror. Joanne blinked, her vision doing a sick little dance between blur and clarity. What she saw sobered every nerve in her body.

They stood in a compound that looked like it had been forgotten by time—and sanity. Concrete walls loomed high, barbed wire snarled at the top like the crown of a psychopath king. Ahead of them, a row of metal cells crouched in the shadows, windowless and quiet, the kind of quiet that screamed. They weren't in a police station. This was a *safe house*—that most ironic of government euphemisms. Safe for torturers, hell for everyone else.

A guard shoved her forward with all the grace of a bouncer tossing out last-call drunks. Joanne stumbled into the cell, catching a glimpse of peeling paint, old blood stains, and a single bucket in the corner that promised no mercy. She screamed. Of course she did. It was the only human thing left to do.

Her voice bounced off the concrete like a bird hitting glass—loud, tragic, pointless.

They locked the door behind her with a clang that sounded like the world giving up.

And then, the collapse.

Joanne crumpled onto the cold, wet floor, her legs collapsing like a pair of church ushers hit by the Holy Ghost. Beside her, Anselm whimpered and Helen clutched her hand like it was the last light in a blackout.

She was scared. Of course she was. But worse than that—she was starting to get used to it.

And then the door creaked open, the heavy iron scraping against the floor with a sound that made Joanne's stomach churn. Her heart sank as the shadowy figure of Bafudde in his signatory multi-striped t-shirt stepped into the cell, his presence as unwelcome as the rats that plagued the corners. His frame filled the small doorway, and though he wasn't particularly tall, his aura of menace made him feel enormous. Joanne felt Helen stiffen beside her, and Anselm pressed his face into her chest, as if trying to disappear entirely.

Bafudde's smirk was the first thing Joanne noticed. It wasn't a pleasant smile—there was no warmth in it. It was the smirk of a man who had all the power in the room and knew exactly how to use it. Joanne's stomach twisted when their eyes met. He remembered her from last night—how could he not? Last night, they'd almost killed him. It was Joanne's pleading with Shawn that had spared his life, tying him to a tree instead of ending him. And yet, here he was, alive and well, standing in her cell with vengeance burning in his eyes.

Joanne bit her tongue, resisting the absurd urge to ask for her underwear back—the same pair she'd stuffed into his mouth last night to shut him up.

Without a word, Bafudde snapped his fingers, and two armed guards stepped forward. They wrenched Anselm from Joanne's arms despite her frantic struggle to hold onto him. Helen joined the protest, her voice high-pitched with desperation, but Bafudde was unmoved.

"You don't know what's going to happen to you here," Bafudde sneered. "You don't want your innocent son to see any of it."

Joanne's arms felt empty as the guards carried Anselm away. She bit back the scream clawing at her throat, knowing that any sign of weakness would only fuel Bafudde's cruelty. Helen, on the other hand, was sobbing openly, her cries echoing off the cell walls.

"Please," Joanne begged. "Please, just let him stay with us. He's just a child."

Bafudde waved her off as if swatting at a fly.

"Spare me the theatrics. I don't have time for it. I'm here for one thing and one thing only—the truth. The same truth I asked for last night, and the same truth you two decided to deny me."

Joanne's jaw clenched. She met Bafudde's eyes, refusing to show him the fear that gripped her.

"What truth?" she asked. "What do you want us to confess to?"

Bafudde stepped closer, his boots splashing in the puddle on the floor. He leaned down, his face inches from hers.

"That American boyfriend of yours," he hissed, "killed the president. And you and your sister helped him do it. You will also tell me where the president's corpse is hidden. Because, as I told you last night, it's missing. And I know that man knows where it is."

Joanne's lips curled in defiance.

"And if we don't know?"

"Then I bring in my men," Bafudde said simply. "They'll beat the truth out of you until you remember."

Helen gasped, her hands flying to her mouth. Joanne glanced at her friend, her heart aching at the terror etched into her face. Turning back to Bafudde, she asked, "And what happens if we say we know?"

"Stop playing games with me!" Bafudde snapped, his voice rising. "You know exactly what I want. Say what I want you to say, and I leave."

"Why don't you just take my confession?" she said. "Leave my sister out of it. She wasn't even with us last night."

Bafudde laughed—a low, chilling sound that echoed in the filthy cell.

"I don't care what your sister knows or doesn't know. You both need to say exactly what I tell you to say. Now."

He pulled a small recording device from his pocket and held it up.

"I'm rolling the tape. Start talking before I lose my patience."

Joanne stared at him, her blood boiling. She wanted to scream, to fight, to claw at his smug face, but she knew it would accomplish nothing. Bafudde was a predator, and they were his cornered prey. Her mind raced, trying to think of a way out, but the cell walls pressed in on her, suffocating her hope.

She looked at Helen, whose wide eyes were brimming with tears. Joanne knew she had to stay strong—not just for herself, but for her friend and her son. Taking a deep breath, she steadied her voice.

"I'm not confessing to something I didn't do," she said firmly. "No matter what you say. No matter what you do."

Bafudde's smirk faded, replaced by a dark, dangerous glare.

"Then you've just made this a lot harder for yourself," he said. "Let's see how long that defiance lasts."

He turned to the guards and barked, "Bring them in."

Joanne's stomach dropped as the door creaked open again, the sound of heavy boots echoing down the corridor. She braced herself, knowing the nightmare was far from over. She counted eight bare-chested, filthy men as they entered into the cramped, stifling cell, their predatory gazes sweeping over her and Helen. The walls seemed to close in further with their arrival, the sour stench of unwashed bodies mingling with the cell's ever-present dampness and decay. Joanne's breath hitched, her fists clenching as she stood protectively in front of Helen, whose trembling hands clung to her arm.

Bafudde settled into the rickety chair, his hulking form barely fitting into its fragile frame. He adjusted his shirt, trying to smooth the wrinkles, a self-satisfied smirk stretching across his face as he eyed the women before him. The battered recorder he placed on the table seemed to carry the weight of their fate. Joanne clenched her fists at her sides, the fight still burning in her chest despite the despair weighing her down. But Helen's voice broke through, pleading once again.

"Please, Bafudde," Helen said. "We will say whatever you want. Please… we just want to leave here alive."

Joanne's stomach churned. She knew what Helen was doing, playing into Bafudde's ego, stroking the delusion he wrapped himself in like armor. She hated it, but she also knew they had no choice. Bafudde leaned back, his chest puffed out like a king on his throne, exuding an air of cruel satisfaction. His sneer deepened, curling the corners of his mouth as though he had already won a game no one else was allowed to play.

"Leave us," he barked at the men.

One by one, the filthy men shuffled out of the cell, their heavy boots thudding against the concrete floor, leaving behind a silence that felt heavier than their presence. The air seemed to thicken with tension as the cell door clanged shut, and Bafudde leaned forward, his cold, calculating eyes locking onto Joanne and Helen.

"That's more like it," he said. "But from now on, you will address me properly. I am Honorable Abwoli Bafudde, Minister of Youth and Entertainment. Don't forget that title—ever."

Joanne swallowed hard, bile rising in her throat. The audacity of this man—this butcher being a minister—made her blood boil, but she forced her voice to remain even.

"Yes… Honorable Bafudde."

"Good," he said.

He clicked the recorder on, the faint hum filling the room.

"Now, listen carefully. I will not repeat myself. This is what you will say."

He leaned forward, his hulking frame casting a shadow over them. Joanne resisted the urge to recoil.

"You will say that the man, Shawn, the one we arrested you with, is an American assassin. He told you this himself. You will say that he admitted to killing the president as part of a plot to overthrow the government. You will also say that he has hidden the president's corpse, but thanks to the General—our esteemed leader—the plan was thwarted, and you were captured alongside the American."

Joanne exchanged a glance with Helen, whose wide eyes betrayed her terror. Joanne could feel her chest tightening, the panic threatening to take hold, but she forced herself to remain still. The weight of what Bafudde was demanding sank into her like a stone. To confess to these lies would not just implicate Shawn—it would seal their own guilt in the eyes of the regime. She could almost see the noose tightening around their necks.

"Did you hear me?" Bafudde snapped, slamming a hand on the table, making the recorder wobble precariously.

"Yes, Honorable Bafudde," Helen said quickly. "We understand. We'll say exactly what you want."

"Good," Bafudde said, sitting back and spreading his arms in triumph.

"Then let's begin. Speak clearly into the recorder, and don't you dare stutter. I want this to be perfect."

The first take was stiff and halting. Helen stumbled over her words, her voice cracking with every sentence. Joanne followed, her words coming out like ash in her mouth. Bafudde grumbled and cursed, demanding they start again. The second attempt was no better. He slapped the table in frustration, his patience wearing thin.

"One more time!" he barked. "Get it right, or I'll call my men back in."

By the third take, both women had their lines memorized, their voices steady as they recited the fabricated confession. Joanne's stomach twisted with every word, but she forced herself to focus, knowing they couldn't afford to falter again. When they finally finished, Bafudde leaned forward, clicking off the recorder with a satisfied grin.

"That'll do," he said, pocketing the device. "The General will be pleased. Once he approves this, you'll be free to go. But don't think this means you're off the hook. If you so much as breathe the wrong way, we'll find you. And next time, there won't be a cell—only a grave."

With that, he stood and sauntered out, leaving the cell door open just long enough for the stench of the hallway to waft in. Joanne watched him go, her fists clenched so tightly her nails dug into her palms. She wanted to scream, to lash out, to fight, but she knew it would only make things worse. Beside her, Helen sank onto the bench, burying her face in her hands. The sound of her muffled sobs filled the silence.

CHAPTER 22:

Shawn

SHAWN'S first stop in handcuffs was Kibuli, the headquarters of the intelligence security organization—a place where nightmares weren't just born, they thrived. The slap of boots against concrete echoed around him as two officers dragged him forward. He could taste blood in his mouth, iron-heavy, bitter. Probably from the welcoming committee's fists back at the arrest site.

A sack had been over his head for the past hour, and when they yanked it off, the sudden blast of light made him squint. The first thing he saw was a faded sign: *Intelligence Security Organization*, (ISO). His stomach sank. Not police custody. Worse. Much worse.

As they shoved him through the reception area, one of the officers barked, "This is the American!" Heads turned. Whispers slithered through the room—some in Luganda, some in English. He could feel it in the air: that electric tension of predators circling a fresh kill.

Then he saw him.

A man, sitting in the far corner, cradling a chipped mug of tea like he had all the time in the world. Striped t-shirt, wide frame, a smirk like he already knew what was coming. Bafudde. Or was it? Something was off—the colors were wrong. Last night, the bastard's stripes were red, yellow, and white. This one? Pink, purple, white. Shawn felt a smirk threaten to rise despite the dread coiling in his gut. Did the guy just buy his striped shirts in bulk?

The moment was short-lived. A bruising hand yanked his arm.

"Keep walking."

They led him down a hallway where the fluorescent lights flickered like they were dying slow, painful deaths. The walls were peeling. It was the kind of place where hope came to rot.

Then he heard it.

A scream. Not just any scream. A raw, throat-shredding howl of agony. Someone begging in Luganda, voice hoarse from overuse. Shawn cocked his head, listening.

"*Please! Forgive me! I'll tell you! I'll tell you everything!*" The voice was shredded, barely human.

The answer came swift—a sharp, wet slap—then the sound of someone breaking apart, sobs bubbling up like something rotting from the inside.

Shawn swallowed, his throat dry as old paper. The fear was there now, settling in deep, curling cold fingers around his ribs. He'd been trained for this—black-site drills, CIA mind games, the whole brutal manual on how to keep your shit together when they started carving pieces off you.

But the truth? The truth was simple. You never really knew what kind of man you were until the pain came. And it was coming.

They shoved him inside a cell. The door clanged shut behind him. The cell smelled like piss, fear, and old blood. The single bulb above flickered like it might just give up and die any second. Shawn leaned against the damp wall, forcing his breath to steady. Panic was an enemy he couldn't afford. He closed his eyes, picturing Joanne. Her son. Whatever hell he was in, theirs was worse.

Then Bafudde strolled in.

"Mr. America," he sneered. "Yesterday, you won. Today, you lose. You're going to tell me where the president's corpse is. And you're going to confess to killing him. On camera."

Shawn tilted his head.

"You'll have better luck getting my balls in your mouth."

Bafudde's smirk twitched, but he held it. Instead, he gestured to the doorway. Three men entered. Two were built like trucks, batons at the ready. The third? Wiry, pale, with hollow eyes and pants already half-down.

"See, Shawn," said Bafudde, "Isa here's the General's special delivery man. He's got a knack for, let's say, re-arranging the rear of our fine male guests. He's the one who's popped open the backside virginity of every poor soul that's ever landed in this hellhole. The General trusts him to crack open tough nuts like you—guys who think they're too hard to break.

"But don't worry, Shawn. The first scream's always the hardest. After that, it's just… surrender."

Bafudde chuckled, a wet, ugly sound, and jerked his thumb toward a tripod in the corner.

"And that fella over there? He's our Spielberg, gonna catch every second of your, ahem, debut on tape. Proof for the General that Isa's given you the grand tour of hell.

"You have one last chance to cooperate before they get… creative."

Shawn let his gaze drop—slowly, deliberately—to Isa's semi-erect penis. He raised an eyebrow.

"Looks like he needs some help keeping it up. Maybe Honorable Bafudde should give him some foreplay."

Bafudde's face darkened. "Kill him."

Isa stepped forward, grin widening.

Shawn moved first.

A swift kick—brutal, precise—collided with Isa's groin. A sickening crunch filled the cell. Isa shrieked, high-pitched and inhuman, as blood spurted from between his legs. He collapsed, hands clutching what used to be his balls, his screams dissolving into pitiful, hiccuping sobs.

Shawn wasn't done.

He stomped on Isa's chest, feeling ribs snap like twigs. The man spasmed once, then stilled.

Bafudde's confidence shattered.

"Kill him!" he shrieked. The guards lunged.

The first swung his baton, but Shawn ducked, grabbed his wrist, and twisted. A pop. A howl. The guard's arm dangled uselessly at his side. Shawn followed up with a knee to the stomach, sending him crumpling.

The second hesitated. Mistake. Shawn drove his head into the wall. Blood splattered. The guard slid down, unconscious.

The first guard—one arm hanging limp—scrambled backward. "Please! Mercy!"

Shawn crouched, staring into his swollen, pleading eyes. Then he punched him. Once. Hard. The man collapsed, out cold.

Bafudde? He was already halfway out the door.

Shawn wiped the blood off his knuckles and grinned.

Game on.

The sound came first. Boots hammering against concrete, the kind of rhythm that meant trouble, the kind of sound you heard in nightmares when the monsters were coming but your legs wouldn't move.

Shawn knew that sound. He knew what came next. Three more guards flooded the doorway, rifles locked, eyes wide and blood-hungry. One of them—a wiry bastard with a face like an old hunting knife—shouted, "Stop, or we'll shoot!"

Shawn lifted his hands slow, measured, his breath a controlled burn in his chest. He could feel the sweat slicking his skin, mixing with the blood. Not all of it was his. Behind the guards, Bafudde lurked like the world's shittiest ghost, his face pale, his fear barely hidden under the thin armor of arrogance.

"The General said not to kill him," Bafudde barked. A little too desperate. "He's American. Just beat him into submission."

The guards hesitated. Their fingers twitched on the triggers. It was a moment. A sliver of time, small as a needle's eye, but Shawn knew—hell, he could feel it—that if he didn't take it, it would disappear.

The walls weren't just walls; they were tombstones

waiting to be carved. He wasn't done fighting—not yet. The silence stretched, thick and strangling. Someone groaned—a man on the floor, his body curled in on itself like a crushed insect. The kind of sound that sticks to you, that crawls inside your ears and stays there long after the screaming stops.

Shawn's eyes cut to the three guards. He saw the fear, saw the hesitation. And he saw his opening.

He moved.

The baton was still there, slick with blood, half-forgotten beside an unconscious guard. He snatched it, twisting his body just as the first gunshot exploded, missing him by an inch, punching a hole into the concrete wall behind him. Shawn didn't stop moving. He threw the baton like a spear. It caught the first guard in the wrist, the rifle clattering to the floor as he howled.

The second guard barely had time to react before Shawn was on him. Three fast steps. A hand on the barrel, wrenching it up, twisting hard. Another shot rang out—useless, wild, slamming into the ceiling. Shawn drove his knee into the man's gut, felt the air rush out of him in a sharp, wet gasp.

Then the third guard. He hesitated. Just a heartbeat. Just a moment too long. Shawn swung the rifle like a baseball bat. The crack of bone was loud, sickening, final. The man collapsed like a sack of rotting meat.

Bafudde was screaming now. Something about killing him, about shooting him, but no one was listening. The last guard—clutching his shattered wrist—didn't even bother pretending he wanted to fight. His rifle was close. Too close. Shawn could see the calculations running through the man's head, could see the moment he decided he wanted to live more than he wanted to die in this room.

"Leave," Shawn said, his voice low, even.

The guard left. Running.

Bafudde was alone now. The man's confidence had cracked wide open, split down the middle like old wood left too long in the sun. He stumbled backward, hands up, eyes wild.

"Wait—wait—the General—he needs you alive!" His voice was high, breaking apart like a bad radio signal. "You can't kill me! They'll hunt you down!"

Shawn took a slow step forward. The look in his eyes made Bafudde take three steps back.

"You should've thought of that before you threatened me."

He grabbed Bafudde by the collar and slammed him against the wall so hard the air left his lungs in a wheezing rush.

"You think you can break me?" Shawn hissed, his breath hot against Bafudde's ear. "You think fear is your weapon?" He bared his teeth. "Let me show you what fear really looks like."

He threw Bafudde. The man flew across the room, hit the table, sent the recorder and papers flying. He groaned, tried to crawl, but Shawn was already there, gripping the back of his neck, shoving his face into the table hard enough to splatter blood across the wood.

"Where's Joanne? Where's Helen?"

"I—I don't know!" Bafudde choked, his voice muffled against the table. "The General—he took them! I swear, I don't know where they are!"

Wrong answer.

Shawn slammed his head again.

Bafudde sobbed. "Please! I don't know!"

Shawn leaned in close, his voice a whisper. "You're going to tell the General that I'm coming for him. And when I find him, he's going to wish he never met me."

The heavy stomp of boots thundered from the hallway. A lot of them. Shawn let go. Bafudde crumpled, a heap of blood and whimpers on the floor. He grabbed a rifle, slung it over his shoulder. Then he turned to the door.

More than thirty men. Rifles ready. The air so thick with death it was choking.

Shawn exhaled.

Outnumbered. Outgunned.

CHAPTER 23:

Joanne

JOANNE had always thought hell would be hot. Fire and brimstone. Sinners roasting like skewered pork over Satan's Sunday barbecue. But this was hotter. Hell in a Ugandan jail cell came with gray walls, rusty bolts, and this state agent Bafudde, whose talent wasn't violence—though he had plenty of that—but worming fake confessions out of prisoners like a priest collecting sins he'd helped commit.

Bafudde came back that morning wearing a grin that should've been illegal.

"Got good news and bad news," he said, licking his bottom lip like a lizard tasting despair. "Your son gave you away."

Joanne blinked. "What?"

"The General had a little chat with him. Seven-year-old boys crack fast when you stick their fingers in electricity and show them what loss feels like."

Joanne froze. Her mouth moved before her brain caught up. "Why would you torture a baby? He's just seven."

Bafudde shrugged, as if she'd asked him why the sky was blue. "Because the law doesn't say we can't. Uganda's parliament never banned torture. So technically, we're just… innovative parenting consultants."

Helen reached for Joanne's hand, but it was like trying to hold onto mist.

"He says you two are… everything to him. No dad. Just Mom and Mom. Like a little queer fairytale. The General wants to know, are you two lesbians?"

"Please," Joanne begged. "Do whatever you want with us. Just don't touch the child. Please bring him back—he's just a kid. He doesn't even know how to lie properly."

"Oh, honey," Bafudde said, "you'll see him again. When he walks in here and puts a bullet in your face. The General's teaching him how to shoot. You know how we make soldiers here, right? Start 'em young. Kill the parents first. The rest's easy."

Joanne collapsed against the wall like her bones had turned to ash. Helen held her, barely breathing.

"Anyway," Bafudde said, stretching his back like a cat. "This has been lovely. Now for the morning's entertainment."

He nodded.

The door slammed. The lock clicked like a judge's gavel. Then came the hiss.

Joanne's brain knew that sound before her ears did.

Gas.

It slithered in through the ceiling vent—creeping, acrid, invisible death. The air turned metallic, like chewing on nails and regret. Helen screamed something about covering mouths, but Joanne was already coughing so hard her ribs felt like they'd snap.

Helen dragged her toward a corner.

"Stay low!" she rasped. "Gas rises!"

Did it matter?

The cell shrank. Every breath was punishment. Their lungs clawed for oxygen that didn't exist. The tear gas didn't just sting—it invaded. It took their eyes, their throats, their dignity. Joanne's face was soaked in tears and mucus and humiliation. She clawed at her own skin, wishing she could tear the pain off like an old t-shirt.

Helen tried banging on the wall, but the wall didn't care. The wall had seen hundreds like them and never moved a muscle.

Eventually, their screams dissolved into choked whimpers. Their bodies curled together like wounded animals in a trap. Time stopped making sense. Seconds became centuries.

And then—just when dying started to sound like a mercy—the door creaked open. Bafudde stood there, grinning like Christmas morning.

"Pull 'em out."

Rough hands yanked them into the light. Oxygen hit their lungs like a slap. They gasped, wheezed, blinked through tears that felt like acid. Their eyes were puffy red slits. Their throats were raw meat.

But they were alive. And in this place, that wasn't always the good news.

*

If Joanne had thought the morning was hell, she was in for a rude awakening in the afternoon. Literally.

The door to their concrete coffin creaked open again with all the drama of a B-grade horror movie, and in stepped Bafudde's favorite pet monster—the man with the melted plastic fetish. Joanne didn't know his name. She didn't want to. Some men you don't name. You just assign them a place in your nightmares and hope they stay there.

He was holding a jerrycan. Of course he was. Because lunch in this place was always served with a side of fear and fumes.

Joanne and Helen were already on their knees, wrists bound so tight behind their backs it felt like their bones were whispering secrets to each other. The concrete was cold, damp, probably flecked with the blood of guests past. She gave Helen a sideways glance, and Helen gave her one back. The kind of glance that said: *If we ever get out of here, let's never talk about this again.*

But they weren't getting out. Not today.

The man loomed over them like a cartoon villain with budget restraints—shadowy and silent except for the occasional creepy chuckle, which didn't help his case. Joanne noticed he tested the jerrycan's weight like it was a bottle of fine wine. She half-expected him to swirl it, sniff the fumes, and say, *Ah, yes, vintage torment, 2025.*

"Get them up," he said to no one and everyone. The hands that obeyed were rough, impersonal, like he'd outsourced the lifting to Satan's interns. Joanne's legs folded like cheap scaffolding. She stumbled forward, dragged like an old rug toward the low wooden bench in the middle of the room—a bench that had seen things. It looked splintered and stained with sins no bleach could absolve.

"Fold them," he said. Like they were napkins at a sadist's dinner party.

Joanne felt herself pushed down, bent over the bench until her spine screamed and her wrists yanked against the ropes. The pain wasn't even polite anymore. It was a houseguest that had kicked off its shoes, cracked open a beer, and decided to stay.

She could hear Helen breathing—fast, panicked, like a deer who finally realized the headlights aren't slowing down.

And then came the pour.

The first sound wasn't a scream. It was a hiss. Like the devil himself had spat on the floor. The molten plastic hit Helen's back with a wet slap, and the sound that tore out of Helen's throat wasn't human.

Joanne didn't flinch. She *couldn't*. Because the moment you let fear in here, it took the whole house.

Then it was Joanne's turn.

The plastic hit like a comet, a fiery trail of pain that lit up her nerves with cruel precision. Her scream exploded from her mouth before she could stop it. Her skin boiled. Blisters ballooned and burst. The air filled with the smell of burnt hair, singed hope, and whatever part of the soul cooks first when it's under direct flame.

And still, the bastard poured.

She screamed again—ragged, primal. Somewhere deep

inside her, something gave up. Something else woke up. She wasn't sure which one she'd miss more.

The man emptied the jerrycan with the slow satisfaction of someone finishing a puzzle or burning old love letters. When it was finally done, he set it down with a soft thud—too soft, like the last note of a funeral song.

Then came Bafudde. Of course. The man had impeccable timing when it came to showing up after the horror was over, like a manager checking in after the ship's already sunk. He peeked into the cell and asked the torturer, as casually as one might ask about the weather, "How is their situation?"

The tormentor shrugged. "They've learned their lesson."

Bafudde nodded and, like some overworked landlord, said, "Good. Close the door behind you."

And just like that, darkness returned. The door clicked shut. The silence pressed in. Joanne lay there, back scorched, tears dried on her cheeks, thinking: *If this is what learning feels like, I'm ready to stay stupid forever.*

*

Later that evening, the cell door creaked open again, loud and slow, like the sound of a knife being sharpened in the dark. Joanne didn't look up. No point. You didn't need to look at the devil to know he was standing in the room.

She and Helen were huddled against the wall, bruised and battered, barely holding themselves up. Their backs were a mess—raw, blistered, and sticky with dried blood. Joanne could smell it all: the sharp stink of burnt skin and something worse. Her own sweat made her gag.

Footsteps clicked across the floor—heavy, unhurried.

A man stepped inside, wearing a white coat that looked like it had seen a few too many crime scenes. His face was hidden behind a clean surgical mask, but his cold eyes gave him away. He wasn't here to help. He was here to make sure they survived just enough to suffer some more.

The General had sent him. A "doctor," they called him, but Joanne knew better. He wasn't there to heal; he was there to patch them up just enough for the next round of pain.

A nurse followed close behind him. She wore a crisp uniform, neat and spotless, like she hadn't just walked into a torture chamber.

"Hold them steady," the doctor muttered, like he was ordering coffee.

Before Joanne could even curse, the nurse grabbed her and slammed her against the wall. Joanne's back screamed. She screamed louder.

Helen was hauled up too, her head hanging like a broken doll. She whimpered softly, too tired to fight.

The nurse dipped a cloth into a metal bowl. The smell hit first—sharp, sour, and wrong. Joanne barely had time to brace herself before the cloth slapped against her back.

It burned like hell.

Joanne shrieked, a raw, wild sound that bounced off the stone walls. She felt the blisters pop under the rough scrubbing, pus leaking down her sides. The pain was so sharp it blurred her vision.

"You bitch!" she spat at the nurse.

The nurse didn't even blink. She just kept scrubbing,

harder this time, like she was cleaning a dirty floor.

Across the room, Helen was getting the same treatment. Joanne heard her soft, broken sobs.

The doctor wasn't finished.

He picked up a small scalpel and got to work, slicing away dead skin like a butcher trimming meat. Joanne bit down hard, but the pain tore another scream from her throat anyway. It felt like being skinned alive, piece by piece.

Helen didn't even have the strength to scream anymore. She just shuddered and whimpered, small and hopeless.

When they were done, the doctor peeled off his gloves with a sharp snap and said, almost cheerfully, "That should do it."

The nurse handed each of them a few grimy tablets.

"Antibiotics," the doctor said. "And some painkillers. You'll need 'em."

Then they left, leaving the door swinging slowly behind them, like the last laugh of a bad joke.

Joanne and Helen slid back down to the floor, bodies shaking, the taste of blood and salt thick in their mouths.

Neither said a word. There was nothing left to say.

CHAPTER 24:

The General

THE General knew—like a rotting tooth you can't stop tonguing—just how hard his old man had worked to hammer him into something resembling a real man, using boot camps, backdoor deals, and enough disappointment to fill a graveyard.

Before the president found Twitter—sorry, **X**—for him, he mostly just found disappointment. And not the subtle, quiet kind. No, this was loud, public, teeth-grinding failure. The kind that makes a father grip his whiskey glass hard enough to shatter it. The boy was dull. A wet match in a thunderstorm. The people ignored him like a pothole they'd grown used to swerving around.

The president, who fancied himself a blend of warlord and wise grandfather, had done all the right things—by dictator standards. He'd oiled the machinery, laid the bricks. He'd shipped the lad off to Sandhurst, the British womb for future coup-makers and ceremonial dictators. But the academy spat him out like a bad oyster after just one year. Reason? *"Intellectual capacity insufficient for command responsibilities."* That's British for "*the boy was dumb as soup.*"

Panic set in. The president, no stranger to coups or cover-ups, scrambled for another boot camp that would accept his undercooked progeny. And God bless Africa—it never disappoints. Egypt, under old mummy Hosni Mubarak, opened its arms. The president's warning was clear as day and sharp as a bayonet: "If you fail here, don't ever mention my name again." The boy emerged months later with a piece of paper that said he could command a battalion. No one bothered to ask if it was his own handwriting.

Still not satisfied, Daddy rang his buddies in Langley. Mr. Taylor—CIA spook with a neck like a tree stump—hooked him up with a slot at Fort Leavenworth, Kansas. That's where the U.S. trained its foreign military friends—the ones that smiled for cameras by day and broke skulls by night. The General graduated. Barely. His grades so low they had to be excavated.

Back home, the president, desperate to turn the boy into something—anything—decided to mold him into a public figure. He hired speech coaches, media whisperers, ex-BBC anchors, even a former Miss Uganda who once read the weather on WBS Television. Still, every time the General opened his mouth in public, it was a horror show. His hands trembled like a leaf in a blender. He couldn't pronounce words. Once, he called "sovereignty" *soup-ver-nanny* and the room went so silent you could hear careers dying.

But then came the *miracle:* Twitter. Well, **X**. Rebranded like a shady funeral home. The president's advisors—witchdoctors in suits—pitched a bold idea: give the boy a Twitter account. Hire a comedian ghostwriter. Make him sound dangerous. Sexy. Unhinged. Like Idi Amin with a smartphone.

Enter the ghostwriter—a washed-up tabloid journalist who once faked an alien sighting in Karamoja and got sued by a Catholic bishop. The guy was perfect. He knew how to stir the pot with one tweet and have the country boiling by lunch.

The General gave him ideas—half-mumbled thoughts between sips of imported whiskey—and the ghostwriter turned them into gold. Tweets like: *Kenya has two weeks left. Consider this your final warning. #WeMarchAtDawn*

The country gasped. The president "fired" the General. He even sent an apology to Kenya. A public scandal. Oh no, Daddy can't control his baby boy! The media gobbled it up like pigs at a buffet.

But behind the curtain, the ghostwriter kept churning out wild, headline-drenched tweets. The General was now lusting after Beyoncé and Ayra Starr like a horny war god in fatigues. He made bizarre threats about airstrikes on Tanzanian Bongo Flava concerts. People were horrified. People were *entertained.*

And then came the real twist—the opposition leader, Omubanda, got in on it. He knew the tweets were fake. Knew about the ghostwriter. Knew the whole thing was political theater with ketchup for blood. But he played along. Fired back tweet after tweet, roasting the General like he was auditioning for Comedy Central. His replies were savage. Viral. Millions watched the online cage match.

And it worked. The narrative shifted. The people stopped looking at the president's failures and instead gawked at the bickering clown show between the stammering General and the pop-star opposition. It was genius. It was madness. It was Uganda's very own Shakespearean farce… if Shakespeare had access to Wi-Fi and trauma.

The General, who couldn't give a speech without sounding like a haunted fax machine, had finally found his voice. Not in real life. But in X's toxic little echo chamber. And as long as no one unplugged the router, the show would go on.

One afternoon, the General dropped a tweet like a live grenade into the digital cesspool, then sat back to watch the world twitch.

It was a good tweet. A dangerous tweet. The kind of tweet that made diplomats sweat and sycophants cheer. The kind of tweet that rewrote history—or, at least, rewrote the version of history that people were dumb enough to believe.

The General had decided on the narrative. And once the General decided, reality bent to fit his will. So, he had fired off the tweet: *Fellow Ugandans, I'm sorry to tell you this, but we are going to have a big problem with the U.S. I hereby order the U.S. ambassador in Uganda to apologize to my father within 24 hours, or I'm going to lead a massive demonstration to the embassy. We shall not leave until we throw him out of our country.*

He let out a long breath, watching the ripples spread

in real-time. His Twitter hounds descended upon the digital town square, their hashtags flaring up like an aggressive rash: *#ApologizeToUganda #USOut.* A wave of patriotic bile surged across the internet, his supporters howling for diplomatic blood. They didn't know why, exactly. They just knew the General had said so, and that was enough.

Whenever the General thought about his digital lapdogs—the sad, angry men who'd weaponized poor grammar and loyalty in his name—his mind always came crawling back to Bafudde. God bless him, the dumb bastard. Bafudde, who replied to every single one of the General's tweets with the wide-eyed enthusiasm of a televangelist on meth. It didn't matter if the tweet was a policy announcement, a selfie, or a typo-ridden insult to a foreign ambassador—Bafudde would be there under it, clapping like a seal on cocaine, writing things like *Well said, sir, the truth as always!*

The General often compared him, in his more literary moods, to that pitiful horse in *Animal Farm*. Boxer, was it? The one whose response to every disaster was, "I will work harder," right up until the pigs sold him for glue. That was Bafudde. Loyal to a fault. And the General knew—hell, he *knew*—that when it was time to toss Bafudde under the bus, he wouldn't hesitate. He wouldn't even slow down.

The signs were already there. Women online had started accusing the man of things the General didn't want to touch, not even with one of his burner accounts. Sexual assault, harassment, the usual cocktail. And the General? He didn't so much as tweet a defense or send a ghostwriter to draft one. He let Bafudde flail.

After all, loyalty was useful. Right up until it wasn't.

While still chewing on Bafudde's smug little reply, the General's phone lit up again. Another tweet. This one didn't come from some bored local blogger with Wi-Fi and a death wish. No. This one came with the blue-checked gall of the U.S. State Department.

He clicked it open. The words blinked at him in sterile Helvetica, clean as a hospital bed and just as cold: *We want to warn the Ugandan Commander in Chief that any escalation or harm to the U.S. ambassador will result in serious consequences.*

That took some of the wind out of his sails.

The General scowled at the screen. *Serious consequences.* Americans loved that phrase. It was so maddeningly vague. Like a father telling his son, *"We'll talk about this when we get home."* It meant nothing and everything at the same time.

His phone buzzed again. Not a tweet. A call. His uncle and father-in-law. Bernard Musinga, aka Sayyid.

The General hesitated. Sayyid wasn't the kind of man who called for small talk. When he finally answered, Sayyid's voice came through the line, thick with tension.

"Please, son, don't make this worse."

"Uncle, do you even know what they did to the president?" The General clenched his jaw.

Silence. Then, cautiously, "I've been trying to reach my brother for three days. I can't get through. What have they done? Have they… have they killed him?"

Now that was the question, wasn't it?

The General toyed with the idea of answering in the affirmative. His father, the president, martyred by the Americans. The perfect rallying cry. A surefire way to consolidate power. But something stopped him. Maybe a survival instinct. Maybe a deeper understanding that even lies needed the right timing.

"These are serious security matters, Uncle," he said, letting the words ooze with importance. "I can't talk about them over the phone."

He hung up before Sayyid could press further. The phone buzzed again. Sayyid, relentless.

The General sighed and picked up.

"Son," Sayyid said, "I don't care what's happening in the State House or the Nile Hotel or whatever bunker you're hiding in. But could you do me one favor? Kindly delete that tweet about the U.S. ambassador."

The General drummed his fingers on the desk. He wanted to argue, but even he knew when to take a tactical retreat.

"Okay, Uncle," he said, slipping into his most obedient tone. "I'll delete it."

And he did. Just like that. Gone. Like it had never existed. Of course, his followers would concoct their own reasons for the disappearance. Some would say it was a calculated move. Others would insist the U.S. had buckled under the pressure and apologized in private.

The truth? The truth was that the tweet had done its job. It had set the stage for the next act. And the General was already writing the script.

After the tweet crisis, the General summoned his top army generals, including the cold and calculating Katamba, into the room. His fingers tapped an idle rhythm on the armrest, the slow, deliberate kind that made men sweat. He had spent years perfecting the art of intimidation—staring down officers, ministers, even foreign dignitaries, until they either stammered out confessions or pissed themselves. Right now, though, his patience was wearing thinner than Katamba's hairline.

Katamba stood at attention, stiff as a corpse left too long in the sun, hands welded behind his back like he was holding his own spine in place. Sweat gathered in the hollow of his throat, a small, glistening swamp of fear. The General's stare bore into him like a slow-moving bullet.

"So," the General said. "What's the latest on the American prisoner?"

Katamba swallowed hard. That was never a good sign. Swallowing in front of the General was what men did right before they choked.

"Sir," he began, carefully, "there has been... an incident."

The General arched an eyebrow, fingers pausing midtap.

"An incident."

"Yes, sir." Katamba cleared his throat. "But it has been resolved. Amicably."

The General let the silence stretch, watching Katamba shift ever so slightly.

"Define 'amicably.'"

Katamba hesitated. The General didn't miss it.

"Sir... the American overpowered three of our men. Two are in critical condition. One is—" he cleared his throat again "—deceased."

The General's fist came down on the desk with a crack, making the half-empty bottle of Waragi jump. "And you let him live after that?"

"Sir, we were under orders not to kill him."

"From who?"

"You, sir."

The General exhaled again. The worst part was that Katamba was right. He had given the order to keep the American alive. But alive and turning his men into punching bags? That was not part of the plan.

"Go on."

"We sent in the special forces, sir," Katamba said hurriedly. "They subdued him. He's under strict watch now. He won't get another chance."

"Is he talking?"

"Yes, sir. He's responding to interrogation."

The General leaned forward, eyes narrowing. "And?"

Katamba hesitated again. Bad news always came in installments, like a series of poorly written horror sequels.

"He hasn't revealed the location of your father's corpse yet," Katamba admitted. "The team believes it's best to take a systematic approach. Extract all the names, networks, and—"

The General slammed his fist down again, hard enough to make the lights flicker.

"I don't give a damn about networks! I want my father's corpse. Do you understand me?"

"Yes, sir," Katamba said quickly. "We will deliver."

The General exhaled sharply, leaning back again. His mind spun, calculating. This American was a pain in the ass, but maybe that wasn't a bad thing. He could use this—turn public anger against the Americans, tighten his grip, become the only answer to a crisis of his own making.

"I want him moved," the General said suddenly.

"Kibuli is compromised. Find somewhere remote. Somewhere no one will look."

"Sir, we have a facility in Bukogolwa, Butambala. Secure. Isolated."

The General considered, then nodded.

"Do it. But hear me, Katamba. If this American escapes or dies before I get what I want, you will take his place in that cell."

Katamba swallowed hard. "Yes, sir."

"Good." The General waved a hand. "Now get out. And send Douglas in with my Waragi. I need another drink."

Katamba saluted sharply, turned to leave, but the General's voice stopped him cold.

"And, Katamba."

Katamba turned, standing rigid.

The General's voice was calm, like the silence before a bomb goes off.

"If I don't have my father's corpse soon, I'll have yours instead."

Katamba nodded, his face drained of color.

"Understood, sir."

The General smiled thinly. Not a warm smile. Not a reassuring one. The kind of smile you see before the world goes dark.

"Good. Now go."

CHAPTER 25:

Shawn

SHAWN woke up to the sickly glow of a bug-zapper in the corner, crackling with the occasional sizzle of doomed insects—like tiny souls getting fried on their way to hell. His body felt like it had been worked over with a crowbar—his ribs ached, his face was swollen, and the handcuffs had chewed into his wrists for so long, he half-expected to see bone. He forced himself upright, his movements stiff and mechanical, like some battered old wind-up toy that refused to die.

The cell was packed beyond reason. Fifteen men stuffed into a space meant for two, their bodies pressed together like some grotesque human jigsaw puzzle. Shawn scanned their faces, sunken eyes and hollowed cheeks, and it didn't take long to figure out who they were. Political prisoners. Men who had spoken out against the General. Men who, in this part of the world, were considered about as valuable as a roach infestation. And now, Shawn was one of them.

He leaned toward the man closest to him, his voice scraping against his throat like sandpaper.

"Where are we?"

The man turned his head slowly, his dark eyes flat.

"Bukogolwa jail," he said. "In Butambala."

Shawn swallowed hard. Bukogolwa. The name was unfamiliar but heavy with doom. A place where people went in but didn't come out. Not in one piece, anyway.

Before he could ask more, a guard appeared at the edge of the cage. His uniform was wrinkled and stained with sweat, his rifle slung over one shoulder like a lazy afterthought. He tossed Shawn a rusty metal pail and a dented tin plate, grinning like he was handing out Christmas gifts.

"Welcome," the guard sneered. "The pail's your toilet. The plate's for your food. Don't mix them up."

Shawn stared at the objects in his hands, trying to process what had just been said. He looked around and noticed similar pails scattered across the floor, some brimming, others in various states of horror.

The stench hit him full-force, a toxic wave that curled his stomach and made his eyes water.

In the next cage over, a prisoner squatted over his pail, bare-assed, making use of his "amenities" without a shred of shame. Shawn turned away, gagging. Back in Boston, he wouldn't even fart in an empty elevator for fear someone might step in right after. Now? Now he was being forced to embrace a whole new level of public exposure.

He gripped the edge of the pail, fingers whitening. The contrast between his old life and this new waking nightmare was almost laughable—if he weren't living it. The stench, the filth, the degradation—it was all part of the plan. This wasn't just a prison; it was a meat grinder for the soul.

Once a day, the prisoners were allowed to empty their pails into a communal sewer hole. The guards stood by, rifles in hand, watching the process like it was some grand entertainment. No toilet paper, no dignity. Just a daily march of shame.

Shawn tried reasoning with one of them when food was finally doled out in a dented saucepan.

"Please, can we get some toilet paper?"

The guard looked at him like he'd just asked for champagne and a cigar. He let out a short, humorless laugh.

"The government's broke," he said. "We give you food. That's all you need to stay alive. Toilet paper isn't a necessity." He smirked, tilting the saucepan so that the slop inside sloshed dangerously close to spilling. "You won't die if you don't wipe yourself."

The other prisoners didn't say much. They didn't have to. Their silence spoke in volumes. They were already dead—just waiting for the paperwork to catch up. Each morning, one of them was dragged into the courtyard and shot, a little breakfast show for the rest of them. It wasn't about justice. It wasn't even about efficiency. It was about breaking them. And from the look of things, it was working.

A guard smirked at Shawn from outside the bars.

"The examination room is being cleared for you," he said. "Hope your memory's sharp. Passing the examination is your lifeline."

Shawn's throat went dry. Examination? The hell did that mean? He glanced around, locking eyes with the prisoner he had mentally dubbed the least likely to stab him in his sleep.

"What's the examination room?" he whispered.

The man sighed, like a teacher tired of dumb students.

"It's the torture room," he said. "Most people who go in don't come out. And if they do, they wish they hadn't."

Shawn felt a prickle of cold sweat.

"Do you have family?" the man asked suddenly. "Anyone you wanna leave a message for?"

Shawn blinked. His ex, Katie. Their kid, a boy who was probably still too young to even know he existed.

And Sasha—Joanne—whatever name she was going by today. He hadn't realized how much he thought about her until now. But thinking wasn't going to save him.

Before he could answer, the iron door creaked open. Two guards emerged, dragging something between them. A body. Or what was left of one. The prisoners fell silent as the thing was hauled past them, leaving a trail of dark red stains on the floor. No one spoke. No one even breathed. But their eyes followed the corpse like it still had a soul worth mourning.

Shawn turned away, swallowing back bile. He was an American. He had been told—repeatedly—that his citizenship made him untouchable. But staring at that mangled body, he wasn't so sure anymore.

The friendly prisoner leaned close again, his voice barely a whisper.

"Pray," he said simply. "To whatever god you believe in."

Shawn didn't respond. His eyes were on the iron door, now shut once more, like the gaping maw of some ancient beast waiting for its next meal. His mind raced, fighting for some semblance of control. Torture. The word sat in his head like a disease. It turned men into broken things. It didn't just hurt—you left pieces of yourself behind in rooms like that, pieces you never got back.

A voice inside him, cold and detached, whispered: *You've been trained for this. You've survived worse.* But had he? Had he really? Because whatever waited for him on the other side of that door, he was pretty damn sure he wasn't ready for it.

One of the guards returned, his keys jingling as he stopped in front of Shawn's cage.

"You," he barked, pointing at Shawn. "It's time."

Shawn hesitated, his legs feeling like lead. The other prisoners avoided his gaze. No one offered words of encouragement. They knew better. He forced himself to stand, his movements slow and deliberate. Every muscle in his body screamed in protest from the beating he had endured earlier, but he ignored the pain.

As the guard unlocked the cage and grabbed him by the arm, Shawn cast one last glance at the friendly prisoner. The man gave him a small, sad nod, as if to say, "Good luck." Then the door slammed shut behind him, and Shawn was led toward the iron door.

The hallway stretched ahead of him, dimly lit and suffocatingly narrow. Each step felt heavier than the last, the echo of his boots against the floor sounding like a countdown to his doom. Shawn gritted his teeth, forcing his mind to focus. If this was a game of survival, he would play. If this was his test, he would pass.

The examination room was a stark, oppressive chamber, its every detail screaming calculated cruelty. The centerpiece was a chair—ominous, metallic, and undeniably tied to something far worse than discomfort. Shawn couldn't ignore its resemblance to the execution chairs he'd seen in movies, complete with frayed wiring snaking down its sides. How such an abomination had found its way to this remote corner of Butambala was a puzzle that momentarily distracted him from the dread pooling in his chest.

Two men in crisp white coats loomed nearby, their air clinical but far from benevolent. They weren't doctors in any sense Shawn trusted; they were artisans of agony, torture doctors trained not to heal, but to break. Their accents were peculiar—a blend of Luganda with something foreign and formal, perhaps picked up from training in Cuba, Russia, or elsewhere. Shawn doubted their knowledge came from the States or the UK, but their expertise was unmistakable. They were professionals in dismantling a person's will.

"Mr. American," one of them said, his voice smooth but laced with menace, "are you here to cooperate, or shall we proceed to more persuasive measures? We know what to do in all situations."

Shawn kept his gaze fixed on his feet, refusing to acknowledge the man's words. A wave of contempt rose within him, but he tamped it down. Showing any reaction would only fuel their sadism.

"We need you to point out that CIA body tracker hidden inside you," the man continued. "We wouldn't want your country's F-15 jets lighting up this humble prison to collect you. So, Mr. American—are you cooperating or not?"

Shawn clenched his jaw, saying nothing. Silence was his only weapon now, a fragile shield against the tide of pain he knew was coming. His captor stepped closer, his expression sharpening.

"If you're not talking," the man hissed, "I'll have to call in our dentist."

A sharp nod from the speaker summoned his partner, who approached with a toolbox that rattled ominously. Shawn's heart sank as the lid was lifted, revealing an array of gleaming dental instruments. These weren't tools of care; they were implements of torment. The "dentist" selected a plier-like device with unsettling ease.

"This," the man said, holding up the instrument, "is a tooth puller. I'll be examining each tooth for that pesky little tracker."

The pliers clamped down on Shawn's front tooth, the cold metal biting into the enamel. Shawn braced himself, but when the tooth was wrenched free, pain like fire exploded through his skull. He screamed, unable to hold it back, but his tormentor merely chuckled.

"Save your tears, Mr. American. This is just the beginning."

One by one, his teeth were ripped from his mouth, the agony compounding with every pull. Blood pooled on his tongue, the metallic taste mingling with the coppery stench filling the room. Shawn begged for anesthesia, for mercy, but his pleas were met with cruel laughter.

"We don't know that word here," the dentist replied.

Six teeth were gone before the man paused, inspecting one particularly jagged specimen.

"Hmm. This one looks promising," he muttered, turning it over in his hand. Without another word, he left the room, leaving Shawn slumped in the chair, barely conscious and wracked with pain.

Minutes—or hours, Shawn couldn't tell—passed before the man returned. He tossed the tooth onto the floor and smiled. "We found what we were looking for," he said casually, "but my boss insists we be thorough. There might be a second tracker. So… we'll continue."

Shawn's broken body wanted to cry out, to plead, but his will wouldn't allow it. The dentist resumed his work with unrelenting precision, and Shawn's world dissolved into a haze of pain. Tooth after tooth was yanked, each extraction another step toward oblivion. By the time the torture ended, Shawn's mouth was a bloody, empty cavern, and his consciousness teetered on the brink of collapse.

The last thing Shawn registered was the dentist's voice, calm and clinical.

"We'll need to move him to the next phase of interrogation. Prepare the equipment."

The world faded to black.

*

Several hours later, Shawn's mind clawed its way back to consciousness as muffled voices filtered through the haze.

Two women, their tones hushed but distinct, were speaking with a man whose gruff voice carried authority.

"Won't it be an overdose, sir? We don't want to be responsible for this American dying," one of the women said.

Shawn's breath hitched as realization dawned. He was the subject of their conversation.

The man's reply was cold and clinical.

"We need him awake for the next interrogation. Give him another injection. It'll wake him up and keep him sensitive to the pain we need to inflict for answers."

Panic surged through Shawn. Another round of torture. More pain. His instincts screamed at him to move, to fight back, but he forced himself to remain still. If they thought he was still unconscious, it might buy him time. He tried to piece together what kind of drugs they were pumping into him, but his foggy mind offered no answers.

Footsteps echoed on the cement floor, growing louder until two women entered his field of vision. Shawn cracked his eyes open just enough to spy on them. Dressed in white gowns, they looked like nurses, though their conversation betrayed anything but a nurturing demeanor.

The taller one frowned as she took his hand, muttering under her breath, "I hate these people with invisible veins." Her fingers were clinical, prodding his battered hand, searching for an entry point. "Why did you remove the cannula last time?" she asked, irritation lacing her voice.

The shorter one shrugged.

"I thought he was all set. We never have to give multiple injections, and those torture guys don't want syringes left on their victims."

"But how does a man have an erection with no veins?" the taller one asked, her tone both incredulous and teasing.

The other woman snorted, her laugh cutting through the oppressive silence of the room. Shawn struggled to pinpoint who was speaking or laughing as their voices intertwined, their conversation bizarrely mundane.

"My auntie warned me never to marry a man whose veins are hard to find," one of them quipped. "She said they always struggle to, you know... perform."

They kept talking as if he weren't there, their conversation drifting to the absurd. Tales of ancestors, aunties, and pseudoscience poured out of them, the kind of idle chatter that might belong in a village square, not a torture chamber.

Shawn's mind raced. Did they genuinely believe the nonsense they were spouting about veins and erections, or was it just their way of coping with the horrors of their work? Either way, their laughter grated on his nerves.

"Never undress for a man if you can't find his veins," the woman with the syringe said, giggling as she prepared to insert the cannula. "It means even down there, there are no veins."

She gripped his hand again, jabbing the needle into his skin with a roughness that made him wince. Pain shot through his arm, sharp and immediate, and he instinctively flinched.

"He's awake!" the taller one shouted, her voice filled with both alarm and triumph. "Call the Kitalya torture team! He's awake—we don't need to add more drugs!"

The other woman dropped the syringe, her eyes wide with alarm. Their chatter evaporated into silence, replaced by a panicked flurry of movement as they backed away.

Shawn lay on the cold, blood-stained examination

room floor, his body a broken husk of pain. Every muscle screamed, his chest heaved with shallow breaths, and his vision blurred with exhaustion. The voices drifted toward him, sharp and commanding, slicing through the fog of his misery.

"Bring a bench into the examination room," a man's voice barked. It was the same voice Shawn had heard before—the one who always gave orders, the one who seemed to enjoy this brutal theater.

The boots came first—two pairs, heavy and unhurried, thudding like coffin nails into the cracked cement floor. Shawn, who at this point had about as much structural integrity as a wet sock, didn't bother pretending he could stand. He was done with heroics. His body had gone on strike.

They picked him up like he was yesterday's trash, limp and leaking, and plopped him onto a splintery wooden bench that had clearly seen more back sweat and blood than a medieval rack. His ribs screamed in protest as his spine kissed the timber. It was the kind of kiss that came with teeth.

Then came the cuffs—cold, metallic, and mean. His arms were yanked behind him and shackled underneath the bench, leaving his chest and face tilted skyward like he was about to receive some divine revelation. Spoiler: he wasn't.

The legs were next. Rope this time. Old-school. Thick, scratchy, and knotted by men who clearly spent their weekends strangling goats. The fibers dug into his shins, his ankles, hell—even his pride. It felt like the bench was hugging him with hate.

He lay there, gift-wrapped for whatever horror was next, a human offering to bureaucratic sadism.

The tall man entered, his shadow stretching over Shawn like a predator looming over its prey. He was calm, almost conversational, as he loomed above him.

"Mr. American," the man said, all syrup and snake oil, his voice so polite it made Shawn's skin itch. "I'm a CIA trainee, just like you. Except my little corner of Langley happens to be right here—in sunny Kitalya prison." He smiled then, the kind of smile you'd expect to find carved into a jack-o'-lantern after a very bad day.

"I trained at Camp Peary," he went on, casual as a man discussing gardening. "The Farm. Williamsburg, Virginia. Lovely place. Learned a lot about breaking things that don't want to break. You see, we've got this sweet little American-sponsored gig going on—helps your government sleep at night while mine sharpens the knives."

He leaned in, and his breath smelled like rotten eggs. His voice dropped low, like he was sharing a bedtime story for psychopaths.

"Tonight's activity is something I picked up during my exchange semester with your folks. It's called waterboarding. Cute name, isn't it? Almost sounds like a sport. You familiar with it? No? Don't worry—you will be. Now... you can start singing, and I'll keep the water in the jug. Or we can get active."

He straightened up, whistling a cheerful tune as he reached for the bucket.

"Personally, I hope you choose poorly. I need the practice."

The man's words hit Shawn like a blow—trained in the

U.S., using American methods. This wasn't just some local brutality; it was exported expertise, turned against him. He didn't respond. He kept his gaze fixed on the ceiling, his mind racing despite his exhaustion.

The tall man gave a sharp nod. That was all it took. His two little helpers moved with the giddy precision of kids unwrapping a Christmas present they knew would scream.

They draped a rag over Shawn's face, not delicately, but with the affection of a man putting down an old dog. The cloth clung to his mouth and nose like it had unfinished business. Shawn jerked, twitching like a dying bug, but his limbs were tied tighter than a sinner at a church revival.

Then came the water.

Not a splash. Not a pour. A flood. The water slammed into the cloth with the grace of a falling cinderblock. Shawn's body panicked before his brain could catch up—his chest bucked, mouth gasped, and water shot down into his lungs like it had paid rent.

It was drowning for people with nowhere to drown. The mind screamed while the body begged for breath that didn't exist. Gulp. Choke. Sputter. Gulp again. Somewhere in the back of his mind, a voice—maybe his, maybe not—was laughing. Welcome to Uganda, buddy. How's that American training holding up?

The edges of the world curled inward. Vision went tunnel-black. Thoughts scattered like roaches in light. The last thing Shawn registered was the drip-drip-drip of the water hitting the floor, like a ticking clock counting down what was left of his sanity.

And then, mercifully, everything went away. But they

weren't done with him.

The man straddled Shawn's stomach, pressing down hard, forcing water and bile to spew from his mouth. Shawn coughed violently, his chest convulsing as he vomited. His tormentor leaned in, his voice cold and clinical.

"Are you ready to talk, or do we need to repeat this treatment?"

"Sir… I can't speak… I have no teeth."

"Do you want a pen and paper? I know you can write."

"Yes, sir," Shawn whispered, his body trembling uncontrollably.

They handed him a pad and a pen, and Shawn scrawled the words, his handwriting jagged and uneven.

I left the truck with the president's corpse on the road.

The tall man snatched the paper and read it, his eyes narrowing.

"Where were you taking the corpse?"

"To Jinja," Shawn wrote. "The same spot where the General is sending bodies of political prisoners and protesters to the crocodiles."

The man's face twisted into a snarl.

"Did you plan to feed our president's corpse to the crocodiles as well?"

Shawn shook his head weakly.

"My orders… were to drop the body there. Others had different orders. I don't know them. You know how it works… You only know what you need to."

"Your answers are not helpful."

Shawn braced himself. The cloth returned to his face. The water followed.

And darkness swallowed him whole.

CHAPTER 26:

The General

THE General sat alone in his private office, the air thick with the scent of old Waragi and power. His tongue, still rough from last night's drinking, ran absent-mindedly over his upper teeth. The texture was… unpleasant. Sticky, like something had died in his mouth overnight. It took him a moment to realize that, yet again, he had skipped brushing his teeth.

It had become a habit. He told himself it was because he was too busy running a country and, more recently, hunting for his father's missing corpse. But deep down, he knew the real reason. He simply did not care.

Yet, somewhere in the back of his mind, he could almost hear the familiar scolding voice of his dentist—a curvaceous woman called Rehema, whose body alone could start a coup. She had a way of chastising him that almost felt like a plea.

"Please, General, remember to brush and floss every day. You're the image of the country, and we need you in good oral health."

The General chuckled at the memory, a faint smile creeping across his face. He'd once entertained the idea of hiring her as his personal teeth cleaner, doubling—no, tripling—her government salary. But the thought of his wife Charity marching into his office, screaming about impropriety and embarrassment, made him reconsider. His wife had a knack for ruining his better ideas.

Charity was his first cousin, Bernard Musinga or Uncle Sayyid's daughter. In many African cultures, it would have been unthinkable to marry her—a taboo so ingrained that the idea itself was revolting. But not in their family. The generals were different. Once they had ascended to power, they had also granted themselves the privilege of bending tradition to their will. Customs, like rules, were for the powerless.

For them, marriage within the family was not only acceptable, but encouraged. It was a matter of security and preservation, they claimed—a way to keep wealth, influence, and secrets confined within their bloodline.

Charity had the entitlement of a royal cat—sleek, lazy, and convinced the General existed solely to refill her bowl. Being the daughter of the General's uncle didn't help matters. That made things familial, which in their world was just a polite word for *inescapable*. Divorce? Not an option. Murder? Tempting. But, alas, also frowned upon at family functions.

One humid afternoon, while Charity was in the shower humming some off-key gospel tune like she was washing her sins down the drain, the General's eye caught her phone buzzing. Pure reflex, he told himself, as he picked it up. He wasn't snooping. No. He was conducting reconnaissance.

And there it was. A contact in her phone labeled *Stupid Man*.

The General's eyebrow twitched. Curiosity flared. Who was the poor bastard? A boyfriend? A lover? A fool? He hit dial. His own phone rang back.

The line went cold. So did his spine.

Stupid Man... was him.

The General stared at the screen like it had slapped him. His own wife—well, his cousin-wife—had assigned him a name better suited to a dog who licked sockets. He didn't scream. No, he took it to Sayyid, her father, the old family lion with a cane and a temper like fermenting jet fuel. Sayyid roared. Charity shrugged.

She changed the name, sure. But not to *Darling*, or *Sweetheart*, or even something halfway romantic like *Bae*. No, her compromise was cold, calculated, and surgical: *Father of Daniel*. Like she was labeling a specimen jar.

And just like that, the General knew: Even dictators get demoted in their own damn house.

The General had always viewed the family's inmarriage tradition with disdain. He had played along at first, out of obligation more than conviction, marrying Charity as his father had suggested. She was beautiful, no doubt—graceful, with sharp features and an air of sophistication that matched her privileged upbringing. Yet, to the General, she felt more like a transaction than a partner. There was no fire, no challenge, no thrill. Loving Charity felt like eating food without salt—necessary, perhaps, but utterly uninspiring.

For the General, love was not just about family duty or preserving power—it was a battlefield, an intoxicating conquest. He desired women who radiated strength, who commanded attention, and who, above all, carried themselves with grace and beauty.

That was what had drawn him to Josephine.

Josephine was nothing like Charity. She was bold, outspoken, and undeniably beautiful. She could light up a room simply by walking into it, her confidence radiating like the sun. Her father, Lubwama, an opposition leader and a thorn in the General's side, had not approved of their union. But Josephine's fierce independence and beauty had captivated the General in ways no one else ever had. His usual conquests—musicians with honeyed voices and politicians with sharp tongues—were fleeting passions. But Josephine had drawn him in with her intellect, her power, and her rare ability to make him feel like a king without ever compromising her own dignity.

At first, his relationship with Josephine had been casual. He had approached her with the same intention he had for countless women before her: sex. It was supposed to be a fleeting affair, a dalliance to satisfy his cravings. But Josephine had been different. She had shown him a side of herself he hadn't expected—a softness, a humility. Despite her outspoken nature in parliament, where she had argued fiercely against his father's policies, she never raised her voice to him. She knelt when she served him food, a gesture he didn't think he cared about until he saw her do it. And then, as if fate had conspired to tie him to her, she became pregnant.

The General decided he would also marry Josephine, even if it meant going against his family's wishes. His love for her felt natural, untainted by the politics and power games that had dictated his marriage with Charity. He wanted Josephine not as a calculated move, but as a matter of pure desire.

Still, he was a man who wanted everything his way. He would not discard Charity; he would simply take them both. Polygamy was hardly unusual for a man of his status, and he had never been the sort of man to ask permission. He owned the country, and in his mind, that meant he owned everything—and everyone—in it.

But Josephine brought with her complications, ones that the General had not foreseen. Chief among them was her past—a boyfriend who had been in her life before him. The General had learned of the man called Godfrey through his network of informants, and the knowledge had festered like a wound.

The General could not abide the thought of another man having shared Josephine's affection. It disgusted him, enraged him. In his eyes, a woman's love should belong to him and him alone. There was no room for rivals, even those from the past.

To the General, men like Josephine's ex-boyfriend were a liability. To him, ex-boyfriends were like thieves holding a spare key to a woman's heart, ready to unlock it and slip inside whenever they pleased. They knew exactly which buttons to press, which strings to pull, the exact ways to ignite her passion. The thought of Josephine's ex resurfacing, of even having the audacity to think he still had a place in her heart, was intolerable.

The General made up his mind. Godfrey had to be eliminated—not just removed, but erased entirely. He summoned his most trusted henchman, a cold and efficient killer named Shafic.

"Find him," the General ordered, "and make sure he never resurfaces. Ever."

The plan was set in motion with precision. Shafic tracked the ex-boyfriend to a small neighborhood in Kampala. Godfrey, unaware of the shadow looming over him, went about his life as if he weren't marked for death.

One night, Shafic and his men abducted him from his home, driving him to a run-down lodge on Salaama Road. There, they carried out their orders without hesitation. A single gunshot ended the man's life, and they left his body in the lodge, arranging the scene to look like a sordid accident. The narrative was carefully crafted: he had died after a night of drug use and sex with prostitutes.

The lodge owners were instructed to play their part, as were the man's family. Shafic visited the family personally, delivering the General's warning in a tone that left no room for negotiation.

"If you speak out," he told them, "if you challenge the story, the General will kill all of you. And no one will dare mourn you."

The family fell silent. They grieved in private, afraid to even whisper the truth to one another. Meanwhile, the lodge owners spread the official story, and soon, the whispers of drug abuse and immoral behavior surrounded Godfrey's name. No one dared question the General's version of events.

The General had ensured his control over Josephine was absolute. With her past erased, she was now entirely his. Yet, as he sat in his office, reflecting on the events, he felt no satisfaction. The act had been necessary, he told himself. A king could not share his queen with anyone, past or present. He smiled in approval.

His smile faded when his private phone buzzed, shattering the quiet hum of the air conditioner.

Few people had that number. Fewer still dared to use it.

The name Taylor flashed on the screen, and the General felt his jaw tighten, a dull pulse throbbing at his temple. His free hand drummed on the desk—a slow, deliberate beat, like a man contemplating whether to answer or shoot the damn phone instead.

With a sigh, he picked up. No greeting. No pleasantries. Just a flat, irritated: "Mr. Taylor, I deleted the tweet."

A pause. Then came Taylor's voice, smooth as a snake slithering into a warm shoe.

"Mlevi, I am so embarrassed by you and whatever the hell you're trying to do in Uganda."

Ah, there it was. The classic Taylor approach. Passive aggression, coated in a thin layer of diplomatic horseshit.

The General leaned back, rolling his eyes. He knew exactly where this was going. Taylor had been his father's fixer in Washington for decades, working behind the scenes to make sure the old man's dictatorship smelled just sweet enough for the West to keep holding its nose. A professional meddler. A man who thought he could control everyone—including Mlevi.

Taylor's voice sharpened. "Your father, the president,

was my friend. How dare he die, and you keep it to yourself? I have spent decades crafting a program to make you his successor, to keep Washington and London on your side. And then you go and try to handle this alone?"

The General snorted. "I don't care about Washington at present, Uncle Taylor. Your Washington chose Nairobi and left us behind. Let them keep their alliances. I'll go to Moscow and Beijing."

Taylor let out a laugh. A genuine, delighted laugh. "Moscow and Beijing?" he echoed, like a teacher humoring the dumbest kid in class.

"Mlevi, they can't protect you. You think you'll last twenty-four hours without us? You're surrounded by Washington in every circle that matters—diplomatically, economically, militarily. We've had this conversation before, and I'm too tired to explain it again."

The General sighed dramatically. "But you told me my father was openly Marxist when he rose to power. Secretly reached out to the U.S. and London, sure, but only after he was secure. He kept the Marxist flag waving while cashing your checks. Why can't I do the same?"

Taylor groaned. "Mlevi, I swear to God, I'm not in the mood for a history lesson."

"Then why are you calling me?" The General's patience was running on fumes now.

Taylor's voice dropped to a business-like coolness.

"Because you're holding an American citizen in your jails. A man named Shawn. You need to release him. Now. Once you've done that, I will establish a communication line between you and Washington to determine what comes next."

The General leaned forward, gripping the edge of his desk. "Should I ask you something first, Mr. Taylor?"

Taylor sighed, exasperated. "Go ahead."

The General's voice turned into a low growl. "I want my father's corpse."

A silence stretched over the line, thick and heavy.

"Your CIA men have it," the General continued, his tone deadly. "I want it back before I announce his death. Before I make preparations for my coronation."

Taylor didn't speak right away. Then, when he did, his voice had softened, turned almost fatherly. Patronizing as hell.

"Mlevi, you have to be a dealmaker. Your father was a dealmaker. That's why he lasted as long as he did. For forty years, we stood by him, kept our promises. And if you prove you're as shrewd as he was, we'll do the same for you. You'll rule until your son is old enough to take over. That's what your father wanted."

The General said nothing.

Taylor continued, his voice smooth as poison. "You'll crush your political opponents. We'll ensure the media stays quiet. But you have to work with us."

Still, the General didn't respond. His grip on the phone tightened, his mind racing. His father had been a dealmaker. But Mlevi wasn't his father.

"When are you releasing Shawn?" Taylor's voice snapped him out of his thoughts. "I have other things to do."

The General exhaled slowly. "I'll do it today." His tone was neutral, empty.

"Good." A click, and the line went dead.

The General placed the phone down, slow and deliberate, like he was lowering a coffin into the earth. His temples throbbed. A dull ache curled behind his eyes, threatening to split his skull into neat little fragments.

He had asked Taylor in the politest way to speak to American intelligence, to at least attempt to bring his father's corpse home. Not much to ask, right? Just the return of a body, a bit of dignity, a final resting place that wasn't a cold slab under fluorescent lights. But Taylor, the ever-smooth, ever-useful Taylor, who had spent two decades lobbying Washington to keep his father in power, suddenly found himself incapable of doing this one thing. Two decades of whispering in senators' ears, ensuring his father's rule stretched on like an unwelcome party guest, but now? Now Taylor had nothing to say.

What was so difficult about advocating for the dead when he had spent his entire life advocating for the living tyrant? Had Taylor already forgotten what his father had meant to him? Or was that just how these things worked—allegiances turning to dust the moment the breath left a man's lungs?

The General had spent his life understanding one undeniable truth: strangers are wolves in borrowed skins. And now, somewhere in a sterile, fluorescent-lit room, his father's corpse lay cold in the hands of strangers. What were they doing to him? Talking to him? Running tests? Laughing? He clenched his fists, feeling the nails bite into his palm. His father had taught him one thing: never let your enemies touch your bones, even in death.

His mind slipped into memory, dark and jagged. He had seen it before—the desecration, the humiliation. Gadhafi. The great colonel, reduced to a whimpering heap on a dilapidated pick-up truck, dragged around by a mob and sodomized on the roadside. Oh, they had called it justice. But justice had a funny way of looking like revenge with a camera crew.

The General had watched, his stomach twisting as the rebels jeered, their fingers digging into the dead man's flesh, their laughter echoing across the airwaves. And then they shot him. Like a dog. Like a sick joke where the punchline was always death.

And now his father—his own flesh—was in the hands of these same people, these Americans. Oh, they acted like friends, grinning with their white teeth and clean suits, but they were hyenas. They never had friends. They had assets, and assets could always be liquidated. His father had once been an asset too, whispering secrets into their ears, feeding them information, thinking that loyalty meant something. It didn't. The Americans had turned on Gadhafi. The Americans had turned on Mobutu. And now? Now they had his father's corpse. And corpses—especially powerful ones—were useful in ways he didn't even want to imagine.

The headache surged again, a sharp, electric burst of pain. His skull felt like a pressure cooker about to blow. He pressed his forehead against the desk, cool wood against burning flesh. His reign had barely begun, and already, the ghosts were circling.

He exhaled, slow and measured. If the Americans thought they could play this game, they had forgotten one thing: he was his father's son. If they didn't return the corpse, he would remind them. He would turn east, where the bear and the dragon waited with open arms, their claws eager for Africa's gold, oil, copper—whatever they wanted. Russia and China didn't care about democracy. They didn't pretend to be friends. They understood power. And power, the General thought, was the only thing worth trusting.

CHAPTER 27:

Shawn

SHAWN'S eyelids fluttered like moths trying to escape a jar—twitchy, drunk, and determined to stay shut. His head throbbed with a slow, deliberate rhythm, as if some impolite demon had taken up residence in his skull and was practicing the drums. The pain was a symphony of suck: dull bass behind his eyes, stabbing violins in his temples, and the occasional crash cymbal whenever he tried to move.

He had no idea how long he'd been out. Could've been hours. Could've been days. Could've been a decade and nobody bothered to tell him. The world came back in pieces—first the sterile burn of antiseptic in his nose, then the sour taste of dried blood on his lips. He blinked, and the blurry outline of a hospital formed in his mind. Sort of.

But something was off. Hospitals usually didn't look like they'd been cleaned last during the Idi Amin government. The walls were more peel than paint, the air thick with despair and a faint hint of moldy cotton balls. An IV bag drooped like a suicide note pinned to the wall, dripping mystery juice into his arm. An oxygen tank hissed beside him like a tired snake, its tubes wrapped around his face like someone was trying to keep him alive just long enough to regret it.

This wasn't a hospital. This was a prison infirmary pretending to be one. A Frankenstein of medical care where hope came to die and paperwork came to breed.

Shawn moved a fraction, and his body screamed louder than a preacher in a tent revival. Every rib, every muscle, every inch of skin sang a hymn of agony. He bit back the noise, survival instincts slamming into place like a switchblade snapping open. Pain meant he was alive. Noise meant someone might come back to make that less true.

And then he saw the silhouette at the foot of the bed. A man in a white coat, his back turned, fiddling with something on a tray. Calm, methodical. The kind of calm that only came from practice—either patching people up or pulling them apart. Doctor? Sadist? Maybe both. Shawn's busted brain tried connecting dots with chewed-up crayons.

The man turned.

George.

Of course it was George. The square jaw. The eyes that always looked like they were playing three games of chess and one of Russian roulette. The quiet confidence of a man who'd survived things normal people couldn't pronounce. Last time he'd been Fred. Now he was George. In the spy game, names were like condoms—use once, throw away.

This was the same man who'd been in the tunnels with him under the Ugandan State House, guiding him through the stink and gunfire like Virgil leading Dante through Hell. They'd hauled a dead president through an armored toilet truck while bullets turned the air into Swiss cheese.

And now here he was, playing dress-up as a prison doctor while Shawn lay broken like a piñata at a biker bar. Shawn's brain screamed, *Why?* but all he could manage was a croak.

"Operation rescue the president. Black Tiger," George said, voice low and surgical.

Shawn's lips moved like dead fish.

"Black Tiger," he rasped. The code still held. Thank whatever dark gods watched over fools like him.

George leaned in, his tone conspiratorial.

"I'm here as your doctor from the outside. But this time, the patient is you. Just like we got the president's corpse out, I'm getting you out. That's the plan."

Shawn's throat felt like it had been sandpapered, but he pushed out a word.

"How?"

George's eyes flicked to the door. "I've greased a few palms. Promised some favors I can't afford. But there's a hitch."

Of course there was.

"What hitch?" Shawn asked, half-expecting George to say they had to fight their way through werewolves or something.

"My family," George said, jaw tight. "Twelve people. Six kids. My wife. Four parents—yes, we collect elders like baseball cards. If I help you and the General finds out, they're toast."

Shawn blinked. "Twelve?"

George nodded. "You know how it is. No one ever dies alone in Uganda—they take the whole family for company. I need assurance from Taylor. They get U.S. visas and they are whisked away by air. No deal otherwise."

Shawn's headache doubled as he processed that.

"What's Taylor saying?"

George pulled a tiny camera from his pocket.

"He wants proof of life. That's why I'm here. You give him the sales pitch, we get the green light."

"You want me to audition for my own rescue?"

"Smile for the camera, superstar."

The red light blinked. Shawn summoned what little dignity he had left.

"Yo, my people," he croaked, "please get me out of here. You said at all costs—well, the cost is George's family. Let them in. I need to get back to my son. Also, this place sucks."

George clicked off the camera.

"That'll do, Shakespeare."

He leaned in close again.

"Now we wait. If Taylor agrees, we leave this dump. If not..." He didn't finish. He didn't have to.

Shawn let his head fall back. The beeping monitor kept time like a countdown. Somewhere out there, a decision was being made. He just hoped it didn't come too late—or with too many body bags.

When George came back about thirty minutes later, he looked like a man trying way too hard to play doctor. A cracked old stethoscope hung around his neck like a worn-out souvenir from a hospital that should've been shut down years ago. It clinked as he walked, and Shawn, half-delirious, found himself wondering how many people that thing had actually helped. Probably none.

Shawn was still lying flat on the cot, his muscles aching, his ribs feeling like someone had gone at them with a hammer. His lips were dry and cracked, and every breath burned just a little. But he was alive. Barely.

"Alright," George said casually, like they were in a real clinic and not a grimy prison cell pretending to be an infirmary. "Let's check your vitals."

He pressed two fingers to Shawn's wrist, shining a flashlight—one that looked like it came from the 1990s—into his eyes.

"Still alive," George muttered. "Unfortunately for you."

Shawn didn't answer. His eyes stayed on the peeling walls, his ears tuned to every little sound. Same buzzing light. Same faint moans from other cells. Same hopeless stink in the air.

Then George leaned in and dropped his voice to a whisper.

"Langley gave the green light," he said. "My family gets out tonight. Airlift. They're going to the U.S."

Shawn blinked, trying to process it.

"It's happening, Shawn. But now it's your turn. We get you out next."

"How?"

"You're going to play dead."

"Come again?"

"You heard me," George said, straightening up. "You're going to fake your death. At 8 p.m., when the guy who collects the dead comes in, I'll pronounce you gone. No heartbeat, no breath, nothing. He'll put you in a body bag and take you out with the others."

Shawn raised an eyebrow.

"Others?"

"Yeah," George said with a shrug. "They're moving six bodies tonight. You'll be one of them."

Shawn's stomach turned.

"And the rest of the bodies—how long have they been…?"

George didn't sugarcoat it.

"A few days. Some maybe a week. It won't be pretty. The smell alone might knock you out. But if you want to get out of here, that's your ride."

Shawn took a slow breath, steadying himself.

"Then what?"

"You'll be taken to the morgue at Gombe Hospital. About two miles from here. Later, I'll show up pretending to be your cousin. I'll bribe the staff, get them to release the body to me, and then we disappear. Simple."

Shawn closed his eyes for a moment, thinking it through.

"And until you show up, I have to stay still. No movement. No breathing."

"Exactly," George said. "You move even a little, you twitch, you make a sound—they'll check you again. And if they realize you're faking it? They'll make sure you're dead for real."

Shawn felt his heart thudding in his chest. He'd done fake-death training before, but not like this. Not in a pile of rotting bodies, not in a prison with real bullets and no second chances.

"I'll manage," he said.

"Good. But prepare yourself. The bodies won't just lie next to you. They'll probably be on top of you. Heavy. Cold. Maybe still leaking. You need to breathe slow. Barely breathe at all, if you can."

Shawn's face stayed calm, but his hands curled slightly under the blanket.

"Got it."

"8 p.m.," George repeated, adjusting the stethoscope around his neck. "Be ready. Don't die before then."

He turned and walked out, his footsteps fading down the hallway.

The light overhead buzzed again. The smell of bleach and blood mixed in the air like a warning.

Shawn stared up at the ceiling, his mind racing. He had to be a corpse. Still. Silent. Not just pretending—but really *being* dead.

For hours.

Under real bodies.

He didn't know if he could do it.

But he had to try.

Because this was the only way out.

And if he failed, they wouldn't bother checking a second time. They'd just zip up the bag… and bury him for real.

Shawn heard George before he saw him.

That voice—booming, full of fake authority and too much theater—ricocheted down the hallway like a drunk preacher at a funeral. Then came the knock. Hard. Metal on metal. It rattled through Shawn's bones, even though he was doing a damn good job of being a corpse. His body stayed still, colder than it should've been, limbs locked like rigor mortis had already moved in.

He couldn't blink. Couldn't twitch. Couldn't breathe too deep. One slip and he wasn't faking a corpse—he *was* one.

The door groaned open like it hated its own existence, and there was George, white coat glowing like a misplaced halo in the sickly flicker of the hallway light. He walked in like he owned the joint, but Shawn could smell the nerves under that aftershave. There was something rehearsed in the way he moved. A man not used to lies, but good at telling them when he had to.

George dropped to his knees beside the mattress—Shawn's own little island of filth and blood-stained cotton. Two fingers to the neck. The whisper of rubber tubing. Cold metal to the chest. Show time.

There might've been a smirk twitching at George's mouth. Or maybe it was just Shawn's brain trying to keep itself entertained.

Then the performance kicked into full gear.

"We've lost the American," George barked, loud enough to wake the dead, which in this place was more of a metaphor than it should've been. "He's dead."

The hallway stiffened. Boots shuffled. A guard coughed—guilty, confused, stupid.

"Dead?" one said. "When… when did that happen?"

Shawn almost rolled his eyes. If he were really dead, the idiot would've asked the same thing.

George turned slowly, the glare on his face hotter than the Ugandan sun.

"When was the last time *you* checked on him?"

"Uh… an hour ago?"

"An hour?" George exploded. "You left a high-value American operative—an asset from the *General* himself—untouched for a whole hour? Jesus Christ on a sugar cane field. This is on you. You want to explain that to the General? Be my guest."

The guards looked like toddlers who'd just broken a window. Ashen faces. Sweaty brows. One scratched his neck like lice had just moved in.

"What should we do?" one mumbled.

"Nothing," George said. "Dead is dead. Gunney boy will come for the body. I'll report it."

Then he was gone, sweeping out like a man who'd just buried a king. The door slammed. The silence pressed in again. Until the gunney boy arrived. He couldn't have been older than seventeen, face hard like he'd seen too much, hands moving with that numb, practiced detachment of someone who knew what corpses felt like. He didn't even flinch when he rolled Shawn's body onto the stretcher.

The canvas scraped Shawn's cheek—rough, smelling like bleach and old blood. Then the stacking began.

One.

The weight settled onto his legs. Cold.

Two.

Heavier. Smelled worse. Rancid meat in human shape.

Three.

The final one landed with a wet sound that made Shawn's stomach lurch. His chest compressed under the weight. Something—fluids, God knows what—seeped through his shirt and touched skin. His nerves screamed, every instinct yelling, *Move! Gasp! Fight!*

But he stayed still. He had to.

The stretcher jerked into motion, rattling down the hallway like a shopping cart full of butchered pigs. Every bump sent shocks through his ribs. The gunney boy said nothing. Neither did the guards. They just watched the dead go out the door.

The truck ride was worse.

Darkness. Stench. The clatter of the road. Potholes felt like earthquakes. The bodies shifted with each turn, pressing down harder, as if they wanted to drag Shawn into death for real. One body groaned. Or maybe that was in his head.

He didn't know what was real anymore.

At Gombe Hospital, the mortuary doors opened like the jaws of hell. The bodies were dumped—no reverence, no care. Just flesh thudding against tile. When Shawn hit the floor, the shock vibrated up his spine. The cold tiles bit through his shirt. The stink was thicker here—death without windows, without mercy.

Around him: bodies. Piled like laundry. Limbs bent wrong. Eyes open.

Nobody looked twice at Shawn.

The doors clanged shut. Dark again. Just him and the dead.

He counted heartbeats. Shallow breaths. Tried not to think. But his mind didn't care. It painted pictures: bloated fingers twitching. Cold lips whispering secrets. Hollow eyes watching him, jealous.

Hours passed. Days, maybe. He couldn't tell.

Then the doors creaked again.

One more body dumped. The thud echoed. Shawn didn't flinch.

And finally—finally—midnight came. The door opened and in walked George, face set like stone, sorrow thick in his voice. He murmured words in Luganda, the local tongue, soft and heavy. Shawn didn't know what he was saying. Probably something like, *"This was my cousin. God bless his brave soul."*

The guards nodded, hands on his back, consoling him. He was good. Maybe too good.

Then George started checking the bodies.

When he touched Shawn, his fingers froze for a heartbeat too long. It was the signal.

"This one," George said, choked with fake grief.

The guards helped him lift the "body." Back onto the stretcher. Into the car. One of them whispered a prayer—Shawn caught *"may his soul rest"* in English. It almost made him laugh.

They drove off into the dark. Ten minutes later, after the last checkpoint, George checked the mirror.

"Alright," he muttered. "Sit up."

Shawn uncoiled like a man clawing his way out of a grave. He sucked in air, sweet and damp and heavy with exhaust. Every muscle screamed. He flopped into the passenger seat, breathing hard.

"Where to now?" he croaked.

"Mityana," George said, eyes on the road. "We'll hide out there. Regroup."

Then he glanced over, gave Shawn a crooked grin that didn't quite reach his eyes.

"Congratulations," he said. "You're officially dead."

Shawn stared out the window. And for the first time

in his life, being dead felt like the safest thing he could be. On the road, the car's dashboard lit up with a call. The name flashed: Taylor.

George, eyes on the road but smirking like he already knew, said, "Looks like the case manager wants to talk to you. Or maybe just confirm I haven't driven you into a swamp."

"Go ahead and answer," Shawn muttered, spitting something—blood or tooth-dust—into a napkin.

Taylor's voice cracked through the speakers like a cheerleader with a bullhorn.

"Well, well, well—look who got himself whipped."

Shawn wiped his mouth, wincing. "I barely got my teeth in my damn mouth, Taylor."

Taylor cackled. "Yeah, and whose fault is that? You blew up a clean op 'cause you couldn't keep it in your pants. What's she got, magic pussy? You better let me meet this firecracker. Hell, she must be carved by angels."

Shawn stared out the window, biting back what he really wanted to say—that Joanne had a wife, Helen, and the kind of eyes that made a man rethink everything. But Taylor wasn't the type to understand that.

"You bet," he muttered, rubbing his busted lip. He could feel George listening, pretending not to, but soaking it up like a sponge.

Then Taylor's voice dropped to that bureaucratic danger tone. "Tell me you didn't use the agency card for her shit. Please, for the love of bourbon and budget reviews."

Shawn smirked.

"Whores in Uganda don't take credit cards, Taylor. What—you think I swipe it through their assholes?"

George made a small choking sound. Caught red-handed listening, but trying to keep his eyes straight ahead.

Taylor actually laughed. "You win, boy. Still, you better account for every cent. Helps us clean up your mess. Keeps the bureaucrats fed and sleepy."

Shawn leaned back, pain blooming in his cheek like a fresh bruise. "Where's George dragging me now?"

"To a clinic in Mityana. They'll patch you up," Taylor said. Then, with a grin in his voice, "And, George—get him a damn dentist. I don't wanna hear him whistling through his gums like a goddamn scarecrow."

George gave the textbook Ugandan, "Yes, sir," which translated to: *I'm gonna do it, but also go to hell.*

Then came the shift. Taylor's voice dropped like a trapdoor.

"Shawn… listen. The agency wants you to meet the General before you fly out. No threats. No guns. Just a talk. You're the one handing over his daddy's corpse."

Shawn sat up straighter. "Wait—you still got the corpse?"

Taylor didn't miss a beat. "Yep. Kept it on ice. Leverage. You know how we play."

"And Joanne? Helen? The kid?" Shawn asked.

Taylor didn't hesitate. "They're not my damn responsibility. And don't blow the mission again trying to play knight in shining armor for some whores with sad eyes."

The line clicked dead.

The car filled with silence. The kind that pressed down on your chest like a cinderblock. George didn't speak. Shawn didn't ask.

They just kept driving through the red dirt and dying light, toward a town with a doctor, a dentist.

CHAPTER 28:

The General

IT wasn't the cold—though there was plenty of that in his office, where the windows stayed shut and the air conditioner wheezed like a dying animal. It wasn't even the silence, thick and syrupy, clinging to the walls like mildew. No, it was the stench of fear that gave it away.

And Douglas reeked of it.

The man shuffled in like a student caught cheating, all elbows and apologies, his sweat soaking through the armpits of a shirt one size too big. The General didn't look up from the reports spread across his desk. Numbers. Operations. Deniable assets. But he *felt* Douglas—the way a dog senses a storm brewing far off, behind the hills.

"Say what you came to say," the General murmured, "or get the hell out."

Douglas opened his mouth. Closed it. Opened it again. The General finally glanced up. The old man's lips trembled like fish meat.

"S-sir… we've lost the American."

Silence.

The words hit the room like a thrown corpse. Wet and final.

The General didn't move. Not at first. He simply stared at Douglas as though weighing how long it might take to strangle him with the telephone cord.

"What do you mean, 'lost'?"

"He… he died."

That did it. The General rose from his chair slowly, the old leather groaning beneath him. He was a tall man, broad-shouldered, but alcohol had pressed into him like a thumbprint—left him heavier, slower, but not softer. Never softer. His presence filled the room like gas before a spark.

"Who killed him?" he asked.

"I—I don't know. I just got the report—"

"He was *leverage*," the General snapped. "Leverage doesn't die, Douglas. It *waits.* It *breathes.* You keep it alive even if you have to stitch its organs back in with barbed wire. Jesus Christ. Who signed off on this?"

"Sir, I think—"

"Katamba," the General growled. "Where is that fat bastard? Butambala was *his* idea. He said it was secure. He swore to me."

"There's… more," Douglas added.

The General froze again. A silence grew so thick, even the flies on the windowsill seemed to hold their breath.

"The body. It's… missing."

Now the General laughed. A low, humorless chuckle,

like the scrape of a shovel in grave dirt.

"Say that again."

"The body disappeared after he was declared dead. It was removed from the prison before we could verify it. The guards said a doctor came with your signature—"

"My signature?" The General's voice dropped to a dangerous whisper. "You're telling me *someone forged my name*, walked into my prison, and waltzed out with the corpse of the most important bargaining chip we had?"

"Yes, sir. He showed credentials. The guards believed him until—until it was too late."

The General walked to the window. Outside, the compound stretched like a scar—towers, fences, soldiers in black boots too clean for the work they were supposed to be doing. He stared out as if expecting the impostor to walk through the gate, dragging the American by the hair.

"Do you know what the Americans will do," he said quietly, "if they find out we've lost one of their men?"

Douglas didn't answer.

"They'll keep my father's corpse," the General said. "They'll leave it to rot in that hole they are keeping it. No burial, no peace. Just dust. Do you understand now?"

"Yes, sir."

"I want that body found," the General said. "I don't care if it's burned, buried, floating in Lake Victoria. I want it found." He turned, his eyes gleaming like wet coal. "And the impostor?"

"Vanished," Douglas murmured. "Like a ghost."

The General smiled then. A terrible, mirthless thing.

"Ghosts leave footprints. And if he left one, I'll find it."

He sat back down. Cracked his knuckles. Stared hard at the red circle drawn over Butambala on the wall map. A mocking little ring of ink.

"Tell the men: No rest. No food. No excuses. Find the body. Find the man who took it. Bring him to me alive. Or dead. I don't give a damn which. Just make sure he *talks* first."

"Yes, General."

Douglas turned to leave, but the General wasn't finished.

"And Douglas?"

The old man turned.

"If you see Katamba," the General said, his voice low and slow, "remind him I don't like being made a fool. Remind him I *remember*."

"Yes, sir."

The door shut.

The General sat alone, the rage in him coiled and writhing like a snake under his skin. The office stank of sweat and fear and something darker—something he'd carried with him since the war.

He looked at the map again. Whispered to no one: "You think you're clever, American? You think you've tricked me? You've only bought yourself time."

His fingers tapped the desk again. One. Two. Three.

"Because I'll find you. I always do."

CHAPTER 29:

The General

THE General kept his ghostwriter strung tighter than a piano wire in a burning church. He fed him tweet ideas the way a madman feeds stray cats—constantly, compulsively, without a shred of mercy. Every time the poor bastard sent back a draft, the General demanded another, like some jittery demon with a Wi-Fi addiction.

It was his therapy, his methadone, his sacrament. The more anxious he got, the faster the ideas came, until he'd stockpiled a digital armageddon—rage-filled, headline-snatching hellfire just waiting to drop. And when the voices in his head quieted down for a minute, that's when he started posting. One apocalyptic tweet at a time.

For an hour, he tweeted relentlessly, pausing only to refill his glass. The subjects of his tweets ranged from threats to grandiose declarations, each one tailored to whip his online base into a frenzy. After the hour passed, he set his phone down and leaned back, a smug smile spreading across his face. Now it was time for his favorite part—checking the impact.

He opened the app and scrolled to his notifications, satisfaction blooming as he saw the relentless activity. His trolls, especially his most loyal supporter, Bafudde, had been hard at work. Each tweet had been retweeted multiple times, the validation replies piling up like soldiers answering a rallying call.

The General scrolled through the comments, nodding approvingly at Bafudde's zeal. *Master stroke, sir*, one comment read. *Only you have the courage to speak the truth*, said another. The trolls were doing their job well, amplifying his voice and ensuring his message dominated the online space.

Two tweets, in particular, stood out, each having gone viral with over a million impressions in just an hour. The first read: *I'm going to kill all the white mercenary soldiers in the Democratic Republic of Congo. If anyone comes under my area of mineral mining and operations, they are dead.*

The second was even more audacious: *As soon as I get authorization from my superiors in the United States, I'm going to lead an army to overthrow the government in Khartoum in one week.*

The General's chest swelled with pride. These were the kind of tweets that reinforced his image as a fearless, no-nonsense leader. The numbers spoke for themselves. But as he read them again, a sliver of doubt crept into his mind. The first tweet, in particular, could cause problems. His British enablers had always been sensitive to any rhetoric that targeted their interests, and the mention of "white mercenaries" might not sit well with them.

He paused—just long enough to let the Waragi burn a hole down his throat—then muttered for the ghostwriter to draft a follow-up tweet. Something to mop up the digital blood. Damage control, his favorite dirty little hobby. Over the years, he'd become a maestro of walking back disaster, a kind of PR arsonist who set fires just to show off how well he could piss on them later. Diplomacy? Provocation? Please. He didn't walk that line—he danced on it in steel-toed boots.

I respect the United Kingdom for many reasons. You'll never hear me saying anything bad about that country. I got the best officers training at Sandhurst 25 years ago. I will always seek closer relations with the UK.

He hit send and set the phone down, his mind already moving on to the next crisis. The apology was vague enough to soothe British nerves without retracting his earlier statement entirely. It was a balancing act, one he performed daily as he navigated the treacherous waters of international politics and his own volatile personality.

As he poured himself another drink, the General felt a familiar sense of triumph. The tweets had done their job, stirring the pot and keeping his name at the center of the conversation. For now, that was enough.

Then the door creaked open, and Douglas stepped in, his face pale and hands trembling. "General," he stammered, "Uncle Bernard Musinga… He… he's at the door. He's insisting on coming in."

The General, half-drunk but still alert, frowned deeply. "Uncle Bernard?" he asked, his voice slurring slightly. "Sayyid?" The name alone summoned the ghost of their rebel days—when Sayyid was lean, mean, and pretending to be Muslim to schmooze Muammar Gadhafi. Now? Now he was more like a haunted parade float pumped full of Big Pharma and regret.

Before the General could argue, the door swung open wider—as if mocking him—and in rolled a man pushing a wheelchair with what looked like the swelling version of the Bernard he once knew.

Sayyid didn't walk anymore. He oozed into the room.

He was massive, but not in any way that inspired awe—just in the way that made chairs creak and elevator doors hesitate. Bloated by meds, his face was a pale moon of puff, his belly a continent, his arms swollen logs. He was a one-man cautionary tale about medical science and its lack of aesthetic priorities.

His skin had the sheen of a wax fruit left too long in the sun. His breath rattled like something was stuck in the plumbing. There was no neck. Just head, shoulders, and a roll of flesh with a heartbeat.

The General, who once kicked open bunkers and executed traitors before lunch, actually flinched.

"Uncle Sayyid," he said, wobbling up from his chair like a drunk trying to salute. "What an honor."

Sayyid's voice, though it sounded like it had to claw its way out of his throat, still held that signature bite.

"Don't flatter me. You're bad at it. I'm dying, and there's business to finish. Can we ask Tweedledee and Tweedledum here to step out?"

He motioned toward Douglas and the poor aide who looked like he was still processing what he'd just rolled in.

The General hesitated, always the tactician, always

playing chess even when the pieces were melting.

"Douglas is family, Uncle. My cousin—Mother's side."

Lies, of course. Douglas was kept around to parrot praise like a budget parrot.

But Bernard wasn't buying the sales pitch.

"No," he said. "This is old war business. Family can wait outside."

Douglas slithered out, and the door clicked shut behind him like the final note in a hymn.

Sayyid wheezed, then tapped his phone like a man defusing a bomb. Bluetooth connected. The massive flatscreen on the wall flickered alive—and there, in full suit-and-tie misery, was Taylor: the middleman between Washington's clean hands and Africa's dirty deals.

"This is a three-man meeting," Sayyid muttered. "Two in Kampala, and one dying of stress in D.C."

Taylor didn't argue. His voice crackled through the speakers like it had been through too many meetings already.

"Son," Taylor said, exasperated, "why the hell are you tweeting like a twelve-year-old on Red Bull? Before we talk shop, let's start with your brain-dead posts about Khartoum and Congo."

The General's eyes narrowed like a cat who just spotted a rival on his lawn.

"Khartoum is mine," he growled. "You want to hand it to Nairobi? I conquered Kigali, Bujumbura, Kinshasa—twice. I sent the rebels of Juba scurrying back into their huts, propped up their puppet government with one hand, and kicked Al-Shabaab's teeth out with the other. I built Somalia from scratch! Now you want me to sit still while they give my prize to some Kenyan desk jockey with a smile like a crocodile?"

Taylor rubbed his temples, looking like a man trying not to murder a child in church. The General kept going, voice rising, hands trembling around his glass of cheap gin like it was a hand grenade.

"Uncle Taylor, tell the Americans in Langley that if they screw me, I'm done. I've given them the best damn military in East Africa. You made me a monster—don't act surprised when I bite."

Sayyid said nothing, but his hand twitched on the wheelchair's armrest like it wanted to slap the General back to childhood.

The silence that followed was thick enough to suffocate a goat. Shadows lengthened around them as the chandelier swayed, a pendulum ticking down the last beats of someone's career—or maybe their life.

Sayyid broke the silence first. His voice was raspy, but it cut through the thick tension in the room like a knife. "Before you two head into Khartoum with your plans," he said, "I want the truth. If my brother is dead… then where's the corpse?"

The General tightened his grip around his Waragi glass. His knuckles turned white.

"Uncle Taylor knows where the corpse is," he said, nodding toward the video screen.

Taylor raised an eyebrow. "Let's start with how he died. What happened?"

"You want to know how the old man died?" the General said. "Fine. Sit tight." He stared at Taylor on the screen like a man looking through glass. "He died with three prostitutes in his bed," he said, the words falling out like spare change. "Three. No foreign plot. No political assassination. No tiny syringe in the neck or poisoned cognac. Just… ego. Plain, good old-fashioned, Third World presidential ego."

He took a slow sip of his Waragi, the local moonshine that smelled like regret and made your liver write its will.

"He swallowed three Viagra pills—100 milligrams each. You don't have to be a pharmacist to know that's overkill. He thought: one pill, one girl. Like he was ordering food at a buffet and didn't want to leave anything behind."

He gave a humorless chuckle. The kind that comes from watching your father die with his pants down and your nation hanging by a thread.

"When the girls got to work," the General said, "his heart gave out. He lasted four minutes, maybe. Dropped dead mid-thrust like a puppet with its strings cut. Eyes open. Boner up. Like he saw death coming and thought she was the fourth girl."

There was a beat of silence.

"The girls screamed, of course. One ran out naked. The other two rifled through his pockets and took his presidential watch. I don't blame them."

Sayyid groaned again, as if to say, *Jesus Christ.*

"That's how we lost our 81-year-old president," the General said. "Not in battle. Not in some noble stand against tyranny. Just a man who wanted to prove he still had it and didn't."

"I gave up on women—and that damned blue pill—when I hit fifty," Sayyid said, rocking back in his wheelchair like a king on his last throne. "Fifty! And I'm still fifteen years younger than your father."

Taylor spat out his drink. "You? Gave up? On *sex*?"

"Eh," Sayyid waved him off. "Every time I took that pill, it was like someone lit a charcoal stove inside my skull. First my head would boil, then my heart would hammer like a condemned man's last drumbeat. I'd think, 'This is it—goodbye world.' I'd manage to get it up—briefly. But by the time I turned the woman around to, you know, *begin proceedings*—zap! Vanished," he paused for dramatic effect—"and just like that, I had to swallow another pill and drag myself back through the same carnival of misery."

The General was clutching his ribs now, tears running down his face. "You mean to say—" he gasped between bursts of laughter—"you survived the woman, but nearly died from the *pill*?"

"That's right," Sayyid said with a shrug. "One day, I figured I'd rather die peacefully than with my trousers halfway down. So I quit sex. Just like that."

The General and Taylor were in stitches—real stomach-clutching, nose-snorting laughter. Sayyid had that gift: he could turn the grim autopsy of his sex life into stand-up comedy, even while dying slowly and visibly from a terminal case of corruption and cholesterol.

The truth? No pill was going to save Sayyid. His belly was killing him. That oversized gut had become the final vault of the family's plundered wealth—the place where the country's stolen rice, oil, and IMF loans went to die. Every starving South Sudanese child, every Ugandan peasant gnawing on cassava peels—they all lived rent-free in Sayyid's stomach.

Of course, the General couldn't say any of that out loud. Instead, he went for the low blow.

"Uncle," he said, "now that you know the pill is the family's leading cause of death, maybe you should advise your daughter Charity to stop demanding I swallow two every night. She wakes me up like an army drill—one hand with the pills, the other with a bottle of water. Says she wants *more action*."

The moment the words stumbled out of his mouth, the General knew he'd gone too far. You don't joke about banging a man's daughter—especially when the man's your uncle *and* your father-in-law.

Taylor's frozen Zoom screen showed him mid-flinch, mouth open like he'd just watched someone lick a car battery.

But the General could see through it. Taylor might look shocked, but deep down, he was loving every cursed second of this circus. This kind of chaos—the incestuous power plays, the bedtime pills, the obesity-induced senility—this was exactly the brand of madness Washington wanted running the African continent. Predictable. Containable. Hilariously dysfunctional.

Fortunately, Uncle Sayyid had started to snore—possibly from exhaustion, possibly from death inching closer with every laugh or maybe from sheer disinterest in his son-in-law's bedroom struggles. Either way, he missed the punchline.

Taylor, ever the diplomat, tried to steer the madness back to the original agenda. "General," he asked, voice dry as desert sand, "who exactly confirmed your father's death?"

"His doctor," he said.

The General leaned over to his desk phone and dialed a number. He turned back toward the screen.

"Let's let the man with the stethoscope explain how a nation lost its father to a pill meant for a hard-on."

The call connected.

"Dr. Peter Jacob Kafeero," the General said, "I've got two men here: my uncle Sayyid, and a friend from America. Please tell them how the president died."

A tired voice came through, clear as confession.

"Gentlemen," Dr. Kafeero said, "Viagra was created to help men feel young again. But in our case, it just helped our president die with a little enthusiasm."

He cleared his throat.

"A standard dose is 50 milligrams. The president took 300. That's not passion—that's a chemical suicide pact. See, Viagra affects blood vessels. Not just down there—everywhere. Drops your pressure. Makes your heart beat like it's running a marathon it didn't train for."

He paused, clinical but not cold.

"Now imagine that heart. Eighty-one years old. Probably stiff as an old boot and full of plaque. You throw in three sex workers, three pills, and the stress of trying to perform like a man half his age... You've got a cardiac event waiting to happen."

He took a breath, like he'd said this all before.

"What happened is called a myocardial infarction. Heart attack. The heart tightened up, screamed for oxygen, and then gave up. He probably gasped, clutched his chest—maybe even smiled for a second. Then collapsed. Dead before the girls even realized he'd stopped moving."

Silence again. Heavy. Final.

The General rubbed his temples.

"Tell that to the historians," he muttered. "Tell them the revolution ended because the man at the top thought he could fuck three girls without consequences."

Taylor blinked, holding back a reaction. His voice was smooth but hollow.

"My condolences," he said. "He was a friend to the United States. We mourn his loss."

The General smirked.

"Friend? You mean puppet. But I'm fine being a puppet... as long as I get to rule forever—just like him."

Taylor didn't answer right away. Sayyid was coughing now, his whole body shaking in the wheelchair. When he finally got his breath back, his voice was sharp.

"So... what happened to the girls?"

The General didn't flinch.

"We killed them," he said flatly. "That was the rule. Any girl who saw him like that—struggling to get it up—they couldn't be allowed to leave. They were warned. Fail, and you don't make it out alive."

Sayyid nodded slowly, his face grim.

"I've known about that rule for twenty years. But he had told me himself he hadn't touched a woman in decades. Said he was done with that."

"That was the plan," the General said. "I don't know why he changed his mind. Maybe he wanted to prove something. I'm just the son. I wasn't told."

Taylor leaned in closer on the screen, his face carved into something colder now—less diplomat, more detective.

"And what else did the doctor find?" he asked, voice low but sharp, like he was afraid of the answer and curious anyway.

Dr. Kafeero didn't even blink.

"Lipstick," he said flatly. "On his frail, eighty-year-old penis. The girls were… committed. I'll give them that. They gave it the old college try."

For a second, no one said anything. Even Bernard seemed to hold his breath.

The General gave a soft, sardonic chuckle and leaned toward the tablet.

"I think we can let the good doctor return to the sick and dying," he said. "Thank you, Dr. Kafeero. That'll be all."

With a flick, the screen went black, like a light going out in a morgue.

Taylor stayed quiet a moment, then glanced back at the General.

"So," he said slowly, "what do you plan to do with the doctor's… knowledge?"

The General didn't answer right away. He stared at the blank screen like it was still watching. Then he smiled, but it was the wrong kind of smile—the kind you'd see on a man holding a knife behind his back.

"He's going to die," the General said simply. "You know how we do things here. Anyone who knows more than they're supposed to… dies."

Taylor didn't blink.

"He's useful, for now," the General added. "Under house arrest. But once I'm officially sworn in, I'll give the order. Quiet. Clean. A car crash, maybe. Or food poisoning. We've got options."

He swirled the Waragi in his glass and watched it like it could tell the future.

"General Mlevi," Taylor said, "listen close, son. This is what Washington wants if you ever want to sit on Daddy's bloodstained throne without getting electrocuted."

The General tilted his head, eyes narrowing like a man watching a child attempt algebra with crayons.

"First—delete those idiotic tweets. All of them. Every last emoji-laced tantrum. You sound like a hormonal brat with a god complex and a cracked iPhone. They want a president, not a meme with legs."

The General remained still, eyes locked on the screen like it owed him money. He wanted Taylor to feel it. To know, without a shadow of doubt, that on the other end of that glowing screen sat a man who was listening. Not just hearing. *Listening.*

"Second—release the American. Yes, him. Shawn. The poor bastard's the only one trusted to bring back your father's corpse. Trust him. You don't have to like it. Just open the cell, shake his hand, and pretend you're not planning to kill him later."

A beat passed. Then he smiled. Not warm. Not kind. The kind of smile that warned of locked doors and shallow graves.

"Once the old man's carcass is home, you can weep on national TV, lower the flag, wear something black, and let the world mourn him like he was Saint Bloody Mandela. Meanwhile, you prepare. Quietly. Carefully. Because once the crying stops, all eyes will be on you."

He sat back, voice flat as iron.

"History's not written by the best men, son. Just the ones who survive the funerals."

There was a pause, the kind that stretches just long enough to let evil catch its breath.

Then Taylor's voice crackled through the screen line like the Devil lighting a cigarette.

"Two last pieces of advice, General," he said. "Now that we've confirmed you as the next president—*our* president—you need to start doing what your father did best."

The General grunted. Somewhere between a laugh and a snarl.

"Which is?"

"Lie," Taylor said, flatly. "Lie like it's foreplay. Lie like your life depends on it—because it does. You need to start downplaying everything. On the media. On your X posts. Confuse the masses. Make them argue among themselves while you're rearranging the country like furniture in a murder scene."

He chuckled. "Become a serial liar. Your father was one. A damn Picasso with falsehoods. Lying was his superpower—well, right after murder."

The General didn't argue.

"Remember how he used to tell them he'd only stay for two terms? Ten years max, and then he'd retire to his cows. Real humble shepherd-of-the-nation crap. Forty years later he was still up there, ruling like a goddamn vampire pope, sucking the country dry and mumbling about livestock."

Taylor went on,"You should try the same line. Tell them you have no intention of being president. That once you're done playing commander-in-chief, you'll go back and tend to your cows."

The General grunted again, this time more amused.

Taylor's voice lowered to a whisper, the kind that gets carved into stone tablets.

"And by the time they realize *they* are the cows you've been referring to, it'll be too late."

The line went quiet, save for the hum of tyranny in the background.

The General nodded slowly to no one, like a man who'd just accepted a bloody inheritance.

"Understood."

"Good," Taylor said. "Goodbye, Mr. President."

He hung up.

CHAPTER 30:

Shawn

SHAWN came to like a man clawing his way out of a grave. Not all at once, but piece by painful piece. First came the weight—the dull, oppressive heaviness in his limbs, like he'd been nailed to the mattress. Then the smells: antiseptic, sweat, and something faintly metallic, like blood or rusted iron. His mouth tasted like cotton soaked in bleach.

He opened his eyes. The world was a smear of low orange light, dancing shadows on pitted walls. A kerosene lamp guttered in the corner. No monitors. No nurses. No soul-sucking hum of machinery. Definitely not a hospital. This place breathed slower, older. Like it remembered war.

A soft voice floated in.

"You're awake."

He turned his head—a bolt of pain shot through his temple like a sniper round—and saw a woman. She wore a gomesi, all flowing fabric and quiet authority, like a queen pretending to be a nurse. Her dark eyes didn't blink much.

"You can call me Nurse Sophia."

"Where the fuck am I?" Shawn's voice came out dry, like someone had poured sand down his throat.

"Uganda. Kawempe."

He blinked, letting that sink in. Kawempe. He knew the place: a rabbit warren of crumbling concrete and suspicion. A good place to vanish. A terrible place to heal. He tried to sit up, only to find his body felt like it'd been stitched together with barbed wire. His teeth—previously a jigsaw puzzle of fractures—felt smooth now. Alien in his mouth.

"Thought I was headed to Mityana?"

"Plans change," Sophia said. "You needed to be kept somewhere quiet. And alive."

"Is this even a real hospital?"

"It's a home," she replied. "But for now, it's your hospital."

He let out a breath and leaned back. His head throbbed with phantom memories—gunshots and screams. Jesus.

"You've got a message," Sophia added. "From your headquarters. On your phone. Want it?"

"Yeah. Might as well hear what hell has in store."

She handed it over like it was a loaded pistol. One message blinked on the cracked screen.

CALL ME—TAYLOR.

Shawn scoffed.

"Fucking Taylor," he muttered, and hit dial.

The line picked up fast, like the guy had been sitting with the phone clenched in his fist.

"Jesus fuckin' Christ, Sleeping Beauty finally wakes up," came the voice. American, nasal, caffeinated. "You alive or what?"

"I'm breathin'," Shawn said. "And about to start kicking."

"Good. Listen up. You got two days, tops. Wrap your shit. Langley wants you on a plane by Tuesday."

Shawn winced, more from the tone than the message.

"Two days? That's not a mission. That's a goddamn death sentence."

"Well, maybe you shouldn't have let yourself get Swiss-cheesed in the first place. Now shut up and listen. You're working with the General."

"Wait, *that* General? I thought we were keeping distance from him."

"The original plan was to uncover the truth about his father. Now we've pivoted—to grooming him as the next dictator."

"Is he even on our side? Honestly, he seems too dumb to know which side he's on."

"He's on whatever side keeps his ass in the presidential seat. He plays ball, we pretend he's legit. You scratch his ego, he lets you do your thing. And maybe—*maybe*—he gets to go hunting in Khartoum with our blessing later."

"Great! So, I'm babysitting a power-hungry warlord with daddy issues."

"Exactly. Return his daddy's corpse and make it look like a goddamn honor parade."

"How do I reach him?"

"Check your texts. His number's there. Make the call. Don't fuck it up."

Then he hung up. No goodbye. Just static and the low hum of a dying connection.

Shawn stared at the phone for a second longer, then let it fall onto the blanket. His stomach gurgled loudly. He glanced at Sophia, who was still standing there like a painting that had come to life.

"What's cooking?" he asked, eyes narrowing as the scent of roasted meat and spice crept under the door.

She smiled.

"Neighbors. They're making dinner."

"Smells too damn good to be from the neighbors."

"In Uganda, we still cook. Real food. Not that frozen shit you Americans microwave into oblivion."

"Yeah. Forgot what food smelled like. You'd think in the land of plenty, someone'd invent a burger that didn't taste like cardboard and regret."

"Want some? I can tell them to send over a plate."

He hesitated. The places he'd been, food was a currency. A risk. Nobody gave anything away without strings.

But Sophia—she just waited, arms folded, like she had all the time in the world.

"In Uganda," she said softly, "we share."

"I'll take it."

She left quietly. A few minutes later, a bowl arrived—matooke, beans, meat so tender it practically wept when touched. He devoured it like a man starved of more than just calories. When he finished, the warmth in his belly settled into something close to peace. Almost human.

Then he made the call.

"General Mlevi," he said when the line picked up. "Name's Shawn. Working for Mr. Taylor. I'm the guy bringing your old man's corpse back."

The voice on the other end was smooth. Too smooth.

"I will be very happy to receive it," the General said. "I am also working for Uncle Taylor."

"Good," Shawn replied, his voice hardening. "Then here's the deal. You bring back the girls and the boy—your men took them with me. You want your father's remains? That's the price."

There was a pause. The kind that felt like a hand reaching through the phone to check your pulse.

"Understood," the General said at last. "And… I'm glad you're still breathing—my boys had already written your obituary."

The line clicked off.

Shawn leaned back, closed his eyes. The food had dulled the edge, but only just. The real game was beginning now—and this time, it wasn't just his life on the line.

It was their lives too.

CHAPTER 31:

The General

THE General was in a mood.

Not the kind of mood where a man opens champagne and hugs his mother. No—this was the quiet, sinister kind. The kind of mood where a man knows, deep in his reptilian gut, that everything he's ever schemed for is finally falling into place.

Washington had practically handed him the keys. Not with a parade, of course. Real power never traveled in limousines or public statements. It crept in through backroom doors, on whispered calls and encrypted emails. And when Mr. Taylor—the man behind the curtain, the one even presidents feared—called him "Mr. President," it wasn't flattery.

It was confirmation.

The General had grinned at the phone like it had handed him a loaded gun and a pardon in the same breath.

He knew what Taylor's blessing meant. The Americans had chosen. And he knew what kind of man Washington wanted in Africa.

Not a freedom fighter. Not some Nelson Mandela with tear-streaked speeches and a moral compass.

No. They wanted a bastard in a tailored suit. The kind of man who wore patriotism like a Halloween mask—cheap, shiny, and made in China.

They wanted someone who could sell out African dreams and make it look like nation-building.

And the General was ready.

He'd studied under the best. Mobutu Sese Seko—Zaire's own Dracula in designer sunglasses. After feeding Patrice Lumumba to Western wolves, Mobutu had crowned himself the Messiah of African pride. Banned Western names, Western suits, Western haircuts—hell, he probably would've banned gravity if he thought it was too European.

And all the while, he let the West mine his country into a skeleton. Gold, diamonds, uranium—all of it carted off like souvenirs, while the people starved in patriotic rags.

The General's father, Joel Katila Muaji, had learned the Mobutu playbook by heart. The man could fake a revolution better than most men could fake a marriage. He'd shouted communist slogans from the bush while writing love letters to London bankers and Washington diplomats. When the Western dollars poured in, he didn't waste time.

He sold every damn thing with a flag on it. Banks, factories, national pride—all stripped and shipped off under a fancy name: **privatization**. It sounded clean. Sanitized.

Like selling your mother's coffin and calling it downsizing.

Muaji hadn't just enforced capitalism in Uganda. He'd exported coups like they were pineapples. If a neighbor resisted Western control, Muaji sent in troops, called it "regional stability," and smiled for the cameras.

But if there was one man the General admired more than his father, it was *Uncle Piloto Kaguume*—the smiling executioner of Rwanda.

Kaguume's whole résumé was soaked in blood. He started in Uganda, slicing through Luweero in the '80s during the guerrilla war. Half a million dead, and the West called it a security operation. Then he upgraded to Rwanda, pulled off a brutal coup, and crowned himself a peacemaker.

That word again. *Peacemaker.* Western journalists loved it. They printed it like scripture.

Meanwhile, Kaguume marched into Congo, turned the mineral-rich jungles into mass graves, and told the world it was all in the name of stopping tribal hate. Ethnic cleansing wrapped in a press release.

His secret weapon? Golf. The man played nine holes with Wall Street billionaires, smiled through dinner, then signed orders to flatten a village by dawn. And the West kept building his skyscrapers, praising Kigali's clean streets like they couldn't smell the blood beneath the asphalt.

That was the blueprint. That was the standard. And now it was *his* turn.

The General wasn't pretending. He wasn't apologizing. He didn't need to.

If Mobutu could sell his people for oil contracts, if Muaji could privatize Uganda into oblivion, if Kaguume could slaughter his way through three countries and still get glowing op-eds in *The Guardian*, then surely he could do the same. CNN sees a skyline and calls it "Africa Rising." They don't ask where the cement came from—or whose bones are buried beneath it.

He didn't need to be loved. Just respected. Feared worked better anyway. So yes, he was celebrating. Quietly. Ruthlessly. He would lie. He would loot. He would rule.

And as long as the real gods of power—those faceless suits in Washington—kept calling him "Mr. President," he'd do it for a very, very long time.

*

The General was slumped in the plush living room of his hotel suite—if you could call the gaudy mess of gold curtains and blood-red carpets a "suite." It looked more like a brothel designed by a retired priest with unresolved rage issues. He tapped his boot impatiently on the marble floor, and he checked his gold-plated knockoff Rolex—the kind you buy off Russian arms dealers who pretend it was once owned by a Saudi prince—and saw that it was 6:54 p.m. Six goddamn fifty-four. Almost time.

Where the hell was Bafudde?

That moron. That walking, breathing embodiment of African time.

Bafudde had the punctuality of a dead goat. Always late. Always sauntering in with the oily confidence of a man who believed time was a colonial invention and that lateness was his right as an African. The General despised him for that. He despised him the way a lion despises a gazelle that dances too long before getting eaten.

He checked his phone. No messages. No missed calls. No nothing. Bastard.

He was supposed to make the exchange at 8:00 p.m. sharp in Nalumunye—two girls and a son for a corpse. Not just any corpse, mind you. *His father's corpse*. A man so feared in his lifetime that even the soil seemed scared to swallow him. Now he was missing.

Panic fluttered somewhere deep in the General's chest like a trapped bat, but he strangled it with the same hand he used to sign off on extrajudicial killings. Panic was for peasants. Panic was for women in labor and village priests without visas. Not for a man like him. Not for *the General.*

Still, just to prepare for Bafudde's eventual arrival, he picked his punishment stick from the bedroom. A polished, barkless, thoroughly satisfying rod of justice. It had flogged ministers, wives, houseboys, and once even a pastor. Tonight, it would be Bafudde's turn. Maybe in front of the girls. That would teach the bastard. A hundred strokes, like the Prophet recommended for adulterous women—except Bafudde had cheated on time.

He placed the stick beside him like a trusted advisor and turned on the television, thinking he'd kill time with the headlines before he killed Bafudde.

Ah, the news.

There they were again—Omubanda, the pop star turned political messiah, and his rebel-turned-rebel-again Vice President Erasmus Muwanga—fighting at a funeral. The poor dead man they were arguing over was some low-level agitator, the kind they called *foot soldier* in local slang. These two political clowns claimed they were the "rightful mourners," as if mourning had a lease agreement.

Each accused the other of aiding the government in the killing, when in truth, the only killing being done was of time and brain cells.

The General chuckled, a low, wet sound from somewhere deep in his gut. He loved these kinds of distractions. While the masses gawked at the funeral circus, he and his boys could quietly prepare the real show: the transition of power from the dead president to his favorite son. Smooth, controlled, silent. Like a syringe slipping into a sleeping arm.

The fools didn't even know the president was dead, let alone that his body had vanished like a whistleblower in a swamp. But they played their parts well. That was the beauty. Good boys. Loyal puppets with strings wrapped in Ugandan flags.

They'd show up later tonight for their cheques, as usual. He had even told them to bring lists of new recruits—those overzealous dreamers, frothing at the mouth with ideas of change. The General would kill them, disappear them, eat them with matooke and groundnut sauce if he had to.

He had developed a soft spot for Omubanda lately. The boy had talent. Not just musically—no, no—*politically*. The man could fake opposition like an angel fakes innocence. And his fans? Cult-like. Devoted. So loyal they'd follow him into Lake Victoria and drown smiling.

Take, for example, the time they convinced Omubanda to make Rugasira, one of the president's many bastard children his party's secretary-general—a position meant to spy on his every move. The fans? They lapped it up like a stray dog at a baptism.

The General had laughed until Waragi came out of his nose.

This "orphan"—as Omubanda described him—had studied in the Kiruhura presidential mansion, graduated from Oxford, gotten a masters from Harvard, and trained in Israel. *Televiv*, he called it. Probably meant Tel Aviv, but the peasants didn't know better. They barely knew how to spell *hope*. And anyway, the kid looked like the president's clone. Same forehead, same sneer. A walking DNA test.

Yet the fans never noticed. Or didn't care. Fanaticism was stronger than facts.

Also, Omubanda agreed to contest in every rigged election like a willing bride in an arranged marriage. His job was to legitimize the lie—to make dictatorship look like democracy with just enough lipstick to fool the world.

The General adored it. Omubanda had gone from calling the regime bloodthirsty monsters to softly telling BBC how the president was "misunderstood," a "visionary" who had simply overstayed his welcome.

Yes, he admitted, the son taking over wasn't ideal. But who else could lead?

Torture, murder, mass graves? Not the real issue. The problem, apparently, was overstaying one's welcome. Like an uncle who refused to leave after a funeral.

The General wondered what the pop star's adoring, half-starved fanbase would do if they ever woke up and realized the whole opposition movement was fake.

All those tear-gassed students, those disappeared bloggers, the bleeding bodies dumped like garbage in Mabira, were in vain.

Maybe the singer would come out smiling that crooked, tobacco-stained grin of his and serenade them with that same tired hit—"Kiwaani!"—that sleazy little number he claimed was a protest song.

The General could almost see it now: the singer, that skinny little Bob Omubanda standing onstage singing:

"Kiwaaaani! Everything here is kiwaaaani!"

Oh, they'd cheer. They'd cry. Some would even believe they were being enlightened.

Now, the General was tired—with a grunt, he jabbed the button and changed the channel.

A talk show. There sat Douglas, the General's favorite cousin and official bootlicker-in-chief. He was sparring with some mouthy Muslim MP. A real spitfire. Used to be friends back in the newsroom days, until Douglas decided he was too smart to be broke and joined the ruling machine. Now he was the mouthpiece of three governments and a rebel group—Uganda, Rwanda, Congo, and soon, Burundi.

Douglas was in top form tonight, his mouth a machine gun:

"Why are you the ones telling us not to kill our people? That's imperialism 101!"

God, the General loved this man. Like his father used to say, *"Tell the Americans to eat their mother's something-something."* And there were no consequences. The real power wasn't in Brussels or human rights offices. It was in Langley and Wall Street. A well-fed CIA man could topple a government with a blink. A human rights report? That was toilet paper in diplomatic language.

The Muslim MP pushed back:

"Even if they are our people, how can they speak if they are all dead or too terrified to talk?"

Douglas didn't flinch. In fact, he grinned the way crocodiles grin before they spin.

"You reason like a thug who skipped school. Madarasa education can't help you here, my friend."

Then came the pièce de résistance:

"This anger isn't about killings or democracy. You're just mad that the Baganda aren't in power. You're jealous of the Bachwezi."

Ah. There it was. The old reliable—tribal warfare. Turn every criticism into tribal envy and laugh as the tribes kill each other over ancient ghosts. The General was proud. That was his playbook. Divide, distract, dominate.

The Baganda were hated anyway. Once upon a time, their king rolled out the red carpet for the British colonizers like he was greeting a lost uncle. Sent Baganda men to beat the other tribes into submission. They became the empire's chosen sons—privileged, resented, isolated. Now they wanted sympathy? Justice?

The General snorted. They should apologize first. For centuries of being good little house slaves. And when Douglas mocked them on national TV, it wasn't just rhetoric—it was strategy. Mock the old snake until it strikes. Then tell the world, "Look! It's biting!"

The General's father had flipped the script. His own tribe, the Bachwezi, were the new chosen sons—not by God, but by American imperialism wearing a Gucci suit.

The Americans didn't want big tribes with old kings and long memories. They wanted orphans of empire, eager to prove themselves with bullets and oil contracts.

The General was still admiring Douglas's smug little face when the living room door burst open.

Bafudde. Sweaty. Panting. Looking like he'd been chased by guilt and caught by consequences.

"We're sorry, sir. The doctors were cleaning up the girls. Their wounds… the torture…"

The General sprang up. Forgetting the stick. Forgetting the flogging. He needed to go—now.

"Get me Shafic and Cyrus. We move."

But just as he reached the door, he turned back, dark eyes narrowing like a predator remembering the taste of blood.

"Oh, and Bafudde…"

The man froze like a schoolboy caught stealing lunch.

"Keep my stick. Leave it right here. When I return, remind me to give you your punishment."

Bafudde nodded like a church usher on judgment day.

"Yes, sir. I will be so happy to receive your punishment."

And he meant it.

Because in this country, pain was currency, and Bafudde had just taken a loan with interest.

CHAPTER 32:

Shawn

SHAWN arrived at Nalumunye Valley just as the sun bled out like a stuck pig behind the hills, leaving the sky bruised purple and the earth holding its breath.

It was 8 p.m., or close enough, but the silence was unnatural—not the quiet of peace, but the kind that presses into your skull, a vacuum of life, like even the crickets had packed up and fled. No traffic. No footsteps. Just two hills cradling a secret the world had no interest in discovering.

This was the place.

The General had been told to come alone. That was the rule. Leave the meatheads with guns behind or the deal was off. A father for a family. A corpse for the living. Fair trade in the arithmetic of grief and vengeance. But Shawn had been around long enough to know that men like the General never truly came alone. They brought their shadows with them. Their secrets. Their sins.

A half-mile back, he'd watched it unfold—Joanne, Helen, and the boy Anselm shoved out of the General's black SUV like garbage bags dumped at the curb. The headlights flickered briefly, like the car itself hesitated before vanishing down the dirt road, finally easing to a stop half a mile away—swallowed whole by the dark.

Shawn sat in his battered Peugeot. Watching. Waiting. Breathing. Trying not to think about the ache in his chest every time Joanne's silhouette moved.

He rolled forward, gravel crunching under bald tires. The girls turned at the sound, faces lit in the faint orange glow of a dying streetlight—faces pale, lips tight, haunted.

"Joanne! Helen! Anselm!" Shawn called through the open window, his voice too loud in all that hush. "Get in. Now."

Joanne didn't hesitate, but her eyes were storms. She climbed into the passenger seat like someone stepping into a trap, rigid and burning.

"Where are you taking us this time?" she asked, not as a question but as an accusation. Her voice cracked through the air, brittle with fury.

"I'll tell you," Shawn said, calm as stone. "But first, we deal with the General. Did you see where he went after he parked?"

Helen, holding Anselm close in the back seat, nodded toward the left.

"There's a path. He went that way. But he wasn't alone. Two men followed him."

Shawn's hands clenched the wheel. Of course. A coward never shows up without his shadows.

He killed the lights. Shifted into gear. The Peugeot rolled forward like a predator creeping up on prey. The trees whispered to each other overhead. Somewhere in the distance, a dog barked once and then went silent. A bad omen, maybe.

Up ahead, three shapes moved along the dirt path. The General walked like a man heading to his own execution—shoulders stiff, legs heavy. The two guards flanked him, heads swiveling, eyes carving the night into slices of suspicion.

Shawn reached under his jacket, his fingers curling around the cold steel of his pistol. It was comforting. Familiar. Like the embrace of an old friend who never let him down. He inhaled once—deep and slow—and pulled the trigger twice.

Pop. Pop.

The night answered with silence.

Both bodyguards hit the earth in unison, marionettes with their strings cut. Their limbs sprawled, necks twisted. The General froze, rifle tumbling from his grip, his face washed in moonlight and disbelief. He looked like a boy who'd just realized monsters were real and that they wore human skin.

Shawn stepped out of the car, the pistol still steady in his hand.

"On your knees."

The General obeyed. Quickly. Like a man who'd pissed himself already and didn't want to find out what else his body could betray.

Shawn could feel the shift in the air—the moment

when death arrives and decides to linger. It was colder now. Not just temperature, but something deeper, like the world was retreating. Like God had looked away.

"Joanne! Helen! Out. Bring the cuffs."

Helen came first, eyes empty, mouth tight. Her kick landed hard and low—no ceremony, no warning. Just a burst of pain and control. The General doubled over, coughing up air. Helen dragged him up and threw him into the car trunk.

Joanne followed. She didn't speak; she *howled.* A sound more animal than human. She yanked off her heels and rained them down on his skull. The thumps were wet and sharp.

"For my son!" she screamed.

"For the hell you made me live through!"

"For *everything*!"

"Joanne—enough!" Shawn barked. His voice cracked like a whip in the valley.

She stopped, breathing in jagged sobs. Her hands shook. Her eyes bled rage.

Shawn turned to Helen.

"Collect the weapons. Don't leave anything behind. Dead men talk when you give them bullets."

Helen nodded and went to work. She was efficient, the kind of woman who'd seen too much and decided she'd never flinch again. She stripped the guards of guns, knives, and ammo. One of them was still twitching. She put a bullet in his brain without blinking.

By the time she climbed back into the Peugeot, the dust had begun to rise. Shawn started the engine. The wheels spun on loose gravel, and then they were moving, the dead shrinking in the rearview, the General mumbling prayers in the trunk.

They had him now. But Shawn knew this wasn't over.

This wasn't the end of the night.

It was only the beginning.

CHAPTER 33:

Joanne

THE house in Mutundwe was the kind of place you'd expect to find a dying secret—not keep one alive.

Two-bedroom concrete box, no fence, no gate, just the lonely skeleton of a swing in the yard and neighbors close enough to count your teeth through the window. Joanne had seen safer places to hide a man. Like under a moving truck.

"Keep it quiet, in and out," Shawn had whispered like some B-movie spy. "We don't want the neighbors asking questions."

He said it like the neighbors weren't already peeking through their curtains, placing bets on whether this was a drug bust or a sex cult.

The plan was to keep the General inside at all times, like a very dangerous housecat with an attitude problem and a war crime or two. Joanne didn't like it. Not the house. Not the plan. Not the way Shawn said "Washington" like it was a person and not the most powerful zip code on earth.

"Are we prisoners now?" she asked. "Prisoners of Washington?"

"No, no," Shawn replied with that CIA smile—tight lips, lying eyes. "Washington just wants to make sure you and your son are safe before you go back."

Joanne stared at him.

"Because nothing says safety like hiding out with a bucket-pooping general in an unsecured house in Mutundwe."

Helen, who'd been quieter, finally said what they were all thinking. "I'm hungry."

"There's food," Shawn said, waving vaguely toward the kitchen like it was Narnia. "Macaroni in the fridge. Peeled matooke in the saucepan. Help yourselves."

Before they could claim their fate as night chefs, Shawn insisted on giving them a tour of the house, which felt less like hospitality and more like showing off his haunted Airbnb. The bathroom was a crypt. Just a hole in the floor and a jerrycan for sympathy.

"This," he said, gesturing like a man ashamed of his toilet, "isn't really… built for long calls."

Joanne raised a brow.

"You mean number two?"

"Yes. That." Shawn cleared his throat. "You'll have to, uh, go outside for that."

"And the General?" Helen asked.

"We give him a bucket," Shawn said, like that made everything okay. "And one of you will take it out."

Helen backed away like he'd offered her a dead rat on a tray.

"I'm not some pickup girl for the General's crap. Delete my name from that list."

Joanne raised her hand, not in agreement but protest.

"Me too. I've seen a lot of shit, but I draw the line at actual shit. Especially general-grade."

"Listen," Shawn snapped, his patience thinning like a discount condom. "We can't be here all night discussing the General's bowel movements. It's inappropriate. Even if he *is* our prisoner."

Joanne folded her arms.

"So how long have *you* been staying in this circus tent?"

"Today's my first day," Shawn said too quickly. "But the president's corpse was here yesterday. Some people stayed here before. It's… one of our operational houses."

Joanne narrowed her eyes.

"Who are you really, Shawn?"

"We're Americans. Friends of the president."

"That's vague."

"The rest is classified."

"Classified by who?" Helen asked.

"The government of the United States."

Joanne didn't like puzzles with guns. She liked them with chocolate and clues. But she kept quiet… until she noticed the shelf in the bathroom. Rows of pills like a traveling pharmacy. She picked up a bottle and read the label aloud like she was announcing bingo numbers.

"Stool softener. Anti-diarrhea. Melatonin… What's this one?"

"Melatonin helps you sleep," Shawn replied.

"And Tylenol Extra Strength—is that your Viagra?"

"No. That's to help me stay awake during the day."

Joanne blinked. "So let me get this straight. You people take a pill to sleep, another to stay awake, one to crap, one to *stop* crapping, one to get it up, and probably one to stop getting it up. You people are pill-powered sex robots."

Shawn didn't laugh. Joanne didn't expect him to.

"Anyway," he said, gesturing like a tired camp counselor, "get your son some food before he starts eating the walls. It's already 10 p.m."

The house creaked around them. The fridge hummed like it knew things. Outside, the darkness pressed against the windows like a jealous lover. And inside, three fugitives, a sulking General with a bucket, and a corpse from yesterday all waited for Washington to make the next move.

Joanne just hoped it wouldn't involve her holding that goddamned bucket.

CHAPTER 34:

The General

THE General was pissed—not the mild, simmering kind of pissed you nurse over whiskey, but the kind that curdles your guts and makes you want to punch a hole in the sky. Shawn had hurled him from the truck like a sack of rotting potatoes straight into a strange, peeling little house, barking strict orders about keeping his mouth shut unless he wanted the nosy neighbors sniffing around.

The irony burned hotter than acid in his stomach. *Safe house*, they called it—like the ones his own goons had been tossing Ugandans into for years, black-bagging them right off the street and dumping them where even God lost track. But now? The hunter had become the meat. Served up cold.

Dragging his half-cuffed legs like a drunk zombie, the General turned to Shawn, trying to salvage some dignity.

"Are you going to take these cuffs off now? I usually

tell my boys to treat prisoners with some respect inside a house."

"We're not your boys," Shawn shot back, his face as warm as a tax collector's.

"I know you're CIA goons. What is this? A job interview to bless me as Uganda's next president? You want a speech?"

"Reserve those stupid questions of yours," Shawn snapped. "Your old man's missing corpse is rotting in that room. Go have your moment. You've got thirty minutes to weep, wail, and confess your sins."

The General limped into the room, the door thudding shut behind him like the slam of a prison cell—heavy, echoing, and full of dread.

And there he was. His father. The president. The missing corpse. Uganda's great imperial puppet, lying there stiff and ugly, stinking of the past and cheap formaldehyde.

The General already knew the old bastard was dead. Hell, he knew more about how he died than any of these idiots suspected—things he would carry to the grave rather than whisper to any CIA pencil-pusher in a gray suit. Still, when he laid eyes on the corpse, a few pathetic sobs leaked out of his traitorous mouth.

He sat there, realizing something ugly: He wasn't just visiting the missing anymore. *He* was missing. Missing like his father's corpse. Swallowed by the same CIA machine they had both oiled and fed for decades. How the hell had it come to this?

His mind, as mean and sharp as a rusted blade, wandered back to the glory days when MI6 and the CIA lifted his father into power like a pig hoisted to the butcher's hook. They gave him guns, money, and a long bloody leash. His father played the role perfectly—the regional sheriff for Western interests, the hitman in a cheap suit. When the banks wanted African economies crushed under debt? His father signed on the dotted line. When corporations needed cheap coltan and gold? His father rolled tanks into Congo, greased the fields with blood, and handed over the mines like Christmas presents. When piracy in Somalia threatened cargo ships carrying TVs and Twinkies to the West? His father sent poor Ugandan boys to die on foreign beaches for someone else's shopping malls. And all along, he was celebrated—the golden boy of imperialism.

Until he wasn't. Until now, when his "friends" tossed his carcass in a stinking room and chained up his son like a mad dog.

Good job, Dad. RIP

The General thought, not without a bitter chuckle curling in his throat, *What more does an African leader have to do to win the West's love? Sell his soul twice? Kiss their boots clean? Shit diamonds on command?*

Apparently, it was never enough. It was never going to be enough.

The longer the General stood there, stewing in his own sweat and anger, the more it became obvious: the Americans had used his old man like a cheap rubber glove, and now they were in the process of yanking him off too—and not even with the decency to do it slow. No, it was going to be the old heave-ho straight into the garbage chute of history.

He had to break free.

But first… he had to survive the damn night. If he

made it through till morning, if he somehow wormed his way back to the Nile Hotel and his command center (still filled with half-competent sycophants and armed guards who could barely tie their boots), he was going to call China. Yeah. Big, booming China.

Because, sure, a man needed an imperial master—but why not pick the one on the rise, the one winning the tech wars, launching extreme ultraviolet lithography like some giant nerd god tossing lightning bolts?

If China really won the battle of chips and AI, the U.S. would either have to share the world like a grumpy kid sharing toys or get dragged kicking and screaming into second place.

And the General was a practical man: If you had to sell your soul, sell it to the highest bidder. But even as that half-assed plan warmed in his brain, an ugly little thought wriggled up from the sewer of his mind. Was it really any better to be a lapdog for Beijing than a punching bag for Washington?

At least the Americans didn't try to colonize with their bodies. They sent dollars, not daughters.

The Chinese? They brought the whole damn family. Already Uganda was crawling with them—a million, by some accounts—and if he sold his soul to Beijing, the General figured it was only a matter of time before he was asked, ever so politely, to naturalize another million. Uganda, already dirt-poor and overstuffed, would be asked to host a Chinese birthday party that never ended.

And then what?

Would the Chinese let him rig elections like Daddy used to, stuffing ballot boxes and disappearing nosy journalists into ditches? Hell no. The Chinese, once their numbers got big enough, would vote him out faster than you could say, "Ni hao."

Maybe Russia then?

He toyed with the idea like a drunk fiddling with a loose tooth. Maybe Moscow would take him in, make him their shiny new agent in Sub-Saharan Africa.

But no sooner had the thought crawled into his head than reality came stomping in with muddy boots.

The Americans—slicker than grease and twice as slippery—were already buying off the Russians.

Not because they gave a damn about freedom, sovereignty, or any of the other pretty words they liked to spray around like cheap cologne. No, their real wet dream was isolating China.

China, the new dragon in the yard, puffing smoke and snapping its jaws at the old world order. *Poor Ukraine*, he thought with a grin. *Poor, dumb Ukraine.*

All that flag-waving, anthem-singing, chest-beating patriotism—and now Washington was cozying up to the very monster they told Ukraine to fight. Because when it came to picking between "doing the right thing" and "strategic advantage," America always chose strategic advantage. Every. Single. Time.

In the grand game of imperialism, loyalty was for suckers.

Pulling Russia out from under China's umbrella was a bigger prize than all the burnt-out Ukrainian cities put together.

That was the real game. The real war.

And Russia, the slippery bastard, was only too happy

to play along—throwing open its front door for America, all smiles and handshakes, while leaving the back door wide open for China to creep in whenever it wanted. A whore with two beds and no shame.

The General chuckled darkly to himself, a low, bitter sound. Russia wasn't a Plan B. Hell, it wasn't even a Plan Z.

America and Russia were now just two arms of the same fat, greedy octopus, strangling the world one slimy tentacle at a time. Switching camps wouldn't save him. It would just change who got to tighten the leash and yank it when they felt bored. The General knew better. He wasn't some green recruit with piss in his boots.

As for independence? *Ha.* The very thought made him want to laugh in front of his father's corpse. "Independence" was a bedtime story for the masses—the kind whispered to crying children to keep them from noticing the monsters gnawing at the door. No, thinking Uganda could actually be independent was about as realistic as expecting the butcher to spare the pig because it squealed in perfect English. The axe always falls.

In East Africa, every neighbor had long since picked a master—and if you dared to step off the leash, they'd tear you to pieces just to earn a pat on the head from Washington, Beijing, or whoever else was signing the checks that month.

So… no grand plans tonight.

First things first: *Escape.* Scheme later. Survive now.

Finally, the door creaked open, and Shawn, looking like he'd rather be anywhere else, barked, "You done with your prayers?"

The General hadn't even touched the body. Hadn't opened the damn bag to make sure it was really his father and not some poor bastard off the street. No, he'd spent the whole half-hour standing there, tangled in cold, sweaty thoughts about Chinese migrants and Russian betrayals.

"One more minute," he croaked.

Shawn shrugged with all the mercy of a guillotine. The General unzipped the body bag just enough to see the face. Yep. That was him. Dead two weeks, and already turning the color of bad meat left in the sun. Satisfied—or at least as satisfied as a man could be under these circumstances—the General nodded.

Shawn grabbed him by the arm, yanked him into another dingy room, and shoved him onto a three-legged stool that looked about as stable as a promise from a politician.

"This is your bed," Shawn said.

The General sat down hard, the stool creaking under his weight, and realized grimly: He was going to spend the night sitting on that goddamn stool, cuffed like a dog, with his father's ghost breathing down his neck.

Happy freaking Independence Day.

CHAPTER 35:

Shawn

SHAWN had been in a lot of strange houses lately—safe houses, trap houses, houses with blood in the drains and history in the floorboards—but this one… this one felt different. Like it hadn't just held secrets, but swallowed them.

It was quiet now, the kind of quiet that makes your ears ring. The General was handcuffed to a pipe in the storeroom, sullen and sweating. Joanne was upstairs, whispering bedtime stories to her son in a tone that tried too hard to sound normal. Helen was in the bathroom, scrubbing at her skin like she could scrape the General's torture off her body—like pain could be washed down the drain with enough soap and scalding water.

Shawn, meanwhile, wandered into what passed for a study—an old den with a half-dead ceiling fan and wallpaper that had seen things and didn't want to talk about them. And there it was. A president's corpse on the floor, zipped into a body bag like yesterday's garbage. And lying right on top of it, with all the casual arrogance of a cat sunbathing on a grave, was a printed autopsy report.

He pulled the report from the corpse like it was a thank-you note from the grave.

Summary of Circumstances:

Eighty-one years old. Viagra. Three companions. Died at 2:17 a.m. No resuscitation. Not a fairy tale ending.

Shawn scanned the lines with a flat stare, something cold curling at the base of his spine. He didn't know whether to laugh or vomit. Maybe both. According to the General—His Excellency's very own son—the old man had ridden out on a wave of lust and cheap glory. But this report? This report told a story that reeked of crushed pills and quiet, opioid-drenched death.

External Examination:

Pinpoint pupils. Cyanosis. Frothy sputum. No trauma.

Hell, the guy didn't go out in a blaze of bedroom glory. He drowned in his own lungs like an old dog sedated for its final vet visit.

Toxicology:

Oxycodone off the charts—triple the top of the therapeutic range. Viagra? Just a whisper of it. Enough to say, *Yes, Your Excellency tried.* But not enough to kill a squirrel, let alone a man who used to have nations trembling at his cough.

The whole thing read like a damning poem:

Here lies a king,
Choked not by love,
But by pharma-grade sleep.

Shawn folded the report slowly. Real slow. Like it might bite him. His fingers itched to slap the General with it, page by page, until the man coughed up the real story. But not yet. Not here. Not with Helen and Joanne still moving around upstairs, still pretending the world could make sense for one more night.

He slid the report into a drawer. It creaked like it didn't want the truth locked inside.

Later, when the house was quiet and the women were asleep, he'd sit the General down. No threats. No shouting. Just Shawn, the ghost of a dead man, and the paper that proved a son had lied about his father's last breath.

And God help him, Shawn was going to enjoy every second of it.

He waited until the girls' room went dark and still. Helen had started snoring—that was his cue. Joanne had gone quiet, the kind of silence that could either mean sleep or deep thinking. With her, you never really knew. He hoped it was the first.

Time to stir the ghosts.

Knock? No—no need for that. Shawn pushed open the dark storeroom door without hesitation. It felt colder than it had any right to be. Concrete walls, no insulation, just a chandelier swinging gently from the ceiling like the last drunk at a wake. It gave off a jittery yellow light, enough to make the shadows twitch. The General sat in the middle of it all, head down, arms folded like he was praying over his sins.

Shawn brought a second stool, dropped it with a scrape loud enough to wake the dead—or at least the guilty. The General stirred, lifting his head like a dog caught sleeping on the furniture. His eyes were red-rimmed; not from tears, but from the weight of whatever secrets he'd been marinating in.

"I've got some questions," Shawn said, his voice soft, but not kind. "Taylor wants answers. We keep it low, so we don't wake the girls. But this? This is what decides if Washington lets you run for Daddy's chair."

He flicked on the recorder. That tiny red light pulsed, steady and judgmental.

"Let's start with your greatest hit. You said the president went out on a wave of Viagra. Three pills. Three girls. Heart exploded. You made it sound like a royal orgasm."

The General blinked. A flicker of a smile, maybe. Or a tic. Hard to tell in the shaky light.

"That's what I saw, Shawn."

Shawn didn't laugh. He slapped the autopsy report on the table, loud and deliberate, like dropping a revolver between them. The papers fanned out, stark black ink screaming one ugly word: *Oxycodone.*

"No, what you *said* you saw and what the lab *actually* saw are different creatures," Shawn said. "No Viagra overdose. Barely enough in him to raise a heartbeat, let alone the flag. What killed him was Oxy. 320 nanograms per milliliter. Enough to drown his lungs in pink foam and regret."

The General's hands twitched on the edge of the table. His knuckles turned white. But the bastard didn't flinch. Not outwardly.

"You're mistaken," he said. "I was there. I saw the blue pills. The girls were laughing. His face was red as hellfire before he dropped."

Shawn leaned in, close enough to catch the sour breath, the dried sweat.

"Pinpoint pupils. Frothy mouth. That's not Viagra, General. That's opioids. You didn't mention Oxy. Not once. Why's that?"

The walls seemed to lean in with him, closing the space like a jaw. He tapped the report again. A rhythmic *tick-tick-tick*, like a countdown.

"Toxicology doesn't care about your bedtime story," Shawn said. "His heart was clean. It wasn't lust that killed him. It was a chemical pillow pressed over his lungs until they forgot how to breathe."

The General's jaw clenched, muscle twitching like a bug caught in amber.

"You're overreacting," he muttered. "My father was reckless. If he mixed his pleasures, that's not on me."

Shawn's grin was more barbed wire than warmth.

"This isn't about what he mixed. This is about what *you* served. Those girls and your doctor saw Viagra, yeah. Because you showed it to them. The stage was set. No one asked about the real show. Not until the body hit the table."

The air felt heavier now. Like the walls were listening.

"Someone gave him the Oxy," Shawn said. "Someone who knew he'd take it. And someone who knew he wouldn't get back up."

And there it was. A flicker in the General's eyes. Not fear, exactly. But something close. Recognition, maybe.

"You're out of line," the General snapped, louder than he should've been. Then, softer, almost to himself, "That man was my father. I would never—"

"Never what?" Shawn's voice dropped to a whisper. "Never poison him? Never lie to save your ass? Washington doesn't care about your grief, General. They care about the truth. And this story? It's got more holes than a dictator's back after a coup."

The silence that followed pressed in like a wet blanket.

"What do you plan to do," the General said, "if I told you I gave him the Oxy myself? Would you recommend Washington backs someone else?"

"That's not my job," Shawn said flatly. "I write the report. Washington picks the puppet."

The General nodded, as if they were just two men talking over bad coffee and not confessing to murder. "Okay," he said. "I did it. It was part of a revenge. A little present for my mother. You know the story—they say my father shot her. Shot her with his own damn hands."

"Wow," Shawn muttered, because there wasn't a better word for it. *Wow* worked for weddings, funerals, and confessions of generational trauma wrapped in Oxycodone.

He was about to ask a question—something sharp, something that would make this whole thing make sense—when a sound snapped the moment in two.

Footsteps. Light. Careful. Close.

Shawn froze, the silence snapping like a wire. His hand went to his sidearm, just beneath the hem of his shirt. The General straightened too, eyes flicking toward the door like it might bite.

Another step. Closer this time.

He held his breath, listening. Was it Helen? Joanne? Or someone a little less friendly and a hell of a lot more armed?

Shawn didn't move. Didn't speak.

Not yet.

CHAPTER 36:

Joanne

JOANNE was awake. Wide awake. It wasn't just the strange bed, though that didn't help. It wasn't just the horrors of the past week, though those had sunk into her bones like old sickness. It wasn't even their son, though the thought of what happened to him in the General's prison sent jolts of grief through her chest, raw and electric. No, it was something else, something more primal. Something she couldn't name.

The rain pounded on the iron sheets, hammering a dull, rhythmic terror into the night. Wind howled through the cracks in the walls, slithering across the floor like something alive. When she was a child, nights like these had been a lullaby, the rain a drumbeat of comfort lulling her into deep sleep. But not tonight.

And then, as if the universe was conspiring to keep her nerves on edge, the power went out.

The house plunged into blackness, so thick and absolute that for a moment, she couldn't even tell if her eyes were open. Typical Uganda. Load shedding. The country had been drowning in darkness for years, thanks to the pathetic, dead-handed leadership of President Katila Muaji. And now Muaji himself was dead, his corpse lying just beyond the door in the living room.

Joanne swallowed, the saliva thick and slow in her throat. No wonder she couldn't sleep. Who could, knowing that a corpse—*that* corpse—was just a few feet away? The man had been a monster in life, and she doubted death had made him any kinder.

Dead was dead, she reminded herself, but still—something about his presence in the house felt wrong.

And then there was the problem of her bladder.

She could hold it maybe. Wait until morning. But the thought of lying there, restless and needing to go, made her skin crawl.

She considered waking Helen. Her love. Her partner. The woman snored lightly beside her, at times stirring just enough to let out a long, rattling fart. Joanne almost laughed. Even now, Helen found peace, something soft in the middle of all this horror. Joanne didn't want to wake her, to drag her into this unsettled night.

That's when she remembered the small basin beneath the bed. A habit from the village, carried over from childhood. Back then, they'd used basins because stepping outside meant risking running into Katila Muaji's security men, drunken and searching for homes to loot. Now, decades later, she was still afraid to step outside, though this time, it wasn't the living Muaji she feared—it was his corpse.

She slid her feet over the edge of the bed, careful not to make a sound. The wooden floor was cool against her skin. Her fingers groped beneath the bed until they found the plastic rim of the basin. Relief was near.

And then she heard the voices.

Her body went rigid. The sound came from the other room. Low murmurs, thick with urgency. Her breath hitched. The ghost of the president? Had death not been enough to silence that wretched man? Or was his handcuffed son talking to something—someone—in the dark?

She strained to listen, her heartbeat thundering in her ears. The voice was unmistakable. General Mlevi, the dead man's son. His tone was urgent, desperate. But who the hell was he talking to?

A trick of the wind, she told herself. The storm outside. The mind playing games in the dark.

She emptied her bladder quickly, barely caring that a few drops missed the basin. The moment she was done, she shoved it back under the bed and rushed beneath the sheets, curling into herself, trying to steady her breath.

The house had gone silent again. But the fear remained, curling up beside her like an unwanted lover.

Dead was dead, she reminded herself. Then why did it feel like something in this house had just begun to wake up?

Joanne continued to overhear voices in the night, the low, murmuring exchange between the General and—God help her—Shawn. Shawn, of all people.

This American man, the one who had been crushing on her, trying to wedge himself between her and Helen, was in the dark, whispering to the enemy. The brutal son of a dictator, whose corpse lay stiff and unrepentant on the cold, unforgiving floor in the living room. Her stomach twisted. What the hell were they talking about?

She strained to make sense of the words, but between the rain hammering against the iron sheets and Helen's steady, oblivious snoring, it was impossible. Damn it. She had to do something.

She reached over and shook Helen's shoulder. Once. Twice. Instead of waking, Helen only sighed and rolled closer, her arm lazily draping over Joanne's stomach like they were back in the safety of their own bed.

"Wake up, Helen, wake up," she whispered urgently.

Helen stirred, groggy, and muttered, "Do you want the top, or should I go on top?"

Was she serious? Did she think they could make love in this godforsaken house, with the body of a dictator stiffening just feet away, his son—a man who had beaten them, terrorized them—now conspiring with their supposed friend? Was she out of her mind?

"Silly, we can't make love in this place!" Joanne hissed. "I need you to listen. The General—he's talking to someone. And it's Shawn."

That got her attention. She sat up, pushing her wild curls out of her face, and they both fell silent, straining to hear.

"... Who made up this story about the president dying of a Viagra overdose? Who's trying to fool the CIA and the USA?" Shawn's voice was sharp, demanding.

A pause. Then the General, his voice dripping with arrogance: *"I made up the story. But I didn't do it to fool the CIA or the USA. I just wanted to be the president."*

Joanne sucked in a breath. Her hand found Helen's arm, gripping it tightly.

"Wow, wow," she whispered. "The Viagra story was a cover. This guy—he killed his own father."

Helen shoved her lightly, her way of telling her to shut up. She wanted to listen.

The voices from the other room dropped to an even lower hush, their words now slipping beneath the sounds of the storm, lost in the night. Joanne and Helen sat there, tense, listening to nothing—and everything.

When Helen could no longer hear what the General and Shawn were saying, she swung her legs out of bed and ordered Joanne to follow her. They were going to go to that room, face them head-on, and find out what the hell they were conspiring about in the dead of night.

Barefoot, they moved silently across the floor, careful not to make a sound. When they reached the door, Helen didn't hesitate. She raised her foot and kicked it hard. The wood splintered, the door swinging open with a groan.

She stormed inside to find Shawn seated beside the General, the dim glow of an iPhone flashlight casting long, eerie shadows against the walls. The General still had his handcuffs on, and Shawn turned in shock, his mouth parting as if to ask what was going on.

Helen didn't give him the chance. She lashed out, kicking the table between Shawn and the General, sending a pistol flying across the room and scattering papers like dead leaves in the wind. Joanne rushed for the gun, snatching it up before anyone else could reach it.

Shawn lifted his hands. "Jesus, what the hell—"

Helen wasn't listening. She spotted an extra pair of

handcuffs on the floor, scooped them up, and in one swift move, snapped them onto Shawn's wrists.

Now both men were restrained, but to Helen, that still wasn't enough. Her eyes darted around the dimly lit room opposite the storeroom, landing on the bed. She grabbed a bedsheet, twisted it into a makeshift rope, and wound it tightly around Shawn, binding him to the chair. The General, she realized, was already chained at the legs and handcuffed. He wasn't going anywhere.

She turned her attention to the scattered papers, crouching down to collect them.

"Sorry, Helen," Shawn said, voice measured. "This interview, these papers—they're classified by the United States government. You can't read them."

"Classified my ass," Helen snapped, fire in her voice. "This is my country. Everything you people are doing here affects me and my countrymen, not you Americans. Stop coming here and classifying our oppression and plunder."

"I'm sorry, Helen, but if this is about Joanne, don't take it out on me." Shawn sighed, his head tilting back against the chair. "I gave up on your girlfriend a long time ago. Just let me do my job so I don't get fired."

Helen ignored him. She turned to Joanne, hand outstretched.

"Give me the gun."

Joanne hesitated for only a moment before relinquishing it. Helen checked the weight in her hand, then leveled it at Shawn's chest.

"Listen, Shawn," she said, her voice steady. "From this moment on, I call the shots. Neither your country nor that bastard son of the dictator rotting on the floor in the living room has any say. You are both going to listen to me."

Shawn exhaled through his nose.

"By the way," Helen added, cocking the pistol, "whose side are you on, Shawn?"

"I'm on the people's side," Shawn said carefully, "but you know the U.S. is my country."

"And this is our country," Helen said. "We have interests, just like your country does. And in this room, the interests of my country now take precedence."

The General's bewilderment deepened, his eyes practically bulging from their sockets as Helen moved toward the door. She turned back, a wicked smirk curling her lips.

"I'm coming back for you," she told him.

The electricity had returned, banishing the shadows. No more iPhone torches, no more hiding in half-darkness. The General looked like he wanted to drop to his knees and beg Joanne to control her unhinged partner, but the chains held him fast. If he tried, he would just topple over, and Helen might see it as defiance. Instead, he turned to Joanne, his eyes wet and pleading.

"Please, please tell her I'm not a bad guy."

Before Joanne could respond, Helen burst back into the room. In one hand, she held a pistol. In the other, a gleaming kitchen knife.

"Where's your phone?" she asked.

The General gestured with his head toward Shawn.

"Where's his phone, Shawn?" she demanded, voice rising.

Shawn jerked his chin toward a small bag. "There."

"Joanne, get that phone out and power it on."

As Joanne rummaged through the bag, Helen pulled

a stool up to the General, her expression darkening. "Do you remember Princess Shakira?"

The General swallowed hard.

"Yes, the singer."

"You assaulted her on your birthday, didn't you?" Helen's voice was dangerously soft. "Tell us what you did to her."

"Nothing, nothing, I swear," the General pleaded, shaking violently.

Helen sneered. "I've heard that word 'nothing' from a lot of rapists. Say it again, and I'll cut off your dick. Joanne, pull down his pants."

Joanne hesitated, but at Helen's sharp glance, she stepped forward. That was when the General broke. "Okay, okay! I'll tell you everything."

"Only the truth," Helen warned. "Start."

The General's breath came in ragged bursts.

"I just… I just used my fingers. I swear. Nothing—nothing like what you're thinking."

Helen's lips curled back. "Which fingers?"

He stammered, then lifted his right middle finger. But as Helen raised the knife, he panicked and switched to his left middle finger.

Helen scoffed. "Both fingers go then."

With a swift, merciless motion, she brought the knife down. The blade sliced through flesh and bone, severing the right middle finger. Blood spurted in dark rivulets, pooling onto the floor. The General screamed, a high, animalistic wail. Helen barely hesitated before turning to the left hand, repeating the act with brutal efficiency.

Joanne had seen many kinds of horror—but nothing

prepared her for this.

The General screamed, a sharp, wet cry that curdled the air like spoiled milk. His knees thrashed against the floor, blood pumping from the stumps where his middle fingers used to be. Helen stood over him, blade in hand, her eyes not just angry—but possessed. It wasn't rage anymore. It was something colder. Older.

Joanne backed away instinctively, her breath hitching in her throat. "Helen…" she whispered, but her voice sounded like it belonged to someone else. Far away.

Even Shawn seemed shaken. He blinked slowly at the gore, muttering, *"Wow."*

Helen turned to them, the blade dripping, her silhouette haloed by the weak glow of a lantern they'd propped in the room. Her lips curled into something that wasn't quite a smile. "When you two start sympathizing with this monster," she hissed, "after everything he's done—you piss me off."

The General whimpered at her feet, blood soaking into the floor carpet like ink into parchment.

Helen raised the severed fingers, holding them like trophies.

"This," she said, her voice low and dangerous, "is for Princess Shakira, the singer he raped. The one whose silence made the world comfortable. She cried for help in that *X* video—remember that? And you made her pull it down. You made her apologize. Her fans… her family… They were helpless. All because *you* had the power."

She dropped the fingers with a soft *plop.* The General curled in on himself like a dying insect.

Joanne watched, stunned. She had always seen Helen

as the quieter one—soft-spoken, sometimes moody, but never like this. Never on fire.

"You turned this entire country into one giant chamber of pain," Helen went on. "Rape was your war strategy—just like your army did in Congo, in Somalia, in Rwanda, Sudan... You used women's bodies like message boards. And even when the UN wrote reports, you buried them in silence."

She kicked the General in the ribs, hard. He coughed blood, a dark spray that gleamed in the lantern light.

"No more silence."

Joanne stared at her friend. It was like watching someone step through a door into another world—and leaving the person you knew behind. Helen was glowing now, not with joy, but with something ancient and terrifying. Righteousness twisted into revenge.

"And don't you dare talk to me about mercy," Helen snarled. "We've all seen what's in those torture chambers. What *you* ordered. Rows of corpses—skin flayed, eyes gone, plastic burned into their flesh like twisted tattoos."

She turned back to Shawn.

"You, me, Joanne—we all carry the marks. You think he gets to walk out of here with just a bruise and a sob?"

Joanne felt her arm twitch—like the burns were remembering too. The smell of scorched plastic suddenly filled her nose, even though there was no fire. Just memory. And pain.

"I still have scars," Joanne whispered. "From where they melted that jerrycan plastic into my back. They told me I screamed like a dying dog."

Helen nodded, grimly.

"And God knows what they did to you, Shawn. Wherever they took you."

The General was trying to crawl now, dragging himself like a slug through the dust, weeping.

Helen reached down, grabbed him by the collar, and yanked him back like a dog on a chain.

"You ran your kingdom on fear," she whispered in his ear. "Now feel it."

Joanne looked at Helen, and then at the General—the man they'd once feared more than death itself—and realized something bone-deep and chilling.

Helen had become his nightmare.

And Joanne wasn't sure who she feared more anymore.

Princess Shakira had her justice.

Helen stood over the sobbing, writhing man.

"Now, let's talk about justice for Uganda."

Joanne felt her stomach churn as Helen turned to her, the gleam of the blood-slicked knife catching the light. The General whimpered, his remaining fingers twitching against the armrest of his chair, the bloody stumps trembling like the last convulsions of a dying animal. His breath came in ragged gasps, his entire body soaked in a sickly sheen of sweat.

"Joanne," Helen said, her voice smooth but sharp as a razor. "Bring me his phone."

Joanne stepped over the pooling blood, careful not to slip. The phone was in Shawn's bag, just as he'd said earlier. She pulled it out, feeling the cold weight of it in her palm. When she turned back, Helen was looming over the General again, her presence a dark shadow swallowing the room.

"Give Joanne your password," Helen barked, her patience stretched thin. "If it doesn't work, I'm cutting another finger."

The General swallowed hard, his Adam's apple bobbing like a drowning man struggling for air. His lips trembled. "Six fingers," he whispered, barely audible.

Joanne typed it in. The phone unlocked with a soft chime.

Helen smirked. "Good boy. Now, Joanne—go to his X account."

Joanne hesitated. She could feel the weight of the moment pressing down on her like a crushing force. This wasn't just violence anymore. This was history being rewritten in blood.

She found the X app, opened it. The General's account was right there, still logged in. Helen leaned over her shoulder, voice low and steady. "Type exactly what I say."

Joanne's fingers hovered over the screen.

I am here announcing that my father, President Joel Katila Muaji, is dead. The circumstances surrounding his death are going to be investigated. I want the people of Uganda to follow the right procedures as stipulated in the constitution to replace my father, and that means making his vice president... the next president. I have no intentions whatsoever of being the president of Uganda.

Joanne hesitated for half a second.

"Send it," Helen ordered.

Joanne's thumb pressed the button. A moment later, the words were live.

The General slumped, his breath coming in short, shallow bursts. Helen wasn't done. She turned back to him, stepping close enough for her breath to brush his face.

"Now," she said. "You're going to make some calls."

The General blinked, still trapped in that haze of shock and agony.

"You call the vice president first," Helen said. "Then the army commander, then the intelligence chief. You're going to order each one of them to facilitate the swearing-in of the new president."

The General didn't move.

Helen lifted the knife.

"If you give them the slightest hint that you're being forced, I take another finger."

The phone trembled in his grip as he dialed the first number. Joanne watched him struggle to sound normal, his voice tight, controlled. "Ms. Vice President," he said, a slight waver in his tone. "I need you to begin the transition process immediately. My father… has passed. We must follow constitutional protocol."

He hung up and immediately dialed the next number. The army commander. The intelligence chief. Each time, his voice grew steadier, forced into a kind of eerie calm.

By the time he set the phone down, the world had changed.

Helen and Joanne stared at each other for a long, breathless moment.

Then Helen exhaled a short, sharp laugh.

"We did it," she whispered.

Joanne let out a stunned breath. For the first time, the Ugandan constitution had been respected. The government had changed—without a coup, without another general grabbing the throne. For the first time, power was shifting into the hands of a civilian. And for the first time, the military had been ordered to protect the constitution, not break it.

They switched on the television. The news channels were scrambling to keep up. Breaking headlines flashed across the screen: *PRESIDENT JOEL KATILA MUAJI DEAD. NEW PRESIDENT TO BE SWORN IN SOON.*

A civilian president. A woman.

Helen grinned at Joanne, eyes wild with something between triumph and madness.

"Now," she said, "let's see if they try to take it back."

CHAPTER 37:

The General

THE General sat still. His breath came in shallow, rattling gusts, like a man hiding from death but already brushing its cold fingers. His mutilated hand—two fingers gone, hacked off with a soldier's glee—throbbed in sync with his heartbeat, a drumbeat of agony pulsing through his arm. The filthy rag wrapped around the stump was soaked through now, red and stiff. Pain should have been his focus. But pain wasn't the problem. Not anymore.

Power was.

They'd made him call. Forced the words out of him like bile from a poisoned stomach. A blood-soaked surrender. He'd handed over the presidency of Uganda—his birthright—through crackling phone lines and threats barked in bad English. They thought they'd broken him. Thought they'd severed more than flesh.

But fools never understand crowns.

His father's death was supposed to be the turning point. The stage had been set, the guns oiled, the generals bought. The throne of Uganda was dangling above him like a golden lure on a rusted hook. And now—gone. Slipped through fingers that no longer existed.

Still, the General wasn't finished.

Uncle Pilooto Kaguume. The name rang in his head like a hymn and a curse. His father's old comrade, now the iron-fisted ruler of Rwanda. They had raised him, funded him, installed him. And now it was time for him to return the favor. To restore the General to Daddy's old throne in Uganda. Then, someday, when Pilooto's little monster slithered up to take the reins in Kigali, the General would scratch his back too.

Dictatorship, it turns out, runs on favors. And blood. Mostly blood.

The plan had always been simple in its ambition: one tribe, one region, one destiny. The Bachwezi, the chosen, the ancient bloodline meant to rule the Great Lakes like gods among cattle. Every neighboring president, placed like a chess piece. But these Ugandan upstarts had knocked over the board. Installed a nobody. A non-Bachwezi.

That mistake would cost them more than fingers.

Uncle Pilooto—Kaguume to the world—had never tolerated disorder. He'd already bathed parts of Congo and Burundi in fire and bone, toppling regimes like a gardener pulling weeds. And now, with Uganda slipping, he'd see the danger. He'd act. He always did.

All it would take was the right story.

He'd come in, of course, under the banner of peace—to protect the Bachwezi, like he'd protected "his people" in

Eastern Congo. The old playbook never failed. He'd seize Uganda's gold and copper, funneling it through Kigali, and tell the world he was stabilizing the region. And the world, as always, would listen. Because Pilooto knew how to play them. Knew the difference between slaughter and security, at least in the language of press releases.

Let the lakes fill with corpses. The rivers run red. It would all look clean once it hit CNN.

The General could already hear the script: "A man of peace," they'd call him. Bloggers would swoon in Kigali cafes. Western journalists would write profiles that smelled like cologne and power, not blood. Over and over they'd say it—he's a man of peace—until even the bodies stopped complaining.

It had worked before. It would work again.

The Europeans would throw tantrums, release toothless reports, wave human rights flags that fluttered like torn rags in the wind. Maybe even sanctions. But none of that mattered. Not with America on their side. The superpower had picked their winners. And once chosen, winners never bled in the headlines.

The General shifted in his chair, pain making his spine feel like it was carved from glass. He stared at the girls who'd tortured him, smiled a little. They didn't understand yet.

They'd made their final mistake.

He just had to survive this prison, this blood-crusted cage. He just had to get a message to Kaguume.

And then—

He'd wear the crown.

CHAPTER 38:

Joanne

THE world outside had turned into a cacophony of celebration, like the gates of hell had been flung open and even the demons were doing the Electric Slide. Joanne could hear it all, even from deep inside the battered safe house in Mutundwe—drums pounding like gunfire, laughter ricocheting off tin roofs, and ululations rising like smoke from the mouths of women who'd spent decades speaking in whispers.

On TV, chaos masqueraded as joy: crowds choking the streets of Kampala, Gulu, Jinja, Arua—hell, even in Karamoja where people usually didn't gather unless it involved cattle or death. Now they were dancing like the dictator's ghost was watching. The same army and police that had once specialized in tear-gas baptisms and boot-kick communion had joined the party. Apparently, even torturers needed closure.

Footage kept spilling in from across the Great Lakes region—Kenya's Nairobi, DRC's Kinshasa and Goma, Juba in South Sudan, and yes, even Mogadishu, where people had mastered the art of celebrating amid rubble. It was like someone had unplugged a monster and the entire continent had exhaled. As if President Joel Katila Muaji hadn't just been Uganda's plague, but the neighborhood's shared infection.

Joanne sat cross-legged on the floor, the General's old iPhone in her hand. Technically it was her phone now. She scrolled through X posts with the detached intensity of someone reading obituaries for the living. World leaders—some with names longer than street addresses—were sending congratulatory messages to Ugandans. A few even attached confused Ugandan flag emojis that looked more like the German one flipped sideways. France, Britain, the African Union—congratulations poured in.

Omubanda, the so-called opposition singer, hadn't reposted anything from the General's account about handing over power. Probably still calculating how to monetize the revolution—or perhaps stunned that his side gig as controlled opposition had been exposed like a magician caught stuffing rabbits into his hat backstage. He'd been too busy fighting with his rebel vice president over government bribes to notice that the real game was over.

On the television, the scene switched to Uganda's Parliament—a zoo with furniture. MPs, ruling party goons, and assorted political barnacles were hugging and dancing like they'd all just escaped death by PowerPoint. The speaker—a tiny woman with the unfortunate complexion of someone who'd tried to erase her melanin like it was a bad memory, most of her face bleached into a patchy, ghostly shade of off-white, like she'd fallen asleep face-first in a bucket of expired paint—struggled to get them to shut up for the swearing-in.

Helen appeared from the kitchen, her face streaked with emotion, like someone had turned on her tear ducts and left the tap running. She flung herself onto the sofa beside Joanne, hugged her hard, and began sobbing with joy.

"This is really happening," Helen whispered, snot and all. "Let's bring them here," she continued, meaning the General and Shawn. "They should see this. History is happening."

Joanne nodded. She didn't particularly care if Shawn wanted to watch the fall of an empire, and she knew the General would pretend not to care while secretly logging every second into that cold reptilian brain of his. Still, she agreed.

They stormed the storage room like it was a rescue mission. Shawn and the General were dumped unceremoniously onto the couch. Shawn looked half-awake. The General looked half-dead. But both of them stayed silent, watching.

The ceremony finally began. Cameras zoomed in on the new interim president: Jane Akello, formerly the vice president with all the power of a teaspoon in a hurricane. Now she was flanked by soldiers in pressed fatigues and men in suits too expensive for their conscience. General Katamba—bigger than God, quieter than guilt—walked beside her to the raised podium. The chief justice, a man whose eyes looked like they'd read too many lies, held out the Bible.

Joanne didn't blink. Jane placed both hands on the holy book like she was about to perform an exorcism.

"I, Jane Akello," she began, "do solemnly swear—"

It was done.

Uganda had its first female president. A woman who yesterday couldn't get a seat at the real table was now the table. She'd been the vice president of a dictatorship that thought ruling was a birthright, a monarchy dressed up in multiparty makeup. And now, by sheer force of fate—or perhaps good old-fashioned paranoia—she was sworn in as interim president for the remainder of the deceased president Joel Katila Muaji's term.

As she walked to the next podium to deliver her first speech, Joanne leaned back and whispered, "God help her." And then, after a pause, "God help us all."

Helen waved a hand at Joanne like she was swatting a fly and hissed, "Oh, shut up—just listen, will you?"

Fellow Ugandans,

I won't pretend I came here with a perfectly polished speech. I have none. Because nothing about the past few days has been polished. Nothing about what we've been through as a nation has been neat, or clean, or easy. But I will speak from the heart.

I never thought I would stand before you as your leader. Not in this way. Not after the blood, the whispers, the betrayals. Not after the dust settled on a battlefield we never asked for. But history has placed us here, and history will judge what we do next.

I take this position not as a ruler, but as a caretaker. This is an interim government, a bridge between the past and a future we must build together. Five years. That is all. Five years to tear down the walls of tyranny, to break the chains that bound us for four long, dark decades. And I give you my word—I will not contest the next election. I am not here to rule. I am here to heal.

I know the anger that burns in many of you. I see it in your eyes, feel it in the air. The old regime did not just govern—it crushed, it strangled, it buried. And now that the door is open, some of you want revenge. But I ask—no, I plead—let us not become the very monsters we fought to defeat. Vengeance will not rebuild our villages. Bloodshed will not educate our children. Retribution will not fix what has been broken.

But justice? Justice will.

That is why, effective immediately, I will be signing a series of executive orders. The first—an end to political imprisonment. Every man and woman locked away for daring to speak, for daring to dream, for daring to resist—your time in the dark is over. Uganda must be a nation where no one is jailed for their ideas.

Second, I am establishing the Department of Equity and Inclusion—a commitment that in the new Uganda, no tribe, no gender, no class will be left behind. We rise together, or we fall apart.

And finally—to those who still lurk in the shadows, waiting for chaos, hoping to drag us back into darkness—I see you. And I warn you. Uganda will never kneel to dictatorship again. Not while I have breath in my body.

My people, we have wasted enough time in fear. Now, we build. Now, we work. Now, we become the Uganda we were always meant to be.

There is no time to waste. Let's get to it.

God bless Uganda.

Epilogue

TUESDAY evening, under a sky smeared with Kampala smog and irony, Helen and Joanne handed over Shawn and the General like they were dropping off spoiled groceries—rotten, dangerous, and long past their sell-by date. The authorities, not known for generosity unless it was embezzled, gave the women a flashy 4x4 ride back to their dusty little corner of Nateete. A "heroes drive," they called it. Heroes, huh? Helen and Joanne just wanted a shower and to not be tortured again.

They weren't generals. They weren't politicians. They weren't even verified on Twitter. Just two stubborn women with no appetite for corruption, no thirst for power—just a burning, bile-flavored urge to see things put right. When offered a backroom deal that would've made any politician sell their own mother to sign, they spat it out and chose honor instead. That kind of thing gets you killed in Uganda. Or worse—forgotten.

And the revolution? Well, it didn't roar in like an action movie climax. It slipped in quietly. No bloodbaths, no shootouts, no TikToks of teenagers dancing on tanks. Just two women, a dead regime, and an entire nation blinking in disbelief.

Their tale of courage and decency deserved headlines, maybe even a Netflix miniseries. But this wasn't how history worked. If a superpower didn't sponsor your revolution, it didn't count. And if CNN didn't show up, it never happened. These women were never supposed to win. But they did. Without fame. Without fortune. Just quiet satisfaction watching their country—finally—look like a real country and not a crime scene dressed up as a democracy.

Meanwhile...

Shawn got scooped up by the U.S. Embassy faster than a CIA asset in hostile territory (which, to be fair, he was). They slid him onto the next flight out of Entebbe, passport stamped, ass covered, and tongue sealed. America always knew how to clean up after a mess—especially when they made it.

The General? Oh, he got the deluxe welcome package from the justice system: 867 charges, give or take a few war crimes. Treason. Murder. Torture. Rape. Corruption. Embezzlement. Even unpaid parking tickets. Victims lined up like they were at a damn concert—men who'd been electrocuted in his basement, women silenced with violence. Even Princess Shakira, the pop star he assaulted and gagged with power, came forward. Then came the neighbors—Congo, South Sudan, Burundi, Somalia, Sudan—all wanting their pound of flesh. The General had basically run a regional genocide buffet, and now the bill was due.

And then came the spooks.

The American intelligence agencies flew in like vultures who'd missed the kill and wanted to know how the hell two broke women from Nateete pulled off what their multi-billion-dollar budgets couldn't. They poked around, hoping to find Putin's fingerprints, or maybe a secret Chinese plan… even North Korea would've made sense. But nope—no shadowy mastermind. Just two pissed-off women and a country sick of being stepped on. This was worse than Iran in '79. Worse than the Soviet fiasco in Afghanistan. This was African self-determination, raw and unsponsored. And that terrified them.

Because if Africans could pull this off without foreign intelligence, without tanks or tweets or funding from Washington… then what if others tried the same thing? The continent might start thinking for itself. Unacceptable.

The question now was: Do they let this new government breathe? Or do they strangle it in its crib?

The agencies were already drafting Plan B: build a new opposition—one that actually bites, unlike the court jester Bob Omubanda, who'd been as useful as a condom with holes. They needed a real threat this time. Something sharper, funded, trained, and with just enough local flavor to look homegrown.

Because if Africa starts believing it can save itself?

Well, that would be a goddamn catastrophe—for the people who profit from keeping it broken.

One Last Thing, Before the Lights Go Out

WELL, look at you—still here, all the way to the end. That says something. Not just about the story, but about *you*. You've got guts. You've got curiosity. Maybe even a little fire in your belly. And maybe, just maybe, you understand that literature isn't just for sipping tea with pinkies up—it's a weapon. A flashlight in the dark. A slap in the face of the powerful who think they own the narrative.

I write alone. No big publishers whispering sweet nothings. No government grants. No committee deciding whether I've behaved well enough to be published. Just me, my words, and whatever spare change I can scrape together.

So here's the deal:

If this book moved you—made you laugh, cry, or want to punch a politician—then help me keep the fire burning. I need your help to:

- Print more copies of this book (so they can't erase it)
- Turn it into an audiobook (for the ones who can't read, but need the story anyway)
- Publish the final beast in this series: *The President's Funeral*—and brother, he's going to need a proper burial—with a front row of readers.

How to Donate (aka, Keep the Revolution Alive):

- **Bank Transfer**
  Account Name: Black Writers Ink LLC
  Account Number: 48884415
  Routing Number: 211391825
- **PayPal:** yasikak@gmail.com
- **Venmo:** @Yasin-Kakande
- **Cash App:** $YasinKakande

A dollar. Ten. Fifty. Hell, even the price of a bad cup of coffee. It all helps.

And if you're broke but still burning with belief—spread the word.

Leave a review. Shout about it on Amazon, Goodreads, Instagram, TikTok—spray-paint it on a wall if you must (just don't say I told you to). Every whisper counts in a world that's trying hard to silence the truth.

Thank you for reading. Thank you for resisting.

See you in the next book—if we're both still standing.

—Yasin Kakande
Writer. Thinker. Independent as hell.

A MURDER OF HATE
The General's Project Series 1 of 3

When Boston detectives Lisa Garcia and Basudde "Bus" Erias are enlisted to solve the brutal murder of an African president's exchange-student niece, the two rival investigators unravel not only the identity of the killer, but also expose deadly ties between Washington elites and the dictators they support.

THE PRESIDENT'S FUNERAL

The General's Project Series 3 of 3

WHEN the long-serving, iron-fisted president of a resource-rich African nation finally kicks the bucket—likely from old age, poison, or choking on his own lies—the world doesn't send condolences. It sends panic.

This wasn't just any dictator. This was *their* dictator—the West's favorite bulldog, who kept the coltan, cobalt, diamonds, and oil flowing like blood through an open wound. Not just from his country, but from every trembling neighbor who owed him—or feared him. He didn't rule just one nation; he managed a whole damn resource cartel disguised as East and Central Africa.

Now that he's gone, every vulture in a tailored suit—from Beijing to Washington—wants a piece of the rotting pie. The global powers return to the African chessboard, and this time the board is soaked in oil, gold dust, and the ghosts of a thousand coups.

Enter the spies, the warlords, the fake rebels, the IMF saints, and the Twitter patriots. The new Scramble for Africa is here—just bloodier, greedier, and with more PowerPoint presentations.

The President's Funeral is a dark, twisty mystery where nations lie, spies bleed, and funerals are less about grief and more about grabbing power while the casket's still warm.

Because whoever buries the president… owns the future.

COMING SOON

CRIME THRILLER
The President's Funeral
The General's Project Series 3 of 3
Yasin Kakande

Printed in Dunstable, United Kingdom

67633639R00221